The CRYSTAL STAR

Vonda N. McIntyre

BANTAM BOOKS
NEW YORK • TORONTO • LONDON • SYDNEY • AUCKLAND

STAR WARS: THE CRYSTAL STAR

A Bantam Book / December 1994

SPECTRA and the portrayal of a boxed "s" are trademarks of Bantam Books, a division of Bantam Doubleday Dell Publishing Group, Inc.

Library of Congress Cataloging-in-Publication Data

McIntyre, Vonda N.
    The crystal star / Vonda N. McIntyre.
        p.   cm. — (Star Wars)
    ISBN 0-553-08929-3
    1. Imaginary wars and battles—fiction. I. Title.
II. Series: Star Wars (Bantam Books (Firm) :
Unnumbered)
    PS3563.A3125C79   1994
    813'.54—dc20   94-28939
                                                        CIP

Published simultaneously in the United States and Canada

PRINTED IN THE UNITED STATES OF AMERICA

BVG   0 9 8 7 6 5 4 3 2 1

For Leigh Brackett

Thanks to:

Kevin J. Anderson
Rebecca Moestra Anderson
Mark Bourne
John H. Chalmers
Jane Hawkins
O. Henry
Marilyn Holt
Andy Hooper
Kate Schaefer
Amy Thomson
Janna Silverstein

Chapter

1

The children had been kidnapped.

Leia ran headlong toward the glade, leaving behind the courtiers and the chamberlain of Munto Codru, leaving her attendants, leaving the young page who—completely against protocol—had stumbled into Leia's receiving room, bleeding from nose and ears, incoherent.

But Leia understood her: Jaina and Jacen and Anakin had been stolen.

Leia ran, now, through the trees and down a soft mossy path that led into her children's playground. Jaina imagined the path was a starship course, set to hyperspace. Jacen pretended it was a great mysterious road, a river. Anakin, going through a literal phase, insisted that it was only a path through the forest to the meadow.

The children loved the forest and the meadow, and Leia loved exclaiming in wonder at the treasures they brought her: a squirmy bug, a stone with shiny bits trapped in its matrix—rare jewels, perhaps!—or the fragments of an eggshell.

Her vision blurred with tears. Her soft slipper snared in

the tangled moss. She stumbled, caught herself, and plunged onward, holding the skirts of her court robe high.

In the old days, she thought, in the old days, I'd be wearing boots and trousers, I wouldn't be hampered and tripped by my own clothing!

Her breath burned in her throat.

And I'd be able to run from my receiving room to the forest glade without losing my breath!

The green afternoon light shifted and fluttered around her. Before her, the light brightened where the forest opened into a water-meadow, the meadow where her children had been playing.

Leia ran toward it, gasping, her legs heavy.

She was running toward an absence, not a presence, toward a terrible void.

She cried out to herself, How could this happen? How is this possible?

The answer—the only way it *could* be possible—terrified her. For a short time, her ability to sense the presence of her children had been neutralized. Only a manipulation of the Force could have such an effect.

Leia reached the meadow. She ran toward the creek where Jaina and Jacen had splashed and played and taught little Anakin to swim.

A crater was ripped into the soft grass. The leafy blades had been flattened into a circle around the raw patch of empty dirt.

A pressure bomb! Leia thought in horror.

A pressure bomb had gone off, near her children.

They aren't dead! she told herself. They can't be, I'd *know* if they were dead!

At the edge of the blast area, Chewbacca lay sprawled in a heap. Blood flowed bright against his chestnut coat.

Leia fell to her knees beside him, oblivious to the mud. She feared he was dead—but he was still bleeding, still breathing. She pressed her hand against the deep gash in his leg, desperate to stop the flow of blood and save his life. His powerful pulse drove the blood from his body. Like the page, he also bled from ears and nostrils.

A dreadful, grieving, keening sound escaped him, not a groan of pain but a cry of rage and remorse.

"Lie still!" Leia said. "Chewbacca, lie still! The doctor is coming, you'll be all right, what happened, oh, what *happened*?"

He cried out again, and Leia understood that he felt such despair that he wanted to die. He had adopted her family as his own, his Honor Family, and he had failed to protect the children.

"You can't die!" He must live, she thought. He *must.* Only he can tell me who stole my children. "Come back! Come back to me!"

Her aides and the chamberlain hurried out of the forest, trampling the delicate high grass, exclaiming in outrage when the slender blades cut them. Leia's children had wandered the meadow at liberty, neither leaving footprints nor receiving any harm. The grass parted before them like magic.

Magic, for my magic children, Leia thought. I thought I had protected them, I thought they could never come to any harm.

Hot tears ran down her cheeks.

The courtiers and advisers and guards gathered around her.

"Madam, madam," said the chamberlain of Munto Codru. Out here in the wild sun and the wind, Mr. Iyon's face was flushed and he looked uncomfortable.

"Did you bring the doctor?" Leia cried. "Get the doctor!"

"I sent for her, madam."

Mr. Iyon tried to make her get up, tried to take over staunching the flow of blood from Chewbacca's wound, but she pushed him away with a sharp word. Chewbacca's pulse faltered. Leia feared he was failing.

You will not die, she thought. You must not die. I won't *let* you die!

She drew on her inadequate knowledge to strengthen him. She bitterly regretted the responsibilities of statecraft that had prevented her from being properly trained in the ways of the Force.

Leia knew that if she allowed Chewbacca's hot blood to gush past her hands, his life, too, would stream away.

The doctor ran across the field. Her wyrwulf loped behind her, carrying her equipment and supplies. The doctor's wyrwulf reminded her that Mr. Iyon's wyrwulf had been playing with her children.

It had disappeared as well.

Dr. Hyos knelt beside Leia. She observed Chewbacca's wound and Leia's first aid with a glance. "Ah," she said briskly. "Good work."

"Come away, now, Princess," the chamberlain said.

"Not yet!" Dr. Hyos exclaimed. "I have only four hands, after all. The princess is quite all right where she is."

The wyrwulf sat on its haunches between Leia and Dr. Hyos. Leia shuddered. The wyrwulf turned its massive head, slowly, gently, staring at her with great limpid liquid blue eyes. Its coat was thick and brown, with long coarse black guard hairs.

The doctor's wyrwulf panted and slavered, its tongue lolling over its pitted fangs. Its face was grotesque. Its hot bitter breath made Leia flinch.

Dr. Hyos's four hands, so languid at rest, moved quickly over the panniers strapped to the wyrwulf's sides.

"Do you see what I am doing, my dear?" she said softly. "The bleeding is most important. Our princess has stopped it."

The doctor spoke to the wyrwulf, explaining everything she did.

Dr. Hyos drew pressure bandages from one compartment as she chose the proper medicine from another. Always, she told the wyrwulf what she was doing. Her long gold fingers were deft and sure.

Leia allowed herself a moment of hope, even with her hands covered with Chewbacca's hot blood. He had closed his eyes; he had stopped moving.

"As the bandage seals itself, my princess," Dr. Hyos said, "move your hand from the wound."

Leia obeyed. Dr. Hyos pressed the bandage to Chewbacca's flank. The bandage pressed itself against Leia's hand, clasped itself to Chewbacca, and wound its connectors through his fur. The wyrwulf watched, its tongue lolling.

Leia sat back on her heels. Her hands were sticky and her robes were smeared and she viewed everything in the clarity of horrified belief.

Dr. Hyos examined Chewbacca, frowning over the drying streaks of blood that had trickled from his nose and ears.

"Pressure bomb . . ." she said.

Leia remembered, as if from a distant dream, the sound of a single clap of thunder. She had thought—her thoughts had been so slow—that the morning must have turned from fair to rain; she had thought, fondly, that Chewbacca would soon bring the twins and Anakin in from the meadow. She could take a moment from her duties to cuddle them, to admire their newest treasures, to see that they had their lunch.

Now it was mid-afternoon. How could it be so late in the day, when such a short time ago it had not yet been lunch-time?

"Madam—" Chamberlain Iyon said. But he did not try again to make Leia come away.

"Close the port," Leia said. "Block the roads. Can the page be questioned? Check the port controller—is there any chance the kidnappers have left the planet?"

As she spoke, she feared any measures she might take would be useless, and if not useless, too late.

But if they've fled, she thought, I could chase them in *Alderaan*. I could catch them, my little ship can catch any-thing—

"Madam, closing the port would not be wise."

She glared at him, instantly suspicious of a man she had trusted only a moment before.

"They took your—" She hesitated, unsure what to say.

"My wyrwulf, madam," he said. "Yes."

"Your wyrwulf. Don't you *care?*"

"I care very much, madam. *And* I understand our tradi-tions, which you—I beg your pardon—do not. Closing the spaceport is unnecessary."

"The kidnappers will try to escape Munto Codru," she said.

Mr. Iyon spread his four hands.

"They will not. There are traditions," he said. "If we follow them, nothing will happen to the children—that too is the tradition."

Leia knew of Munto Codru's traditions of abduction and ransom. That was why Chewbacca had been staying so close to the children. That was why extra security surrounded and guarded the ancient castle. For the people of Munto Codru, coup abduction was an important and traditional political sport.

It was a sport in which Leia did not care to participate.

"It's a most audacious abduction," the chamberlain said.

"And a cruel one!" Leia said. "Chewbacca is wounded! And the pressure bomb—my children—" She fought for control of her voice and of her fear.

"The coup-counters detonated a pressure bomb only to prove that they could, madam," Mr. Iyon said.

"But no one is supposed to be injured, during your coup abductions!"

"No one of noble birth, Princess Leia," he said.

"My title is 'Chief of State,' sir," she said angrily. "Not 'Princess.' Not any longer. The world where I was a princess is long destroyed. We live in a Republic, now."

"I know it, madam. Please forgive our old-fashioned ways."

"They must know they haven't a hope," Leia said. "Of receiving a ransom, of escape. And if they should . . ." She could not bring herself to say the word *harm*.

"Please allow me to advise you in this matter," the chamberlain said. He leaned toward her, intense. "If you apply the rules of the Republic, disaster—tragedy—will be the result."

"The ransomers," Dr. Hyos said, with every evidence of approval, "must be very brave. But young and inexperienced as well. The family . . . which would it be?" She glanced at Mr. Iyon. "The Sibiu, perhaps?"

"They have insufficient resources," the chamberlain said.

Whoever it was, Leia thought, needed only the resources of the Force. The dark side of the Force.

Mr. Iyon gestured to the broken ground, to Chewbacca. "This required a skiff, a tractor beam. Connections with arms smugglers, to obtain the pressure bomb."

"Ah. The Temebiu, then."

"It could be," the chamberlain said. "They are ambitious."

"I'll show them ambition," Leia muttered.

"Madam, please. Your children will not be harmed—*cannot* be harmed, for the ransomers to achieve their goals. They may look upon the event as a great adventure—"

"Our friend Chewbacca has been wounded nearly to death!" Leia cried. "My children will *not* find that amusing. Nor do I!"

"It is a shame," the chamberlain said. "Perhaps he did not comprehend the information on our traditions? He was meant to surrender."

"Close the port," Leia said again, her voice tight. She was too angry to respond to the chamberlain's comment. "I won't take any chances that they'll leave Munto Codru."

"Very well," Mr. Iyon said. "It is possible . . . but we must do it carefully. We must do it . . . in a way to amuse rather than offend. . . ." His voice trailed off thoughtfully.

Dr. Hyos checked Chewbacca's pulse at the large vein the wound had come so close to piercing. "Stable. There. Good. To the surgery with you."

Chewbacca, barely conscious, gazed at Leia with uncomprehending eyes.

"Battlefield medicine," Dr. Hyos said. "Haven't done any in a long time. Didn't think I'd ever have to see a battlefield again."

"Neither did I," Leia said.

The wyrwulf howled.

Leia had seldom worried about the safety of Jaina and Jacen and Anakin.

Thought about it, made arrangements for it, certainly; talked about it, with the children's nanny, Winter, and with Han and Luke and with the supreme worrier, See-Threepio.

But Leia herself had seldom worried. She would be aware of any danger. Her lack of training would not hamper her perception of her children. Besides, if she somehow did not know of the danger, Luke surely would. Winter would protect the children with her life. And when Chewbacca accompanied Leia's family, as he so often did, he spent much of his time with the young ones. Who better to ensure their safety?

And Han, Leia's dear Han, had helped orchestrate the spreading peace. All children, not just the children of the people who brought down the Empire, should be safe.

Or so Leia had thought.

Leia followed Dr. Hyos's assistants as they carried Chewbacca back to the surgery in the ancient Munto Codru castle.

She felt very alone. Han and Luke had left on an adventure, with her blessing. Winter had taken the opportunity of this peaceful tour to attend a conference on runaway children. She too was worlds away.

The coincidence did not amuse Leia.

She waited outside the surgery, where Dr. Hyos and her assistants worked to heal Chewbacca's wounds. Courtiers and aides hovered until Leia, with careful courtesy, sent them away.

The wyrwulf sprawled before the surgery doors. Dr. Hyos had spoken to it, told it that it could not enter the surgery until it was older, and left it on guard. It dozed, and its head tipped forward until it balanced on the tips of its awful fangs.

Chamberlain Iyon hurried into the stark stone waiting room.

"There's no sign," he said. "No sign. They are very bold, very clever. Madam, we must wait for them to communicate."

"Wait?" Leia exclaimed. "That seems . . . unwise . . . to me." When she was younger she would have chosen a more intemperate description: Stupid. Ill-advised. Idiotic.

"The ransom demand will come in the morning," the chamberlain said, trying to reassure her.

"Morning! By morning the kidnappers could escape!"

"They cannot escape, madam. The port is closed. And furthermore, they will not escape. They have no reason to."

"But it's been two hours," Leia said. "The people who stole my children also stole two hours!"

Mr. Iyon frowned. "How, stole? Madam, you worked through the noon hour. The chronos are correct, the sun is in its proper place . . ." He let his voice trail off, aware that his feeble joke had failed to lighten the mood.

"They stole two hours," Leia said again. "These were no ordinary kidnappers! Ordinary kidnappers could never get through our defenses, they couldn't get past Chewbacca, they couldn't steal time from us!"

"But, madam, as I explained—Munto Codru produces kidnappers of rare quality." He looked at her sadly.

He thinks I'm reacting from fear and grief, Leia thought. If I tell him I suspect a follower of the dark side is responsible for this outrage, he'll believe I've lost my mind.

The doors of the surgery opened; Dr. Hyos patted the wyrwulf's heavy head, came to Leia, and took her hands. The doctor held each of Leia's hands pressed between two of her own.

"Chewbacca," she said. "He'll be fine. His hearing will take time to recover from the effects of the pressure bomb. He'll be weak while he builds up his blood."

"Did he tell you—"

"He's not in any shape to tell anyone anything. Leia, my princess, he must sleep or he'll be in danger."

"Did you send my message to Han and Luke?" Leia asked the chamberlain.

"Yes, madam, but I regret—they are too close to Crseih Station. The star system is most violent. The black hole, its quantum crystal companion—their influence blocks communication."

"Then we must send a ship out after them."

"Madam, the port is closed."

"I closed the port! I can order a ship to leave the planet!"

Concerned and gentle, he touched her hand in comfort.

"We must maintain an illusion," he said. "The port is closed because of a malfunction in the tracking equipment. If a ship leaves, if the emergency is revealed publicly to be a sham, we will have offered the ransomers a mortal insult."

"But you said they'd know—"

"The kidnappers," Dr. Hyos said. "They know, and we know. Everyone else may guess. No matter. Perception, that's what matters. Not reality."

"Dr. Hyos is correct, madam," the chamberlain said. "I beg you, madam, carry on with your afternoon's appointments as if nothing had happened. Call on the bravery for which we all honor you. For the sake of the children."

Leia struggled to hide her trembling, struggled to think clearly.

By the time a ship could reach Han, she thought, whatever happens will have happened. I gain nothing by sending for him.

"I'll go back to the receiving room," she said. "I'll finish my appointments. If we haven't heard from—if we haven't heard anything by sundown—"

"By morning, please, madam." The chamberlain's face was anxious. "By morning, I assure you, we'll have instructions."

"I'll finish my appointments." Leia left the waiting room.

"Leia—" Dr. Hyos said.

"Madam—" the chamberlain said.

"What!" She faced them both, glaring.

Mr. Iyon gestured, unhappily, wordlessly, at her bloody hands, her muddy skirt.

I've met ambassadors and heads of state in worse clothes than this, Leia thought. Worse clothes, and dirtier.

Leia scrubbed Chewbacca's blood from her hands. Her gown was a lost cause, bloodied and mud stained, its delicate fabric slashed by the grass blades. She threw it into the recycler, and her slippers after it. In her bathing room, as she stood in her shift, she started to tremble. She lowered her eyelids, blotting out the reflection of her own disarranged hair and stark face and staring eyes, reaching for calm, reaching for certainty.

The fluting warble of Artoo-Detoo drifted into the room. The droid came closer. At the same time, Leia heard a person's voice, high and childish and uncertain.

"No, I don't remember, I don't remember . . ."

Artoo-Detoo sang.

Leia hurried toward the voices. As she entered her bed-chamber, the silk rugs soft beneath her bare feet, a young Codru-Ji, a native of this world, backed erratically into the room.

"I don't know, I don't remember," she said.

Artoo-Detoo's front foot preceded his cylindrical body; finally his domed head and his rear feet appeared in the doorway. He was herding the Codru-Ji to her.

"I only saw that the small ones were gone, and the large one was hurt, I only ran for help."

It was the page who had reported the kidnapping. The blood had been washed from her face, and her abrasions treated, and her torn clothes replaced by a hospital gown.

Leia hurried forward. "Oh, my dear—" The page did not react. Leia touched her upper shoulder.

Startled by the touch, the page jumped straight up and turned around in the air. She came down with all four hands clenched into fists behind her, and backed rapidly away.

She saw Leia. Her eyes widened.

"Forgive me, forgive me—"

Leia took her gently by one lower arm and urged her into the room.

"Why are you out of bed?" Leia asked. "You should be resting—healing."

"The small droid came to me, and I saw I must beg your forgiveness—"

"Artoo, how could you?" Leia said. "Fetch Dr. Hyos—quickly!"

The droid warbled, backed up, came forward, hesitated.

"Hurry!"

With a descending trill, the droid scooted through the doorway.

Leia led the page to a couch and tried to help her to sit. At first the page resisted.

"No, I mustn't sit—"

"It's all right," Leia said. "Please don't stand on ceremony."

Leia tried to urge her to sit, but the page's knees locked. Leia allowed her to remain standing, and stood beside her.

"You saved Chewbacca's life," Leia said. "And you gave the alarm—"

The page stared at her, uncomprehending.

"Milady, I'm sorry, I cannot hear . . ." She put her hands to her ears. She started to cry, her sobs shaking her silently.

"I don't know what happened," she said, her words broken by tears. "They were there, playing, and then—" She shuddered and flinched; Leia wondered if she was experiencing the pressure bomb all over again. "I . . . I must have fallen asleep, madam. I should be exiled! And when I awoke the small ones were gone, and—" She touched the shells of her ears. She made a high-pitched whistling sound in her own language. "That is to say, Mr. Chewbacca was hurt, and—and I cannot *hear*, madam!"

Leia held her—awkwardly, because of the difference in their forms, but tenderly—and tried to soothe her.

Dr. Hyos arrived, indignant that her patient had been disturbed.

"I can't imagine what Artoo was thinking, to bring her here," Leia said. "Of course she shouldn't be up—"

"She shouldn't be down," Dr. Hyos said cryptically. "But you are correct, she must rest and recover."

The page broke away from Dr. Hyos and grasped Leia's hands.

"I am so sorry," she said.

"I forgive you," Leia said, slowly and carefully. "I forgive you. Do you understand me?"

The page hesitated, then nodded, and allowed the doctor to take her away.

Artoo-Detoo remained in Leia's apartment, whistling unhappily and arcing back and forth while Leia dressed. His noise irritated her, but he would not stop and he would not stay still and he would not tell her what was wrong. He followed her from her apartments. When they came to an intersection of corridors, he rolled along one that led outside, while Leia squared her shoulders and trudged toward the meeting room.

Artoo-Detoo whistled insistently.

"I can't," Leia said. "I have to . . . pretend."

She walked into the receiving room. The herald, usually so efficient, glanced at her, dismissed her with his gaze, took a step toward her to show her out, then snapped to attention, recognizing her at last despite her rough clothes.

"Chief of State of the New Republic, daughter of—"

"No time for the whole list!" Leia said. The herald fell silent. Everyone in the room, her aides and advisers and native Codru-Ji alike, stared at her in confusion. The chamberlain took a hesitant step toward her.

Leia crossed the receiving room, her boots loud on the polished stone floor. She took her place in the circle of chairs, leaned back, and crossed her legs. The heavy fabric of her stiff new hiking trousers rasped against itself. She forced herself to look relaxed.

"Your pardon, Ambassador Kirl," she said to the representative from the province of Kirl. "Thank you for your patience. We had a slight . . . a slight domestic upset." She forced her most charming smile. "You know how it is—" Her voice suddenly failed her.

The handsome Kirlian ambassador, who took his name from his province, spread all four hands. He returned her smile.

"I do know how it is," Kirl said. "Many's the time I've interrupted my work—as you say, for a slight domestic upset. No apology is necessary, though you are notably gracious to offer it!"

Always before, his grandiose manner had amused and sometimes even charmed her. Now it felt to Leia as if his words went on forever, each one dragged out like molasses.

The day continued, interminably. Munto Codru's convoluted politics meant that she had to receive ambassadors from an endless number of independent political entities. No wonder the world lay at the edge—outside the edge—of importance to the Republic. It spent most of its energy facing its own international disagreements. Its citizens had little time or attention left over for the larger questions of interplanetary cooperation. They had taken years to agree to choose a chamberlain, another year to settle on Mr. Iyon.

When the evening bell rang, the ambassador bowed and withdrew. As the aides shut the doors of the receiving chamber, the people left in the waiting room whistled and sighed in the native language. The doors closed, shutting off the sound.

"Any word?" Leia asked, her voice tight.

"No, madam," the chamberlain said. "But we must not expect to hear before morning. That is the tradition."

"Those other people," Leia said. "What did they want? Are you sure they weren't the kidnappers, trying to talk to me?"

"What other people?"

"The people still in my waiting room."

"Nothing and no one of importance, madam," Mr. Iyon said. "Small matters—many invented so the petitioner may go home and say, 'I met the princess—I spoke to the Chief of State of the New Republic!' "

"Nevertheless, I'd like to speak with them."

"They will return. Come, now, you must eat. Tomorrow you'll negotiate with the ransomers, and the children will come home, and everything will be as it was."

Leia forced herself to unclench her hands from the arms of her chair.

Her fingernails had torn small crescents into the heavy satin upholstery.

Leia hurried toward the silent surgery. Inside, Dr. Hyos stood at her desk. The doctor's eyes were closed. She dozed, standing up, with all four arms slightly extended, shifting subtly as if in a slow-motion dance or a soft breeze, balancing her. Leia had never seen a native of Munto Codru sleep.

What an odd position, Leia thought. Is that normal? Or unique to Dr. Hyos? Maybe she just fell asleep standing up. I'm about to do the same.

The wyrwulf lay at the doctor's feet. It raised its horrible head and gazed at Leia with its horrible bright eyes. It snorted and laid its head back on its frontmost paws. But it did not close its eyes. Leia had no reason to be frightened of the wyrwulf, but it disconcerted her nonetheless.

Leia let the doctor sleep. Walking softly, giving the wyrwulf a wide berth, she entered Chewbacca's sickroom.

He lay in a hammock that cradled his huge form. Regeneration bandages covered his leg. Leia had been afraid she would find him immersed in a bacta tank, suspended and unable to communicate.

Leia sat in a chair nearby and watched him, impatient with his sleep. His breathing was shallow and fast. She wanted him to wake. She wanted to talk to him, to find out what he had seen, to find out if he too had lost two hours or if he had observed what had happened and could confirm her suspicions about these events.

And of course she wanted to reassure him, to tell him she did not blame him—

A wave of fury rushed across her, so powerful that she gasped.

She *did* blame him. She was furious at him. There was nothing at all in the world that she could say to him.

Leia rose and backed out of the room. She closed the door, turned, and very nearly ran into Dr. Hyos.

"Oh—! I saw you sleeping, I didn't want to wake you."

"Did you speak with Chewbacca?"

"No, I—" How could she admit how she felt about her husband's oldest friend? "Isn't he sedated?"

"Of course. He is badly injured."

"Have you treated Wookiees before?"

"No, Chewbacca is the first of his kind to visit our world."

"Then how did you know how to treat him?"

"It's my job to know. I have never treated a human, either, but when your mission was announced, I made it my business to learn something of the people who would visit us."

"He's lucky," Leia said. He has no worries, she thought, just oblivion. By the time he's healed, and awakes, I'll know . . . and I'll have lived through every hellish moment.

"He's very badly hurt," Dr. Hyos said. "And he lost a great deal of blood. If he were lucky, he would not have been injured."

"Can you wake him? Just for a moment? If he saw something, anything—"

"The page saw nothing. She heard nothing. I doubt

Chewbacca saw anything either. It would be a great risk to wake him."

"But he *might*—"

"An *unnecessary* risk."

Dr. Hyos turned Leia toward the front of the surgery and led her away from Chewbacca's room.

"You've had a long, terrible day," the doctor said. "Try to rest. A coup abduction is never easy. But tomorrow—"

A high keening sound cut off her words. She hurried into a nearby room. Leia followed, all too aware that the wyrwulf followed too. Its claws clacked loudly on the floor.

The page stood in the center of the room, still wearing the soft hospital gown, steadied in her upright position by a harness. The doctor stopped beside her, stroked her soft short hair, soothed her. They spoke to each other in their own language, whistles and warbles that passed beyond the range of Leia's hearing. Soon the page dozed again. Dr. Hyos left her, looking worried.

"Will she be all right?"

"Are you still here?"

"Will she?"

"The bomb damaged her hearing."

"But you were talking to her—she heard you. She'll heal, won't she?"

"I fear she will never recover the highest range. And yet she will live."

"I'm glad," Leia said.

"Are you?" Dr. Hyos exclaimed.

"That she'll live? Of course!"

"Our hearing is more sensitive than yours, and more delicate. Our most intimate communications take place in the upper ranges," Dr. Hyos said softly. "Imagine your body numb. Imagine all your senses reduced by half. *All.* Perhaps you humans could endure such an existence, but her future will be . . . difficult."

"Oh," Leia said. "I didn't know. I'm so sorry." She glanced toward the page with renewed sympathy. "Wouldn't she be more comfortable lying down?"

"Adults don't sleep lying down."

The wyrwulf raised its head and gazed at Leia. "Go," Dr. Hyos said kindly. "Rest."

Leia flung herself onto her bed with a cry of despair. How had she survived this intolerable, interminable day? Her muscles ached with tension that she could not dispel. She regretted, as she had regretted so often in the past, the duties that had kept her from studying the way of the Jedi.

I'll bet Luke just says to his body, Enough, no more being stiff, Leia thought uncharitably. Or he says to himself, I don't feel any pain, and he doesn't.

How can I wait till morning to hear from the kidnappers?

She believed the chamberlain's assurances that a coup abduction was not meant to hurt its victims. And yet she believed her children were in mortal danger. If the kidnappers had, somehow, allied themselves with a practitioner of the dark side. . . .

It *must* be. The chamberlain and Dr. Hyos, whom Leia thought admirable, considered coup kidnappers honorable. But the kidnappers of Leia's children were ruthless and cruel: they had injured Chewbacca and the page when they were already unconscious, helpless.

The pressure bomb! Leia thought. It wasn't detonated to aid the kidnapping—it was detonated to destroy evidence. Evidence that someone used the dark side. . . .

She lay on her back and let the tears come. Above her, the translucent stone ceiling shone with pearlescent light, its delicate, intricate carvings a mystery to her as to everyone. The contemporary societies of Munto Codru used the ancient castles as provincial capitals, or avoided them as haunted places. But a previous civilization had built the labyrinthine palaces. The civilization had written its history on rock walls carved so thin that they looked like water-worn glass. The civilization had disappeared, leaving only its castles and its unreadable stories.

The carvings blurred beyond Leia's hot tears.

In the outer room of Leia's apartment, the annunciator chimed. Leia dragged herself to her feet.

Perhaps there's a message! she thought.

She hurried out of her bedroom. Mr. Iyon stood in the doorway.

"You've heard—?"

"No, madam," he said. "Please, I assure you, they'll communicate by morning."

"They could be anywhere by then!"

"No, they'll be near."

"They *aren't* near!" Leia insisted. "Sir, we've waited long enough. By now they've surely escaped!"

"But, madam, escape is unnecessary—more convenient to stay near. Especially with young children. They could even be in the castle."

"In the castle? How could they be? They aren't!"

"What better place to hide than right beside our ears? The castle is thousands of years old. Its basements and tunnels extend into the ground—even into the mountain—"

"I'd *know*! Don't you see, I'd *know* if they were near! We *must* begin a search."

Mr. Iyon gazed at her solemnly. Gently he took her arm and guided her to a chair. When Leia was seated, Mr. Iyon sat facing her, perched gingerly on the edge of the soft couch.

"If you order it, madam, I will of course obey—"

"I *do* order it!"

"—but I wish to be certain you understand what you are asking."

"I—" She hesitated. "You have more to tell me."

He inclined his head in a slow nod. He gazed at the elaborately patterned carpet.

"If anything disturbs the negotiations," he said, "everyone loses face. The kidnappers will be forced to recoup."

"By hurting the children?"

"They would sacrifice their own ambitions, if they injured anyone of noble birth." He stopped, and continued with difficulty. "But if you refuse to negotiate, the kidnappers may feel inclined to make *some* sacrifice—to demonstrate their sincerity."

Leia could not understand what he meant. How could the kidnappers make a sacrifice, if their own traditions forbade them to hurt her children?

"Your wyrwulf," she said. "You're afraid they'll sacrifice your wyrwulf."

Mr. Iyon raised his head and looked her in the eyes. He said nothing.

"But it isn't coup kidnappers!" Leia said. "Don't you understand, no one from Munto Codru is involved!"

"Are you certain, madam?"

She was—she had been—but she was so tired, and she was so torn by grief, so tempted to believe that in the morning, everything would be resolved, the children would be safe.

I won't answer yet, Leia thought. For a few minutes, I can think about what Chamberlain Iyon has said.

Mr. Iyon clapped his two left hands together. One of his aides entered, carrying a tray that bore a delicate antique stone pot, a teacup, a plate of cookies. Light shone through the sides of the teapot, liquid gold moving gently among carvings of the same vintage as the castle.

"I took the liberty of bringing you some tea. It is soothing."

She had eaten nothing all day. A moment ago she would have sworn she could never eat again, but her dry mouth suddenly watered and her stomach growled, most inelegantly, when she smelled the fragrant tea and the thin nut cookies.

"Thank you, Mr. Iyon," Leia said, grateful for the interruption. "But you haven't brought yourself a cup. There's another, on the sideboard."

"I've eaten already, madam."

"I insist," Leia said, suddenly, reflexively suspicious, and embarrassed at herself for her reaction.

The aide fetched another cup, poured the tea, and withdrew. Leia picked up her cup, and a cookie.

"These are Chef's best sweets," she said. "Have you had them?" She bit into one, confident that the chef would no more let someone adulterate his recipe than he would swing from the sconces above a state dinner. The cookie vanished in her mouth like air, leaving a sweet, spicy flavor and taking the edge off her hunger.

"I cannot eat sweets, madam." He sighed. "But I will join you in a cup of tea." He drank the cupful in one gulp.

Surprised, still suspicious, even wondering if she had

made a mistake by eating the cookie, Leia sipped her tea. She was amazed at her ability to perform any normal action. She felt like she should be running, blaster in hand, chasing the enemy.

In the old days, she thought, we *knew* who the enemy was.

"It is good of you to bring the latest Coruscant fashions to Munto Codru," the chamberlain said, trying to change the subject. "News travels so slowly, this far from the center of government."

"What—?" She remembered what she was wearing: hiking trousers and a soft leather shirt and heavy boots. She started to explain that she had not been able to face putting on another fancy court dress. Then she wondered if he was subtly chiding her for her choice in clothing.

But he was perfectly sincere. Leia blushed. She searched for a way to explain without having him suspect she was making fun of him.

"It isn't quite the *height* of fashion," she said. She sipped her tea again. "But it's comfortable, and—" She shrugged.

Mr. Iyon yawned. His thin lips pulled back from his prominent teeth. He snapped his mouth shut.

"I beg your pardon, madam!"

Leia accepted his apology with a nod, then she yawned too.

"We should have had pepper tea," she said, "instead of this. Delicious though it is."

Leia struggled to remember the question she was trying to answer. Mr. Iyon had said that the children must be near. Leia doubted that was possible.

If they were hidden nearby, she thought, wouldn't I know it? Wouldn't I *feel* it? They *must* have been stolen by a master of the dark side. . . .

Maybe it isn't the dark side after all, Leia thought, desperately seeking comfort. Maybe the castle's built on some unique mineral, maybe it disrupts my perceptions. If ysalamiri can disturb the Force, why not a phenomenon from the depths of a planet?

Leia yawned again. Like a mirror image, so did Mr. Iyon. Sleep drew Leia irresistibly.

"We must . . ." Her words trailed off. She could not recall what she had been about to say.

"Good night, madam," the chamberlain said. His voice was kindly. He rose, pushing himself from the couch like a man exhausted, levering himself with all four arms. He stumbled once on the way to the door. Leia was too sleepy to be surprised by his lapse in grace.

Her need for sleep overtook her dread. She told herself to get up, but the chair was so comfortable . . .

I'll just rest here a moment, she thought.

Chapter

2

J ust like old times, hey, kid?" Han Solo said to Luke
Skywalker.

Sitting in the copilot's seat of the *Millennium Falcon*,
Luke grinned.

"Just like old times except the Empire isn't trying to shoot
us out of the sky—"

"You got that right."

"And Jabba the Hutt isn't after your hide for dumping
that spice load—"

"Yeah."

"And nobody is trying to collect old gambling debts from
you."

"Also true," Han said, thinking, But I might get around
to running up some *new* gambling debts. After all, what's a
vacation for?

"Finally, you can't ogle every beautiful woman who
comes by."

"Sure I can," Han said, then hurried to defend himself as
Luke chuckled. "Nothing wrong with looking. Leia and I

know where we stand with each other, we trust each other, she's not jealous."

Luke burst into outright laughter.

"And you wouldn't mind," he said, "if she flirted with the Kirlian ambassador. Good-looking guy, that Kirlian ambassador."

"Nothing wrong with looking," Han said stubbornly. "Or a little innocent flirtation. But the Kirlian ambassador better watch his hands. All four of them. Hey, kid, listen, flirting is one of the best inventions of civilization." Han grinned.

Luke hated it when Han called him "kid." That was why he did it. He stared out into hyperspace.

"You ought to do more flirting yourself," Han said.

"If I might be of service, Master Luke," See-Threepio said, leaning forward from the passenger seat. "I have an extensive library of love poetry at your disposal, in several languages suitable for the human tongue, as well as etiquette, medical information, and—"

"I don't have time for flirtations," Luke said, "or love poetry. Not right now . . ."

Threepio sat back in the passenger seat. At the corner of Han's vision, the droid looked like a shadow. To disguise himself, See-Threepio had covered his glossy gold finish with a coat of purple lacquer. Han had not yet gotten used to the change.

"Don't be so damned dedicated," Han said to Luke. "Don't Jedi Knights get to have any fun? Little Jedi Knights have to come from *somewhere*. I'll bet old Obi-wan—"

"I don't know what Ben would have done!"

Luke spoke in a tone of distress, not anger. The fundamental loneliness of the young Jedi struck Han deeply.

"I don't know what other Jedi Knights did," Luke said softly. "I didn't know Ben long enough, and the Empire destroyed so many records, and . . . *I just don't know.*"

Han wished Luke could find someone to share his life and his work. Han's marriage to Leia grew and strengthened with each year, with each day. As his own years of happiness continued, Han was increasingly troubled by his brother-in-law's solitude.

"Take it easy, Luke," Han said. "Take it easy. You're doing great—"

"But the *traditions*—"

"So if you have to make them up as you go along, that's not so bad, is it?" Han asked. "We always were pretty good at bluffing. In the old days."

"In the old days." Luke sounded glum.

"And who knows what we'll find when we get where we're going? Maybe some more Jedi Knights to help with the school."

"Maybe," Luke said. "I hope so."

The *Millennium Falcon* swept out of hyperspace, diving through streamers of light into normal space.

The alarms shrieked and the radiation shields snapped into existence around the *Falcon*.

Han swore. He had expected a heavy radiation flux in this region—he had outfitted the *Falcon* to withstand it—but nothing as powerful as the X-ray storms raging around them.

When he had checked the ship's systems to make sure none were damaged, Han took a moment to look outside. He whistled softly in awe.

A dense, brilliant starfield spread all around his ship. Two star clusters collided: Bands of red giant stars, like veins of glowing blood, meandered through regions of white dwarf stars. The stars clustered so closely that they formed one huge chaotic system, spinning around each other, pulling each other into different dances, one snatching star-stuff from the surface of another.

Chaos reigned in the impossible circle-dance of stars; no one could predict the changes each star's pattern would take —if anyone could find a pattern to start with. Soon, measuring by astronomical time, the cluster's stars would fly off in all directions. Or perhaps the whole cluster would collapse in upon itself. It would squeeze its mass into the size of a planet, a moon, a fist, a pinprick. And then it would vanish.

"If I may be so bold . . ." See-Threepio said. "Despite the extra shielding I can feel X rays penetrating my outer shell, all the way to my synapses. I can hardly imagine what they might do to your more delicate biological structure. Crseih Research Station was constructed to withstand this assault. Might I suggest that we get beneath the spaceport's shielding as soon as possible?"

As if to punctuate See-Threepio's comment, a bright flash of light with no apparent source streaked across Han's vision; he recognized it as a cosmic ray traveling across his retina.

"Good thinking, Threepio," he said.

He laid a course for the Crseih Research Station.

Han piloted the *Millennium Falcon* through the strangest star system he had ever approached. An ancient, dying, crystallizing white dwarf star orbited a black hole in a wildly eccentric elliptical path.

Eons ago, in this place, a small and ordinary yellow star peacefully orbited an immense blue-white supergiant. The blue star aged, and collapsed.

The blue star went supernova, blasting light and radiation and debris out into space.

Its light still traveled through the universe, a furious explosion visible from distant galaxies.

Over time, the remains of the supergiant's core collapsed under the force of its own gravity. The result was degenerate mass: a black hole.

The violence of the supernova disrupted the orbit of the nova's companion, the yellow star. Over time, the yellow star's orbit decayed.

The yellow star fell toward the unimaginably dense body of the black hole. The black hole sucked up anything, even light, that came within its grasp. And when it captured matter —even an entire yellow star—it ripped the atoms apart into a glowing accretion disk. Subatomic particles imploded downward into the singularity's equator, emitting great bursts of radiation. The accretion disk spun at a fantastic speed, glowing with fantastic heat, creating a funeral pyre for the destroyed yellow companion.

The plasma spiraled in a raging pinwheel, circling so fast and heating so intensely that it blasted X rays out into space. Then, finally, the glowing gas fell toward the invisible black hole, approaching it closer and closer, appearing to fall more and more slowly as relativity influenced it.

It was lost forever to this universe.

That was the fate of the small yellow star.

The system contained a third star: the dying white dwarf, which shone with ancient heat even as it froze into a quantum crystal. Now, as the *Millennium Falcon* entered the system, the white dwarf was falling toward the black hole, on the inward curve of its eccentric elliptical orbit.

"Will you look at that," Han said. "Quite a show."

"Indeed it is, Master Han," Threepio said, "but it is merely a shadow of what will occur when the black hole captures the crystal star."

Luke gazed silently into the maelstrom of the black hole. Han waited.

"Hey, kid! Snap out of it."

Luke started. "What?"

"I don't know where you were, but you weren't here."

"Just thinking about the Jedi Academy. I hate to leave my students, even for a few days. But if I *do* find other trained Jedi, it'll make a big difference. To the Academy. To the New Republic . . ."

"I think we're getting along pretty well already," Han said, irked. He had spent years maintaining the peace with ordinary people. In his opinion, Jedi Knights could cause more trouble than they were worth. "And what if these are all using the dark side?"

Luke did not reply.

Han seldom admitted his nightmares, but he had nightmares about what could happen to his children if they were tempted to the dark side.

Right now they were safe, with Leia on a planetary tour of remote and peaceful worlds of the New Republic. By this time they must have reached Munto Codru. They would be visiting the beautiful mountains of the world's temperate zone. Han smiled, imagining his princess and his children being welcomed to one of Munto Codru's mysterious, ancient, fairy-tale castles.

Solar prominences flared from the white dwarf's surface. The *Falcon* passed it, heading toward the more perilous region of the black hole.

Han set the shields as high as they would go, and sped through the dangerous radiation. The accretion disk blazed wildly, its light harsh and actinic.

Neither white dwarf nor black hole possessed natural planets, only a few bits of distant debris and a halo of frozen comets. But the white dwarf did possess one artificial planetoid.

Crseih Station had been a secret Empire research facility. During the rule of the Emperor, it had moved from covert place to hidden location to secret destination. Wherever it went, it carried with it a reputation of evil.

Most of the records of its work had been destroyed when the Empire fell. Its researchers had fled, to surrender to the New Republic or to disappear. Han knew only one thing about Crseih for certain. It had been sent to this star system to adapt the destructive power of the black hole to the martial ambitions of the Emperor.

Crseih had failed, but it still existed, hidden out here on the edge of civilization, isolated by the disruption of the exploding, dying stars. Some inhabitants remained, content to be free of the Empire. They also lived outside the New Republic, without the protection of its justice.

Without the protection, or the restraints.

Han plunged the *Millennium Falcon* into the shadow of Crseih Station. He breathed a sigh of relief. Light from the white dwarf still illuminated his ship, but the station blocked the intense X rays of the black hole.

Like a patchwork umbrella, powerful shielding covered half the irregular artificial planetoid of Crseih Station. As the station had grown, the patches had spread. Shielding formed the residence domes, and the corridors of the airlinks. Transparent to the visual spectrum, it protected the equipment and the inhabitants from high-energy radiation. The shielding shimmered in patterns of shadow. Wherever a particularly intense burst of radiation assaulted the shielding, it darkened.

Han set the *Millennium Falcon* down on a bare patch of blasted stone. Crseih had nothing much in the way of a spaceport. A few itinerant hyperdrive mechanics and refuelers. A rental company that specialized in shielding.

Han made arrangements for an extra shield for the *Falcon*. A few minutes later, a crawler shuffled toward them, towing the big transparent sheet.

"Efficient," Luke said.

"Or bored. Sure isn't much traffic." He scowled. "Wouldn't you know? First vacation I ever get, and I come to a backwater."

"Threepio, where's your contact?" Luke asked.

A few dozen other ships of various types and vintages hunkered down on the blasted rock. Most were shielded. A few had been left naked and exposed in the cosmic weather, decaying to derelicts.

"Here to meet us, I'm virtually certain, Master Luke." See-Threepio peered nervously through the viewport. "Perhaps riding out on the crawler?"

See-Threepio fidgeted. A few weeks ago, Han had begun to receive incomprehensible messages. But Threepio recognized the language; he said it was nearly extinct. The messages passed on rumors of strange events at Crseih Station.

"It is my fault we've set out on this investigation," See-Threepio said.

Han had charged Threepio with replying to the messages, using the same obscure language, and with setting up a rendezvous. Now Threepio, being Threepio, took full responsibility for the entire expedition.

"I do hope we are not following a hoax," Threepio said.

"It's all right, Threepio," Han said. "It wouldn't be your fault."

"But I could hardly survive the embarrassment if the rumors turned out to be of no account. . . ."

Han gave up listening to Threepio's worries. Han would be sorry for Luke, of course, if he failed to find the lost Jedi. But Han was content to be here, whether the trip turned out to be vacation or adventure.

He turned his attention to the outpost. The low, oblate airlinks covered and protected and connected the districts of the station, some rich and well kept, some collapsing into piles of rubble. Though the Empire's research facilities had been abandoned, the community that had sprung up around them had continued. Some of the inhabitants had found other ways to thrive, without the presence of the Empire or the attention of the New Republic.

Representatives and ambassadors concentrated their attention on more populous worlds closer to the center of power.

And that's a relief, Han thought. No ambassadors, no court dress. No formal dinners.

The crawler hesitated.

"How will you be wishing to pay for this service?" its operator asked.

"Letter of resources," Han said.

"Hard credits only." The crawler started to back away.

"Wait a minute!" Han shouted. "Do you—" He stopped. He had been about to say, "Do you know who I am?" But he was traveling incognito. Of course the operator did not know who he was.

The thought gave him a feeling of freedom.

"The letter of resources must be deposited, Master Ha—" See-Threepio's memory programming cut off the use of Han's real name just in time. "Sir. Otherwise it cannot be drawn upon."

"I *know* that." Han grinned. "I guess I just wanted to flash it around. All those seals and signatures." And a fake identity.

The crawler headed for the airlinks.

"Come back here!" Han said. "Cash money."

"Show your coin."

Han displayed the rainbow edges of a few bills of New Republic currency. He was glad, for old times' sake, for the sake of his smuggling days, that the Senate had failed to pass a law abandoning physical currency. Smuggling would have been a whole lot harder without hard-to-trace cash money. Of course, that was why the Senate wanted to abandon it.

The crawler pulled forward again and maneuvered until the shield covered the *Falcon*. It disengaged, and the shield settled. The crawler nestled up beneath the *Falcon*.

Han shut down the *Falcon* and set several security devices, some of them cleverer than others.

"Let's go," he said. "And remember who we are. I mean, who we *aren't*."

Threepio had put on the purple lacquer; Han had grown his beard. But Luke had done nothing to disguise himself.

"I don't know, kid," Han said to Luke. "I still think you ought to do *something*. Shave your head, maybe? Otherwise, somebody's sure to recognize you."

Luke gave him a quizzical glance. "I'm not shaving my head. No one will recognize me."

Han felt dizzy. Luke's features suddenly blurred and re-formed. He became, in Han's eyes, a different individual: darker hair, a handspan taller, thinner, his features ordinary and unmemorable.

"Dammit!" Han said. "Don't *do* that to me!"

The image shivered away, revealing Luke.

"All right," Luke said. "I won't affect you. But no one else will recognize me."

"*Okay.*"

They descended.

Han wished Chewbacca was with them, but traveling incognito, it had been too risky. With his beard, Han could probably escape identification. A human man and a chestnut Wookiee traveling together, though: throughout the Republic, that image made people think of General Han Solo and his friend, the Hero of the New Republic, Chewbacca.

At the bottom of the *Millennium Falcon's* ramp, the crawler's entryway was dim. A translucent rod barred Han's path. He pushed it. It moved in his hand. He gripped it harder. It shivered and shook and rattled against the skin of the crawler. Several similar rods, each one segmented, each joint a faceted bulge, snapped across the doorway in front of him.

"Hey!" Han yelled.

"Let go!" the driver said.

"Let him go," Luke said. "You're holding on to his arm. His leg. His appendage."

"How do *you* know?"

Luke just looked at him.

Han let go. "I hate it when you do that," he said to Luke.

"Pay first," the driver said. "Then enter."

Han peeled off several bills and gave them over to the driver.

One of the thin, translucent appendages slid across the doorway in front of him until its four-clawed end hovered before his face. The claws were as sharp and blue as steel, and each was as long as his hand.

"Nice fingernails," Han said. He put the cash into the claws. They closed gently, without piercing the engraved paper.

"Thank you," the driver said. "You will pay more."

"More? Now?" Han exclaimed. "For parking on a chunk of rock?"

"For parking on a chunk of rock under a rented shield," the driver said, "when a new X-ray storm will approach. *My* rented shield. However, I will move it away if you would prefer."

Han had considered the radiation flux strong enough to qualify as an X-ray storm. On Crseih, though, it was normal weather. When the white dwarf neared the black hole, and the black hole began tearing heated gas from its surface, the X rays would intensify into a true storm, an X-ray hurricane.

"An X-ray storm will surely have adverse effects on the systems of the *Mil*—of your ship," See-Threepio said, "if it is left unprotected."

"I *know* that," Han said. He pulled off three more bills and shoved them into the driver's claws. He thought, This is going to leave us pretty short of cash. Never mind, the letter of resources will take care of the problem.

The claws withdrew. Rustling, the other legs parted. Han's eyes were becoming accustomed to the dim light. The driver sat on the other side of the crawler cabin, pulling its legs in around it like a pile of dry sticks.

"The ride to Crseih," the driver said, "will be free."

"Thanks so much," Han said. Behind them, the *Falcon* drew in its ramp and locked its hatch.

See-Threepio peered around the inside of the crawler.

"You have no other passenger?" he asked.

"I will only have room to carry you," the driver said.

Threepio said a few words in a language so strange it hurt Han's ears. Threepio had spoken it to him before, while translating the messages from Crseih Station.

Threepio thinks this guy might be our contact! Han thought.

The driver rattled several appendages, including those with aural sensory hairs, and sharp defensive spines.

"What will you mean?" the driver said to Threepio. "Why will you irritate my auditory organs?"

"I beg your pardon," Threepio said. "I said nothing of any importance. I mistook you for someone else."

The crawler left the starship beneath its shield and headed toward the city.

The driver stopped the crawler in its bay. The airlink moved to meet the door. Han vaulted down and strode into Crseih Station. Luke and See-Threepio followed.

The crawler backed out and rumbled away.

"Spiders," Han said, shuddering. "I'm sorry, but spiders really give me the creeps."

"Spiders?" See-Threepio said. "Are there spiders? Where? I must be careful that they do not spin their webs in my joints. Why, I knew a droid once—"

"I meant the driver," Han said.

"But the driver was not a spider," See-Threepio said.

"Metaphorically speaking," Han said.

"But—"

"Never mind," Han said. "Forget I said anything."

"He *was* a good businessman," Luke said.

Han laughed. "Yeah, you're right. He was pretty grabby."

See-Threepio took a few nervous steps forward and looked around.

"I'm *certain* our contact is here *somewhere!*" he said, despite their being alone in the entry bay.

Han glanced at Luke. "Now what? Do you have any idea where to start looking for your lost Jedi?"

Luke shook his head. His hair fell across his forehead and for a moment he looked like the green kid he had been when Han first met him. But he was not a green kid anymore. Far from it. Over the years, he had developed an otherworldly presence that Han found both touching and alarming.

"I expected to be able to sense—" Luke shrugged unhappily. "There's nothing. Maybe they're shielding themselves. Hiding. After the way the Empire hunted them down, who can blame them?"

"You'd think they'd notice," Han said, "that there hasn't *been* any Empire for years."

"But there are plenty of people who want it to return," Luke said stubbornly.

"Okay, okay." Han did not believe a group of lost Jedi existed. On the other hand, the longer Luke searched for them, the longer Han's vacation would last.

Maybe I'd better go easy on the teasing, he said to himself.

Beneath the transparent radiation shields, the carnival light of the burning whirlpool turned gray and soft. Small shadows appeared and disappeared, dappling the ground.

Han glanced up. As Crseih Station spun on its axis, the black hole and its accretion disk created a violent dawn. The burning whirlpool stretched across a quarter of the sky. When it set, its white dwarf companion would rise. As the white dwarf plunged toward the center of the star system, it and its companion would rise closer and closer to the same time, until they rose together and burned the heavens.

Han was careful not to look directly at the accretion disk of the black hole, even with the protection of the shields. In an instant, the natural fireworks display expended more energy than all the celebrations conceived by civilization since the beginning of history.

He proceeded through the airlink toward the first dome of the station proper. Hot, moist air, tropical and fetid, closed in around Han. He could practically see the air, practically open his fingers and grab a handful of it.

Most of the folks who live here must be from tropical worlds, he thought. It's easy to keep a space station cool—

But not a station like Crseih. Overworked cooling machinery vibrated the floor. The shields protected the living space by absorbing X rays. But the enormous energy re-radiated as heat, and the heat had to go somewhere. The cooling machinery strained to transport it to Crseih's night side, where the heat could be radiated into the vacuum of space. With the black hole on one side of the station, and the white dwarf on the other, Crseih's night side was barely a sliver of shadow.

Han held his palm a finger's width from the surface of the airlink. After a moment he pulled back. Even with the efforts of the cooling machinery, the surface was uncomfortably hot.

See-Threepio hurried on ahead, strutting stiffly, strange in his purple-lacquer disguise. He continued his futile search for his contact.

"I distinctly told our correspondent to meet us," Threepio said querulously. "I cannot understand—"

Luke strode past Han—

He *did* go by me, didn't he? Han thought. Did I see him? Or didn't I? Damn, I hate it when he does that!

"Threepio," Luke said, "it would be better not to broadcast our plans."

"But, Master Luke, I never would—I assure you I wasn't engaging my transmitter!"

"Don't engage your vocal unit, either."

"Very well, Master Luke," See-Threepio said, "if that's as you prefer it." The droid walked on, body language as expressive as words that he had expected to be met at the landing field.

In the humidity and the heat, sweat ran down Han's back and sides and beaded on his forehead without evaporating. He wiped his face and rolled up his sleeves, for once not worrying whether he looked proper.

Over the years, Leia and his own advisers had made him more aware of his clothing. Instead of putting on whatever came to hand out of his closet, in whatever combination the cleaner droid deposited it, he had begun to dress according to his day's duties. Usually he could get away without wearing a formal uniform, unless his schedule included addressing or inspecting regular troops, or a diplomatic reception. Han Solo hated uniforms. He was not particularly keen on speeches or receptions, either.

On this trip, he had not even brought a uniform. And though his frayed pants and comfortable old shirt were too heavy for the climate of Crseih Station, he felt as if he were expanding with freedom.

No uniforms, no speeches, no receptions.

He laughed out loud.

"This is going to be fun," he said.

They rounded a curve of the steamy airlink. It stretched on empty before them.

"Where's Threepio?" Luke said.

"I don't know," Han said. "You probably hurt his feelings by telling him to shut up."

"I just told him to keep our plans to himself."

"Don't you know where he is?"

"I could find him," Luke said, "but I'd better not. I'd better not do anything long-range. I don't want to give us away."

"Why not send up a signal flare? Let the Jedi Masters find us."

"Let's get the lay of the land first," Luke said. "After all, we don't know much about the people I'm looking for. Only the rumors, and the strange stories—"

"You're right, kid," Han said. The longer Luke takes, the longer before I have to put on another uniform. "Absolutely right. Take all the time you want."

"And if they are Jedi—I want to be certain they aren't on the dark side."

"Wouldn't you know it—wouldn't you sense it—if someone using the dark side was near?"

"Sure I would," Luke said.

"Good."

"I think I would." Luke stared through the translucent side of the tunnel. In the distance, domes perched on flat rock between craters. He said in a soft voice, "I hope I would."

Exasperated, Han strode on ahead. "What do I always say?" he muttered. "They're more trouble than they're worth."

He burst through the exit of the airlink and entered the first dome of Crseih Station. Noise and light surrounded him, as thick and exciting as the hot, steamy air.

Luke followed more cautiously, poised at Han's right shoulder, keeping watch.

Han wondered how far Luke could project his illusion of disguise. Did the inhabitants of the station see him as he really was, when they were at a distance, and then think they had mistaken what he looked like when they got nearer? Or did his local effect of disguise surround him like a cloak, and project his image to anyone who glanced at him?

Han could not tell, for Luke had kept his promise to leave his partner unaffected. As far as Han was concerned, the young man beside him was Luke Skywalker, pilot, brother-in-law, and, incidentally, Jedi Knight. He wore his robes, which fortunately were not much different from the everyday garb of many humanoid beings. They did not mark him as Jedi, and they did conceal his lightsaber.

Han stroked his beard, a habit he had picked up while it was still growing. Those last few weeks before he and Luke began this trip, he had been eager and anxious to be on their way. Stroking his beard surely had not made it grow any faster, but the motion was a talisman, a reminder that in two more weeks—if he could just get through this review, then in one more week—if he could just get through this speech—he would be away and on his own again.

The enormous first dome of Crseih Station spread out like a carnival around him. Bands and jugglers, acrobats and merchants demonstrated their abilities or displayed their wares.

A group of Brebishems lay in a heap on the side of the path, wriggling and rolling together, twisting their long snouts and flapping their wide leaf-shaped ears. They squeezed so close together that they resembled one organism, as if their soft wrinkled mauve skins had touched and melded. A low continuous moan emanated from the group. It was impossible to tell if one or all made the sound.

Luke threw a coin into the basket sitting before the Brebishems.

"What's that for?" Han said.

"Appreciation for their art."

"Art?" Han looked at Luke askance, but Luke was perfectly serious.

"It isn't any stranger than dancing, or bolo-ball."

"You're entitled to your opinion," Han said. An image came to him, unbidden, of the last time he and Leia had danced. Some reception somewhere, he could not remember when or even what planet the event had been on. Only that there had been a few minutes free of diplomacy, toasts, and salutations, and he and Leia had held each other close in the mirror-fractured light on the sparkling dance floor. A sharp pang of desire and loneliness touched his heart.

"Please, honors, a small coin left for me?" An individual only as high as Han's hip plucked at the sleeve of his shirt. A long gray-green pelt concealed the being's form. "Has it got a coin in its pocketses for me?"

"No, I don't have any change on me," Han said. He pushed the long thin fingers, like brittle twigs, away from his pockets.

"Wait," Luke said. "I have some." He gave the being a coin. His voice was very gentle when he spoke to the being. The bony fingers snatched the coin, which vanished somewhere beneath the long coarse fur.

The being snuffled and went past them, toward the airlink.

"Other passengers coming?" the being said hopefully.

"Just us," Han said.

Several other beggars, guides, and tchochke-sellers converged on Han and Luke.

"They're mine, mine!" the being cried. "Find your own!"

They all ignored the hairy being's protests.

"No, thanks, we don't want any," Han said, sidling through the group and dragging Luke with him. He imagined Luke passing out all the rest of their spare credits before they made it beyond the entryway.

It did not take them long to escape. The beggars, guides, and sellers retreated to their places near the entryway and waited for more receptive customers.

But the hairy being had followed Han and Luke through the crowd. It circled them warily, muttering, "Mine, mine."

"The droid who came in with us," Han said. "Did you

see him?" He craned his neck to look across the chaos of the welcome dome. In any group of standard humans, Han Solo could look over the heads of most of them. Within the mix of sentient life-forms gathered at Crseih, he was of no more than average height. And he had to remind himself that he was looking for a purple droid, not a gold one.

"Droids never have spare change," the hairy being said. "Droids never have pocketses. No reason to ask droids."

"Maybe you could help us," Luke said. "In another way."

"Help?" the being asked suspiciously. "Work?"

"Just show. Show us where there's a good lodge. Help us get our bearings at Crseih Station."

"I can find us a lodge," Han said, insulted. "I haven't been out of touch so long that I can't even find us a lodge!"

"Shut up!" Luke whispered fiercely.

Startled, Han stopped his protest.

"Lodge, yes, lodge," the being said. "And places to eat and places to buy nice clothes, specialize in human fit." The being loped off, its heavy fur bouncing against its sides.

Luke followed it. Han glanced at the ceiling in supplication. As the ceiling neither replied nor did anything to help, he shrugged and went along, muttering, "Damned if I'll take fashion criticism from a guy in a hairy suit."

The hairy being led Han and Luke through several air-links and as many completely different domes. The noise and excitement of the first dome faded away. They passed into a region of huge machines and warehouses, then into a lush park, where alien vegetation clambered up the walls and moderated the whirlpool light with leaves in all the colors of the rainbow.

"Where are we going?" Han demanded. "There's got to be lodges back in the carnival dome."

"Not for you," the hairy being said. "Not good enough for you."

They traveled farther away from the lights and the noise and the action, into quieter regions. Gardens and low, organically engineered buildings surrounded them. Instead of being excited by the atmosphere, Han felt as if the very air were wrapping him in hot, damp blankets.

"Luke," he said under his breath, "we're never going to find anything, out here in the middle of nowhere."

"Be patient," Luke said.

"Patient! I've been patient! We've been walking half the day."

Except to grin at Han's exaggeration, Luke ignored the complaints and continued on after the hairy being.

They entered the largest dome so far. The top curved so far overhead that small clouds floated at the apex, and a breeze circulated the heavy warm air. The being led Han and Luke to a building that followed the contour of a crater. The front of the building spilled down to a pool at the crater's floor, and rose to a tower at the crater's rim. Two wings of the building followed the rim of the crater.

"Here," the hairy being said. "Here is perfect." It pointed through an irregularly arched opening.

Han stepped over the threshold into a cool dim room filled with the sound and scent of running water. He glanced back. Luke stood in the doorway, silhouetted by the harsh light. Han started. For a moment he could see both Obi-wan Kenobi and Anakin Skywalker, Lord Vader, in Luke's stance. Luke came toward him, gazing around curiously, and the illusion vanished.

Han returned to the entryway and looked outside. The hairy being had disappeared. He scowled.

"Why'd you want to follow that guy all the way out here?" he asked Luke, who sat on his heels at the edge of the indoor pool, scooped his hand through the running water, smelled then briefly tasted it.

"We needed a native guide."

"We're supposed to have one," Han pointed out.

"And he might be useful to us," Luke said.

"I doubt it," Han said.

"And . . . he reminded me of Yoda."

"You think *he* might be one of the Jedi?"

"I thought he might be. Now I don't think so. But he *could* have been."

Han started to make a crack about Luke's highly honed

decision-making abilities, but thought better of it for the moment. Luke's uncharacteristic lack of composure and self-assurance troubled him.

"Hey!" he shouted. "Anybody here? Is this a lodge or not?" It occurred to him that the place might not be a lodge; the hairy being might have brought them to a business or even a private house as a joke.

"Yes, human being, I am here."

An image formed above the pond, flickering, reflecting, shooting shards of light throughout the irregular room. Han could not make out a definite shape amid the hypnotic aurora.

"We want three rooms," Han said. "Two for humans, one fitted for a droid."

"For what duration?" The musical voice took on color, like the image.

"We'll be here indefinitely."

"Payment two standard days in advance, if you please."

Han slammed the door as he entered his room. The lodge now possessed all but the very last of his ready cash.

Not that the room wasn't worth it. It was luxurious, with everything from instant-delivery high cuisine in the alcove to a patio overlooking the spectacular crater lake far below. Nevertheless, if he could not negotiate the letter of resources, he and Luke would be on a dangerously short rein.

He had a bad feeling about the letter of resources. Crseih Station was too far off the spaceways; it had been left too far outside the embrace of the New Republic. The rights and privileges and services he took for granted did not exist here.

Crseih was the kind of place he had known inside out, before he became General Han Solo. The kind of place where he could land the *Falcon*, walk into any establishment, and blend in or stand out, as he chose. He wondered if he still had that ability.

You've gotten too soft, he said to himself. Too complacent, too secure. It's time to make some changes.

And time to repair our finances.

He knew Luke would disapprove of his plan.

As Han grabbed his jacket and left, Luke knocked on the connecting door between their rooms. Instead of answering, Han left by the front door, closed it softly, and hurried away down the corridor.

The letter of resources was a worthless piece of trash in Han's pocket. His immediate impulse was to rip it to shreds and throw it into the nearest crater. But that would be stupid as well as impossible. It was printed not on paper, but on a practically indestructible sheet of archival plastic. The edges would cut his skin before they would tear.

As far as he could make out, no one in Crseih Station was the least bit interested in honoring a letter of resources drawn on the assets of the New Republic. One entrepreneur had negotiated to buy it. Han would have had to be a lot more desperate to consummate the deal; the offering price had been ridiculous. It would have been a fine bargain for the entrepreneur, for it was negotiable by the bearer. Negotiable almost anywhere but here.

"Hell with it," he muttered.

"Have you a spare—"

"No!" he said without looking around. "No spare change!"

"—minute, sir?" The ghostling placed herself in front of him, as delicate as a reed in a spring pond. "I want nothing from you but a moment of your time."

"Sure," he said, "I have a minute." Ghostlings had always mesmerized him. They looked like humans, but were not. Their ethereal beauty tantalized humans and they in their turn were fascinated by human beings. They were as seductive as incubuses and succubuses, but as fragile as spiderwebs. For a human and a ghostling to enter into a physical relationship meant certain death for a ghostling.

But there's no harm in looking, Han said to himself.

The ghostling smiled. Her long fine green-gold hair spread around her head like a halo, and her wide black eyes searched his gaze. She touched his hand with her delicate fingertips. Her gilt-tan skin glowed and her golden fingernails dimpled his skin. Han shivered.

"What do you want?" he asked, his tone harsh.

The ghostling smiled. "Nothing. I want to give you something. The route to happiness—"

"To your death!" Han exclaimed.

"No," she said. "No, I'm not like that, not one of *them*. I used to—" She broke their gaze and looked at the street, at bits of trash that skittered past her bare feet.

She stood on tiptoe. Her feet had never evolved to stand flat. Her feet and legs were more like those of a faun than a human being.

"I used to plague humans," the ghostling said. "I was fascinated with your kind. I followed, I teased—you are so exciting!—and I thought, It might be worth it just to partake of a human, even as the last experience of my life." She smiled again, her expression beatific. "But I saw the error of my ways, of my thoughts, and I've dedicated myself to helping others see the truth! The truth that we are all the same, that we may commune in joy if we give ourselves to Waru!"

Han laughed out loud. The ghostling sprang back, at first startled and frightened, then distressed.

"Sir? I've said something to amuse you?"

"Something to surprise me," Han said. He gestured around him, at the dome, the taverns and lights, the establishments at which one could get anything one wished, if one had the price. "I didn't expect to be proselytized—not here."

The ghostling smiled again, and moved close. "But where better? Come with me, I'll show you. We're the same. Waru will give us joy."

"Thanks," Han said. "But, no. Thanks."

"Perhaps some other time," the ghostling said, her voice a soft promise. She tiptoed away, waved over her shoulder, and vanished into the crowd.

Han chuckled and strolled into the nearest tavern. He forgot about his encounter with the ghostling, as he had forgotten about every other encounter with a ghostling. It was pointless to remember them, pointless to dwell on the impossibilities.

The tavern was hot and dark and smoky; intoxicant incense tinged the air and mixed with the pungent scent of wine. Han sat at the bar and relaxed. He could identify the homeworlds of about half the customers in the place; the other half were unfamiliar to him.

Borderland, he thought. A real borderland.

He smiled to himself, then laughed again.

It had been too long since he had crossed a border.

"Two-element minimum."

Han turned to the bar. No one was there. He looked up, then down; still nothing.

A slender tentacle tweaked his cuff.

"Two-element minimum."

All along the bar, the slender tentacles waved or waited or curved around mugs or wineglasses or flagons. Han rose to look over the edge of the bar, but the slender tentacle stretched before his face and motioned him back.

"If you wish to imbibe, you are in the right place." The voice sounded like a falling stack of steel rods. "If you wish to indulge your curiosity, may I suggest the museum in the next dome?"

"Sorry," Han said, offended.

"No offense taken. Two-element minimum." The tentacle was poised to serve him.

Han subsided onto his barstool. "Then give me two elements," he said. "How about polonium and plumbum?"

"I serve neither here," the voice said.

"Two glasses of the local ale will do," Han said.

"A fine choice for a brave individual." The tentacle snapped out of sight behind the bar.

Han searched his memory for a shy species with many tentacles, but he came up with no one who would suit. He leaned against the bar, content. When he returned home was plenty of time to research the species he had never met, and perhaps to start an expedition to invite them to join the New Republic.

He scouted out the tavern. This was not a family establishment. The light was low, the intoxicant smoke thick, and small groups of people leaned close together over heavy tables and the occasional meeting pond. Han could hear the low tones of many conversations, none loud enough to make out.

Two glasses of ale thumped on the bar behind him; the serving tentacle vanished before Han turned around. Ale sloshed over the lips of the tankards, splashing on the dented wood.

Han took a gulp of ale, expecting watery swill or throat-stripping solvent. Instead, the soft strong ale traced its flavor across his tongue. He swallowed. The ale glowed pleasantly in his stomach. He finished the first tankard and started in on the second, still checking out the patterns of the tavern.

A damp tapping drew his attention. The slender tentacle patted the bar, gently at first, then more insistently, till one of the suckers on the tentacle fastened to the bar and released, over and over, with a loud wet *pop.*

"Careful, you're going to get tangled," Han said. He laughed. The ale warmed him with an agreeable buzz. He could hear the conversations better; he could almost make out the words. He took another gulp of ale.

"You have already proven your bravery, sir human," the barkeep's voice said. "No need to push your luck by failing your obligations."

"My what?" Han said.

"Your obligations! You occupy my space, you ingest my comestibles—"

Han chuckled. "This isn't your native language, is it?"

"Certainly not," the barkeep said in a highly insulted tone.

"It works better if you speak plainly."

"Pay!"

"That's plain enough," Han said. He took a coin from his pocket and tossed it on the bar. The tentacle coiled over it, placed one sucker delicately on its surface, and lifted the coin. The tentacle snapped away behind the bar, and when it reappeared, the coin had vanished.

"What do you folks do for entertainment around here?" Han asked.

"We are doing it." The tentacle waved its tip toward each corner of the room, each table, each meeting pond. "Do you require additional entertainment?"

"I don't mind a game now and then."

"Bolo-ball? There is a league."

"I was thinking of something more sedentary . . . and riskier."

The tentacle twisted into a knotted shape, rising over Han's shoulder, pointing. Han turned around, and ran nose-first into the chest of a giant.

Han looked up. An enhanced human grinned merrily down at him.

"A sporting man?" The enhanced human, her size increased by genetic manipulation and her strength increased by surgery, was a head taller than Chewbacca.

"I've been known to place a bet from time to time."

"Will this suit your fancy?" She opened her hand. In her wide palm lay a deck of cards. A design of complex knots decorated the back. The enhanced human moved her hand, and the deck flipped over. Chance & Hazard, illuminated with gold and emerald paint, topped the stack.

Han grinned. "That will do fine," he said. "Just fine."

Chapter

3

Anakin wriggled furiously in Jaina's arms, trying to get down.

"Bad mens, Jaya!" he said. "Bad mens!"

"Stop wiggling, Anakin," Jaina said. She hugged her little brother, but that just made him struggle even more. His face was streaked with furious tears. He had stopped crying, but he was still so angry and scared that his whole body trembled.

"Papa!" he shouted. "Papa! I want Papa!" He started to cry again.

Jaina was scared, too, and confused. She pretended not to be.

They were on a perfectly circular patch of Munto Codru feather grass. Jacen and Mr. Chamberlain's black-furred wyrwulf slept on the grass beside Jaina. Jaina wanted to wake Jacen up. But she had just woken up. Waking up had hurt. It never hurt to wake up before. Never before in her whole life.

The patch of grass was not part of the meadow anymore. It was in a big metal room. It sat in the middle of the metal floor, as if someone had cut it out with a big round cookie-cutter. Metal walls rose very high above, all around. Jaina could not see any doors. She could not see any windows. Big lights glared down at her from the ceiling.

"Don't cry, Anakin," Jaina said. "Don't cry. I'll take care of you. I'm five, so I'll take care of you, because you're only three."

"Three and a half!" he said.

"Three and a half," she said.

He sniffled and rubbed his sticky face. "Want Papa," he said.

Jaina wished Papa was here, too. And Mama. And Winter. And Chewie. But she did not say so. She had to be the adult. She was oldest. She was almost already getting her grown-up teeth. Her right front tooth was really loose. She wiggled it with her tongue while she thought what to do.

She was two years older than Anakin. Okay, one and a half years older. She was only five minutes older than Jacen. They were twins, even though they did not look exactly alike. Her hair was light brown and very straight. Jacen's was dark and curly. But she was still oldest.

"Down!" Anakin demanded. "Jaya, down!"

"I'll let you down," Jaina said, "if you promise to stay on the grass."

Anakin stuck out his lower lip. His dark eyes sparkled with tears of frustration and anger. He was always stubborn when anyone said no to him. About anything.

"Promise?" Jaina said.

"Stay on the grass," he said.

She let him down. He dashed across the grass. He peered over the edge. Jaina took her gaze off him for a second. She crouched down next to Jacen, wishing he would wake up. The wyrwulf twitched and moaned.

Jaina looked around for Anakin. He was sticking his foot over the edge of the grass. Jaina ran after him and pulled him back.

"I said stay on the grass!"

"*Am* on the grass," he insisted. He pointed toward the floor. "Just a floor, Jaya. No krakana!"

The last place they had been, on Mama's tour, they had not been allowed to swim in the ocean. Mon Calamari was mostly ocean, and its ocean was full of krakana. Krakana would eat anything, even children. *Especially* children.

Now, every time anybody told Anakin "no," he would argue by saying, "No krakana!"

Jaina did not want to scare him. She did not know if there was anything to be scared of yet. She wished she knew how they had gotten here. Something bad must have happened, but maybe getting taken away like this was how they got rescued.

She wished Mama and Papa and Uncle Luke and Winter and Chewie and Mr. Threepio were here. Or even just one of them.

Jacen whimpered. Jaina grabbed Anakin's hand and pulled him across the little patch of grass to her twin's side.

"Hold Jasa's hand," Jaina said. Anakin grabbed Jacen's hand in both his little fists. Jaina took Jacen's other hand.

"Jasa, Jasa, wake up," Anakin said. "Sleepybones!"

Jacen opened his eyes. "Ouch!" he said, just as Jaina said, "Ouch!" She could feel what he felt. He could feel what she felt. Jaina's head hurt, like somebody was screaming in her ear.

Their eyes were filled with tears. Jaina's lower lip trembled. She pressed her lips together to keep from crying. Her front tooth wiggled.

She *made* the scream and the hurt go away. From her and from Jacen, before he was all awake.

She was not supposed to use her Jedi abilities unless Uncle Luke was with them. Jacen was not supposed to. Anakin especially was not supposed to. Uncle Luke was teaching them what to do. How to do it right.

But sometimes it was hard not to do something. Like now.

Jacen sat up. Bits of grass stuck to his homespun shirt. Some were stuck in his curly dark brown hair. Jaina brushed her hands against her own hair, but she did not find any grass blades. Her light brown hair was very straight, so hardly anything ever got tangled in it. Jacen roughed his fingers through his hair, leaving it rumpled as usual. The grass fell out.

"Okay now?" she said.

"Okay now," Jacen said. He looked around. "Where are we?"

"Remember what happened?"

"We were playing with Chewie—"

"—and he jumped up—"

"—and then he fell down—"

"—and then I went to sleep."

"Me too."

"Skiff!" Anakin said. "Jaya forgot the skiff!"

"What skiff?"

"I *saw* it!" Anakin insisted.

"*This* isn't a skiff!" Jacen said.

He was right. The room they were in could hold a whole skiff.

"Maybe the skiff brought us here."

"Where?" Jacen said.

Jaina shrugged. They might be on a spaceship. They might be in a great big building. They might even still be on Munto Codru, underground. Jaina and Jacen had explored under the castle. They had found halls and caves and tunnels. But they had never found any place that looked like this.

"Are you okay, wyrwulf?" Jacen bent over Mr. Chamberlain's wyrwulf and stroked its fur. The black undercoat shone beneath the rougher, duller black guard hairs. The wyrwulf's eyelids flickered. It whimpered and sat up, panting.

"Good woof," Anakin said.

Jacen looked around. "Maybe Chewie is here someplace, maybe he's still asleep too." He jumped to his feet and walked right off the edge of the grass.

Nothing happened.

"See, Jaya?" Anakin said, pleased with himself. "No krakana!" He ran after Jacen. The wyrwulf trotted after them.

Jaina took one step after Jacen and Anakin. She stopped. She was sure that if they stayed on the grass, nothing could hurt them. But she did not want her brothers to go off alone. She was the oldest, after all.

She ran back to the center of the safe patch. She stooped and pushed aside fronds of feather grass. She was looking for her multitool. She knew it was here. She had brought it to the field to look at things with. When Chewie fell down, she had jumped up. Then she had fallen asleep. She must have dropped it.

There!

Jaina snatched up the tool. She shoved it deep into her pocket to keep it hidden. With her multitool she would be safe.

She ran after her brothers.

Her feet clanged on the metal floor. She caught up to Jacen. He was looking at the wall. Anakin did not bother to look. He kicked it.

"Bad wall!"

"Don't do that, you'll hurt yourself," Jacen said.

Anakin glowered and bumped the toe of his shoe against the wall. Not kicking. Not kicking for real.

"There's got to be a door," Jacen said reasonably. "For us to come in."

"Maybe there's a trapdoor," Jaina said. "A secret door." She rapped her knuckles against the metal. The knock was very solid. She looked up. "Here's the support," she said.

Jacen, too, looked up at the ceiling. Narrow metal beams curved over them. The lights hung from the beams.

"We have to look for a door *between* the beams," Jaina said. She walked around the room, knocking on the wall. She found some hollow spots. But she could not find a door. She took out her multitool. She opened the drill part.

"You aren't supposed to do that," Jacen said.

"I didn't!" Jaina said. But she touched the drill part to the wall. She was only supposed to use it on something she was making in the workshop. Not on walls or floors or furniture. Anyway it would not work on metal, only on wood.

She tried anyway, wiggling her front tooth with her tongue while she concentrated. But the drill would not do anything. It hid itself back inside the handle.

When Jaina was seven she could have a multitool that worked on metal. If she was good. If she was *responsible*.

She wished she was seven. Seven was a long time away.

She opened the lens part instead. She used it to look at

the wall as close as she could. She thought she found a seam. A crack?

A door opened.

Jaina jumped back. She grabbed Anakin's hand and pushed him behind her. At the same time she shoved her multitool back into her pocket.

She and Jacen stood side by side, defending their little brother.

The wyrwulf crouched and growled.

Anakin wailed and tried to burrow his way between Jaina and Jacen, to see what was happening.

A tall and very beautiful man walked out. He had gold- and copper- and cinnamon-colored striped hair, very pale skin, and very big black eyes. His face was sharp and thin, all corners. He wore a long white robe.

He smiled down at Jaina.

"You poor children," he said.

He knelt in front of them.

"My poor children! I'm so sorry. Come to me, I'll keep you safe from now on."

"I want Papa!" Anakin shouted. "Mama!"

"I'm very sorry, sir," Jaina said with her best court manners. "We can't go to you."

"We aren't allowed," Jacen explained. "We don't know you."

"Ah, children, don't you remember me? No, how could you, you were only just born. I'm your hold-father Hethrir!"

Jaina stared at him, uncertain. She had never heard of any Hold-father Hethrir. But she and Jacen had lots of hold-fathers and hold-mothers. Anakin had lots of hold-fathers and hold-mothers.

"Candy?" Anakin asked hopefully.

The beautiful man smiled. "Of course. As soon as we get you cleaned up."

Their hold-parents always brought them toys, and treats that were not often allowed otherwise.

"Do you know the password?" Jaina asked. Mama had told her never to go with anyone who did not know the password.

Hold-father Hethrir sat crosslegged on the floor in front of them.

The wyrwulf flopped to the deck, leaning its head on its fangs, and stared at Hold-father Hethrir.

"Children," Hethrir said, "a terrible thing has happened. I came to visit you, to see my sweet friend Leia and my old comrade Han. To meet your Uncle Luke. But when I came, I saw a horrible thing! An earthquake!" He cocked his head at Jaina. "Do you know what an earthquake is?"

Uneasily, Jaina nodded.

"I'm sorry, children. The castle—it was so old! It fell down, and . . ."

He stopped, and took a deep breath. Jaina's lower lip started to quiver again. Her eyes got all blurry. She blinked. She did not want to hear what Hold-father Hethrir had to say.

"Your mama was in the castle. And your papa, and your Uncle Luke. You were in the meadow—do you remember?— and the ground opened up and swallowed friend Chewbacca, and you were about to slide down into the horrible crack in the earth, but I was right there and I swooped down and I saved you. But I couldn't save friend Chewbacca, and . . ." He glanced down, and wiped a tear from his cheek, and looked up again. "I'm so sorry, children, we could not rescue your mama or your papa or your uncle."

Anakin started to wail. "Papa! Mama! Uncle Luke!"

Jaina clutched his hand and pulled him close. "Don't cry," she whispered. Anakin stopped wailing, but he still sniffled and sobbed.

"But Papa and Uncle Luke—" Jacen's voice was trembly, but suspicious.

Jaina *nudged* him. He shut up.

"None of that, now." Hold-father Hethrir smiled.

Somehow, he knew what she had done. And it made him angry, though he was smiling. Scared, Jaina pulled back inside herself. She pretended she had never touched Jacen with her mind.

"If I had landed, if the earthquake had not happened, your mama and papa would have introduced you to me. They would have told me your password. We would have had a party, and we would have been friends!"

He stretched both his hands toward Jaina and Jacen.

"Your dear family is gone, my children. The Republic asked me to take you, to keep you, to protect you and teach you. I am so sorry . . . that your mama and papa are dead."

Jaina huddled together with her brothers. How could it be true? But why would anyone lie about it?

"We—we're supposed to go with Winter," Jaina said. Her voice trembled. "If anything hap—"

"Winter? Who is Winter?"

"She's our nanny," Jaina said.

"She went on a trip," Jacen said.

"Are you keeping us till she comes home?"

"Can we call her?" Jacen said hopefully.

"She'd come right back," Jaina said.

"Her services are no longer necessary," Hold-father Hethrir said. "Children, children! You are important! Your abilities are precious! You cannot be raised, you cannot be *taught*, by a servant."

"She isn't! She's our friend!"

"She has her own life to live, she cannot raise you properly with no one to pay for you."

"We wouldn't eat much," Jacen said hopefully.

Jaina wanted to say Hold-father Hethrir was a liar!—and run away. But she had nowhere to run. And maybe Papa and Uncle Luke *had* come home, while she and her brothers were in the meadow, and maybe the earthquake *had* come before Papa came out to greet them, and maybe Hold-father Hethrir really *had* rescued them.

And maybe Winter really wouldn't come back. Not *ever*.

Or maybe Hold-father Hethrir did not know that Papa and Uncle Luke and Mr. Threepio had gone on a secret mission. No one was supposed to know about the secret mission, except Chewbacca and Mama—but Jaina did! And she had told Jacen, of course, because he was her twin. Maybe no one could tell Hold-father Hethrir because then Papa and Uncle Luke would be in danger. That meant Papa and Uncle Luke might be all right. But she could not say so, because then *she* would put Papa and Uncle Luke in danger.

Anakin huddled against her, sniffling. He was trying not to cry, but his tears left a cold wet spot on her shirt. Mr.

Chamberlain's wyrwulf had edged closer to Jaina, too, and leaned unhappily against her side.

Or maybe, Jaina thought, Hold-father Hethrir isn't who he says he is. Maybe he's making it all up, about the earthquake.

Maybe he stole us.

Maybe Mama and Papa and Uncle Luke and Chewbacca are all right.

Jaina looked at Hold-father Hethrir. His huge dark eyes gleamed with tears. He gazed at her, his hands outstretched.

A second set of eyelids swept across his eyes. Jaina could see through the second eyelids. They looked like smoke. They pushed away the tears. Then they disappeared again.

Without meaning to, without wanting to, Jaina started to cry.

Don't cry, she said furiously to herself. Don't cry. If you don't cry it means Mama is alive!

She made herself stop crying.

"Jacen," Jaina said, "*you* have to say whether we believe him. Because *you're* the *oldest*."

"I'm oldest," Jacen said. "*I'm* oldest, Hold-father Hethrir!"

"I remember," Hold-father Hethrir said. "I remember when you both were born, your mama and papa were so happy, they said to me, 'Here is Jacen, our firstborn son, and here is Jaina, our beautiful daughter.' "

He's a liar! Jaina thought. A liar!

"We believe you, Hold-father Hethrir," Jacen said.

For just a second, Jaina thought maybe Jacen really meant it. But then she thought, No, that's stupid. She was afraid to *touch* him for reassurance, because Hold-father Hethrir would know.

She started to cry again.

It's all right to cry *now*, she thought. Because I'm just pretending, because I have to, and Mama and Papa and Uncle Luke and Chewbacca are all alive!

She and Jacen and Anakin huddled together, all of them crying, Anakin wailing, "Papa! Papa!"

Hold-father Hethrir took Jaina's hand. He took Jacen's

hand. He squeezed gently. His skin was very cold. He pulled on Jaina's hand. She had to move nearer to him. She wanted to move away from him.

I don't believe he's really my hold-father! Jaina thought. I'm not going to call him that anymore.

Hethrir put his arms around her and her brothers. Jaina shivered.

"Poor children," he said. "Poor little children. I'm so sorry your mama and papa are dead."

Anakin cried harder.

Jaina and Jacen cuddled him. He sniffled. He started to hiccup. He fell asleep with his cheek pillowed on Jaina's shoulder. He hiccupped again.

"There, there, poor children," Hethrir said. "You've had such a hard day. Come along, it's time for bed."

Jaina stood up. She picked up Anakin. He was heavy.

"We always have our supper before we go to bed," she said.

Hethrir stood up. He was very tall. He smiled down at her.

"But you live with me now," he said. "And at my house, it's time for bed."

He urged them toward the doorway. Jaina saw another person standing in the darkness. Scared, she stopped.

"Come forward, Tigris," Hethrir said. "Don't stand there hiding in the shadows."

Tigris took a step forward. He was not scary at all. He was not even grown up, only twelve or thirteen. He wore a brown robe. Jaina thought it was ugly. It needed to be washed, and the hem had come down.

He had striped hair like Hethrir's, but his was silver and black. It needed to be washed, too. And combed. Her mama would never let her go outside looking like that. He had pale skin and big black eyes, also like Hethrir's.

"Don't make our new sister carry the child," Hethrir said. "Show your manners."

Are they brothers? Jaina wondered. How could they be, Hethrir is so *old*. And Hethrir doesn't act like Tigris's brother. I'd never talk to Anakin in such a mean way.

Tigris tried to take Anakin from Jaina. She stepped back. Jacen jumped in front of her to help protect their little brother. Together, they created the barrier Uncle Luke had taught them to make. No one would be able to get through it. They would not let Tigris take Anakin!

The barrier *shimmered* around Jaina.

And then it fell apart like a sand castle in the tide.

"Now, now," Hethrir said. "None of that! Didn't your uncle ever tell you not to behave like that? You're being very, very bad."

He knelt down in front of them again.

"I'll teach you to use your abilities. The same as your Uncle Luke. But you must only use them under my supervision, until you're grown up."

Jaina hugged Anakin tighter.

"Do you understand?"

Jaina knew what was going to happen. She knew she could not stop it.

"Do you understand?" Hethrir demanded.

Jacen had backed up right against Anakin. Their brother was protected between them. The wyrwulf growled.

Suddenly the wyrwulf slid across the deck and crashed against the wall. Jaina cried out. The wyrwulf yelped and lay still.

"Woof!" Anakin cried.

Hethrir took Jacen's shoulders and pulled him forward, away from Anakin. He pulled him aside. He did not even bother to move Jacen with the Force powers he had revealed. He did not need to. He was a grown-up. Jacen tried to wriggle free, but Hethrir would not let him go.

"Do you understand?"

Tigris took Anakin from Jaina's arms. His eyes were sad and hopeful. Jaina could not stop him. She could not move. She could not extend her mind to her brother's. She did not know what Jacen was thinking. He looked back at her, scared. She did know one thing. He did not know what she was thinking either.

"Jacen!" she said. "Anakin!" She could talk! But she did not talk to Hethrir.

"I see that you understand," Hethrir said.

He grabbed Jaina's hand and Jacen's hand. He pulled them along after him.

"What about Mr. Chamberlain's wyrwulf?" Jacen shouted.

"You're too old to keep a pet," Hethrir said.

The door closed. Behind them, the wyrwulf howled.

Hethrir was so tall and he walked so fast that Jaina had to run to keep up. Tigris strode along after them.

Jaina could hardly see anything. She tripped. Hethrir jerked her to her feet and kept going.

"Stop!" Jaina shouted. "Stop! No! Help!" She screamed.

"Help!" Jacen shouted along with her. "Help, leave us alone!"

"Jaya, Jasa!" Anakin cried.

Jaina dragged back on Hethrir's hand. She struggled to look over her shoulder. Anakin wriggled to escape Tigris's arms. Tigris held him tighter. Tight enough to hurt. Anakin's dark eyes were bright with tears.

"You leave my brother alone!" Jacen shouted. He too fought to get away from Hethrir.

Anakin *pushed* at Tigris.

Tigris yelped with pain. He nearly dropped Anakin. He held on to him till Anakin's feet touched the ground. Then Tigris grabbed his own hands together. He shook them and rubbed them against his grubby robe.

Hethrir stopped. He dropped Jaina's hand, and Jacen's.

Jaina ran to Anakin. She hugged her little brother. He burrowed against her shoulder. Jacen knelt on the floor beside them, hugging them both. Jaina knew his determined look.

Hethrir loomed over them. He looked angry. He stared, intent, at Anakin.

Then he smiled.

He crouched beside them. He stared hard at Anakin.

"As I hoped," he said softly. "As I expected, from the Skywalker line."

He reached past Jaina and stroked Anakin's hair. The tangles smoothed out under Hethrir's touch. Suddenly he grabbed a lock of Anakin's hair and yanked it *hard*.

Anakin screamed in surprise and pain and outrage. Furious, Jaina bit Hethrir, right through his robe. Jacen pummeled Hethrir's arm with both his fists.

Hethrir did not even flinch. And Jaina had bitten him hard.

Anakin's abilities erupted around them all. The dark hallway lighted up. Light shone through Hethrir's fingers. Jaina gasped. Hethrir's hand looked like a skeleton's.

Anakin's light went out.

Jaina felt as if a wet cold blanket had fallen around her.

Tigris pulled Jaina and Jacen away from Hethrir. Jaina's loose tooth fell out and stuck to Hethrir's sleeve. Jaina was so surprised she stopped biting. Anakin stared at Hethrir, his eyes wide.

"Be quiet!" Hethrir said softly before Anakin could say a single thing. Hethrir's voice was scary.

Jacen grabbed Jaina's hand. She could hardly feel his fingers.

Staring up at Hethrir, scared, really scared, Anakin shivered. Jaina tried to go to him, she was responsible, she was oldest. But Tigris took her by the shoulder and stopped her.

"Do what you're told," he said. "Then nobody will hurt you, nobody will hurt your brothers."

No one had ever treated her this way before. Jaina could not understand why anyone was treating her this way now.

Uncle Luke could affect her abilities, and Jacen's, and even Anakin's. A good thing, too! Anakin was too little to always know what he was doing. But Uncle Luke never made Anakin's light go away. He never smothered Jaina and Jacen with a horrible wet cold blanket that Jaina could not even see, or grab, or pull off and throw on the floor. Uncle Luke helped guide her abilities so she used them properly and learned more about them. Sometimes he even added to her power to help her, to show her how to do what she was trying to do.

Not like this!

"Take these two to their rooms," Hethrir said to Tigris. "Then return to me."

"I will obey, Hethrir," Tigris said. His voice was full of admiration.

"I want my tooth," Jaina said.

Hethrir shook his sleeve. Her tooth fell on the ground. Tigris would not let her go get it.

Hethrir picked Anakin up. Jaina's little brother did not resist. He *could* not resist.

"Please let him stay with us," Jaina said. "He's only three—"

She stopped for a second. Anakin would say, "Three and a half!" But he said nothing.

"We'll all be good if you let him stay with us," Jaina said desperately.

Hethrir gazed down at her. Now she knew the kindly look in his eyes was all a lie, and so was everything else he had said.

"If you're good," he said, "I might let you visit with your brother. In a few days. Or a week."

He turned, his long white robe swirling at his heels, and carried Anakin into the darkness. The last thing Jaina saw of her little brother was his wide, scared eyes.

Tigris pushed Jaina and Jacen along the hallway, then around a turn. The wet cold blanket of Hethrir's power still surrounded Jaina.

"It's freezing," she whispered.

"Nonsense, it's perfectly warm," Tigris said.

Jaina felt hurt and embarrassed, scared and mad. Even when she was little, no one had ever treated her like this. She always tried to use her abilities properly. To be *responsible.* As soon as she had understood what the word meant, she had known it would be important in her life.

She wished she had Mama to talk to. She was never, never, never allowed to use her abilities to hurt someone. But what about if she *had* to, what if it was to keep somebody from hurting her or Jacen, what if it was to defend her little brother? She was as responsible for Anakin as she was for the right use of what she could do.

She was *supposed* to use the barrier for defense. But she already knew that would not work.

Hethrir can stop the barrier, Jaina thought. He wouldn't do that, if he was really our hold-father. I don't believe he knows Papa and I don't believe he's friends with Mama.

Finally she thought—the thought was like the sun coming

up, here in this dark hallway—And I don't believe Mama and Papa and Uncle Luke are dead!

This time she really believed it.

She tried to catch Jacen's eye, to see if he knew Mama and Papa were alive.

She turned her head to look at Jacen. Tigris put his hand on the side of her face—his hand was warm, and he was not mean, but his purpose was clear—and made her look forward again.

"Here we walk straight and tall," he said. "With our eyes straight ahead, to see what we must face."

"That's silly," Jaina said. "Then you miss a lot!"

"And we do not contradict our elders," Tigris said.

"What's 'contradict'?" Jacen asked.

"Don't be impertinent," Tigris said.

"What's 'impertinent'?" Jaina asked. She did not know what either word meant, so if Tigris was trying to tell her that they meant the same thing, she *still* did not know what he meant. Now he acted as if he was angry, saying nothing and urging them faster into the dark.

Jaina wondered if she could burrow her way through the wet heavy blanket. It followed her and stayed wrapped around her. It was invisible, and when she touched her own arm she could not feel anything surrounding her.

But all the time, she felt like Hethrir had his cold hard hand on her shoulder. She kept trying to wriggle out of it, like Anakin wriggling out of her arms when she carried him. Trying to get free exhausted her.

The corridor ended in a big square stone room. The room was dim, but at least it was not all dark like the corridor. Faint gray light glowed from the ceiling. The ceiling was very low compared to the ceilings Jaina was used to. If Tigris reached up, he would be able to touch it. Hethrir would hardly have to reach to touch it.

The stone room had no walls, only wooden doors. Each door touched the door on each side of it. All the doors were closed. There were no windows. Jaina wondered if she could find her way outside, somehow, back the way they had come.

Or I'll have to try every single door, she thought. There must be at least a hundred. Maybe seven thousand!

One of them must lead outside, she thought.

Then she realized, If this is a spaceship—which she had not been able to figure whether it was or not—then getting out won't do us any good at all.

She was so tired. She tried to pretend she did not want to take a nap—naps were for little kids, like Anakin—but her eyelids kept drooping.

Tigris urged Jaina and Jacen into the big stone room. It echoed all around. He stopped, standing between the twins. Jaina was so sleepy that she leaned against him. She almost fell asleep standing up.

Tigris's hand lay on her shoulder. It was the only warm thing in her whole world. For a second—just a second—his touch felt like a friendly hug. Jaina thought he might pick her up and carry her to a place where she could take a nap, and tuck her in like Winter did. And everything would be all right.

Then she remembered where she was and what had happened, and maybe Tigris remembered that too, because he shook her shoulder and made her wake up.

"Here!" he said. "None of that. Here we don't sleep unless we're in our beds. There's no time for lazy napping!"

"I wasn't asleep!" Jaina said, which was sort of true.

"Me either," Jacen said.

He sounded as sleepy as Jaina felt. He must be wrapped in one of Hethrir's heavy cold blankets, too.

But when we're in bed it will be all right, Jaina thought. It will be warm and I can sneak my hand out of the covers and he can sneak his hand out of his covers and we can hold hands. And even if we can't think at each other we can whisper.

Jaina's eyes filled with tears and her vision blurred. She had never before had to think about sneaking just so she could hold her brother's hand. She never had to think about sneaking before at all! And she could not remember the time before she could *think* at Jacen. She felt so cold and tired and hungry and lonely that she almost burst into tears again. She only kept from crying because she knew that pretty soon she could talk to Jacen and they could figure out what to do.

Tigris urged them forward. They reached one of the little doors. Tigris opened it. Jaina thought there would be another long corridor beyond it. She did not think she could walk down another long corridor.

There was hardly anything at all beyond the door. Only a tiny room, just the width of the door and only about twice as deep.

Jaina stopped, confused. Maybe there was another door at the back of the tiny room. But she could see no handle, no automatic controls, no mark where the door's edge would be. The open door was heavy, scarred wood, while the inside of the room was the ugly, gray-glowing rock.

Tigris let go of Jacen's hand and pressed him a few steps forward into the little room.

The door thudded shut behind him.

"Jacen! Jacen!" Jaina cried. She snatched herself out of Tigris's grasp and ran to the door, grabbing for the handle. But Tigris pulled her away. From the other side, Jacen cried out her name. She could barely hear him.

"Come now," Tigris said. "Don't be a baby. Here we don't shout and scream. We're brave."

Jaina turned around furiously. "I *am* brave!" she said.

She tried to hit him, but he caught both her hands and held them still, and she could not *do* anything.

"I *am* brave, and I want my brother!"

"It's time to sleep," Tigris said. "You won't act so foolish in the morning. Come along."

Maybe I can still talk to Jacen through the wall, Jaina thought desperately. Maybe it won't be too bad. . . .

She turned hopefully toward the door next to Jacen's.

Tigris led her away from Jacen's room, all the way across the huge square hall. He opened a door to a tiny room just like Jacen's, but as far from her brother's as it could be.

Tigris let go of her hand. She looked up at him.

"Show me that you are brave," he said. He glanced into the room and Jaina knew he wanted her to go inside without being told.

She looked up at him, directly into his large dark eyes.

"I want to go home," she said.

"I know," Tigris said softly. He hesitated, then gestured to the tiny room. "But . . . you cannot."

She went in. She had no other choice. He closed the door behind her.

The ghostly gray stone faded toward darkness. Jaina searched for another opening. Another exit. A way to take apart the lock or the hinges of the big wooden door. She could find nothing, except a few splintery scuff marks where someone had kicked at the wood.

Jaina walked around her tiny room. She touched the walls. She found nothing. She knocked on the side walls, but the sound was very hollow, and she received no reply.

At the back of the room, her feet sank. She dropped to her knees and felt the floor. It was soft and squishy. The ghost glow was almost gone. She could see her fingers, but the floor was dark. She could push the floor down. The soft spot was just big enough for her to curl up on. She tried it out. She was cold, but that was because of Hethrir's invisible blanket. She wanted her own bed. She wanted her own comforter, and Eba, the soft Wookiee doll Chewbacca had brought her, with a twin doll Aba for Jacen, after his last trip home.

The light went out. The room was very dark. Jaina shivered.

I'll pretend, Jaina thought. We're on a campout. But all the camping stuff got lost. Or maybe it fell in the water. It's all wet. We have to fix it.

She thought of a soft camp mattress under her, just dried out, nice and warm. And her smart camping blanket. It knew when she was cold and it knew to warm up. It knew to snuggle down around her to keep out the wind. It liked to get wet sometimes—it liked to swim. Then it lay flat on the ground, because it did not have any feet. And it wriggled and shook until its fur was dry and warm and Jaina could wrap it around her shoulders and go to sleep. When she was little she even liked to sleep with it at home.

Mama is on the camping trip, too, Jaina thought. And Papa, and Winter, and Chewbacca, and Uncle Luke, and Mr. Threepio, and Artoo-Detoo didn't come because he doesn't like getting dirt in his treads, but he's back home all safe. We had toast over the campfire, and Anakin is sleeping over there, and Jacen is here too, and we made cocoa . . .

A small warm point of light appeared before her, flickering like flame. She reached her hand out, and Jacen wrapped his fingers around it, and Jaina stopped shivering. . . .

Tigris hurried back to Lord Hethrir's chambers.

I was foolish, he thought. Foolish and weak to coddle the children. I did them no good, to try to comfort them. I only make them foolish and weak as well!

He knelt at Lord Hethrir's door. He did not knock. Lord Hethrir knew he was here. The Lord would acknowledge him when he was ready, when the time was appropriate.

Tigris used the waiting time to consider the errors he had made.

Finally, when Tigris's knees had begun to ache, Lord Hethrir's door swung open. Tigris felt the weight of Hethrir's gaze upon his shoulders. He raised his head and looked into Hethrir's eyes.

"You took longer than necessary," Hethrir said.

"Yes, Lord Hethrir."

For a moment, a moment only, Tigris thought to lie, to blame the extra time on the little children. For they *were* contrary and impertinent. But their impertinence had not caused him to take the extra time.

"I erred, Lord Hethrir. I spoke to the children. I instructed them, as you wished, but I spoke to them at unnecessary length. I was . . . weak and foolish."

Hethrir loomed over him. He did not express anger. He never expressed anger. Tigris wondered if he ever felt anger, or if his mind was too advanced for any such defect.

"You disappoint me, Tigris," Hethrir said.

Tigris felt the disappointment. He was disappointed in himself. He never pleased Hethrir; he always failed.

"But you have confessed your error, so I will give you another chance. Get up."

Tigris obeyed. Hethrir returned to his chambers, then glanced back impatiently.

"Come along!"

Astonished, Tigris followed Hethrir. Hethrir seldom invited him inside. He felt mightily honored to be brought into the beautiful receiving room, with its thick patterned carpet over golden tiles, its polished body-wood walls, its curving pipes of light tracing designs on the ceiling.

The smallest new child, Anakin, sat quietly in the middle of the rug. His energy was much diminished since Tigris last saw him. He had begun to shine again, with a weakly flickering light.

"You have confessed your weakness," Hethrir said again. "That will help you find your path to strength. I will forgive you. What do you think of this child?"

Tigris regarded the little boy.

"He could be very strong," Tigris said. "His light shines. You have placed him within a veil."

Hethrir nodded. "An adequate observation."

Tigris was thrilled by the compliment. Not precisely a compliment, but as near as Hethrir ever gave him. For once he had not displeased his master!

"Thank you, Lord Hethrir."

"I shall take him to be purified," Hethrir said.

"To be purified?" Tigris said, so startled he forgot his place.

This child, an Empire Youth? he thought. If my lord will present this contrary child for purification, why won't he present *me*?

"My lord, he has no training—he isn't a Proctor, he isn't even a *helper*—!"

Hethrir gazed at him, without anger or comment. Terrified, Tigris fell silent.

"I will take the child to be purified," Hethrir said again, as if Tigris had never spoken. "Take my message to the helpers: they are to prepare my ship."

"Yes, Lord Hethrir," Tigris whispered.

Tigris rose, then hesitated.

Lord Hethrir cannot have forgotten the reception tomorrow morning, Tigris thought. Is he testing me again? I long to serve him some other way than carrying messages! I long to earn the right to be purified. I'm not afraid of the danger!

Perhaps, Tigris thought, Lord Hethrir believes *I* forgot the reception. Perhaps he thinks my hopes are so arrogant that I cannot remember my duties.

"Is a member of the Empire Youth in residence, my lord?"

"Certainly not. They are all working for the Empire Reborn, undermining the New Republic." Lord Hethrir sounded impatient.

"Then, sir, shall I ask the Head Proctor to negotiate with your guests?" Tigris asked.

"My guests—?" Hethrir said. "The Head Proctor?"

"Tomorrow morning, sir."

Hethrir paused.

"I'd no more leave the Head Proctor to receive my guests than I'd leave you, foolish Tigris!" he said sharply. "I have no intention of departing *before* my guests arrive! Why did you think I might?"

"I misunderstood," Tigris said quickly. "I beg your forgiveness."

Hethrir sighed. "You continually apologize, but you never change in such a way as to make apology unnecessary. That is what you must strive for!"

Tigris hung his head. He could not think of anything to say, except that he was sorry, and he did not want to say he was sorry again. He was aware of the depths to which he had disappointed Lord Hethrir. He picked at the cuff of his ragged brown robe, knowing how far he was from replacing it with the rust-colored tunic of a helper, or the light blue jumpsuit of the Proctors.

Hethrir rose. His white robes rustled. The soft fabric slid across itself as the Lord moved. The sound made Tigris shiver.

The whining hum of Lord Hethrir's lightsaber filled the room, and the silver-gray light of the blade cast shadows on Tigris's empty hands. Tigris raised his head, to gaze in wonder as he always did at the radiance of Lord Hethrir's saber.

The blade vanished.

"Try once more," Lord Hethrir said, and gave the handle of the lightsaber to Tigris.

The handle of the saber felt warm in Tigris's grip. The

lightsaber was too large for Tigris's hands, but he clasped it as best he could.

He knew what Lord Hethrir wanted him to do.

The blade of Lord Hethrir's lightsaber could only be activated by the use of the Force. Hethrir would not accept anyone into his inner circles who could not complete the circuit and generate the blade.

Tigris tried, how he tried, to make a connection to the Force, to extend himself, to *create* the blade.

The child Anakin raised his head and watched with interest.

Nothing happened. The saber remained cold and dead.

"Mine!" Anakin said, stretching his hands toward Tigris.

Lord Hethrir smiled fondly at Anakin. "No, little one," he said. "You have no need of my lightsaber."

He returned his attention to Tigris, and sighed again. He took back his saber and fastened the handle to his belt, beneath his outer robe. Tigris caught a glimpse of the second lightsaber he carried, a smaller one, which Tigris had never seen him wield. Tigris was convinced that if Lord Hethrir would let him try that lightsaber, the smaller one, he would be able to succeed. But Tigris had tried to hint at the possibility, just once. The memory of his lord's abrupt silence kept Tigris from ever again making such a suggestion.

"Go," Lord Hethrir said.

"Yes, Lord Hethrir," Tigris said.

He had disappointed his mentor. He had disappointed himself. And he was frightened.

Children who could not touch the Force did not deserve to remain in the presence of Lord Hethrir.

Jaina woke up because she was so hungry. It was very dark! Where were the moons and the stars?

Maybe it's all cloudy, Jaina thought.

And then she remembered what had happened.

She gasped and sat up. She stuck her hands out in front of her—Jacen had been holding her hand, hadn't he?—but she could not see him and she could not hear him and she could not *find* him.

The soft place in the floor turned solid again. Startled, Jaina jumped up. The spot the room used for a bed had disappeared.

She felt her way to the door. It was still the same splintery wood. The hinges were outside and so was the latch.

"Let me out," she said. The door did not respond. "Open," she said. "Please." Nothing happened. She tried a couple of other languages. None of them made any difference.

She sighed.

I didn't *really* think it would work to ask, she thought.

She was scared to use her abilities to explore the door latch, but she was more scared not to try.

The moment she *reached* into the latch, the heavy cold blanket of Hethrir's power fell around her.

Jaina flinched and pulled away. She had managed a brief glimpse of the latch. It was simple but very big and heavy. A handsbreadth of wood stood between the latch and Jaina.

I *could* take it apart, she thought. I know I could. If I could just get to it. I could even put it back together and not have any pieces left over.

She shivered again. Hethrir's blanket lay cold and wet around her. She guessed it would go away again, if she was good. She pushed her cold hands into her pockets. She just wanted to get warm.

Her fingers closed around her multitool.

She snatched it out of her pocket.

How could I forget? she thought. She opened the wood tool. She touched it to the door. She was not supposed to use her multitool on houses or furniture. But surely this was different.

A few splinters fell away.

The door cracked open. Dull light washed over her. She jumped back and shoved the multitool into her pocket to hide it.

"Ow!" It was so dark in her room that the light hurt. She squeezed her eyes closed.

"Come out," Tigris said. Jaina could not see him but she

recognized his voice. Blinking and rubbing her eyes, she came outside.

Tigris closed the door behind her.

She saw Jacen across the room, standing in front of his door. His shoulders drooped.

She ran toward him. Tigris grabbed her and stopped her. She wriggled but she could not get away. He made her stand in front of her door. She looked around the room. A child stood in front of each door, all different children from all different worlds. None of them moved. They all looked scared and tired, and their clothes were ragged.

Older children in rust-red tunics stood straight in a double line in the middle of the big stone room.

"We do not run, here," Tigris said. "We wait for permission from the Proctor."

Tigris pointed toward the front of the big room. A tall young man wearing a light blue jumpsuit stood at the entryway, watching everything. He folded his arms.

"And then the helpers show us how to line up, and we walk where we are told."

The helpers fanned out, precise and expressionless, spacing themselves as if they were herding the ragged children. The children turned obediently to face the Proctor. Across the room, Jacen stayed stubbornly where he was.

Jaina glared at Tigris and did not move.

"Why?" Jaina asked. "I want Jacen! Where's Anakin?"

"I told you we are not impertinent here!"

"I wasn't, I don't even know what it *means*!"

"Turn!" Tigris said sharply.

Jaina glared at the floor, just like Jacen across the room.

"Do you want your breakfast?" Tigris asked.

Jaina looked up. "Yes!"

"Then do as you are told."

Jaina scowled and looked at the floor again. Tigris had to push her around. One of the helpers did the same to Jacen.

"Walk!" Tigris said. The other children walked forward, all in step. Tigris pushed Jaina along with them.

But she did not walk in step.

Jaina scuffed her feet on the concrete. Tigris tightened his long sharp fingers around her shoulder. But he did not tell her to stop, so she kept scuffing. The noise came in between the regular *tramp, tramp, tramp* of the other children's marching feet. A second scuffing added itself to the sound. Out of time with her own!

Jaina shot a glance across the room. Jacen grinned at her. Then the helper beside him turned Jacen's head straight forward.

But the damage was done. Jaina skipped a few steps, one foot, hop! the other foot, hop! All around her, other children broke step and hopped and skipped and jumped.

A red-gold centauriform child tapped her hoofed feet in a quick dance. She cantered in place, flicking her long tail across her spotted flanks. She raised her head and yodeled a joyful howl, and both Jaina and Jacen answered her.

Tigris hauled Jaina back.

"Stop! Be quiet!"

His fingernails dug into her skin.

"Ow!" she shouted. She could pretend it did not hurt, but she saw no reason to pretend she was not outraged. "Stop it! That's mean!"

His grip opened for a moment, then tightened again, even harder. He made her stand still. Her abilities trembled at the brink of exploding, but she controlled herself. Hethrir's power had begun to ease away. She was scared it would come back.

The other children stood still. Across the room, a Proctor clamped one hand around Jacen's arm.

"We all must accept discipline," Tigris said. "You're a child. You can't know what's right for you. You must obey me, as I obey the Proctors and Lord Hethrir."

"Why can't I skip? Why can't I run? Why can't I shout?"

"Because it is bad discipline. You must learn to control yourself."

That stopped her. Classes with Uncle Luke were mostly about learning to control what she could do.

"But Uncle Luke let me run and skip!" she said. "That didn't have anything to do with—"

"Luke Skywalker is dead," Tigris said.

"But—"

"No more argument!" Tigris said. "Stand in line quietly and follow the child in front of you."

Jaina was glad Tigris had interrupted her. She had almost told him she knew Uncle Luke was alive!

And Mama too, she reminded herself, and Papa, and—

Suddenly Hethrir was beside them. Jaina imagined that she could see silvery symbols on his robe, across his shoulders and his chest.

"Lord Hethrir!" Tigris exclaimed. He fell to his knees.

"What is this commotion?" Hethrir demanded.

"I was explaining our ways to the child," Tigris said, keeping his gaze on the floor.

"Do not explain," Hethrir said. "Command."

"Where's my brother?" Jaina said. "Where's Anakin?"

"You have behaved badly," Hethrir said. He raised his voice so all the children and the helpers could hear. "I have canceled breakfast because of the behavior of this child. You will all proceed directly to the study hall."

"That isn't fair!" Jaina cried. "No breakfast—no breakfast for anybody—because *I* skipped?"

"Hush!" Tigris whispered.

Hethrir strode from the room without speaking to her again. His white robe swirled across the floor.

Jaina was so hungry her stomach growled. She and Jacen had had nothing to eat since lunch yesterday. Her mouth watered when she remembered the chowder and sandwiches, and the fruit for dessert . . .

"It isn't fair!"

"You broke the rules." Tigris climbed to his feet. "You're part of a group. The rules apply to the whole group."

"But—"

"Be quiet," Tigris said. "Lord Hethrir hasn't canceled lunch—yet."

Jaina looked around at all the other children. She thought they would all be mad at her. No one said anything or looked at her. She saw, for the first time, how thin they all were, as thin as they were ragged, and she thought how hungry they must all be. She wanted to say she was sorry. But she was afraid if she spoke, Lord Hethrir would take their lunch away too.

She subsided. When the line of children moved forward, she walked along with everyone else.

But her steps were a little out of time.

Jaina was so hungry she could hardly think, and so bored she could hardly stay awake. She did not understand why she had to sit in this tiny cubicle with no sunlight and no fresh air, memorizing information that popped up in the air in front of her. Most of it she knew already, like her letters, and her times tables. The stuff she did not know, she could not understand why she would want to know. She stopped bothering to remember it. The score of wrong answers mounted in big numbers hovering over her head. She did not care.

She fell asleep.

"You must be a very stupid little girl."

Jaina jumped, wide awake. She had not heard Tigris come up behind her. She stood and glared at him.

"I am not! I'm smart! Why are you so *mean*?"

He stabbed one finger into her ghostly score of wrong answers. His fingernails were dirty and bitten.

"You mustn't think of me as mean," Tigris said. "I'm only helping you learn discipline."

"You *act* mean."

"If you don't want me to act mean, then you have to answer the questions."

"They're stupid questions!"

"You're an impertinent child. Do you think you know what's better for you than Lord Hethrir does? You're very ignorant!"

"I'm not! I'm not! I like to learn things! These are dumb things!"

"How high is the highest waterfall on the world of Firrerre?"

"I know how to decide what stream is the headwater of a river," Jaina said hopefully. "I know how to figure out how high a waterfall is, even if you can't get to the top!"

"But Lord Hethrir didn't ask you those questions," Tigris said. "He asked, 'How high is the highest waterfall on the world of Firrerre?' "

"I don't know. That's a dumb question, too—who cares what the answer is? I can look it up."

"It is one thousand two hundred sixty-three meters high. Lord Hethrir thinks all educated people should know these facts. Sit down at your screen and learn what he offers."

She could not see that she had any choice.

"It's still a dumb question," she whispered.

Chapter

4

L eia dreamed in sounds. She was surrounded by darkness, but whistles and warbles came to her from all directions. The voices formed shapes in the night. She cried out, reaching for the shapes, three small figures, so fragile and precious.

Leia gasped and woke with a start. She had fallen asleep in the chair. The lights sensed her motion and brightened.

What a horrible nightmare, she thought.

Then she remembered: it was not a nightmare.

At her side, Artoo-Detoo whistled plaintively.

"Oh! You frightened me," she said. "What's the matter, Artoo? Is there news—?" There was not. "Did you wake me up to go to bed?" She smiled sadly. "I don't think it matters where I am anymore." She pushed herself to her feet. Tension stiffened her neck and her back.

She felt lethargic and groggy. It was the middle of the night. Still hours till dawn.

"Mr. Iyon *did* drug me!" she exclaimed. She shook her head, trying to fling away the daze of sleep. "Why, I'll—!"

Then she remembered that Chamberlain Iyon had drunk the tea along with her. That was why he had yawned, that was why he had stumbled. And perhaps he had hurried to his room and collapsed into drugged slumber.

She was angry to have been sedated without her knowledge. But considering his beliefs, and his fears, she could hardly blame him.

Artoo-Detoo rolled toward the doorway.

"Good night," Leia said.

Artoo-Detoo rolled toward her, then away again.

"What's the matter?"

The droid whistled peremptorily. It whirred toward the door.

It waited.

"Where are you going? Do you want me to go too?"

Artoo-Detoo scooted through the doorway.

Leia followed.

"But where are we going? Is Chewbacca awake, is that it?"

She followed Artoo-Detoo into the corridor. The castle was silent and dim. In the corners of her vision, the carven figures on every surface shifted and played out their stories. When she looked at them straight on, they remained still, mere carvings in the stone.

Artoo-Detoo did not take the path to the surgery.

"This way," Leia said.

The droid rolled off without stopping. Curious, troubled, Leia hurried to follow.

Balmy night air flowed around her as she followed Artoo-Detoo out of the castle. She had not even known this doorway existed. The castle was so big, so labyrinthine, that she had only memorized routes to the places she needed to reach.

Above, the several moons of Munto Codru waltzed in the sky. The cries of night creatures eased the silence.

"Where are you going?" Leia whispered.

Around her, all sounds ceased. She stopped, spooked by the change. She stood quietly, and the night sounds slowly began again, first distant ones, then nearer cries, finally small chirpings almost at her feet.

Artoo-Detoo whistled. The droid's voice blended with those of the night creatures. They continued their calling, unafraid.

Artoo entered the woods and rolled along the trail that led to the meadow. At the edge of the field where the children had disappeared, Leia hesitated, then plunged ahead. When she entered the woods on the other side of the clearing, she suddenly gasped for air. She had been holding her breath.

You're acting like a scared child, she said to herself. Then added, Or a terrified mother . . .

Soon she realized where Artoo-Detoo was going. She caught up to the droid.

"What's at the field? Artoo, do you know where the children are? Are they hidden in one of the ships?"

A few spaceships stood in the small landing field on the castle grounds. Larger ships had to put down at the main spaceport, for the facilities here were primitive. But if the kidnappers had access to one of the local ships, they might have hidden here. No one would have thought to look, because they could not take off. Not without clearance from the main spaceport, and the main spaceport was not giving clearance to anyone.

"Tell me, Artoo!"

Artoo-Detoo did not reply.

Three ships stood on the small landing field. One was a courier, the ship she had wished to send after Han and Luke. The second was an antique local craft of intricate design, a Munto Codru vessel put at the disposal of the chamberlain.

The third was *Alderaan,* Leia's pride and joy. *Alderaan* was a sleek little ship with hyperdrive capabilities. Luke had chided her for spending the time to learn to fly it that she could have used to study the ways of the Jedi. But the truth was, it was much easier and faster to learn to fly *Alderaan* than to learn to be a Jedi Knight. And a great deal more fun. Maybe that was why she loved the little starcraft so much. Her responsibility to the Republic kept her from having much fun.

The same was true of everyone she knew. Luke worked himself to exhaustion. Leia thought that he deliberately worked himself beyond exhaustion, either to test himself or to take himself to another level of achievement. But he scared her, sometimes. She wished they had grown up together; she wished she had known her brother as a child, so she could understand him better.

Han did not deliberately push himself beyond his endurance. He had passed plenty of tests in his life; he never needed to give himself more. But he did press himself to his limits without meaning to. Often Leia would come home after a diplomatic reception or a long meeting with her advisers to find Han facedown at his desk, snoring. Once he fell asleep in his bath. Leia was convinced that if she had come in five minutes later, he would have drowned.

That was why he and Luke had gone on a quest together. They were both burning out. They needed time off.

She doubted Luke would find any other Jedi Knights on his quest, but she hoped he would find some rest. And she hoped Han would let loose, like in the old days.

Leia followed Artoo-Detoo onto the field. She expected the droid to stop at the courier. When Artoo-Detoo passed the courier she drew in a long, distressed breath. Could the droid be heading for the chamberlain's ship? He had always been kind and helpful to her. Even when he drugged her he had meant well. But if the children were in his ship, if he had kidnapped her children to increase his prestige on Munto Codru . . .

Artoo-Detoo passed the chamberlain's ship and continued on toward Leia's.

Leia ran after the droid.

No one can get into *Alderaan* without my consent! she cried to herself. *No one!* Not even Han. And certainly not the twins or Anakin! The kidnappers couldn't have forced them to open the ship, because they don't know how to do it.

Her heart raced. A powerful practitioner of the Force might be able to get into her ship without setting off the alarms.

She calmed herself. Wait and see, she thought. Wait and see.

Artoo-Detoo stopped beside *Alderaan.*

Leia laid one hand on the silver flank of her ship. No distinguishing mark marred its limpid finish, which looked like puddled mercury. It was registered to a person who did not exist, a second identity Leia had established so that someday, sometime, somehow, she would be able to take a few days off and fly away to a pleasant place without being recognized. Its ship's signature did not even list its name, only its number, because the name of Alderaan gave too great a clue to the true identity of the ship's owner. Almost all the citizens of Alderaan had perished in the attack of the Death Star. Only a few had survived. Princess Leia Organa had been one of them.

"Is someone in there, Artoo?" she whispered.

The droid made a soft faint hum, the sound *Alderaan* made as it powered up for liftoff.

"All right. I'll stop them before they can take off. Don't worry."

She executed the entry sequence. The hatch opened. Leia entered her ship and moved silently down its corridor.

She had no feeling of intrusion, no sense that anyone was aboard. Artoo-Detoo followed on silent treads. Leia kept the lights off; she could find her way around in *Alderaan* with her eyes closed if need be. She glanced into her stateroom. Nothing. No one was hiding in the second cabin, in the head, in the storeroom, in the galley. She crept toward the cockpit. Her pulse pounded.

The cockpit, too, was empty.

Could they be hiding in the engines? That was the only possibility left.

At the engine hatch, she stopped and listened carefully. She could hear nothing, no sounds of conspiracy, no cries of frightened children, no shrill squeals of Anakin in one of his brief, intense tantrums. Perhaps they were all asleep.

A soft faint hum surrounded her.

She glanced over her shoulder, expecting to see Artoo-Detoo mimicking the sound of her ship again.

The corridor behind her was empty.

The hum increased. Someone had begun the takeoff procedure.

Leia slammed the hatch and pelted her way back to the cockpit.

Artoo-Detoo had extended connectors into the ship's systems and powered up *Alderaan*'s drive.

"Stop it, Artoo!" Leia exclaimed. "What are you doing, I can't—"

A display flashed into being before her.

The display traced out the spaceways of Munto Codru. Traffic was light around this old world. No ship had arrived or departed for several days.

Except one.

A single distinct trail led from the surface. It reached escape velocity, streaked away from the planet, reached for hyperspace, and disappeared.

"What is this, Artoo?"

The droid trilled at her.

Leia gasped and sat down hard in the pilot's couch.

She was looking at the trace of a ship that could belong to the kidnappers.

"Why didn't anyone show this to me before?"

Artoo-Detoo showed her that the information had disappeared from the spaceport's records. The only uncorrupted information lay within Artoo-Detoo's compact shell.

"They got away . . ." Leia whispered. "How did you know, how did you find out?"

Artoo-Detoo sang her an explanation. The droid might have to navigate through local space at any time, and, as a precaution, made a habit—or an instinct—of tracking spaceship traffic. When the kidnappers struck, Artoo compared memory banks to the spaceport report, and noted a disparity.

Artoo-Detoo believed the contradiction was a clue to the kidnappers.

Leia agreed with Artoo's conclusion. Munto Codru attracted little starship traffic. The disparity in the records, coming as it did just at the time of the children's disappearance, was too suspicious and too convenient.

The hum of *Alderaan*'s engines increased.

Leia knew she should shut *Alderaan* down, return to the castle, and confer with her advisers. Talk for hours, trying to decide what to do, what was prudent, waiting on the whim of the people who had stolen her children.

Arguing with Chamberlain Iyon about whether it was a coup kidnapping . . .

"You understand, don't you," Leia said, as much to herself as to Artoo-Detoo, "if we leave, and if we're wrong—if it really is a coup kidnapping—we're risking Mr. Iyon's wyrwulf."

Artoo-Detoo warbled a descending call.

Do I hear uncertainty? Leia asked herself. Or is it *my* uncertainty I feel?

It would be so much easier for her to believe Mr. Iyon, to wait for a few more hours, negotiate with the Munto Codru family, see her children rush happily into her arms. Followed by Chamberlain Iyon's massive and horrifying black-on-black wyrwulf.

But she did not believe. She did not believe a coup kidnapper could penetrate her security and whisk her children from Chewbacca's protection. She believed the kidnappers to be altogether more powerful, more sinister.

They wounded Chewbacca and set off the pressure bomb to disguise their true actions and their true intentions, Leia thought. They made us oblivious to the passage of two hours' time. And they abducted Mr. Iyon's wyrwulf—to add to their illusion of a coup kidnapping, to distract us, while they escaped.

If this was true, the children were far from Munto Codru, and they were in deadly peril.

She laid one hand gently on Artoo-Detoo's carapace.

"Yes," she said. "You're right. I have to take the risk."

Artoo-Detoo emitted a shrill of agreement.

"Mr. Iyon, I'm sorry," Leia whispered. "I hope I'm right."

She dragged the safety straps across her body and fastened herself in and engaged the controls. She went through the countdown sequence fast, pushing the safety margins. Her ship came alive around her.

Activation.

Alderaan lifted off.

As soon as *Alderaan* rose above the clouds, the spaceport sensors reacted. A sleepy traffic controller sent her a message.

"Munto Codru Spaceport to WU-9167, do not proceed."

If Leia replied, they would know who piloted the ship. She would have to explain, justify herself—and she could not justify herself. She only knew she had no choice.

But she could not let it become known that the Chief of State of the Republic had begun to behave erratically.

"Munto Codru Spaceport to WU-9167, return to your base, the hyperspace supervision systems are under repair. Proceeding could be dangerous to your health!"

"Tell them we have our own supervision systems," Leia said to Artoo-Detoo. *Alderaan* streaked upward through the atmosphere. Its skin grew hot.

Artoo-Detoo warbled a transmission.

"Munto Codru Spaceport to WU-9167, that isn't an acceptable response. You risk censure, a fine, and confiscation of your spacecraft."

Artoo-Detoo replied with a soothing explanation.

The chamberlain's secrecy worked against him now. As far as the spaceport police knew for certain, she was only breaking an administrative order. They could record a fine against her. They could plan to confiscate her ship or take her license, when and if she returned. But this was not a police matter. They did not suspect that she was an escaping kidnapper, because they did not know anyone had been kidnapped.

"Munto Codru Spaceport to WU-9167, if this is an emergency, we can send a tractor after you."

"Oh, Artoo!" Leia said. The last thing she needed was to have to dodge around a space tug and its tractor beam.

Artoo-Detoo broadcast a loud electronic raspberry and shut down the transmission.

"Got that one from Han, did you?" Leia said.

Alderaan reached the upper atmosphere. In the thinning air, heat dissipated rapidly. The temperature of the ship's skin dropped, from very hot to very cold.

The blue sky turned indigo, then purple, then black. The stars came out.

One of the stars moved: light glinted off the battered skin of the orbital space tug as it changed its path to intersect Leia's.

Setting itself to stop her, it put a tractor beam between *Alderaan* and the hyperspace point through which the kidnappers had escaped.

"How strong is it?" Leia asked. "How far do we have to go to avoid it?"

Artoo-Detoo evaded her questions.

"And here I thought you were perfect," she said.

Instead of changing *Alderaan*'s course, Leia accelerated. Artoo-Detoo whooped in warning.

"I don't care. We have plenty of power. If the beam grabs us we'll just have to break it."

"Munto Codru Spaceport to WU-9167, we're tracking you. Stay calm, we think we can counteract your acceleration. Pilot, are you injured? If you can pull the plug on your engines you'll make our work a lot easier."

The controller kept his voice calm. If *Alderaan* had been in distress, Leia would certainly have appreciated the reassurance.

Alderaan accelerated toward the tug's tractor.

Leia's display showed her the beam, waiting to surround her ship with an energy field as thick as molasses. She poured on more power.

At least we aren't in combat, she thought. There's no risk to them, trying to stop me. I don't have to worry about their safety.

Her own safety struck her as inconsequential.

"Munto Codru Spaceport to WU-9167, secure yourself for tractor, it's going to get rough in five, four . . ."

Artoo-Detoo snapped treads into the safety recess and hunkered down. Leia glared at the droid.

"Why do I think you *do* know the strength of the tractor beam?" she said.

". . . three, two, one, *engage!*"

Alderaan shuddered violently as the tractor beam grasped and slowed it. Leia pushed the engine to its limits. *Alderaan* quivered around her. The strain on her ship hurt her.

Alderaan's shields resisted the tractor. For an instant, Leia's little ship slid free. The space tug, responding with surprising speed for such an old and obsolete vessel, snatched at

Alderaan again. *Alderaan* struggled in its grip. The shields wavered, compressed to the edge of their strength.

Alderaan slowed, plowing through the beam as if through a powerful current.

If I were in trouble, Leia thought, I'd be desperately grateful for whoever's keeping that tug in such good shape . . .

The shields rallied. *Alderaan* seized more distance, another step toward escape.

Alderaan shuddered.

The tractor beam broke. The change buffeted *Alderaan* and flung Leia into the pilot's couch so hard it knocked the breath from her. Struggling against the streaks of pain through her vision, she corrected her ship's course.

Alderaan responded, steadied, and plunged.

"No!" the spaceport controller cried, at the end of his reassurance. "I'm sorry—"

Every star exploded into a multicolored line, radiating around *Alderaan*'s path.

"We made it!" Leia exclaimed.

A cry of distress and relief echoed through the ship.

"What was *that*?" Leia exclaimed.

She snatched away the restraint, jumped up, and ran to the rear of the ship.

In the second cabin—the cabin that had been empty when she checked it for kidnappers—Chewbacca lay in the bunk.

"What—how—?" Leia cut off her words.

Artoo-Detoo rolled past her and stopped beside Chewbacca, warbling happily.

"You *let him in*?" Leia exclaimed. "How could you? Is that why you let me think my children were hidden under the engines? So you had time to let him in? He's hurt! How is he going to heal? What am I going to do with a wounded Wookiee?"

She stopped. She tried to calm herself. She was so angry she could barely speak, much less make sense.

Chewbacca roared.

Leia still had to concentrate hard to understand him. She had listened and learned for a long time, to be able to communicate with her husband's oldest friend. She still could not pronounce Chewbacca's language, but she had made some headway in comprehending it.

Chewbacca expressed distress and regret and sorrow that he had failed Jaina and Jacen and Anakin, but not a moment's remorse that he had come along.

"I'm not going back," Leia said to Artoo-Detoo. "I'm not taking him back to Dr. Hyos. I hope you thought to bring enough medicine!"

Alderaan carried medical stores, of course, but Chewbacca was large and his wound was serious. Leia herself had only the most rudimentary of medical training, picked up on the fly in the old days.

She crossed the cabin and stood beside Chewbacca, gazing down at him. He moaned.

"I'm sorry you're hurt," she said. "And I know you want to help. But I wish you'd stayed back on Munto Codru. Everyone will recognize you, that's why you couldn't go with Han! Even when you're well enough to get up, you're going to have to stay in the ship."

Chewbacca snarled a quick retort.

"I suppose you're right," Leia said reluctantly. "You and Han, people would recognize. You and me . . . maybe not. I'll have to think about it."

His huge palm touched the back of her hand; his fingers, very warm and gentle, curled around her wrist. Leia jerked away, fighting her anger at him, but losing.

"Go to sleep," she said. "You're *supposed* to be *asleep*."

She fled before her anger could hurt him any more.

Leia flung herself into *Alderaan*'s pilot's chair.

She breathed deeply, slowly. The exercise felt ragged, for she was still angry and distressed. The calming ritual was one of the few Jedi abilities she had begun to learn, though when she had told Luke she knew how to do it, he had replied that no one ever completely understood Jedi techniques.

"Every time you reach a new stage," he had said, "you realize that you really don't understand anything, you have to go back to the beginning, to the most basic practice, and learn what you didn't see the last time through."

"That's very encouraging," Leia had said in a dry tone that Luke chose not to acknowledge.

"It is," he said. "It's wonderful, isn't it? There's always something more to learn. There's always something new."

Her pulse and her breathing slowed and steadied. For the first time since morning, she felt a glimmer of hope, a glimmer of the presence of her children. The center of her being yearned toward them.

Behind her, Artoo-Detoo entered the cockpit.

The glimmer vanished.

"I'm not speaking to you," Leia said.

With a plaintive whine, Artoo-Detoo rolled away.

She had to start all over again. In a state of calm, or in a state of frenzy, she could begin to use her untrained potential. She had more control when she was calm, more power when she drove her potential with fury. With fury came great danger.

Hyperspace glowed and writhed around her. Somewhere in its patterns she would find a trail.

She *must* find it.

She thought she saw it, she grasped for it, it eluded her and disappeared.

Relax, she said to herself. Relax, and maybe you can find them.

That was like ordering herself to stop worrying: it was impossible.

She abandoned her quest for detached calm. She discarded her pretense of composure.

Instead, Leia loosed her rage and terror and pain. Tears sprang to her eyes, blurred her vision, and rolled down her cheeks. Anger spiced the terror. She pounded her fists against her pilot's chair. She began to sob, to groan, to mutter the basest curses of Han's roughest smuggler friends.

Leia screamed.

Rage and terror and pain all shattered around her, and disappeared. The force of her love and grief broke through into a brilliant blue-white reality.

A vivid scarlet line streaked across the glowing blue-white domain and stabbed into the soft rainbow colors of hyperspace: Leia saw it, felt it, heard its color. She tasted and smelled it.

She snatched the controls of *Alderaan* and plunged along the bloodred trail.

Artoo was *right,* Leia thought. The children did come this way, it *wasn't* a coup kidnapping.

Leia shivered with relief, and with fear. She had made the correct choice. But her children were in even more danger than Mr. Iyon's wyrwulf.

Just outside the cockpit, Artoo-Detoo rolled nervously back and forth, whistling with confusion and distress.

The crystallizing white dwarf plummeted toward Crseih Station, falling toward the black hole. The two stars rose and set in opposition, creating long days, short nights.

Grateful for even a few hours of relative coolness, Han strolled into the lodge, along the pathways between the quiet streams and glassy pools.

In his room, the only illumination was the reflection of shore lights off the crater lake.

Han threw down his jacket, kicked off his boots, and flung himself onto his bed. It was a long walk from the first dome of Crseih Station to the park dome of the lodge. He felt tired but exhilarated.

The humming whine of a lightsaber startled him. He whirled around. The blue light filled every corner of the room and even lit a dust-mouse beneath the bed, as if the light were too powerful to cast shadows.

"Where've you been?"

Luke slouched on the deep couch in the corner, wrapped in his robes, his legs extended. The lightsaber flicked off again, plunging the room into darkness.

"Out enjoying my vacation," Han said easily. "How about you?"

The hum of the lightsaber pierced Han's inebriated brain as the blade snapped into existence.

"That really hurts my head," Han said.

Luke performed a couple of ritual cuts. A slash, a parry, a thrust. The air vibrated. The blade barely missed the wall, and a hanging tapestry, and the arm of the couch.

In the light of his blade, Luke looked haunted. He let the energy blade withdraw.

"What were you doing?" Luke asked.

"Repairing our finances." Han raised the light level in his room. He grabbed his jacket, reached into the pockets, and pulled out handsful of credits. He let the bills flutter to the bed, to the floor, even over Luke's feet.

Luke gazed at the bills dispassionately.

"We didn't need our finances repaired," he said.

"We're on the border!" Han exclaimed. "You show a letter of resources on the border and they laugh at you. And maybe knock you on the head in an alley to grab it and take it someplace they can use it."

"But gambling winnings," Luke said dryly, "are perfectly safe."

"I couldn't lose tonight, kid," Han said. "They thought they could lure me in and take me, but I couldn't lose. I could have made us rich instead of just comfortable, but I thought, No, why be greedy? Why risk one hand too many? So I picked up my winnings and I thanked them for a fine time—and fine ale—and here I am. Safe, and sound, and flush."

"I was worried about you!" Luke said. "You disappeared without a word—"

"I didn't want to argue with you," Han said to his brother-in-law. "You wouldn't have come along—"

"How do you know? You didn't ask."

"Would you?"

"No."

"See?"

"It's beside the point! I've got a mission here, a purpose, I—"

"What's wrong?" Han said, suddenly concerned. "What are you so upset about?"

"Something strange is happening at Crseih Station," Luke said. His voice was tight and intense. "Something strange, and I don't know what it is. I think we should be careful."

"I'm on vacation," Han said, trying to make a joke of it. "Being careful is the last thing on my mind."

Luke stared in silence out the dark window.

"I'm tired," Han said. "I'm going to sleep. In the morning I'm going to sleep in, and have breakfast in bed, and maybe

I'm going to have lunch in bed too. And then maybe I'll go back to the tavern." He yawned. "Do the same thing, kid. Relax. If there's anybody here for you to find, you'll find them. Or they'll find you."

He sat up long enough to pull off his shirt, but he was too tired to take off the rest of his clothes. He flopped back onto his bed.

"And tomorrow you can try to find Threepio," he said to Luke.

"I already did that," Luke said, matter-of-fact.

"Oh yeah?" Han mumbled, half asleep. "Where is he?" He fumbled for the edge of the blankets to pull them around himself before he fell asleep.

"Right here, Gen—sir." Threepio stepped into Han's room, almost invisible in his new purple skin.

"Fine, great," Han said sleepily. "Tomorrow you and Luke can get on the hunt and find our mysterious informant." His eyelids drooped and he heard himself snore just as he fell asleep.

"I have done that, sir," Threepio said. "She is here."

Han woke with a snort. He sat up, still half asleep.

"Her? Here? What'd you bring her here for?" Struggling to wake up, he thought back over what they had said. Luke had been playing with his lightsaber—had he even been using his disguise?—and Han had not been careful with his tongue. Maybe the informant already knew Luke Skywalker and Han Solo were investigating the strange reports from Crseih Station.

"Because we need to speak." The new voice was light and soft, but very serious.

Han turned over, rolling himself up in his blankets with a groan of exhaustion, hiding himself from the intruder.

"Come back in the morning," he said through the muffling bedclothes. "On second thought, come back in the afternoon."

"We have no time to waste, Solo."

He bolted up, snatching the bedclothes away from his face. She *did* know who they were—

Luke's saber hummed, and the blade stroked a line of light across Han's dim hotel room. In the ghostly illumination of the Jedi weapon, Han saw their informant's face. He did not recognize her.

"You no longer know me, Solo," she said with resignation. "I should not be surprised, but I am disappointed that you wiped me from your memory."

It was her voice that let him remember. He caught his breath.

"Permit me to introduce—"

"Xaverri? Xaverri!" Han said to Threepio, "We've already been introduced."

Luke let his lightsaber blade vanish. The room turned pale with the dawn of the burning whirlpool.

Han finished untangling himself from his blankets and stood up. His heart beat wildly; he felt as if he had run a race.

Xaverri faced him. She was nearly his height. She used to look him straight in the eye, but she was not wearing the high-heeled boots that had been so much a part of her style in the time he had known her. Nor was her heavy, curly black hair elaborately dressed, for she had cropped it into short, tight curls. Instead of revealing silks, she wore homespun trousers and shirt.

"I do remember you, Xaverri," Han said softly. "Of course I remember you. I could never forget you."

When he had known her, she had acted both carefree and careless, avoiding any responsibility, moving on a whim. She took extraordinary risks. For a long time, Han believed she simply sought excitement because she enjoyed it. Exhilarated, they had taken the risks and experienced the excitement together.

Finally, Han discovered that she did not care if she lived or died. He had not understood why, back then.

But now he did understand.

Xaverri had risked her life against the chance that she could outsmart and outrun high officers of the Empire. She had always won.

Han had begun to wonder, in those heady days of excited terror, if she won because she did not care if she lost. If she lost, she would die, and her grief would end. When she won, revenge eased the grief a little.

She had changed. When he knew her in the old days she

had hidden herself behind makeup and expensive clothing and jewels. She had heightened the gold glow of her skin and disguised the round lines of her smooth face. She had concealed the soft brown of her eyes behind iris-enhancers of opaque silver, piercing green, or eerie faceted diamond.

Yet her beauty and intensity had always glowed through her veneer of sophistication. Now she no longer hid behind anything, and her spirit shone as strongly. Han would not have recognized a picture of her. But her voice was the same, and her strength.

"How did you know it was me?" he asked.

"How could I not?" Xaverri asked. "I sent you the message."

"Why didn't you say it was you? Why didn't you use a language I know?"

"Because I did not want my message to be easily read." She hesitated. "And . . . I did not know you would respond, if you knew the message was from me."

Han started to protest, but kept his silence.

She might be right, he thought. I'm ashamed to admit it, but she might be right.

"At first I did not know you," she admitted. She touched his beard. "But as soon as you spoke—"

Han felt as if he had plunged back into the old days, when his thoughts and Xaverri's mirrored each other with eerie precision.

He could not speak directly about those old days. He was surprised at the turbulence of his feelings and the strength of his pain.

"What have you been doing, all these years?" he asked. "What have you been doing in the Republic, now that all the Empire officers are gone?"

"They are not gone, Solo," she said.

She had always called him Solo. In the society of Xaverri's birth, the given name came last, after a long list of ancestral references. She had assumed his given name was Solo, and that he was of low class or an orphan, with only a single prename. Once they got that straightened out, she was used to calling him Solo and he was used to hearing it.

"They are not gone. Some—some that you fought—are

dead. But many are hiding beneath respectability, waiting and working for your government to falter and fail. Waiting for their chance."

"They'll wait a long time," Han said.

"I hope so. In the meantime, they are as greedy and venal as they always were. They are as susceptible to temptation, when I offer them more wealth." Her smile was joyous and unmerciful. "And they are even more vulnerable, because they have fallen from power. They do not dare draw the attention of your authorities. I wrong them dreadfully—and they cannot complain."

Han laughed, imagining the arrogant Empire officers he had known, brought low by fear and Xaverri's predations. Then he sobered.

"You should tell me who they are," he said. "Who they're pretending to be. So the New Republic can bring them to justice."

"My justice is harsher," Xaverri said, "and more satisfying. Perhaps, when I have taken sufficient revenge, I will tell you the names of the ones I have humiliated and impoverished. And then I will humiliate and impoverish more of them, and tell you who they are. Thus I will have my justice, and the Republic will have its justice."

Han wished he could ease her memories, and her need for vengeance. But he could not help her in the old days, and he could not help her now. He wished he had embraced her as soon as he recognized her, but now he felt awkward about doing so. He backed away a step, and looked around for his boots. His exhaustion had vanished.

"You've met Luke and Threepio, I see," he said. He sat on the edge of his bed to pull on his boots.

"Yes." Xaverri inclined her head to Threepio. "I am not often received with such diplomacy." She turned toward Luke. "And I had not expected the New Republic to respond to my warning with such illustrious investigators."

"We decided—"

"—that the report deserved a serious response," Han said quickly, cutting Luke's words off. Luke might have said the same thing. Then again, he might have let it slip that Han was using her strange report as an excuse for a vacation.

He did not want her to know he had not taken the message seriously.

"Your report," Luke said. "You wouldn't tell us the source of the strange phenomena. Will you now?"

"No," Xaverri said.

Luke jumped to his feet. "But you must! Who—?"

"I will show you," she said.

"Just *tell* me!" Luke exclaimed.

"You would not believe me. You must see for yourself."

Jaina trudged down the hallway, one of many in the long line of children. The helpers made sure the line stayed straight, while a Proctor oversaw the whole group. Tigris walked nearby.

Is that what they always have for *lunch*? she thought. She could still taste the rancid grease of the soup she had been given. She had tasted one bite, and then—politely, as she had been taught, she *did* have good manners no matter what Hethrir and the Proctors said—she had said it was rotten. She did not mean it tasted bad—well, yes, she did mean it tasted bad. It was also spoiled.

She had not eaten it. Everyone else had. She had given hers to the red-gold centauriform child. But a little bullyboy named Vram had snatched it away and thrown it on the floor and gone and told on them. The helpers had given him a piece of fruit as a reward. They liked Vram.

Jaina's stomach growled. She was very, very hungry.

Someone nudged her shoulder. She glanced back.

"Play, soon," said the red-gold centauriform child. "Play, now." She spoke with a heavy accent, but Jaina understood her.

She cantered one quick step in place, just as she had when Jaina skipped across the gathering room. Her dainty hooves tapped on the stone.

Tigris glanced back to stop the cheerful noise. But the red-gold child was plodding along with everyone else by then. Her tail switched briskly.

Jaina wondered what the red-gold child meant.

Play? she thought. I don't believe nasty mean Tigris will ever let us play. Why can he tell me what to do, he isn't a Proctor, I don't think he's even a helper!

The children marched down another long hallway. Jaina wondered why it was so far between places, in these endless underground tunnels. They must have been hard to build. The castle at Munto Codru had been honeycombed with tunnels, but the tunnels connected hundreds of rooms and storage chambers and spy-windows and secret places. Here the tunnels had no windows, no doors, no twists or turns. Each had only a beginning and an ending, with maybe one curve or corner in all its long length.

Jaina saw light! Real light, white and full of color, not this ghostly gray. It blazed down at her, silhouetting the children ahead of her. She wanted to run toward it. She wanted to shout with joy.

Ahead of her, the other children climbed stairs and walked out into the light. It washed over them, bathing them in radiance. But they just kept walking. When Jaina saw the sun, she would raise her face to it and let it pour down over her. She would run into the brightness—

"Stop."

All the children stopped at the Proctor's command. Jaina was only a few steps from the dazzling brightness at the bottom of the stairs. She caught her breath. She feared they would take her back into the darkness.

The Proctor gestured sharply to Tigris. Jaina yearned toward the light in dismay, certain Tigris would pull her from the line and make her go back to the dim study cubicle, or the dark sleeping cell.

Tigris raised her chin and turned her toward him and made her look up at him.

"You can walk, in the play yard," he said. "You can speak quietly in the play yard. You can't shout. You can't run. You can't dig the sand. You mustn't pick the leaves. Do you understand?"

She nodded. His grubby fingers pinched her chin. He let her go.

"And you can't go near the fence!" he said.

"Why do you have so many rules?" Jaina asked.

"That isn't a rule," Tigris said. "If you go near the fence—the dragon will eat you!"

A dragon! Jaina was entranced.

The Proctors allowed the children to move forward again, and Jaina climbed out of the pit into the sunlight.

It was bright and hot, much more intense than she was used to. She blinked the sparks away from her vision, looking for Jacen, anxious to see him, trying to discover where she was and how they might escape for home.

Mr. Chamberlain's wyrwulf ran toward her across the sand. She fell to her knees and flung her arms around its neck.

"Oh, you're all right! Did they leave you out here all alone? You're lucky, though, you don't have to study those dumb lessons!"

The heavy black guard hairs of the wyrwulf's coat felt rough against Jaina's face. A heavy metal and leather collar had been fastened around the wyrwulf's throat. Jaina tried to free the wyrwulf.

"I'm sorry," she said. "I can't get it off." Her fingers were not strong enough to unfasten the collar.

The wyrwulf whined and leaned against her.

"Let's explore." Jaina got to her feet. "Let's see if there's a way out of here."

She looked around.

The play yard was the bottom of a canyon. The canyon was not very deep, but its sides were very steep and smooth. They would be hard to climb.

There was some way to get up there. On the cliff high above, the Proctors in their light blue uniforms spun and struck and slashed, practicing with lightsabers.

Jaina stared at them in disbelief. Why did these bad people have lightsabers? Lightsabers were for good people, for Jedi Knights. She wanted to be a Jedi Knight. She wanted to be old enough to build her own lightsaber, and learn to use it. She also wanted to be a mechanic, and a raceship driver, and a drum player.

She turned her back on the Proctors, up on their high cliff, and kept looking around for a way to escape. Mr. Chamberlain's wyrwulf trotted after her.

A fence closed the far end of the canyon. Jaina walked toward the fence. It might not be as hard to climb as the stone cliffs.

She was not on Munto Codru. She was not on any world she had ever visited. It was a very small world. Past the fence, the horizon lay very close. And the horizon curved. The tiny hot sun moved in the sky, so fast the shadows moved.

This isn't a real world, Jaina thought. It's too small. It's a made one, a built one. Otherwise it wouldn't have this much gravity. And it spins so fast, its day is only a couple of hours long!

A few prickly plants struggled to grow in the dry sand. Jaina could not imagine *wanting* to pick their thorny leaves.

There was nothing to play on, only the bare canyon sand surrounding the staircase pit, and the fence locking them all inside.

Someone nudged Jaina from behind. The red-gold centaur child danced around in front of her. Her sides and back were spotted with white. Velvety knobs above her temples poked through her wild, curly hair.

"You're different," the red-gold child said.

"I'm Jaina."

"I'm Lusa." Lusa looked sidelong at the wyrwulf. "Does it bite?"

"No, it just has big teeth. Do you see my brothers?" Jaina looked around, but there were only half as many children in the play yard as there had been in the gathering room.

Lusa took Jaina's hand. "Every day, they mix us up. Every day, it's different. Tomorrow your brothers are in this group, I'm not. Tomorrow, you're in their group, I'm still here."

It took Jaina a little time to figure out Lusa's way of talking.

She tells me different things that could happen, Jaina thought. But that's okay. At least they aren't awful things. Except that I want to see Jacen *now*, not tomorrow or the next day. And I want to know if Anakin is all right.

Hand in hand, Jaina and Lusa walked across the yard. Every few steps, Lusa hopped, springing into the air and coming down on all four feet.

"I want to run," she said sadly when she saw Jaina watching her curiously. "I want to gallop, and jump."

"Me, too," Jaina said. She jumped up in the air, like Lusa, and came down on both feet. It was not the same as running, but it helped. The wyrwulf watched.

The edge of the play area ended ten paces from the fence. All the other children were walking around, but no one entered the undisturbed border.

Jaina took a step toward it.

"Don't!" Lusa said, keeping hold of her hand. "The dragon—it'll eat you."

"I want to see the dragon," Jaina said.

Then she thought, Why should I even believe there's a dragon? Hethrir told me my mama is dead. I don't believe that. I don't believe anything he says. I don't believe anything mean nasty Tigris says.

She looked around for Tigris, but he had disappeared. A few bored helpers stood together and gossiped, hardly paying any attention to the children.

"There's no dragon out there," Jaina said.

"There *is*," Lusa said. "A dragon lives there. The sand hides the dragon!"

Beyond the fence, wind had blown the sand into low rolling dunes.

"There's no place for a dragon to hide," Jaina said.

She took another step.

A huge lizard erupted from the sand. It roared. The sound was like thunder, like wind.

Sand showered up around it, and over the fence, and into Jaina's hair.

She shrieked in fear and delight. The wyrwulf yelped. The other children ran away, toward the safety of the stairwell. Jaina wanted to stay where she was, on the undisturbed ground, to see what the dragon would do. Lusa pulled her to safety. Lusa tried to run all the way to the stairwell, pulling Jaina, but Jaina pulled against her and stopped them both.

Just beyond the undisturbed sand, they turned back to look at the dragon.

It was like Jaina had suddenly turned invisible. The dragon crouched on all fours, lashing its heavy tail. It growled. It peered this way, that way. It was beautiful, Jaina thought, not very graceful but powerful. It had thick, muscular legs and a short heavy tail with a spiked knob on the tip. Its huge long head was mostly mouth. Big jaws and big thick drippy teeth.

Its scales looked like shiny beads, black and tan and pink.

"It hides in the sand," Lusa said. "The sand looks like its scales."

The dragon snorted and blinked. It backed up a few steps, wiggling its tail. It dug itself a basking spot and used its big feet to flip sand up over its back. Lying between two of the low dunes, it looked like a sand dune itself.

"It's wonderful!" Jaina said. She wished Jacen were here. Jacen would love it.

Maybe I'll get a chance to tell him about it, she thought. Just a second is all I'd need, practically.

She almost tried to *think* at him about the dragon. Just the idea brought her up against the hovering cold cloud of Hethrir's power.

She decided to wait.

"What does it eat?" Jaina asked.

"Children," Lusa said, her voice gloomy. "Us when we're bad."

"Oh, silly," Jaina said. "Did you ever see it eat anybody?"

"No, but they told—" Lusa blinked her red-gold eyes. "They told us . . . they made it roar. It didn't *eat* us, it only *roared* us."

She switched her tail and flung back her tangled hair.

"It only *roared* us!"

Jaina grinned.

The other children came cautiously out of the stairwell and gathered behind Jaina and Lusa.

"It didn't *eat* you!"

"I bet it doesn't even eat children," Jaina said. "I bet it eats . . . bugs or fish or plants or something."

"There aren't any fish!" Vram said in a stuck-up voice.

"Sand fish!" Jaina retorted. "Haven't you ever heard of sand fish? You've never been *anywhere*!"

The other children nodded. But no one stepped onto the undisturbed ground. Jaina had to admit the dragon was pretty scary, when it jumped up out of the sand. It might not *eat* her. But it might knock down the fence and step on her, without even meaning to.

Suddenly three ships screamed down out of space and streaked across the sky above the canyon.

"Look!" Jaina cried out with excitement, knowing, just *knowing*, that Papa had come to save her with the *Millennium Falcon*, or Mama had come with *Alderaan*.

The wyrwulf pointed its nose in the air and howled after them.

Jaina did not recognize any of the ships. Two were dark, like the *Falcon*, and one was bright like *Alderaan*, but the two dark ones were shaped wrong, and the bright one was gold rather than silver.

The other children stared after the ships. They all fell silent and scared. Jaina expected one of the helpers to come and tell her to be quiet. Maybe even send them all to bed without dinner. Jaina was so hungry now that she wished she had eaten the icky soup. She was sorry she had shouted.

All the helpers, and the Proctor overseer, had disappeared.

"Don't they watch us while we're out here?" Jaina asked.

The other children looked around. A whisper of fear passed among them.

"What's the matter?"

Without a word, the other children clustered together. Lusa pranced nervously.

"What's the matter, Lusa? What's going to happen?"

Lusa raised her head, her eyes wide with fear. Her long curly mane flew around her face.

"They come for us, they take us—" Lusa put her hands protectively over the velvet knobs on her forehead. "They cut off your horns!"

"You're gonna get sent away!" Gloating, Vram pointed at Lusa; he pointed at Jaina. "You're gonna get sent away-ay, you're gonna get sent away-ay!" he chanted. "Whenever the ships come, Lord Hethrir sends the *bad* ones away!"

Jaina thought, Where could we go that would be worse, why is Lusa so scared?

"Good!" Jaina said. "Who wants to stay in this rotten place?" She grabbed Lusa's hand. "We'll go away together, and my papa will come and rescue us!"

"You don't know anything!" Vram shouted. "You'll all go away to different places! You'll be all by yourself!"

That scared Jaina. Lusa was trembling. They could make Lusa go away. They could make Jacen and Anakin go away!

Vram jumped up and down with glee and pointed at Lusa.

"I heard them say, they're going to take you away and cut off your horns! Cut off your horns *forever*. Serves *you* right!"

Lusa cringed away from him.

I don't have any horns to cut off, Jaina thought. So what would they do to *me*?

She held Lusa's hand tighter. Mr. Chamberlain's wyrwulf leaned against her.

Lusa edged toward the other children, till she and Jaina became part of the group. Lusa kept pushing between the other children till they reached the center.

If I hold Lusa's hand, Jaina thought, it will all be all right. They won't take either of us away.

Lusa's fingers felt warm in Jaina's hand. The centauriform child was trembling. She hunched down and ducked her head. She shook her hair forward. But no matter what she did she was still taller than the others. And no matter what she did, her velvety horn-knobs poked out through her curls.

"They wouldn't cut off your horns," Jaina whispered. "Why would they? Your horns are pretty!"

"They cut off your horns to make you ugly," Lusa said, her voice shaking. "They cut off your horns to make you obey. But my horns haven't come through the velvet yet." She stared at Jaina, fear in her eyes. "If they cut the velvet, I'll die!"

Jaina hugged Lusa. She wanted to hit Vram for scaring them all, for scaring Lusa. But Mama always said not to hit.

She thought that if all the children stood around Vram in a circle and glared at him, though, they could make him be quiet.

Before she could try to get everyone to test her theory, a double line of helpers marched out of the stairwell. A Proctor overseer followed. The helpers surrounded the children, the way Jaina thought the children should surround Vram.

"Line up," the overseer said. "Line up, and stand up straight and tall."

"He said line up!" Vram pushed one of the smallest children out of the group. The little child stumbled.

Jaina jumped forward to catch her. Lusa pulled Jaina back. Jaina slipped out of Lusa's grasp and ran toward the little one. When Vram raised his hand to slap the little one, Jaina grabbed him. She was right behind him. She pulled his hand over his shoulder. He fell down, almost on top of her feet. She had to jump away.

Lusa pranced beside her, and the wyrwulf growled. All together they faced the bully. Vram flinched down against the ground.

He's scared of us! Jaina thought.

Then she thought, I'd be scared, too, if Mr. Chamberlain's wyrwulf growled at me!

Vram's fair skin looked grayish and his spiky hair flattened against his head. He backed away. The little one scampered back to the group of children.

Vram suddenly straightened up, swaggering. His skin flushed with satisfaction.

"You better get in line," he said.

"Do line up, children."

Hethrir's voice made Jaina shiver.

Hethrir stood at the top of the stairwell. He spoke softly, but there was no mistaking his tone. Frightened, the children broke up their group and shuffled into a ragged line, scuffing their feet in the sand.

Vram ran to Hethrir and gazed up at him. "I was getting them to line up! I was making them, Lord Hethrir!"

"I see that you were," Hethrir said kindly. He placed his hand on Vram's head, ruffling his flattened hair.

The fast-moving sun touched the canyon wall. In a minute it had set. Floodlights came on all around, so bright Jaina had to blink.

Hethrir strode forward. The hem of his long white robe whispered against the sand.

All the Proctors, in their clean blue uniforms, their medals polished and their epaulets glittering, marched behind him. Their lightsabers hung at their belts.

More helpers followed, guiding the second group of children. Jacen's group. Jaina wanted to run over to him, but she was afraid she would get everyone in trouble again.

And finally Tigris climbed to the top of the stairwell. Anakin slept against Tigris's shoulder!

But it was nowhere near Anakin's naptime.

What's the matter with him? Jaina wondered. Did they hurt him? I hope they just made him sleep again. Like they made us sleep in the meadow when they stole us.

The helpers lined up Jacen's group so they faced Jaina's group. The Proctors lined up in front of Hethrir, and the helpers lined up behind him.

In the center of the square, Hethrir turned to Jaina and Lusa and Mr. Chamberlain's wyrwulf. Vram grinned nastily at them. Lusa stamped one hind foot. Vram ran behind Hethrir.

"Get in line." Hethrir's voice scared Jaina.

"No!" She wanted him to be mad at her, so he would send her and her brothers away.

Suddenly she was in line. She felt like someone had slapped her. I won't cry! she thought furiously. I won't!

From the stairwell, Anakin wailed sleepily, then fell silent. Jaina wanted to run to him, but she could not move.

Mr. Chamberlain's wyrwulf growled. Suddenly it yelped and flattened its ears and crouched down, staying very still.

That left Lusa standing all alone. Hethrir froze the centaur child with his gaze.

"Perhaps you will regret defying me," he said. He turned his back on her.

The centaur child fled to the line. She was shaking. The wyrwulf slunk to Jaina's side.

Hethrir nodded at the line of Proctors. One strode forward, strutting with pride.

"You have proven yourself," Hethrir said. "You are worthy to join my spearhead. You are worthy to join the Empire Youth."

Two Proctors marched out and held a knee-length coat for the Youth. The coat was not quite white, but the palest shade of blue. The Youth slipped into it.

He stroked the fur lapel. His face glowed.

"Thank you, my lord! The Empire Reborn!"

"The Empire Reborn!" the Proctors shouted, so loud Jaina jumped.

The Empire Reborn? Jaina thought. What's that?

She knew the Empire had been evil. Why would anyone ever want to bring it back?

Hethrir beckoned to one of the helpers.

"You merit purification." Hethrir placed one hand on his head. "You are now a Proctor. I shall take you to be reborn in the service of the Empire."

Three Proctors surrounded the boy. When they stepped away, he stood proudly in a light blue Proctor's uniform.

Finally, Hethrir put his hand on Vram's head.

"Good boy," he said. "You are now one of my helpers."

A helper came forward, carrying a rust-red tunic. Two other helpers pulled off Vram's stained shirt and his ragged trousers. They lowered the tunic over his head.

Vram preened and smiled and strutted.

Hethrir turned to the children in Jaina's line. He looked straight at Lusa. She cringed back from him, afraid.

Hethrir gestured. Lusa pranced forward nervously.

Hethrir held out a lightsaber. Except it had no lens at its end, only a small glass bulb. Jaina tried to figure out what the fake lightsaber really was.

"Watch," Hethrir said.

The glass bulb lit up, then went dark again.

"Take it," Hethrir said to Lusa.

The centaur child obeyed.

"Turn it on," Hethrir said. "As I did."

Lusa turned it over and around, trying to figure out how Hethrir had activated it.

"Use your mind," Hethrir said. "Watch, again."

He nodded to the new Empire Youth. The Youth drew his lightsaber. Its blade hummed into existence.

His lightsaber was different from Uncle Luke's. He had to turn it on by using the Force. That was what Hethrir wanted Lusa to do with the fake lightsaber.

And Lusa could do it! For a second, Jaina perceived that her friend could touch the Force and use it. She was untrained and inexperienced, but she had the ability. Jaina imagined herself and her friend as Jedi Knights, traveling through the galaxy and defeating evils.

Evils like Hethrir, and his Empire Reborn.

Hethrir's power slipped over Lusa. It blocked her talent. The bulb of the fake lightsaber remained dark.

"No fair!" Jaina cried.

Hethrir's cold wet blanket fell around her. She gasped. Lusa dropped the test machine and sprang to help Jaina. Halfway through the leap, Hethrir's power flung her to the ground. Struggling to get up, she whimpered.

"You have failed," Hethrir said to Lusa.

Two of the helpers pulled Lusa to her feet and dragged her away.

"No." Lusa's voice rose. "No!"

"Do not defy me," Hethrir said. "I'm doing this for your own good."

Jaina struggled up and ran to Lusa and flung her arms around her neck. The wyrwulf ran back and forth, confused and upset and growling. Lusa hugged Jaina and pressed the warm soft knobs of her horns against the top of Jaina's head. Hot angry tears burned Jaina's eyes.

Slowly, slowly, Hethrir's force drew them apart. No matter how hard Jaina tried to stay in one place, Hethrir's power easily overcame her. She felt like she was falling off the edge of a cliff. Jaina's hands slid from Lusa's neck, and down her arms. Lusa braced all four feet. Her hooves dug stripes in the sand as Hethrir pulled her away from Jaina and Jaina away from her.

They grabbed hands and held tight.

As long as I hold her hand, Jaina thought. It will be all right, as long—

Their hands slipped apart.

Lusa screamed. Jaina *reached* to her—and Hethrir's power fell around her again, like a heap of wet sand. Jaina's *reach* vanished, and Jaina lost her balance and fell down.

She could not get up. She lay on the sand crying with rage and despair. Jacen cried out and ran toward her and Hethrir made him fall down, too.

Hethrir made them stay there while he tested all the rest of the children. A few could turn on the little light. More failed. Under the pile of invisible wet sand, Jaina could not tell if Hethrir was cheating with some of them.

Hethrir used his test to divide the children into two groups, one with Jaina and Jacen, the other with Lusa. Lusa stood shivering in the heat, with her head down. Mr. Chamberlain's wyrwulf leaned against her front leg, panting. Hethrir did not test the wyrwulf. He just pointed at it without looking at it, and two helpers came and fastened chains to the heavy collar and dragged the wyrwulf away.

All the children were terrified, crying or keening or hunkering down within their body armor or shaking their fur, however their own people expressed fear and grief.

All the children in Jaina's group were human beings. A few human children had been sent to Lusa's group, but mostly Lusa's group was other species. Jaina thought that was weird. All the Proctors and all the helpers were human, too. Jaina thought that was even weirder.

Lusa looked back over her shoulder at Jaina.

"Take me," Jaina said to Hethrir. "Take me instead, don't take Lusa away, don't cut off her horns!"

Hethrir ignored Jaina. The Proctors marched down the stairwell. Their medals and epaulets glittered. Some of the helpers marched Lusa's group away. Two of them dragged the growling wyrwulf.

Lusa's cry echoed up out of the tunnel.

"Lusa!" Jaina cried.

Vram pointed at Jaina. "You're so dumb, you're so dumb!"

Maybe they're just going back to their places, Jaina thought desperately. Maybe it *is* me that Hethrir is sending away—and Jacen too! and probably Anakin!—because we're too much trouble! We don't have horns to cut off. If Lusa's staying and we're going, she'll be safe!

Hethrir strode over to Jaina. He glanced down at her. His gaze flicked briefly over her face. The smothering sensation of wet sand all around her disappeared. She stood up. Jacen climbed to his feet, too. They hugged each other. Jaina felt very heavy and very tired.

"There," Hethrir said, using his kind voice. He was talking to everybody, not just Jaina. "Go back to your places and study hard. The other children are going away because they are not as good as you. You may stay, because I expect you to make me proud of you."

"I never will!" Jaina shouted. "I never will, Lusa's *just* as good as me, and I'll *never* do anything to make you proud!"

Chapter

5

Alderaan fell out of hyperspace. The scarlet trail led to a cold dark region of space. The nearest star was light-years away.

A burst of pain and fear and despair obliterated the trail. Leia cried out.

If they've hurt my children . . . she thought. If they've harmed one hair— If they've . . .

The memory of pain faded.

I didn't feel death, Leia thought. It wasn't death! And it wasn't Jaina or Jacen or Anakin. Who was it?

The fear she had felt was not fear of death, but fear of continued life. She shuddered, imagining what could happen to a person to create such terror.

Bathed in sweat and weak with exhaustion, Leia drew a long, ragged breath.

Leia extended her ship's sensors outward. She watched and listened.

She found a ship.

"That's it!" she exclaimed. "I have you—!"

She fought back the urge to press toward it immediately. It would not do, to find her children only to fall into a trap.

Artoo-Detoo raced into the cockpit.

"I'm *still* not speaking to you!" she said.

Artoo-Detoo grabbed the new ship's signature from the sensors and traced it in the air. Then the droid traced another signature beside it: the record of the kidnappers' ship.

The two ships were nothing alike.

"No!" Leia cried. "No, this has to be them. I *followed* them here, and there's no trail away! Maybe the ship was disguised—"

She accentuated the visual aspect of the unknown ship. The result struck her silent. The vessel she had found was a huge, hulking passenger freighter, the kind the Empire had used to transport unwilling colonists from star to star. It traveled slowly, carrying its sleeping cargo at sublight speeds. The Empire did not care if the colonists—political prisoners, convicts, and other undesirables—lost touch with families and friends, who lived their lives and aged and died. The colonists slept on, trapped in dreams of a new world that would welcome them, or in nightmares of a world that would kill them. They had been slaves in all but name, sent away to prepare a new world until their masters chose to seek them out again.

We've been looking for these ships, Leia thought. Trying to rescue them. No wonder we couldn't find them, way out here at the end of nowhere!

Leia frowned. The passenger freighter was derelict, drifting, its engines dead and its interior barely functioning.

"What's it ᴄ ing here?" she said. "We couldn't just have stumbled across it, that's too much of a coincidence to bear."

Alderaan's sensors touched a second ship, and a third.

"I don't believe it . . ." Leia whispered.

Fully two dozen ships lay within her perception.

She had found a graveyard of abandoned starships. They hung in a slowly shifting cluster, circling each other in a tangled and chaotic dance.

Chewbacca roared, a cry of grief and understanding.

Leia jumped out of the pilot's chair.

"What are you doing up? What are you doing *awake*? Are

you determined to—" She bit off the words before they left her mouth. If she accused Chewbacca of trying to kill himself, he might agree with her.

He limped forward and lowered himself painfully into the copilot's seat. He gazed at her. She glared at him, but finally her expression softened.

"I'm sorry," she said. "I was blaming you. I shouldn't have. I don't know what happened, but whatever it was, you couldn't have stopped it. I couldn't have. Maybe even Luke couldn't have done anything."

Chewbacca touched the thick chestnut fur at his throat. He raised his chin, combed his fingers through his pelt, and revealed a patch of stark white hair. He let her look at it for a moment, then lowered his head again.

"Is that—?"

He growled in assent.

Chewbacca had been a slave. Not a colonist-slave, but the chattel of an Imperial officer. Leia knew very little about that part of his life. She knew he had been kidnapped from the deep and magical forests of his world. He had been chained, and punished for any defiance, and worked nearly to death.

Young Han Solo of the Imperial Navy had freed him. Han had saved Chewbacca's life, for no Wookiee lived long as a slave.

"Is that what happened here?" Leia said. "Did the Empire hijack ships, did it steal their passengers? That doesn't make sense!" She gestured toward the sensor reports. "Those are *Imperial* colony ships. The Empire wouldn't take slaves from its own ships, it already considered those people slaves. It wouldn't abandon ships like this. It would take them away and use them again. It was evil—but it was efficient."

Leia looked at the reports more closely.

"Oh, no . . ." she whispered.

The ships still contained passengers, and many of them had died. But some were alive. Just barely alive.

Xaverri showed Han the way, along a path that led toward still another dome. The trail led into a dense thicket of tall, twisting bushes. Branches tangled together to form impenetrable walls and a leafy ceiling, and to let in nothing but gloomy deep green light. The path twisted and turned, leading deeper into the thicket.

It feels like a trap, Han thought. I trust Xaverri—I *trusted* her, with my life, and I was never sorry.

But he had also trusted her with his heart.

That was the old days, he said to himself. Everything's different now.

Han walked behind Xaverri, with Luke and See-Threepio following. The pathway could only accommodate one person at a time.

I wish, Han thought, not for the first time during this expedition, that Chewbacca was with us.

"Look, Master Luke," Threepio said. "These leaves are all different shapes. Look how they fall when I touch them."

As Threepio's querulous voice fell a little way behind, Han noticed the leaves for the first time. Threepio was right, they *were* misshapen. Scabrous colors mottled the irregular shapes. He brushed his hand along a branch, and leaves fell fluttering to the ground.

"I wonder," Threepio said, "if we should return to the ship and secure some radiation detectors. I believe more radiation may be penetrating the domes than the station management is prepared to admit." His voice faded as Han rounded a bend in the path. "Why, I can virtually feel my intelligence circuits exploding beneath the assault."

"Your intelligence sounds normal to me," Luke said.

Han chuckled, and lengthened his stride to catch up to Xaverri. He wanted to speak with her privately.

But when he was walking just at her shoulder, he could not decide what to say. He wanted to know what had happened in her life, in the years since they had parted, but he felt uncharacteristically shy of asking.

"You recognized Luke," Han said to Xaverri.

"Yes."

"He said no one would."

"I demanded some proof that he was a true representative of the New Republic. He removed his disguise."

"So he *did* look different to you, at first?"

"Very different. But he released me from his influence."

She shivered slightly. "He is very skilled, Solo. I did not even know he was affecting me, until he let me go."

"He's talented," Han said. "But he never had the chance to finish his formal training."

"Ah," she said. "That's said to be very dangerous."

"Yes. And he's had occasion to realize it."

"I had heard . . . some rumors on that subject," Xaverri said.

"Did you?" Han said. "We thought we'd managed to keep it from public knowledge."

"Perhaps you did," Xaverri replied. "But I am not precisely the public . . . and I put considerable energy into cultivating many lines of communication."

"Some of them are better than mine," Han said, annoyed by the realization.

"Some of them are different than yours, Solo," Xaverri said. "There are many people who will speak to a thief, who might have spoken to a young smuggler . . . who will not speak to a General of the New Republic."

Han did not like to admit he had changed so much from the old days. Admit it or not, though, it was true.

"You could be an asset to the Republic," he said.

"Me?" She chuckled. "No. As soon as I became an asset, I would become valueless."

"Your work would be secret."

"Nothing is secret. And you know it, Solo."

"Then why did you get in contact with us? What do you want?"

"I want nothing from you!" she said angrily. "The Republic has made my work harder. You are worthless as prey—you are all so honorable—so dull!"

Xaverri glared at him a moment, then her anger eased. Her expression turned to worry.

"I heard about phenomena that are strange and dangerous. I investigated them. I think they are a threat to the Republic."

"You just said you don't like the Republic," Luke said.

Han started. Luke had come up behind him without a sound, without warning. He hoped Luke had not heard him discussing Luke's frailties with Xaverri.

"She did not precisely say she did not like the Republic," Threepio said, pedantically. "She said—"

"I have no quarrel with the Republic," Xaverri said. "My profits are less, but I do not need much to live on. Perhaps I shall retire soon."

"But you *said*—" Han said.

"You must remember what it was like!" Xaverri snapped. "When the Emperor ruled, his minions raided our homes. When the Emperor ruled, our only protection was bribery and blackmail. When the Emperor ruled, I required great sums to protect my homeworld from raids, to protect my friends from death, to save their children from the press gangs. And even then . . . sometimes my efforts were not sufficient."

Her voice broke. Han touched her wrist. She twisted her hand so her fingers curled around his; she pressed his hand briefly, then released him.

"Yeah," he said. "I remember how it was."

"So, you see," Xaverri said, in control of her voice once more, "thanks to the Republic, I no longer need huge sums." She grinned. "Only moderate sums."

"How much farther?" Luke asked suddenly.

"It is still some distance," Xaverri said. "Are you tired, Jedi?"

"I'm curious," Luke said.

"Be patient, kid," Han said. Just like the old days, when Luke had been restless and eager as well as green. In recent years, he had developed the ability to fall into a preternatural calm. Han found it disturbing.

They continued on through the garden maze, walking in silence. The path through the bushes grew narrower, lower; Han had to stoop, and the branches scraped against Threepio's purple lacquer with short, high-pitched screeches.

Han's back started to hurt, and the march no longer reminded him so much of the good old days.

Finally, when he was about to give up and call for a rest, the tunnel ended at the side of the translucent dome. Xaverri ducked through an opening and disappeared. Han followed, stiffly. Behind him, Luke's robe rustled quietly against the ground as he stooped.

"Wait, please, I do not bend well that way," Threepio

said. He clanked against the edge of the dome material, scraped through, and joined them on the other side. He clambered to his feet.

Han peered into the new dome. It was almost as dim as the green illumination of the leaf tunnel. But the eerie greenness had possessed a quality of life and growth. Here the twilight was oppressive.

Great gray stones loomed around them. The rocks perched on the edge of a cliff: the steep and partially collapsed side of a huge crater.

Xaverri edged over the top of a great cracked stone. Han slithered up beside her. From their vantage point they could see the whole dome. Its floor lay far below. A small complex of buildings occupied the center of the crater. The buildings were gilt, and brightly lit: the only spot of light and color in Han's view. The delicate lines of the complex traced calligraphy against stone.

Han wondered what the pattern might mean.

Several rough paths led into the crater. On all of them, people picked their way across the desolate lava toward the haven. A constant stream of people from many worlds entered the compound, and no one was leaving.

"That is our destination," Xaverri said.

"What are we looking for? Why's it so special?"

She shook her head and refused to answer. "If you do not see it for yourself, you will not believe."

Luke started forward, heading for a space between two rocks. Xaverri slid quickly down from her perch. She barely touched his sleeve, then snatched her hand back. Luke had already stopped within the protective concealment of the stones.

Han jumped down beside them. "Kid, what's the matter?"

Luke was pale and tense, his gaze far away. One hand rested on the grip of his lightsaber.

Threepio bent solicitously toward Luke. He laid one long purple finger against Luke's forehead. Luke shook his head, barely distracted, jerking himself away from Threepio's touch.

"I fear Master Luke has contracted some ailment,"

Threepio said. "His temperature is abnormally low. Perhaps some form of landfall disorder—"

"Threepio," Luke said patiently, "your sensor's covered with purple paint, that's all."

Chagrined, Threepio inspected the tip of his finger.

"But Threepio's right," Han said. "You look awful. What's wrong?"

"I . . . I don't know," Luke said. "Something . . . there's *something* here, but I've never . . ." He started away again, as if he had never begun the conversation.

"Jedi!" Xaverri said.

Reluctantly, Luke glanced back.

"Let me lead you," she said. "I am accepted. And there is an easy path, farther along the rim . . . I would prefer no one else knew of this escape."

Luke glanced between the stones, as if he might leap between them, slip over the edge of the cliff, ignore the faint steep twisting path, and plunge straight down.

And he probably could do it, Han thought.

"Very well," Luke said.

Tigris answered Lord Hethrir's summons to his receiving chamber. He carried the child Anakin, who slept more than any little one Tigris had ever met.

Hethrir had built his private receiving chamber from the finest wood of all the old Empire. Body-wood, they called it. It resembled the flesh of the people who had inhabited the forest, before the Emperor claimed the world. To his most favored officers he had dispensed the right to exploit certain resources. Hethrir's reward had been the license to export body-wood. Lord Hethrir had begun his fortune from the license. But he used the wood profligately for himself as well. The walls and floor and ceiling of the chamber glowed with it.

The surface of the polished body-wood was the palest pink. Scarlet streaks shot through it, gleaming with light, like cut and polished precious stones. Tigris always thought the wood looked alive, and indeed it was said that the body-wood trees sustained a certain intelligence. It was said that they cried, when Hethrir cut them down. Tigris almost believed that they cried. He knew their wood bled. He had the task, the honor, of cleaning up the scarlet rivulets before they pooled on the floor and stained it.

When will Lord Hethrir allow me to do something important? Tigris wondered. Tigris shifted Anakin to a more comfortable position in his aching arms.

Tigris had been moved and impressed by the promotion ceremony, but he resented being left out.

He wondered when Lord Hethrir would sell him, along with the other inferior children. He could not even pass the first test! He was desperately grateful that his lord had allowed him to stay this long.

In the receiving chamber, Lord Hethrir welcomed his guests. Lord Qaqquqqu, Lady Ucce, and Lord Cnorec bowed low. Hethrir acknowledged their respect with a simple nod. He sat in a chair of gold and fur and satin pillows. He glanced at Tigris and gestured with his chin toward a small rug on the floor beside him.

Thrilled, Tigris took his seat. He had never been permitted to sit at Lord Hethrir's feet before!

As Tigris sat down, Anakin stirred and woke. Careful of the precious burden of the child, Tigris tried to hide his terror. What if he did something wrong, what if he dropped Anakin, or caused him to cry?

But Anakin looked into Tigris's eyes, stuck his thumb in his mouth, snuggled against Tigris's shoulder, and fell asleep again.

The guests approached Hethrir, making a second set of obeisances.

"This one is rather young, is it not, Lord Hethrir?" Lord Qaqquqqu asked, gesturing toward Anakin, smiling wide to show he was joking.

"Yes, too young," Lord Hethrir said easily. "We shall have to let it grow—or send it back to where it came from."

"Back, my lord?" Lady Ucce exclaimed. "Would that be wise—" She cut off her comment a moment too late, as she realized what an insult she had offered to Lord Hethrir. "I mean to say—oh, of course, how silly of me, of course you meant you would wipe its memory and *then* put it back. You *are* so wise."

"Or you may allow me to have it," Lord Cnorec said. "I think it is adorable. You would not be troubled with it, and I would make it worth your while."

"I will keep it," Lord Hethrir said. "It amuses me. You need not worry that it will reveal your existence—or your profession—to the New Republic."

All three guests bowed a third time. Tigris watched with awe as Lord Hethrir's words, words alone, controlled the guests. He toyed with them, for of course he had no intention of giving Anakin to anyone. The child was the key to his plans.

The guests feared Lord Hethrir, though each one owned an armed ship, perhaps even a fleet of ships. Hethrir's guests had saved themselves and their resources from the fall of the Empire. They had hidden themselves, and their great riches, and followers, and starships, invisible to the perception of the usurpers.

They gave their allegiance to Lord Hethrir. When the Lord was ready, when the Empire Reborn vanquished the New Republic, he would become Emperor. These guests and all his other followers would acknowledge him publicly.

Tigris wanted to be at his side when that happened. He wanted to wear the palest blue coat of the Empire Youth, or the light blue bemedaled uniform of a Proctor, or even the rust-colored tunic of a helper.

He wanted the Lord to acknowledge *him.*

Anakin shifted in his arms. Tigris smoothed the little boy's hair and whispered to him, to keep him from disturbing Lord Hethrir's meeting.

I must prove myself, Tigris thought. I must prove that I'm worth more than a nursemaid!

"My time is short today," Lord Hethrir said. "Let us conclude our business quickly."

An image formed between the guests and the glowing wall of body-wood. The image displayed the children culled from the training group. The guests inspected them.

"Soon," Hethrir said, "we will travel to Crseih Station to secure my alliance with Waru. My followers are gathering now. Each one will wish to choose from among these children."

He gestured to the image. The guests examined the children dispassionately.

"You may bid against each other for the license to distribute." Lord Hethrir named the sum at which the bidding must start. He smiled and pointed to the ugly black-on-black fanged creature, now Anakin's pet. "That one is not sentient, so I will give it free to whichever of you wins the license."

"Good woof," Anakin said softly.

The guests glanced at each other uneasily, then back at Hethrir. Even Tigris was shocked by the magnitude of the amount Hethrir demanded.

But Lord Hethrir is always fair, Tigris thought. The group he offers is exceptional, of course—and it will seal the treaty with Waru!

"That is a large amount . . ." Lord Cnorec let his voice trail off without even adding the honorifics due Lord Hethrir.

Hethrir frowned.

"My lord!" Lord Cnorec added quickly.

"Have I not been good to you, Cnorec?"

"Yes, my lord!"

"Have you not prospered through your association with me?"

"Yes, Lord Hethrir! But—" Lord Cnorec stopped himself, too late.

" 'But,' Cnorec? 'But' what?"

"Nothing, my lord."

Hethrir gazed at Lord Cnorec in silence.

Cnorec broke before Hethrir's gaze. "I only meant . . . we grow tired of working in secret, my lord! We grow tired of waiting for the rebirth of the Empire!"

"You doubt me, Cnorec," Hethrir said softly.

"Not at all, my lord! I only wish—I only hope—" He gasped for breath. "I anticipate living—" He struggled to draw air into his lungs. "—beneath—your—" His face grew red, and a tiny trickle of blood flowed from one nostril. He touched it and looked at his stained hand in disbelief. "—your —rule!"

He collapsed and lay still. Tigris stared at him, horrified

that he would question Lord Hethrir, shocked by his punishment.

Lord Hethrir made no gesture, no command, yet two Proctors appeared, lifted Lord Cnorec's body, and carried him from the receiving room.

Stunned, Lady Ucce and Lord Qaqquqqu tried without success to fasten their gazes elsewhere, to behave as if they had not witnessed their colleague and rival's downfall and death.

"He should have been patient a moment longer," Hethrir said pleasantly. "The Empire Reborn is at hand."

Lady Ucce and Lord Qaqquqqu reacted with surprise and awe and anticipation. Lord Cnorec was forgotten.

"You may consider part of your bid as a contribution to the success of the Empire Reborn," Hethrir said.

"I will bid," said Lady Ucce.

Lord Qaqquqqu countered Lady Ucce's bids inexorably. The winner of the auction would be in Hethrir's good graces. The loser might well follow Lord Cnorec.

But when the bidding reached double the original amount, Lord Qaqquqqu began to sound nervous.

"I beg your forgiveness, Lord Hethrir," he finally said. "I cannot obtain such a sum in good time to pay you."

"To contribute to the Empire Reborn," Lord Hethrir said softly.

"Of course I always intended to make a contribution," Lord Qaqquqqu said, "beyond what I might have bid." He named a sum half the original price, then quickly doubled it when he noticed the minuscule lift of Lord Hethrir's eyebrow. He made a low bow to Lord Hethrir. "Please accept this contribution to our cause."

Lord Qaqquqqu turned to Lady Ucce. "You have bested me, madam."

Lord Hethrir made a slight, and elegant, motion of acceptance.

Lady Ucce had won the auction, the group of children, the right to offer them to the Empire loyalists in Lord Hethrir's treaty gathering. If any remained, she could sell them into the trade.

Though the trade supported Lord Hethrir's achievements,

Tigris pitied anyone who could only command loyalty by owning a person's body. Such people enslaved other beings. Lord Hethrir, now . . . Lord Hethrir freed beings into his service.

Tigris felt sorry for the children in the group that Lord Hethrir had just sold. Not because they had been sold. That was their fate, if they were not suited to serve Lord Hethrir directly. He felt sorry for them because their place in Lord Hethrir's plan was now at an end.

The children who remained in the school still had a chance to be promoted, to be purified, to be reborn in the Lord's service, to wear the Lord's colors, to receive his orders.

Tigris glanced down at Anakin. The child was heavy. Tigris's arms ached with holding him. But Tigris bore the pain gladly.

You're lucky, small child, Tigris thought. You'll do much more to help my lord than I can ever hope to.

Lady Ucce transferred the payment from her accounts to those of Lord Hethrir.

"And naturally," she said, "I too will make a contribution, without recompense, to the cause of the Empire Reborn."

Lady Ucce glanced again at the display of her new purchases. She said nothing, but her eyes were hungry.

"Power," Lord Hethrir whispered to her. "Power is what is important."

She gazed at him.

"Power over other sentient beings," the Lord said.

A slow smile curved her lips.

"You may do me a service," Lord Hethrir said.

"Gladly, my lord."

Again, Lord Hethrir's signal was undetectable to Tigris.

The newest member of the Empire Youth entered silently, proud in his new coat, carrying a bottle of fine wine and three delicate glasses on an inlaid tray.

"You may take this boy into your service, and establish him within the Republic."

"It will be my pleasure to secure a position for him, Lord Hethrir."

"I will settle upon him . . . a substantial trust."

The Youth could not hide a smile of pride. He opened the bottle and poured a splash for Lord Hethrir to taste. Tigris admired his lord for never using a food-tester, even when he was away from his own kitchens and wine cellars. His actions demonstrated his bravery, his invulnerability, better than any words.

Lord Hethrir picked up the wineglass. The crystal was so delicate, so fine, that it rang when the Lord touched it. The high clear note filled the chamber. Hethrir put the glass to his lips. The music stopped. Hethrir tasted the wine, closed his eyes, swallowed, smiled.

Lord Hethrir allowed the Youth to fill his glass, and Lady Ucce's. But Lord Hethrir himself filled the third glass, and gave it to the Youth. They all pointedly ignored Lord Qaqquqqu, who watched unhappily.

Lord Hethrir raised his glass. Lady Ucce and the Youth mirrored his gesture.

Tigris bowed his head.

Anakin struggled around to watch, his ice-blue eyes wide.

"To the Empire Reborn!"

"To the Empire Reborn!"

"To the Empire Reborn!"

The airlock door of the passenger freighter slid aside, opening onto darkness. This far from any star system, too little starlight existed to illuminate the cavernous entrance.

Leia's pressure suit clasped her warmly, shielding her from the frigid airlessness of space. Artoo-Detoo followed her, with Chewbacca bringing up the rear. He looked strange and sleek in his form-fitting pressure suit. Cautiously, Leia entered the freighter.

Nothing happened. No security system queried her presence; no light responded to her motion.

The freighter's power had been cut to such a low level that the gravity barely functioned. Leia's feet touched the floor, but she could jump up and bounce off the ceiling, twice her height, if she chose.

Silent in the vacuum, Artoo-Detoo accelerated to pass

her. In the low artificial gravity, the droid's treads catapulted him upward and forward in a long, uncontrolled bounce. Artoo-Detoo landed on the other side of the airlock, bounced off the bulkhead, and finally came to rest. The droid circled slowly and unhappily, searching for danger.

Chewbacca's surprised snort echoed in Leia's comlink. He loomed behind her. He was stiff and sore and he probably could not move very quickly—not that moving quickly was a good idea in these conditions—but she was glad to have him backing her up.

Leia turned on her searchlight. Artoo-Detoo flashed his spotlights into the corners of the big cubical freight-loading airlock. Leia found the interior controls. The last thing she needed was to be trapped inside the freighter with only *Alderaan*'s cleaning droids left to try to get her out. But neither Artoo nor Chewbacca had been willing to stay behind, and she certainly would not send them in alone.

The controls responded to her commands. She set the airlock to cycling.

The outer door slid shut. It made no sound, but its vibration rumbled through Leia's boots. Despite the warmth of her suit, she shivered. The last streak of black space and distant, pinpoint stars vanished.

Air entered the freight dock. The air pressure crept upward. Leia fidgeted, wishing she could run the process at full speed. But the power plant had been damped down almost to nothing. She could not risk draining the life-support systems of the sleeping passengers.

Chewbacca made a plaintive cry.

"I don't know *what* I'm looking for," Leia said. "The kidnappers stopped here, and I don't know where they went next. If you have a better idea I'd love to hear it."

Chewbacca snorted.

Leia's pressure suit sampled the air. It was breathable, though rather low in oxygen. It would be safer to stay in her suit and not worry about contamination—or passing out from anoxia.

Finally the inner door slid aside and admitted Leia to the passenger freighter. The ship was divided into huge sections, each filled with racks of sleep coffins. The life systems balanced on the edge of failure. Some coffins had gone dark; the people inside had died.

Chewbacca moaned in memory and despair. Leia touched his hand in sympathy. These people had been stolen, as he had been. Their fortune had failed them.

Leia rubbed the dust from the transparent carapace of one of the sleep coffins. Beneath the glass, a humanoid lay like a fairy-tale prince. His long hair, striped gold and brown, curled in tangles around his face and grew along his chin, like sideburns.

"From Firrerre," Leia said. She swiped her glove along the windows of several of the other sleeping coffins. All the people were from the same world. "The Empire wiped them all out—wiped out everything on their world. They used a biological weapon . . . but it's so dangerous no one ever dared land there again. I thought the people were extinct. . . ."

If she could save them, find them a suitable world to settle, they could rebuild their civilization.

Leia wished she could find a shipful of people from Alderaan.

Maybe I will, she thought. Maybe one of those other ships carries people from my homeworld. Maybe—somehow—maybe the Empire abducted some of my people. Before it destroyed my world . . .

Leia set the first sleep coffin to "wake."

"Can you find the controls of this ship?" Leia asked Chewbacca. "Can you get the power back?"

He set off down a dark corridor. Leia hurried after him, walking with a low-gravity skiing bounce. Artoo-Detoo followed, whistling plaintively. Every time the droid tried to speed up, he left the ground and spun his treads uselessly until he came to rest.

Chewbacca loped unerringly through several intersections and took several turns through the complex corridors. Either he was familiar with passenger freighters from his own experience, or he had found reason to study their plans. Leia decided not to question him; if he wanted to tell her his experiences, he would.

In the depths of the ship, he found a small chamber with

no portholes, not even any viewscreens to the outside. The room was close and stuffy. Displays glowed faintly with low readouts.

Chewbacca studied the levels for a moment, then traced a pattern into the controls. The ship came alive around them, lights brightening, air *shusshing* through the ventilation. Even the brittle cold eased. Leia's pressure suit stopped straining to keep her warm.

"Good," Leia said. "Thank you. I'm going back to the sleep coffin so the Firrerreo doesn't wake up alone."

Chewbacca growled in negation and showed her a separate readout.

"What is it?"

But he was already loping out of the control room, bounding in long low-gravity leaps along the corridor. Leia followed as quickly as she could. She had little experience in very low gravity or free fall; she did not want to go tumbling in the air like Artoo-Detoo.

Chewbacca's cry of grief and rage echoed through the hallway.

Leia found him in a cabin as white and clean as a surgery. He stared upward.

A Firrerreo hung from strange, writhing webbing that hugged her body against the ceiling.

Her eyes were open and staring. Her sharp-featured face was gaunt. Her long hair, striped with black and silver, drifted in the air currents as if it were alive. The webbing cut into her golden-tan skin. She moved.

"She's alive!" Leia cried.

The webbing tightened, cutting into her emaciated arms and legs. The Firrerreo froze without a sound. Only her eyes moved; her gaze touched Leia for a moment. Nictitating membranes crept across her black irises, making her look blind.

"Get her down, quick—can you reach her?"

Chewbacca stretched upward and tentatively poked at a stray web filament.

"No . . ." The Firrerreo's voice was hoarse, growling.

Chewbacca snatched his hand back as the filament whipped into a spiral that nearly captured him.

Behind them, someone snorted in disgust and amusement.

Leia spun toward the new voice. Chewbacca grabbed for his blaster. Unfortunately, he was unarmed.

The Firrerreo Leia had awakened stood in the doorway, clutching the frame to keep himself on his feet.

"You can't get her down like that," he said. "You can only get yourself tangled in the web."

"It's torturing her!" Leia said. "We have to free her."

Artoo-Detoo extended connectors into the cell's data port. Like a locksmith, the droid tested one connector module, then another.

The data port violently ejected Artoo-Detoo's module. Spinnerets popped out of the wall and spurted web silk over the droid. Artoo-Detoo squealed and spun his treads backward. This time the low gravity aided him, for he backflipped into the air and ripped the webbing away before it could immobilize him.

The Firrerreo laughed.

"Stop it!" Leia snapped. She grabbed the web silk and pulled it away from Artoo-Detoo's carapace. She could remove the soft, delicate fibers, but she could not break them. When she tried, they cut into her skin. She brushed them quickly from her hands, before they drew blood. Artoo-Detoo backed away from the filaments.

Chewbacca growled, glaring at the Firrerreo.

"What's your name?" Leia asked. "How can you think this is funny?"

"I might ask you the same thing," he replied. "After all, you're the intruder."

"I woke you up. I probably saved your life."

"Who asked you to?" he said, his voice a low snarl.

Taken aback, Leia paused to collect herself.

I'm a diplomat, she thought. I can manage this.

"I don't mind telling you my name," she said.

She minded very much telling him her real name. She told him her false identity, the identity that owned *Alderaan*. It felt strange to call herself by her nickname from childhood.

"I'm Lelila, and this is my companion Geyyahab."

She nodded toward Chewbacca, who gave her a quizzical look. She had chosen for him a name from Wookiee mythology, from a story the twins loved to hear. But the character was not entirely heroic. Leia wondered if Chewbacca was offended by her choice—or if it were religiously offensive, even blasphemous, for her to give him a mythological alias.

I don't know much about his people's religion, Leia realized.

The Firrerreo sneered. "I do not care to tell you my name," he said. "But *her* name is Rillao." The name sounded like a snarl, the information like an insult.

Leia gestured toward the ceiling. "Please help me free her."

"She's not my clan," he said. "I owe her nothing. I owe you nothing."

"If I pay you, will you owe me?"

"I have no use for money here."

"What will it lose you, to help me?"

"Nothing," he said. But he did not act.

"What do you want?" Leia cried.

"What *are* you?" he asked. "A pirate? Or an Imperial flunky sent to torment us?"

"I'm neither," she said. "Do I look like a stormtrooper? Did you see troopers when you came down here?"

He regarded her suspiciously. "I want my freedom," he said.

"It's yours," she said instantly. "Please. Help us."

His eyes narrowed till they nearly closed, then abruptly he made a decision and bent over the console that had defeated Artoo-Detoo. He was familiar with its workings, and that made Leia uncomfortable. This cell in the depths of the ship had no purpose other than punishment and torture. Perhaps he was a collaborator. Perhaps the Empire had built the freighter with a prison cell so some of the passengers could wield power over others.

He stood back from the controls and glanced at Leia with a smirk. When he looked over her shoulder, she followed his gaze.

Rillao drifted slowly from the ceiling. The webworks stretched, then contracted, pulling away from her body, pulling *out* of her body. The ends of the silver strands were dark with her blood.

Chewbacca's growl was soft and low and angry and nearly inaudible. He caught Rillao gently. She did not move.

"Let's get her to—to my ship." Leia almost gave herself away by revealing the name of *Alderaan*. It was too good a clue. She would have to give her ship an alias, too.

Jaina flung herself into her study cubicle. She was sobbing too hard to see the display. Even if she wanted to pay attention to it. Which she did not. She wanted to be up in the canyon with Jacen. She wanted Lusa to come back.

Jaina put her head down and cried.

Vram stopped behind her. He jabbed at her shoulder. "Stop crying! Pay attention! Sit up straight!"

Jaina twisted away from him. She made herself stop crying. She wiped her eyes angrily on her sleeve.

"Lord Hethrir wants you to answer these questions," he said. "Who was the greatest leader in our history?"

"My mama, of course," Jaina said.

"You're wrong! You're so stupid. The Emperor was our greatest leader."

Jaina stared at him in horror.

"Who's going to restore the Empire?" Vram demanded.

"No one!" Jaina cried.

"You're wrong! Lord Hethrir will!" Vram said. "The Empire Reborn!"

"No!"

Vram was hateful. Hethrir was hateful. They were all hateful. Jaina sobbed, crying for Lusa and for Jacen and for Anakin and Mr. Chamberlain's wyrwulf and for Mama and Papa and Uncle Luke—not because she believed they were dead, she did *not*, they couldn't be, but because they would be sad and worried and searching for her. And she cried for Winter and Mr. Threepio and Chewbacca and Artoo-Detoo. And she cried for herself.

"You're wrong!" Vram cried with glee. "You're wrong! You have to go to bed without your dinner. And it goes on your record!"

She was so hungry that she almost stopped crying, but she was so angry about Lusa that she could not.

"You're nasty!" she shouted. "How did you get to be so nasty?"

Jaina kicked him in the shin.

He yelled in pain. Another helper came running. They dragged Jaina out of her cubicle and toward her sleep cell. She screamed and kicked and wriggled but none of the other children even looked at her. They hunched down in their places and stared at their displays.

Vram slammed the door of her cell, shutting her into the darkness.

Jaina sat on the cold hard floor—it had not turned soft anywhere yet—and struggled to stop crying. She had to think, she had to figure out a way to escape or send a message.

Hethrir's promotion ceremony had scared her. She could practically still hear the Empire Youth shouting, "The Empire Reborn!"

I *have* to let Mama know about the Empire Reborn, Jaina thought. Somehow. I have to let her know about Hethrir. He sounds like one of the evil tyrants Mama fought against, before I was even alive.

Jaina wondered if the fight would have to happen all over again.

She wiped away her furious tears.

She took out her hidden multitool and held it in her hand. She opened it and felt her way to the door. A splinter scratched her finger. She had found the place where she had begun to drill toward the latch.

While the multitool chipped slowly away at the hard wood, Jaina thought about how she might escape from Hethrir's compound. After she escaped from her cell.

Could I sneak past the dragon? It couldn't see me when it was far away. If it was all the way at one side of the canyon fence, maybe it wouldn't notice if I climbed the fence on the other side.

Jaina really did not believe that would work. The dragon was almost as wide as the canyon mouth. Even if it was all the way at the other side, if it looked over its shoulder it would still see her.

Maybe I could climb the canyon wall. But it's pretty steep, and it's pretty smooth, and I guess the Proctors would see me as soon as I got to the top . . .

Maybe I could steal a spaceship, and program it for home—

If she could escape *and* find Hethrir's skiff.

The trouble was, she did not know where she was, or where home was compared to where she was, or even where Munto Codru was. Maybe the ship would know.

And maybe it wouldn't.

Maybe it would be better to try to send a message.

If I can sneak out of here, somehow, Jaina thought, then maybe I can figure out where they send their messages from. Then I could sneak back in . . .

She felt the wood where she had been drilling. She had made a very small and very shallow hole. The multitool was so hot she could barely hold it.

She sighed. This was going to be hard. She wished she had Jacen to talk to. She wished she could reach past Hethrir's control over her abilities. Then she could open the door, find Hethrir's communications, whatever she wanted.

Can I still do *anything*? she wondered. Anything at all?

She imagined the molecules of air all around her. She imagined one molecule. She imagined it moving, faster and faster. She felt the molecule respond.

Hethrir's power did not react. She knew it was around her, she could feel its attention off in the distance. But it did not notice the tiny motion she created.

She added another molecule, another, doubling and redoubling the number she affected. Soon a small handful of air vibrated with her energy. Its warmth took the chill from her cell.

The swirl of air glowed red, then yellow, spreading light into the corners of Jaina's cell.

Jaina laughed with relief and joy.

Chapter

6

People from many worlds crowded around Han and his companions as they made their way toward the graceful gilt buildings. Han thought he saw the ghostling who had approached him in the welcome dome.

The effect of calligraphy, of esoteric hieroglyphics, was magnified by the entry to the structure. An intricate design traced secrets in gold across the mirrored facade. The building's wings curved around to form a sheltered, quiet courtyard. The visitors gathered just outside, then entered the silent space singly or in small groups.

Xaverri calmly waited their turn. Han passed the time by trying to identify as many homeworlds as he could. After several dozen, there were still individuals left over whose origin he could not guess.

He nudged Threepio. "Where do those folks over there come from?" He did not point; too many people in the Republic found pointing intolerably rude. He nodded toward a multihumped stack of mobile seaweed. "And is it a group, or one person?"

"Why, a group, of course, sir. They are from the fourth

world of Markbee's Star, specifically, from—if I am not mistaken—Zeffliffl. That is to say, from the shallow seas of the smaller southern continent—"

One of the leafy mounds produced a bulging bag, twisted one end, and squeezed liquid from the bag in an arching spray to splash itself and its companions. Some of the droplets rained down on Han. He stepped back, but it was only saltwater. The wet leaves of the Zeffliffl glistened blackly in the gold light of the building. A few leaves fluttered to the ground and lay twitching.

"How about them?" He gestured toward a second group, half a dozen massive, low-to-the-ground ovoidal people with short, powerful legs and eyes on thick flexible stalks.

"They are," Threepio said.

"Are what?"

Threepio did not reply.

"*What?*" Han asked.

"I just told you, sir," Threepio said. "Oh. I beg your pardon. The language exists at a frequency below the limits of your hearing. It is a function of the environment, which is extremely high gravity."

"They're sick," Luke said softly.

"No, Master Luke," Threepio said patiently, "they are speaking a language that human ears—"

"I don't mean them," Luke said. "I mean—there's somebody in almost every group who's ill or injured."

Paying more attention to types of people he was familiar with, Han soon saw that Luke was right. The gathering took on a poignancy that he had not previously perceived. Here a family huddled together, protecting a child or parent or cross-cousin; there a clan group carried a stretcher that supported a moaning, palsied colleague.

Han nodded at Luke, agreeing with his analysis.

Luke doesn't look so hot himself, Han thought. What's happening to him? He never gets sick . . .

"You will understand soon," Xaverri said. Her expression was grim. "It is our turn."

She entered the courtyard. Han followed, with Luke at his side; Threepio brought up the rear.

Silence surrounded them. The golden calligraphy on the

front of the building glimmered against the mirrored sheen of the wall. The perspective changed as Han walked. The calligraphy moved and shifted and writhed, as if it were still being written.

They were alone in the courtyard. The quiet was eerie. Han glanced over his shoulder, taken by the illusion that all the other people had disappeared. They had not; they remained where he had left them, crowded up to the entrance of the courtyard, waiting, speaking with quiet excitement among themselves. But their voices were inaudible.

"Master Luke, I wonder, all things considered," Threepio said, "shall I wait outside?"

"If you prefer," Xaverri said. "But I am accepted. There will be no danger to any of us."

"Danger!" Han said. "Wait just a minute. Who said anything about any danger?"

"No one," Xaverri said, amused. "I said there *is* no danger, if you follow my lead."

"But—"

"I meant," Threepio said, "that this does not appear to be a place likely to welcome . . . my kind."

"All forms of sentience are welcome here," Xaverri said.

"Even droids?"

"Even droids."

"Ah," Threepio said. "Somewhat unusual. Quite . . . enlightened."

They passed beneath an archway at the far end of the courtyard, and descended into bedlam.

Inside, the awed gathering had transformed itself into wailing, begging supplicants. They roiled in an undisciplined crowd toward the back of the wide, low theater, where a high golden altar loomed above them.

"Waru, help us! Waru, heal my child, heal my egg-sister, protect my hearth-friends from the curse laid upon them!"

The pleas echoed in the chamber. Luke grabbed Han's upper arm. His fingers dug painfully into Han's biceps.

"Hey, kid—"

"*Look,*" Luke said urgently.

The altar moved.

Han tensed. "What—? Where is *that* from, Threepio?"

"I confess, sir, that despite my knowledge of all the worlds of the New Republic, and many worlds outside it, I am unfamiliar with this being."

"That is Waru," Xaverri said.

The altar—the being—rose higher with a clenching contraction. It oriented itself toward them.

"Approach me, Xaverri."

The voice was rich and full and clear and very, very soft. It filled the chamber with a whisper, insinuating itself past the pleading of the congregation. Xaverri stepped forward, and the crowd parted for her. Han followed without thinking; all he knew was that he did not want her to approach the strange being alone. He pulled himself free of Luke's restraining hand.

As Han neared the altar, he got a better look at Waru. It was a complex construct of chased gold shields. But beneath the shields, visible from certain angles and at certain movements of the being, lay a slab of raw, uncovered tissue, like chunks of meat. Fluid—blood?—glistened between the massive shields, oozed out, and fell by drops and fine streams onto the stage, where it coagulated into a crusted pool. The blood ran off the stage and formed stalactites that hung nearly to the floor of the auditorium.

Xaverri stopped at the edge of the stage.

"Thou art not alone, Xaverri," Waru whispered.

"I am not alone, Waru."

"Do they wish to be healed?" Waru sounded infinitely tired.

"No, Waru. I have brought new students to study thy revelations, and learn thy truth, and appreciate thine existence. To give thee their devotion."

Thou? Han thought. Oh, fine, what is this, some obscure dialect—? Thou art, thou hast, thou wouldst . . . What did they just say? Thou wouldst hadst beenst . . . ? No, that's not right.

Waru sighed. "I am very pleased. Only thou, Xaverri, hast ever offered me a gift. All others plead for *my* gifts—and I am glad to give them! But . . ."

"Thy generosity is the marvel of Crseih Station," Xaverri said.

No one else responded to Waru's complaint. It was as if the being's whisper reached only Xaverri and her friends. Come to think of it, Han had not heard Waru speaking to anyone else. He had only heard Waru's whisper when the being addressed Xaverri directly.

Good trick, Han thought. It *has* to be a trick—doesn't it? Unless . . . it's what Luke is looking for.

He glanced at Luke, but he could not tell whether this was the lost Jedi Luke sought. Luke's expression was intent, but he revealed no joy.

The golden plates riffled, as sensuous and sleek as an animal's fur. They contracted, and the veins between them closed together. Fluid—Ichor, Han thought, this is the first time I've ever seen anything that should truly be called ichor—ran from beneath Waru's massive base, seeping out to form a new, glistening layer around it. One droplet flowed along the spike of a stalactite, hung at the tip, simultaneously stretched and coagulated, and froze into a narrow, sharp edge at the end of the spike.

As Waru's armor contracted, the being rose even higher, craning toward them. Han searched in vain for obvious organs of sight, hearing, smell, or other sensation. But he could not even tell how Waru produced a voice.

Maybe it perceives us as heat impressions, right on its skin, Han thought.

Or maybe, he thought, it doesn't perceive us at all. Maybe it isn't even alive.

"Thou hast brought me a new creature," Waru said to Xaverri. "I have seen humans before—oh, yes, many humans, humans are so frail—but not this other being." Waru leaned forward. The crusted ichor cracked and flaked away, revealing new edges of gold scales. "Who are you? What are you?"

Xaverri drew See-Threepio forward. "This is my new acquaintance, Purple-Three. I thought perhaps thou hadst not met his like before."

"Welcome, Purple-Three," Waru said.

"Thank you, Mr. Waru," Threepio said. "I am most honored to be permitted into your presence."

Han gave Threepio a lot of credit for picking up on

Waru's use of the standard *you* instead of the esoteric *thou*. The droid had noticed, as Han had not, that Waru used *thou* for Xaverri alone.

I would have put my foot in it, Han thought. Probably offended the hell out of this critter. Why didn't Xaverri tell us—?

"My name is only Waru," the enormous being said, its voice a purr. "Though some call me 'teacher.' It is the only honorific I esteem."

"Then I would be pleased to use it, if you will accept it from me," Threepio said. "I have studied many subjects, in many places. I am an expert on human-cyborg relationships and am fluent in six million forms of communication. I am always grateful for a teacher willing to share esoteric knowledge."

Han found the heat and humidity oppressive. The coppery scent of Waru's ichor prickled uncomfortably in his lungs. Beside him, Luke stared at the being with a fixed, hypnotized gaze.

"Relax, kid." Han's voice was quiet, amused. "It's only a—"

Xaverri shot him a quick, furious warning glance. Luke turned slowly toward him with an icy, inhuman glare, then returned his attention to Waru. Startled, Han shut up, but he finished the comment to himself: This is a *scam*, he thought. It's the most elaborate one I've seen in a while, but it's still a scam. If Luke and Ben Kenobi are anything to judge by, no Jedi would behave like this—and if Waru represented the dark side, Luke would know it.

The best reaction I can give this thing is laughter.

"Xaverri, honored student, wert thou able to study the texts I gave thee?"

"Yes, teacher," Xaverri said.

"Of course thou didst comprehend the connection between the ego-flux and the universal backlight, but I wonder if thou didst make the conceptual leap to the synergy of intellectual realization and quantum crystallization?"

"I am embarrassed to admit that I had not," Xaverri said, "though now that thou hast shown me the path, I can see that the interaction is completely inevitable."

Han repressed a snort of annoyance and disbelief.

Xaverri and Waru conversed in that manner for a few minutes, oblivious to the crowd and the noise and the pleas for assistance. The wailing began to get on Han's nerves. What he wanted to do was leap up on the stage and tell all these people to go home and see their doctors. He wanted to ask Xaverri why she kept flattering Waru. It shocked him to witness her deference to the being.

In the old days, she had never been susceptible to this kind of fraud. She knew too much about fraud to be taken in. She had designed some similar hoaxes herself, though she reserved the healer scam for particularly loathsome Imperial officers. She had never failed to relieve her chosen prey of a considerable portion of their resources.

Did she *believe* Waru's nonsense? If she did, she had changed beyond recognition from the person Han used to know, changed far beyond the physical. If she did not believe —then what were they doing here?

Threepio observed the conversation in uncharacteristic silence. Han frowned. Threepio's expression was impossible to read, but it was seldom difficult to know what the droid thought about any particular situation. Threepio would tell you. Or the droid would dissemble transparently. For a diplomat, Threepio was one of the poorest liars Han had ever met.

On the other hand, a lot of people found it flattering to know they were being lied to, if the lie was to soothe their feelings or acknowledge their status. Threepio was a master of that technique.

Luke watched and listened with the same fixed and intense expression that had possessed him as soon as he encountered Waru. Luke's reaction troubled Han most of all.

Waru completed a philosophical discourse on the state of the universe, which Han had long since lost track of.

"And now," Waru said with every evidence of disappointment, "I cannot further indulge myself in this enlightening conversation."

Xaverri placed her hand on one of Waru's golden scales. She closed her eyes and fell silent and still. The gold scale took on a pink glow and radiated gentle warmth around

Xaverri's fingers. Luke took one step toward her, lifting his hand. Han grabbed him and pulled him back. Luke turned on him, snarling.

With a startled curse, Han nearly dropped Luke's wrist. He wanted to walk out of the assembly in disgust even if it meant leaving his friends to be bilked and shamed.

"Don't be stupid!" Han whispered fiercely. "And don't presume on a few minutes' acquaintance!" He tightened his grip.

Luke looked at Han's fingers clamped around his flesh and squeezing his bones together. Intelligence leaked back into Luke's eyes. He made a leisurely turning movement of his hand; he slipped from Han's tight grasp without apparent effort.

"You're right," he said. His voice was tight. He turned his back on Han and watched Xaverri and Waru, intently, hungrily.

"I hate it when you do that," Han muttered. His fingers tingled, not because of any violence in Luke's motion, but because he had been holding so tightly that his hand spasmed when Luke pulled free.

The marks of Han's fingers remained, first white, then red, on Luke's skin.

Xaverri drew back from Waru. Her handprint glowed, then faded from the golden scale. A drop of ichor oozed from the scale's lower edge and fell with a sticky *plop*. Xaverri made a motion of obeisance toward Waru.

The being's attention left them abruptly, like a release of pressure. Han staggered one step forward, caught himself, and shrugged off the odd effect. But he was curious about how the effect had been produced.

Xaverri backed up. The roiling crowd surged ahead of her, each member keening for Waru's recognition.

Xaverri's knees buckled. Her collapse surprised Han so thoroughly that he nearly let her fall. In all the years he had known her, in the old days, she had never fainted, even at times of exhaustion or pain. Her stamina had always amazed him. His first thought, as she fell, was that she must be sinking to the ground for some deliberate reason: she wanted to make another bow to Waru; she had dropped something and had to retrieve it.

Han jumped forward and caught her before she fell beneath trampling feet. She trembled violently. Luke and Threepio closed in, forming a small circle. Moving against the flow of the crowd, they pushed their way to the back of the theater. Han plunged toward the door, but Xaverri struggled free.

"Stay here!" she said. "I am all right, I only—speaking with Waru affects me for a moment. But you *must* see the ceremony."

"*Affects* you?" Han said. "It knocked you flat. Let's get out of here!"

The color began to return to her golden-tan face, and her shivering ceased.

"You *must* observe," she said again.

"She's right," Luke said. "It's what we came here for."

"All right," Han said unwillingly.

It's all a fraud, he said to himself. But even frauds can be dangerous.

They made their way to the very back of the auditorium. The floor slanted, so they had a view over the crowd. On the stage, in the frozen pool of ichor, Waru waited as one of the small groups of supplicants brought one of their members into the teacher's presence. The Zeffliffl pressed one of the leafy comrades to the top of their heap, then slid the individual forward till it huddled on the ichor. Its color was noticeably paler than that of its companions, a sickly yellow-green rather than shiny and blue-black. It shed a flutter of small wilted leaves whenever it moved.

"Do you wish me to try to heal you, seeker?" Waru's voice, no longer a directed, private whisper, rumbled through the hall.

The Zeffliffl responded with a flurry of sound, like leaves swirled in water.

"She says, 'I entreat you to help me,'" Threepio said.

Now comes the scam, Han thought. Give Waru all your worldly goods—

"Then I will try to help you," Waru said.

Every sound in the auditorium ceased abruptly. The attention of every being focused on Waru and Waru's patient.

Waru leaned over the Zeffliffl. Several of the golden scales liquefied and splashed over the huddled Zeffliffl, covering it with a bright metallic shell. Han watched closely, wishing he were at the front of the auditorium so he could figure out how Waru conceived that effect.

Why'd you bring us all the way back here, Xaverri? he wondered. Were you afraid for me to be too close?

The metallic shell attached the Zeffliffl to Waru like a parasite, like an exterior womb. The raw wound left where the scales had melted gushed bloody ichor. The liquid flowed over the shell, patterning it like the calligraphy on the facade of Waru's compound. The runnels flowed together, creating a translucent chrysalis around the shell.

At the foot of the stage, the Zeffliffl group huddled together, their leaves fluttering as if they were in a windstorm.

The room grew still. All around Han, people were bowing their heads. Even Xaverri, who had never bowed her head to anyone. Stubbornly, Han kept watching.

Waru shuddered. The golden scales touched, ringing together with pure clear tones, like bells enlivened by the wind.

Han divided his feelings equally between admiration for the effects and scorn for the gullibility of Waru's followers.

The shuddering extended into the chrysalis. It trembled. It shook, and expanded.

The solidified ichor exploded. Like silver dust, the fragments hung and shivered in the air. Scars and scratches marred the golden shell. It, too, shivered, then slowly opened like a flower, revealing the Zeffliffl.

The gold petals drew back; Waru's body resorbed them and re-formed the melted scales. At Waru's base, the Zeffliffl lay quiet.

Suddenly it shook itself like a wet puppy. Its groupmates shrilled with excitement. Its leaves, green and dark with moisture, fanned open.

"They say," Threepio whispered, "that their groupmate has returned from the dead."

The healed Zeffliffl scrambled down and disappeared

among the groupmates. The mass of beings backed away, twittering.

The silence of the auditorium ended as every being at Waru's feet burst into speech and song and light.

"The Zeffliffl said thank you," Threepio said, speaking loudly enough for them all to hear, "and—"

"And, 'We will give you all our worldly goods,' " Han said cynically.

"No, sir, not at all," Threepio said. "They acclaim Waru as their benefactor. No mention of monetary recompense has been made."

Han shrugged, unconvinced. "Recompense *always* gets mentioned," he said. "Eventually. Can we get out of here? The gratitude is making me sick."

Xaverri turned away from him and walked out of the auditorium. After a moment of surprise, Han followed her. In the relative coolness and silence of the courtyard, welcome after the tumult of Waru's reception hall, he caught up to her and touched her shoulder.

"Xaverri—!"

She shrugged him off and plunged through the gateway. Outside the calligraphed arch, she spun on him.

"Never speak, inside the courtyard. *Never.*"

"Hey, I'm sorry, I didn't mean to blow your cover."

Threepio joined them. "Master Han, Mistress Xaverri, is anything wrong?"

"No," Han said. "I don't think so. I don't know. Except Luke's still back there!"

Han plunged through the archway and ran through the courtyard, unreasonably anxious considering Luke had been out of his sight for about a minute. Han pushed his way back into the auditorium. At first he did not see Luke anywhere. His eyes were no longer accustomed to the dimness, and the noise and heat oppressed him.

He looked at the place where they had all been. Luke stood right where Han had left him. The young Jedi stared at the stage, where Waru had encysted another supplicant.

"Come on!" Han said. He grabbed Luke by the sleeve and dragged him bodily out of the theater.

Luke did not resist.

Xaverri was walking away, already a couple of hundred paces down the trail to the main entry of the dome. Threepio hovered halfway between, moving a few steps toward Xaverri and calling her name plaintively, then returning. When he saw Han and Luke, he stopped stock-still in relief, then hurried to join them.

"She would not wait, Master Han," Threepio said. "I asked her politely, but . . ." Threepio stopped, at a loss for words.

"You worry too much," Han said. "Purple-Three. Come on."

Han led Luke past Threepio. Only when they had caught up to Xaverri did he let Luke go. Han's brother-in-law had made no attempt to escape. His gaze was distant, his expression blank.

"Luke! What's wrong? Snap out of it! Xaverri, wait!"

She complied, but her shoulders were stiff with anger.

Luke raised his head. Suddenly he was back, his usual self.

"Is Waru your lost Jedi?" Han demanded.

"No," Luke said. "I don't think so . . . I don't know. I don't know *what* it is." He gazed into the distance. "I ought to be able to tell, to sense another Jedi Master. But I can't." He took a deep breath.

"Is it *any* kind of manifestation of the Force?" Han asked Luke.

Luke hesitated, then shook his head. "I'm sure I'd know it if it were. It isn't. It's . . . something else."

He smiled, a luminescent smile that wiped out his hesitation, his apprehension.

"But it *was* amazing," Luke said. "Wasn't it amazing?"

Xaverri nodded. "Every time I see Waru do that, I cannot believe it. But I must."

"I *don't* believe it," Han said. "If that thing isn't a manifestation of the Force, what else could it be but a fraud? I can think of six different ways Waru—whatever it is—could bring off that illusion. Substitute another Zeffliffl for the sick one—"

"But, sir," Threepio said, "the groupmates would not have accepted a substitute for their colleague. They would have reacted to an impostor quite violently."

Han shrugged. "So Waru paid them off."

"The reaction cannot be bought, sir," Threepio said. "It is not conscious. It is comparable to an allergic response."

Han flung up his arms in exasperation. "Then the sick one was the impostor, or a mechanical device. Or they painted the healthy one seasick-green and washed it off in the cocoon. It doesn't *matter* how they did it—what matters is, they *could* have done it. Waru didn't need supernatural healing powers to heal the Zeffliffl because the Zeffliffl didn't need to be healed in the first place!"

Xaverri folded her arms and stared thoughtfully at the ground.

"Do you think I have completely lost my mind?" she asked, her tone cold.

Her contempt goaded him.

"Yeah, that would about cover it," he said.

"I, Xaverri, the best creator of deceptions in the old Empire?"

"We all change," he said. "Look, if somebody had a really fine scam, one even you couldn't figure out—then you'd be easy to fool. You're so good, it's hard to imagine anyone better."

"It is *impossible*," she said.

Luke stared through the archway. Han feared he might have to chase Luke down again to keep him from going back inside.

"There's *something*," Luke said.

"But not your lost Jedi."

"Han, it isn't a fraud."

"Luke is correct," Xaverri said.

"Fine!" Han said. "I give up! Waru is for real, which means you don't need me, because it isn't the Republic's business to interfere in people's worship!" He started down the trail without another word.

"Han!" Luke called. "Where are you going?"

"On vacation," Han said. "I still have some vacation left!"

Threepio hurried after him.

"Master Han, if I may be so forward—"

"What *is* it?"

"Our resources are severely depleted. If you plan to gamble—and I certainly do not wish to imply that I believe you should *not* gamble, or that I believe there is anything *wrong* with gambling, or that there is any possibility that you might *lose*—but *if* you plan to gamble . . . don't you think it would be for the best, merely as insurance of course, for you to leave some of your previous winnings in my care? That way I could pay our outstanding bill at the lodge. I noticed the lodge-keeper toting up our accounts as we left today, and he fixed me with a positively poisonous glare!"

Han pulled a wad of credits out of his pocket and thrust it into Threepio's fingers.

"When you want some money, all you have to do is say, 'Can I have some money?' " Han said. He laughed, thinking about the gaming table, the cards that he trusted to go his way. "Plenty more where that came from."

He strode away.

Leia and Chewbacca did what they could for Rillao, the injured Firrerreo. *Alderaan's* medical equipment expressed confusion when Leia asked for information. The Firrerreo were basically human, but something more, something different. The equipment recommended food that might not be toxic. It failed to suggest a safe antibiotic, but, then, Rillao's injuries had not become infected. She had astonishing powers of recuperation. Once the webbing had withdrawn, her skin began to regenerate and the hairline lacerations closed quickly enough for Leia to watch, with astonishment, as the healing occurred. Silver threads of scar tissue formed across Rillao's golden skin.

But Rillao showed no signs of waking.

"What else should we do?" Leia asked the nameless Firrerreo.

He shrugged, barely moving his shoulders. "She'll live, Lelila, or she'll die." He sprawled in a chair, perfectly relaxed.

"Don't you care, either way?"

"She isn't my clan."

Leia let the subject drop. She brushed Rillao's striped hair away from her thin, fierce face and drew a blanket up around her shoulders.

"Do your people sleep lying down?" she asked the nameless Firrerreo.

"How else?" he said, surprised into replying without an argument.

"How else, indeed," Leia said. She laid one hand gently on Artoo-Detoo's carapace. "Will you watch her for me?"

Artoo-Detoo beeped softly.

"Thank you," Leia said to the droid. She turned to Chewbacca and the nameless Firrerreo. "Are you hungry?"

Chewbacca roared, with relief and hunger.

"Me, too," Leia said.

She was ravenous. She had had nothing since the chamberlain's cookies and drugged tea. She led the way to *Alderaan*'s tiny galley. She wondered if the Firrerreo would refuse to accept food, but he sniffed the bowl of stew she gave him— the analysis had suggested his metabolism required high levels of protein—tasted a bite, and dug in hungrily. He held the bowl near his mouth and delicately plucked the meat up in his first two fingers.

Chewbacca fixed himself a bowl of stew and garnished it with salty dry seaweed and a dribble of forest honey.

The dinner conversation was nonexistent, until Leia scraped up the last of her stew with a spoon. As she watched the Firrerreo drink the sauce from his second serving, she thought, He accepted my food because he *doesn't* accept any obligation. He didn't ask me for food. If I asked him for gratitude, he'd say, No one asked you to offer me anything. I owe you nothing.

"Why do you hate Rillao?" Leia asked.

He licked his lips and glanced at the stew pot, but thought again about overloading his system with a third helping.

"She was in the chamber!" His languor vanished and he leaned toward Leia, angry and intense. "*She* must be the reason we were exiled, Lelila. Why else would the Empire sentence her to spend the trip under torture?"

"Random cruelty." Leia wondered why the Firrerreo used her name—her alias—so often. No matter. It helped her remember what she was calling herself.

"No. No. The Empire is cruel, Lelila, but it directs its cruelty. To create fear, to extort, to increase its power—"

"The Empire is gone," Leia said. "It's finished. Defeated. You're free, you and your people."

If she expected gratitude or even happiness, she was disappointed.

"Defeated!" He thumped his fist on the table. "You said you could give me my freedom—but, Lelila, it wasn't yours to give!"

"I said you were free," Leia said. "That's all I said." If she admitted who she was, she could claim some responsibility for his freedom. Instead, she would remain Lelila.

He growled low in his throat. Chewbacca growled, too.

But Leia remained calm. She smiled at the unnamed one.

"No one asked me for an explanation," she said. "You only asked me for your freedom."

He snorted in disgust, but his contempt lessened, to be replaced with an expression of grudging respect. To her astonishment, he rose and bowed.

Then he walked away.

"Where are you going, unnamed one?" Leia asked.

Without replying—Why did I expect him to reply? Leia thought—he left *Alderaan*'s galley.

She followed him; she caught up to him. He was a head taller than she, sleek and potentially powerful despite his gauntness. He continued toward the airlock without acknowledging her presence.

"Are you going to wake up your people, unnamed one?"

A few paces farther along, he said, "Here, Lelila? To what purpose?"

"To regain their strength—"

"The ship will return their strength while they sleep."

"—and to decide what to do now that you're free!"

"Should we return to our home, Lelila?" he snarled.

He knows, Leia thought. She wondered if the Empire troops had awakened him and tormented him with the news of his world's death.

"No," she said. "I'm sorry. It's quarantined. No one can land, and live . . . nothing can ever leave the planet."

He stopped short at the airlock door. His shoulders slumped. Leia took his elbow, steadying him. The sound he made was the cry of a grief-stricken predator.

And Leia knew how he felt.

"I'm sorry," Leia said again. "I'm so sorry."

He turned upon her. "Lelila, did you have a hand in poisoning my world?"

"No! I—I played a small part in bringing down the people who ordered the poisoning."

"The Starcrash Brigade?"

The Starcrash Brigade had been one of the Empire's elite assault teams.

"Not the Brigade—the Empire." She looked him in the eye. "It destroyed my world, too."

He narrowed his wide black eyes. "Ah. Alderaan, yes, Lelila, I thought perhaps you were from Alderaan."

The airlock door slid open. The unnamed one strode from *Alderaan* into the freighter's echoing entry dock. Leia grabbed his wrist, but snatched back her hand when she felt his muscles tighten.

"What are you going to do?" she asked.

"Continue."

"But you don't have to! Everyone's free, now, within the New Republic."

"The Empire bequeathed us a world. We will continue."

"But it might be—you don't know—what about the other ships stranded here?"

He leaned toward her. In the low gravity, the motion spread his hair around his head like a brindled halo.

"The other ships have nothing to do with me," he said. "And I have nothing to do with them. Do with them as you will, Lelila. As for the new world . . . we are adventurous people. We will take our chances."

"You'll be traveling at sublight," Leia said. "You'll be traveling for years! The Republic could give you hyperdrive, or find a world for you within its bounds—"

"To what purpose?" he asked again. "We will not notice

the length of time. We will not care. We will be asleep. If all memory of the Empire has vanished when we wake—so much the better. If your Republic has vanished when we wake —we will not care."

Leia stepped back. Nothing she could say could change his mind, she knew that. He was doing what was right by his own sense of duty. She could not force him to accept hers.

"Good-bye, then," she said. "And good luck."

"May you always be shielded from the wind, Lelila."

"Why do you keep repeating my name?" Leia asked.

"For power," he said. "Lelila."

The airlock door began to slide shut.

"But I gain only a little power from your false name, Princess Leia," he said. "You wear it uncomfortably." As the airlock door closed, he said, "And your disguise is pathetic."

Han returned to the city domes and sauntered down the street. He wanted some more of the local ale, and he wanted another card game where Chance & Hazard topped the deck. But he also wanted a different tavern from the one he had been in last night.

"Good evening, small human."

He spun around, and once more bumped his nose against the chest of the enhanced human. She laughed down at him, but Han got the distinct impression that her laughter was superficial.

"You left our game far too soon," she said. "The cards began to turn my way, later on in the evening."

"Congratulations!" Han said heartily. "I'm glad to hear your night wasn't a complete loss."

She leaned toward him, and the heavy, entangled locks of her white hair swung down on either side of her face.

"Nor will tonight be," she said. "You are obviously well born and well mannered, so you will give me the chance to make myself even with you."

"I wasn't planning on cards tonight," Han said. "Nope, no cards, I was just taking the air, just came out for a glass of ale."

"Ale will run as plentifully as water," she said. She took his upper arm in her huge hand. Her fingers met around his biceps.

"I mean, I've already had my glass of ale," he said. "Hit my limit—"

He tried to twist his arm from her grip, as Luke had twisted from his. The enhanced human lifted his arm, lifted his whole body. Han stretched on tiptoe to stay in contact with the ground.

"You may drink or not, as you choose," the enhanced human said. "But you *will* play."

"Well, okay, sure, why didn't you say you had your heart set on a game?" Han said. "Fine, let's go. Would you do me a favor? Either put me down or pick me up. This is very uncomfortable."

He thought she might sling him over her shoulder and cart him away. She could certainly do it if she chose. Finally she let him down. But she did not let him loose. She urged him down the street, holding his arm tight enough to bruise.

"I didn't get your name last night," Han said in a companionable tone. "What did you say it was? And by the way, you want to loosen up a little?"

"I did not say," she said, "and you did not ask, but my name is Celestial Serenity. No, I do not want to loosen up at all."

He glanced up at her. She smiled down at him and walked faster, pushing him along.

Jaina ate her breakfast.

She was so hungry she hardly even tasted the rancid grease that floated on top of the thin porridge. When she finished, her stomach still growled. She could smell the ripe fruit and honey and fresh hot bread that the Proctors passed among themselves.

Jaina's mouth watered. She watched the Proctors at the highest table and the helpers at the middle table breakfasting on good food, more than they could eat. They laughed and shouted and threw half-eaten food on the floor to go to waste, and leaned way back in their chairs with their feet on the table.

The children, at the low tables, had to wait to be excused until the Proctors were all finished.

It isn't fair! she thought.

Jaina could see Jacen, but only the top of his head. He was all the way on the other side of the cafeteria. She wished she could talk to him about what she had learned she could do. And she wished she could tell him she had drilled halfway through the door of her cell to the lock. Then she had stuck the sawdust together with spit, *Ick,* and pressed it back into the hole in the door so no one would notice.

Vram sat at the middle table with the other helpers. He wolfed down a piece of fruit, some bread, and a whole bunch of cookies. He picked up a honey-cake and waved it at the other children. At Jaina. Honey dripped down Vram's fingers. He licked it off.

Jaina looked down so she would not have to see him.

On the table in front of her, a bug, a tiny myrmin, tiptoed past on its hair-thin legs.

It isn't *really* a myrmin, Jaina thought. It has ten legs instead of just six, and an extra set of feelers! But it sort of looks like a myrmin. Jacen would know what it is. I bet it's hungry.

Jaina scraped the last tiny grain of porridge out of her bowl. She put it near the myrmin. The myrmin walked around it, tapped it with its feelers, and struggled to lift it and move it and carry it.

I hope that tastes better to myrmins than to children, Jaina thought.

The myrmin balanced the sand-grain-sized bit of porridge and climbed down over the edge of the table.

The myrmin gave Jaina an idea.

Sand got tracked in from the playfield. It lay in the cracks between the stone tiles on the floor, and even in the spaces where the planks of the table touched. Jaina experimented with moving a grain.

I'll pretend I'm a myrmin, she thought. Not a little girl, not Jaina. I don't have any Jedi abilities—I'm just a myrmin! Who would pay any attention to a myrmin?

She pushed the sand grain. It skittered across the table and fell over the edge.

Jaina hunched her shoulders, expecting Hethrir's cold wet blanket to fall around her and cut her off from the world.

Nothing happened. It was just like last night with the air molecules.

Jaina *reached* for sand grains on the Proctors' table. She found none. Someone cleaned their table better. But plenty of sand lay on the platform at their feet. Jaina played with a few grains. They spiraled up into the air. No one noticed.

The Head Proctor picked up a section of fruit. Jaina dropped the scatter of sand grains on it. The Proctor tossed it down to Vram. For a second, Jaina thought the Proctor had noticed the sand, but then she decided not because he did not look mad and he did not look for more sand on the sticky bun he chose from a steaming basket.

Vram popped the fruit into his mouth and gobbled it without even noticing the sand.

Jaina felt a little sorry for him. But only a little.

If somebody gave me a piece of fruit right now, she thought, I probably wouldn't notice sand on it, either.

The second time she moved sand, she dropped it onto the Head Proctor's sticky bun. Jaina felt like she had done something very, very bad, to spoil good food like that.

The Proctor pulled off a piece of the soft, sweet bread and put it in his mouth. He chewed.

His expression changed. Jaina felt glad. Not happy-glad. Jaina felt satisfied-glad.

She *lifted* another handful of sand and scattered it across the Proctors' table, so it fell on all their plates.

The Head Proctor spit out his mouthful of sticky bun.

That's disgusting! Jaina thought. He didn't even cover his mouth with his napkin.

"Grake!" the Head Proctor shouted.

Several of the other Proctors spit out their food, too, and soon they were looking at it and poking it, even the half-chewed bits, and talking to each other and arguing. Jaina watched them, pretending not to. Soon she did not even have to pretend, because all the other children were watching, too.

"Grake! Get out here!"

The door beside the Proctors' stage slammed open, bouncing against the wall.

A huge being thundered through the doorway. Jaina flinched—she thought the dragon had broken into the bunker —then looked again, surprised and excited.

The being in the wide white apron was a Veubg, from Gbu, a high-gravity world. Gbu was the last world before Munto Codru that Mama had visited. The New Republic delegation had not been able to go to the surface, most of them, of course, because the gravity would have squashed them. But the Veubgri had traveled to the meeting satellite. They had liked Jaina and Jacen and Anakin. Jaina remembered the soft touch of their tendrils on her hair. Her mouth watered at the memory of their sweets. She wanted to jump up and wave at the Veubg.

But Grake had never seen Jaina or her brothers. She would not recognize them. She would not care.

"Why are you yelling at me, little blue-clothes?" Grake climbed the stairs, light-footed and powerful, tendrils coiled around a heavy wooden spatula, and stopped behind the center chair. "I work all day for you, and you only yell at me, you are a very unappreciative person."

"There's sand in the food!" the Head Proctor shouted. "Is this your idea of a joke?"

"A joke? Sand—in *my* food?" Grake smacked the Head Proctor on the side of the head with the spatula.

The Head Proctor fell off his chair and scrambled up, staring, stunned.

Jaina gasped. She wanted to hide her eyes. She was sure the Proctors would hurt Grake—use the Force to make her explode! And it would be Jaina's fault.

But nothing like that happened.

Maybe they *can't*, Jaina thought. Maybe all they can do with the Force is just barely turn on their lightsabers, or maybe Hethrir even cheated to let them do that!

Grake leaped to the end of the stage and whacked the Proctor who lounged in the last seat. He scrambled to keep his balance, lurching sideways and forward to grab the edge of the table.

"Take your feet off the table!" The Veubg leaped again, all

the way from one end of the stage to the other, knocking the spatula against the head of each Proctor in turn. "You complain of sand in my food—when you put your feet on the dinner table? You have the manners of dragons!"

The Veubg landed soundlessly—then stamped all six feet. The whole Proctors' table bounced a handsbreadth in the air and forward.

Jaina giggled. She could not help it. She tried to stop and so did all the other children. She knew they would get in trouble for laughing and she knew she would be the cause of it. But she could not help it. And how she wished Lusa were here to see it too!

"Stop it!" the Head Proctor shouted.

Jaina could not tell whether he meant her or Grake.

Grake snatched handsful of fruit from the serving dishes and flung them over the second table and out to the children. Everybody shrieked with excitement and grabbed for the fruit.

Jaina caught a chunk of melon and stuffed it into her mouth. It was the most delicious thing she had ever tasted. It made tears spring to her eyes. She was glad she had not poured sand on the serving dishes, but she would have eaten the fruit anyway.

"Sand! In *my* food!" Grake flung the contents of a whole serving bowl of cookies over the children's heads. Everyone was running around and jumping up to catch the sweets and snatching them off the floor before they got trampled.

Jaina snatched more sand, even though she really wanted a cookie. A little cloud of sand grains floated up from the tiles. She dropped the sharp grains down the necks of the Proctors' uniforms. The sand fell down their backs and into their pants.

At first they did not notice because they were all on their feet, yelling. Then the Head Proctor drew his lightsaber. Its blade hummed and glowed.

Jaina jumped up, horrified. Uncle Luke always said that when she became a Jedi Knight, she should never draw her blade, except for practice, unless she was willing to kill.

Jaina had never even touched a lightsaber.

Grake did not give the Proctor the chance to kill her. She leaped down the stage, down the steps, and through the doorway even before the Proctor could strike, if he was going to. Jaina had never seen anyone move so fast.

The Proctors shouted a few last insults. The Head Proctor put away his lightsaber. Jaina did not know if he would have killed Grake, or if he was only threatening. Or joking. She did not think they should threaten *or* joke with a lightsaber.

The Proctors shouted after Grake, and pushed each other back and forth, and finally sat down again.

None of them put their feet on the table.

"Be quiet!" the Head Proctor yelled at the children. "Sit down and be quiet or we'll come put you in your places."

Jaina sat back down and so did the other children. They might as well, because all the extra food was gone. Everybody was looking around, hoping to find one last tart grape or sweet crumb.

The Proctors sat uneasily at their table, not wanting to dismiss dinner because that would mean they had failed at something. But they did not eat any more of the sandy food.

The Head Proctor frowned and fidgeted and pulled his uniform away from his sides and shook it. Jaina stared down at the table. If she started to laugh before anybody else noticed what was happening, the Proctors would know it was all her fault.

Jaina wished a grape had fallen on the table in front of her so she could eat it. But the table was empty. She carefully looked past the edge of the table. The Proctors were talking together now. They sounded mad. Jaina made herself not smile. Instead she jiggled the sand in the Proctors' uniforms, and looked for more sand.

She had used it all up. The floor tiles, even the cracks between them, were clean.

Except for little black spots moving toward the Proctors' table. They formed a line across the floor like the foam on waves.

The myrmins scurried up the front of the Proctors' stage. As the Proctors squirmed and itched and hissed impatiently at the Head Proctor to dismiss dinner, the myrmins ran over their shoes and into their pants legs.

Jaina could not resist anymore. She looked across the cafeteria toward her brother. She even stood up so she could see him. At the same time, Jacen stood up and looked at her. He grinned quickly. They both sat down again before anyone could catch them.

Jaina knew Jacen had asked the myrmins to climb up the stage.

One of the Proctors leaped to his feet with a shout. He thought he just had sand in his pants. Then the sand *bit* him. The other Proctors started jumping up and yelling and scratching. And stamping, stamping on the myrmins.

"Oh!" Jaina whispered. "Oh—poor myrmins, thank you, myrmins." Some of them were running away now, disappearing into cracks and hiding. But some of them were being killed.

"We're sorry, myrmins," she said, sincerely, the way Chewbacca spoke to insects he sometimes killed, even if he never meant to, when he harvested forest honey. She risked another glance across the hall at Jacen.

Stricken, he started to cry. He cried when Chewbacca apologized to the forest insects, too. But this time it was his fault that the myrmins were being hurt.

Suddenly the myrmins all disappeared. Jaina felt the *flare* of Jacen's abilities, whisking the little creatures out of danger.

Hethrir's cold wet invisible blanket fell down around Jaina— It's not fair, she thought, *I* didn't do anything . . . well, not *much*, anyway—and she knew the same thing had happened to Jacen. She gasped, and shivered, and struggled up out of her seat, and stumbled across the cafeteria to Jacen.

They hugged each other. It was such a good hug. It almost made Hethrir's blanket go away. Or anyway it made it feel only cool and damp instead of cold and wet.

"Jacen, Jacen, they took Anakin, they took Lusa—"

That was the first time she thought that Hethrir might have taken Anakin away *forever*, the way he took Lusa. Where else could their brother be?

"We have to *do* something," she whispered.

"All you children get back to your studies!" the Head Proctor said, scratching the side of his leg. The myrmins were gone, but their bites remained!

"Thank you, little myrmins," Jaina whispered.

"Thank you, little myrmins," Jacen said too, "I'm s-sorry!"

"Back to your studies!"

The children straggled into an uneven line. They could not keep from giggling. Jaina stayed near Jacen. Maybe no one would notice they were together.

"Do something about that line!" the Head Proctor said to his underlings.

The other Proctors all looked at him like they thought he was crazy.

And they ignored him and ran out of the cafeteria. Some of them were already unfastening their uniforms before they got out of the room.

The Head Proctor glared down at the children. And then he winced and started to scratch, in a place it was very naughty to scratch in public, and turned around and strode out of the room. As soon as he vanished, his footsteps speeded up. He ran away.

Chapter

7

The children were alone in the cafeteria.

"Let's go out!" Jaina said. She did not know what she could do once she was outside, but she felt desperate to get away from this cold hard building.

She and Jacen ran down the long dark corridor. All the other children followed them. They burst out into the light, as the tiny planet's tiny sun leaped into the sky. The little planet spun fast, so its days were much shorter than regular days. The children shouted and ran and cheered in the warmth.

Jaina and Jacen held hands and leaned backward and spun around and around, just like the little planet. Jaina whipped her hair back and forth till she felt dizzy. She and Jacen fell down in the sand, panting and laughing.

Jaina jumped up again and Jacen jumped up beside her.

"Jaina, Jaina, you're okay!"

"Jacen, I missed you so much! I don't know where Anakin is!"

"If we could *reach* for him—" Jacen said.

"—we might be able to find him. But—"

"—we have to run far away from that blanket!" Jacen

finished their shared thought. Jaina was glad he thought about it the same way she did, but that did not help them figure out how to get away from it.

"We have to get past the dragon," Jaina said.

"There's no dragon," Jacen said scornfully. "That's just to scare us." He marched straight toward the canyon fence, straight into the blank space.

Jaina ran after him. The dragon jumped out of the sand and roared and bounced against the fence. Jaina grabbed Jacen and pulled him back till the dragon could not see them anymore. She did not have to pull him very hard because he was scared too, but he was also amazed.

The dragon forgot it had seen them and snuffled around the edge of the fence looking for a soft warm patch of sand.

"Wow," Jacen whispered.

"Maybe I could jump up and down and wave and—" She was thinking Jacen could run around behind and climb the fence. But then she would still be stuck inside.

"Maybe I could *tame* her," Jacen said. "And we could ride her away!"

Jaina had no idea how Jacen knew it was a Mistress Dragon and not a Mister Dragon. But he was always right about this sort of stuff.

"*Ride* her?" Jaina said, entranced.

Then Jacen's lips trembled. "But maybe the Proctors would hurt her the way they hurt the myrmins."

"How could they hurt a dragon?" Jaina asked.

"With their lightsabers!"

"They'd be too scared! I bet they wouldn't even get close to her."

"With a *blaster*, then," Jacen said.

"Oh. Yeah."

"Maybe we could distract her," Jacen said thoughtfully.

"We better do it fast," Jaina said.

"I need something to throw," Jacen said. He looked around but there was just sand.

The dragon lumbered to the fence and rubbed her nubbly-scaled shoulder against the wire mesh, closing her eyes and groaning happily.

If Jaina could use her abilities, she could easily distract

the dragon. Together with Jacen, they might even be able to stop the dragon. But Jaina thought that would be a lot to try to do, without Uncle Luke's help.

"I know!" Jaina pulled her multitool out of her pocket.

Jacen grabbed for it eagerly.

"No, wait!" Jaina snatched it back. "Don't throw it." She opened up the lens and caught the light and flashed it on the ground in front of the dragon.

"Isn't she pretty?" Jacen said.

When the dragon opened her eyes, she saw the concentrated point of light from Jaina's lens. She snorted and lowered her head. Jaina gave the multitool to Jacen. He was better with critters than she was.

He wiggled the light near the dragon's front paws. The dragon put her paw on the place where the light was. Then she had to put her other paw on top of her first paw, and still the light was not covered. She pulled her first paw out from under her second paw and lost her balance. She rolled completely over, snortling and wriggling. Then she jumped up and looked around for the light.

Jacen moved it around for her to chase. She jumped forward after it, shaking the ground when she landed, raising great sprays of sand. Jaina laughed with delight.

By now all the other children had gathered behind Jaina and Jacen to watch the dragon play.

Jacen danced the light before the dragon, who gallumphed after it, pouncing to try to catch it. Jacen skipped the light up the cliffside that projected beyond the fence. The dragon scratched the rock with her front feet, ripping loose bits of stone. She roared joyously. She lashed her tail.

All the time, Jacen kept moving closer to the fence, crossing the undisturbed ground till he was right up against the thick metal mesh. Jaina followed him. The other children stayed back, still frightened of the dragon.

"Hey, dragon," Jacen said softly. "Hey, Mistress Dragon." He wiggled the light down the cliff again, and the dragon followed. The light crept toward the fence.

The dragon followed.

Jacen brought the spark of sunlight right up next to the fence. Jaina caught her breath. Her heart beat very fast.

The dragon's snout pressed against the fence. Her big teeth stuck out of her mouth and she drooled in the sand. Her tongue flicked, flicked, flicked between her lips. Her eyes were the size of Jaina's fists, big and gold. The dragon blinked her heavy beaded eyelids. Her hot breath ruffled the sand where the spot of light lay.

Jacen was having trouble keeping the light near the dragon because the sun was already falling in the sky.

As the spot of light faded, Jacen put his hand through the fence. Jaina gasped. Jacen touched the dragon's great eyebrow, and rubbed her smooth scales.

"There, Mistress Dragon," Jacen said. He rubbed harder. The dragon pressed against his hand, and made a low, rumbling, pleasant snorting sound. The dragon did not mind that she could no longer play with the light.

"She likes you," Jaina whispered.

"She's all alone," Jacen said. "She's lonely, she's a little dragon, she wants someone to play with."

"Hey! You children!"

The dragon jerked her head up, startled by the shout. Jaina turned around. The Head Proctor stood at the head of the stairwell. The other children scattered away into the twilight.

The dragon roared. The fence rang as she rose up and crashed against it. Jacen snatched his hand away from the fence, and he and Jaina ran to the playfield. Jacen pressed the multitool into Jaina's hand, and she hid it in her pocket.

The Head Proctor laughed at them.

"Now you'll believe in the dragon, I think," he said. "You children all line up! You've been very bad. I told you to get back to your studies."

"We couldn't hear you, sir," Jaina said respectfully. "We thought you said to go outside."

He glared at her. He looked very uncomfortable. He had swelling red bites on his wrists and his neck. He kept moving inside his uniform as if he wanted to scratch. Jaina looked him straight in the eye without laughing, even though she wanted to laugh.

"That's right, sir," Jacen said. "I thought I heard you say to go outside, and I was much closer to you than my sister!"

"That's right, sir," one of the other children said.

The Head Proctor was wearing a rumpled uniform with a dirty smudge across one arm, and all his medals pinned on crooked.

I bet *he* didn't do his laundry when he was supposed to! Jaina thought. I bet he lets it pile up all over the floor of his room, and he didn't have anything clean to put on when the myrmins and the sand got in his clothes.

Jaina felt very grateful to Winter, who always encouraged Jaina and Jacen to pick up after themselves. She had even shown them how to do their laundry if they needed to, if the laundry droid wasn't working or forgot how you liked your clothes ironed.

"Get in line," the Head Proctor said. All the other children lined up behind Jaina and Jacen.

The Proctors marched the children back inside. Jaina sighed. They had not escaped, and now they would have to spend all day staring at the horrible, dull displays that said how wonderful everything would be when Hethrir made himself Emperor.

Probably Lord Hethrir would come and lecture them, too. She was scared of that. He would probably know that she had caused all the trouble.

Jaina yearned for her classes back home. Sometimes she and Jacen read stories to Winter or to Papa and Mama. Sometimes they made up stories! Jaina was learning number theory and she loved it, it was so beautiful. On Mundo Codru, Jacen had been studying first aid with Dr. Hyos and her child. Jaina bet Jacen was as bored with these dumb displays as she was. She bet all the children were bored.

Instead of taking the children to the study desks, the Proctors herded them back to their rooms. Most of the children groaned.

"Be quiet!" the Head Proctor shouted. "Your discipline is dreadful! Lord Hethrir will never choose any of you as his helpers at this rate."

The children fell silent. Jaina realized she should have groaned, too, but the truth was that she no longer feared the dark of her cell. She was overjoyed that she would have a few hours, maybe all the way until tomorrow morning, by herself, to work and plan.

"You'll spend the day in bed," the Head Proctor said. "So that tomorrow, you'll appreciate the opportunity Lord Hethrir gives you to learn."

He opened Jaina's door and pushed her inside and *slammed* the door closed after her.

Bits of sawdust scattered to the floor. But the Head Proctor had not noticed that Jaina had been drilling the wood.

And Lord Hethrir had not come to lecture them or inspect them.

Finally, outside Jaina's cell, the faint sounds of closing doors and the voices of the Proctors and the sounds of their boots on the floor stopped.

Jaina rubbed some molecules of air together and created a faint light to work with. She brushed the last of the sawdust away from the hole she had made, pulled out her multitool, and began to drill again.

For several hours, the Firrerre passenger freighter hovered in space, coming alive. The first thing it did, long before it reached full power, was to disengage itself from *Alderaan*.

Leia took her ship out of range of the freighter's propulsion field.

"Good luck," she said, transmitting to the nameless Firrerreo.

He did not reply. The freighter hovered in space, gathering itself for its lonely voyage. Even if Leia could do any more to help the Firrerre ship, its inhabitants did not want her aid.

Leia checked on Rillao, who remained asleep. But Artoo-Detoo and the medical equipment thought her body was regaining its strength.

"Thank you for watching her," Leia said to Artoo-Detoo.

Chewbacca came in and looked mournfully at the sleeping Firrerreo.

"What are we going to do?" Leia said. "This is a dead

end! The trail is gone." She tried again, reaching out desperately all around her for any trace of her children.

Rillao's pain had blasted the trail out of existence.

The *kidnappers* tortured her, Leia thought. The nameless Firrerreo was wrong: Rillao wasn't left here by the Empire at all. The kidnappers tortured her so no one could follow them! Unless . . . they're the same people.

That would make sense, Leia thought. And it would explain how they knew where to find the passenger freighters. But it doesn't give me any better clues to finding them.

Chewbacca put one giant hand on her shoulder. The fur of his fingers tickled Leia's cheek. His plaintive groan conveyed his sympathy and his grief. Leia's family was his family, his Honor Family. He had chosen to share his life with the people she loved. She could not remain angry at him.

"The Firrerreo was right about one thing!" Leia said. "Our disguise is no disguise at all. We'll never get anywhere if everyone knows we're Leia and Chewbacca. And if we're up against Imperial loyalists—come on!"

She took Chewbacca to her cabin and pulled out all the cosmetics in the dressing-table drawer. Chewbacca looked at them quizzically.

"You didn't think my eyelids were this color naturally, did you?" she asked. "Didn't you notice the color changes sometimes?"

He snorted.

"No, my skin doesn't camouflage itself!" Leia said.

As she spoke, she pulled the pins from her hair and unbraided the long plait. Chewbacca watched with astonishment.

I so seldom take my hair down, she thought. Hardly anyone has seen me with my hair down in years . . . except Han.

She had thought, over the years, of cutting her hair, but the idea was too radical. On Alderaan, adults grew their hair long and usually kept it bound.

Feeling reckless, Leia brushed her hair loose and free over her shoulders. She stood up. Her hair spilled almost to her knees. She kept brushing it, till it parted down the center and hung on either side of her face and draped down over her breasts. It tended to fall across her eyes, so she looked out through a curtain.

All the better, she thought. All the better to hide me with.

She rummaged through the bottles and packets. Some she had bought on a whim and never even tried. She kept them on her ship because her ship was her place for whims and fancies.

Leia remembered the first time she had taken Han out on *Alderaan*. She shook the stirring memory away. Now was no time for such memories.

Several packets of color-crawlers lay in her hand.

"Aren't you tired of being chestnut all the time, Chewbacca?" she said. She tore open a package of black and a package of silver, mixed them together, and tossed them at Chewbacca. He blew out his breath in surprise, reached up as if to brush them off, then looked at them curiously.

The color-crawlers picked their way over and across and through his fur, leaving intermittent trails of black and silver behind them. Chewbacca plucked one up, delicately, let it crawl along his finger, and watched it streak a patch of chestnut hair with silver. The hair on his chest had already begun to mottle with silver and black.

Amused, the Wookiee let the color-crawlers have their way with his fur.

"Soon you'll just be one more brindled Wookiee," Leia said. "Now. What about me?"

Chewbacca chose several different greens and handed them to her.

"I look terrible in green," Leia said. "I can't imagine why I bought those." She chose, instead, several shades of ordinary brown and let them loose in her hair.

I can't imagine why I bought these colors, either, she thought. I gave Chewbacca the best shades. Oh, well.

She chose one package of very dark green and opened it into her hair.

Chewbacca whuffled with approval.

I'm going to look so *boring*, Leia thought.

But I want to be invisible, Leia reminded herself. There's

no way to make Chewbacca invisible. I only have to make him not-Chewbacca. And I have to make sure no one notices me.

She was glad Artoo-Detoo was a common sort of droid, so she did not have to disguise him, too.

She envied Han his beard. Such an easy way to hide one's face. She considered disguising herself as a man, but only for a moment.

In stories, she said to herself, princesses always disguise themselves as princes. But princesses in stories never have any hips. They never have any breasts. No. I'd look like a woman in disguise; I'd only draw more attention.

Better to be invisible.

Chewbacca gazed at his changing fur with every evidence of fascination. But then he sighed, deeply, woefully. His sigh echoed in the empty space in Leia's heart where she could not find any perception of her children.

"We can't be Leia and Chewbacca anymore," she said.

Chewbacca raised his head slowly. His eyes were dark and sad and questioning.

"We have to be Lelila and Geyyahab—we have to be Lelila and *somebody*, if you don't want to be Geyyahab you can choose another name."

Chewbacca—Geyyahab—indicated that he accepted her choice of names, but did not understand the necessity.

"Whoever stole the children meant it as a strike against me," Leia said. "And against you and Han and Luke. The kidnappers will expect us to come after them. They'll be watching for us. Setting a trap. I think the only way we'll defeat them is with surprise."

Chewbacca whined at her quizzically.

"No," Leia said, in despair. "I don't know who they are. Or where they went." But they *must* be remnants of the fallen Empire, she thought. Who else could hate me enough to attack me through my children?

She grabbed the most lurid vial of eye-paint from the clutter on her bed. She wrenched the vial open and slashed the purple paint across her eyelids, under her eyes, like the kohl of desert fighters. She highlighted her forehead and her cheeks with gold.

"I'll find out," she said. "Maybe Rillao knows who—who hurt her. But if she doesn't, I'll wake up every passenger on every freighter, if I have to. *Someone* must know who they are and what they plan. And where to look for them."

She looked in the mirror. Her hair hung around her face, half hiding her. Her eyes peered out, intense and dark and wild with purple. The paint's gold and ruby enhancers glittered and shifted. She looked less like a desert fighter than a saloon dancer.

It doesn't matter, she said to herself. All that matters is, I don't look like Leia anymore. From now on, I'm Lelila.

Artoo-Detoo buzzed fast over the threshold, hesitated, and hooted as its sensors took in the changes in its biological companions. As soon as the droid recognized them, it reversed and vanished again.

Lelila the bounty hunter jumped up and ran after the droid. Behind her, Geyyahab her client followed along, the change in his fur nearly complete.

Han had to admit that as far as he could tell, the game had been honest. Of course, as far as he could tell, Waru was legit, too, and he did not believe Waru either.

He plodded down the street toward the lodge, reeking of six kinds of smoke, his head aching. He wished he had drunk another glass of local ale; he might feel better. He thought the stuff had magical healing powers.

"Just like Waru," he muttered.

He reached the lodge. The proprietor popped up and greeted him in a friendly manner.

Threepio must have paid our bill, Han thought. Wonder what our cordial host will say tomorrow when we ask for an extension . . . and don't pay for it?

He climbed the steps, tripping only once, and counted doors carefully till he came to his own. It opened for him. The eerie glow of Luke's lightsaber flowed over his feet and across the carpet.

Han quickly straightened his shirt, combed his hair and his beard with his fingers, and strolled casually inside. The blade of the saber hummed and disappeared. Luke sat in the corner, exactly as he had the night before.

"Hi, Luke," Han said, pretending to be much more cheerful than he felt.

"We have to talk," Luke said. "Xaverri and I, we went back to the—the ceremony. Han, there's no mistaking what we saw—what *you* saw."

Unable to maintain his pose, Han flung himself on his bed and covered his face with the pillow. His head ached fiercely.

"Master Han!" Threepio's feet clattered metallically on the floor tiles. "I paid our bills. Thank you very much! I will have other expenses to pay, in the morning, perhaps before you arise, and I wondered—"

"I'll give it to you tomorrow," Han said.

"But I had thought to go shopping early. Were I to lay in some provisions, that would save my human companions from the expense of eating in restaurants—"

"We're on vacation! Half the fun of being on vacation is eating in restaurants!" Han tried to remember when the last time was that he had eaten. Have I been subsisting on local ale? he thought. The stuff is even better than I thought.

"—and it would allow me to serve you breakfast in bed."

"Can we talk about it tomorrow?" Han said. "I really need some sleep."

"Did you lose all the money?" Luke asked.

Han flung himself up. The pillow fell off his face and flopped onto the floor.

"No." He shrugged, and grinned. "Not *all* of it."

"Oh, Master Han," Threepio said. "How am I to go shopping in the morning, if you lost all our money?"

"I *didn't* lose all of it," Han said. "I can get more. I just had a bad evening. Relax. Now can I get some sleep?"

"No," Luke said. "Dammit, Han, wake up!"

"How can I wake up when you haven't given me a chance to go to sleep yet?"

The blade of Luke's lightsaber shivered into being. The ghostly green light filled the room. It brightened, oddly, to pure white; its low hum rose to a shriek. Han shouted in protest.

Luke quickly turned off the lightsaber and slipped the handle beneath his robe.

"What was that?" Han asked. He was wide awake.

"I don't—nothing. It's all right." He sounded uncharacteristically startled. "Han, this Waru . . . if we could persuade this being to come back with us, we could make a tremendous difference in the Republic. The Jedi—and your legions, of course—protect the peace. Waru could directly improve people's lives."

"Waru isn't a Jedi—for certain?"

"No. I mean . . . I'm not getting any of the perceptions I ought to feel." He leaned forward, intent. "When your kids were born, I *knew*, right away, that they belonged among us. Especially Anakin. When I first saw him, and he looked straight at me—" Luke exhaled loudly. "If Waru were Jedi, I don't think I'd make a mistake." He interlaced his fingers, opened his hands, stared at his palms. "But maybe Waru is connected to the Force, by some means we aren't aware of. Some means *I'm* not aware of." He pulled his hands apart and clenched them into fists. "I *just don't know*! And I've got to find out."

"Okay, okay, take it easy." Han rubbed his face. He was so sleepy he could hardly keep his attention on what Luke was saying, despite Luke's urgency.

"Xaverri said she thought Waru was dangerous. A danger to the Republic, she said. And now you want to take him—it—the being—back to the heart of our government?"

"Waru has attracted a lot of followers here. They could form a powerful faction. Wouldn't it be best to cooperate, right from the beginning?"

Han chuckled. "You don't usually sound like a politician." Han doubted that Luke cared one way or the other if Waru's followers formed an opposition to Leia's government. But the young Jedi was fascinated with what he perceived as remarkable abilities; he obviously wanted Waru where he could keep an eye on the being, and perhaps even learn from him.

Han still had no idea why Xaverri thought Waru was dangerous.

Han produced one of his last coins, as if he had brought it out of thin air.

Luke smiled slightly. "Not bad."

"I told you, more where this came from." Han made it disappear again.

Threepio approached. "How were you able to do that?"

Han produced the coin from Threepio's mouth.

Threepio's eyes changed. "Do that again, if you please, Master Han."

Han complied.

"Ah," Threepio said. "Exceedingly dexterous."

"What'd you do?" Han asked. "Slow it down?"

"Indeed I did, Master Han."

"Did you watch Waru that way?"

"I regret that I did not, sir," Threepio replied to Han. "I was so intrigued by what Mistress Xaverri had brought us to see, it did not occur to me."

"Where *is* Xaverri, anyway?" Han asked. "Did she go home?"

"She stayed back at the compound," Luke said. "She wanted to—"

"You *left* her there?"

"Sure."

Han grabbed his boots from the floor where he had just thrown them and wrestled them back on.

"She's lived here for years," Luke said reasonably. "She's been attending Waru's meetings since they began. She knows how to take care of herself."

"You said yourself, something weird is going on—"

"And *you* said it was a fraud!"

"Just because something's a fraud doesn't mean it isn't dangerous. You saw how Xaverri reacted yesterday." He hunted around for his jacket, then realized he had never taken it off.

Han Solo ran out the door.

Rillao lay very still beneath the shroud of medical equipment. Only her eyes moved. Her gaze flicked over everything in the room, searching for weaknesses, searching for escape. A moaning growl shuddered deep in her throat.

Lelila stood in the doorway, regarding the Firrerreo dispassionately.

Compassion was wasted on the nameless Firrerreo, Lelila thought. Besides, I can't afford compassion.

She waited till Rillao's gaze found her.

Lelila moved forward deliberately, and stopped a pace away from Rillao's bedside. Rillao glared at her.

"I saved you," Lelila said.

"Who asked you to?" Rillao's voice was hoarse and rough.

"I saved you from torture, Rillao," Lelila said. She adopted the speech habits of the unnamed Firrerreo who used names to gain power. "I freed you from the web, I took you from the passenger freighter, I brought you to my ship, and I healed you. Rillao."

Rillao's expression changed. Apprehension replaced some of the arrogance.

"You own my name," she said. "Do you also own my body?"

"Perhaps I did, for a moment," Lelila said. "But I give it back to you."

"Magnanimous of you," Rillao said. She glanced around the cabin, with its understated elegance and its up-to-date medical equipment. "You are too rich, I suppose, to worry about the profit."

"Profit?" Lelila said.

Rillao stared at her, disbelieving. She pushed herself up on her elbows, shrugging away the medical equipment's sensors. Her striped hair snarled in sweaty tangles. The medical equipment, noting her recovery, pulled up to the ceiling to protect itself.

"The freighter was taken from its route," Rillao said. "It was hidden, far off trade routes. If you aren't a slaver, how did you find it? What are you doing here?"

Lelila's knees went weak. She locked them, or she would have fallen. She felt herself go cold and pale, and she was glad her hair nearly hid her face. She wished she had put on even more makeup. Behind her, Geyyahab roared in surprise and fury. Lelila reached back, grabbed his hand, and silenced him with a squeeze of warning.

Slavery had existed under the Empire. But the Republic ended the practice. The government she served had sought out the people bound by the ugly Imperial laws. They were free. The Empire no longer existed to sell political prisoners into slavery, to steal their children and sell them.

There *were* no slavers to steal Anakin and Jaina and Jacen!

"How long have you been here?" Lelila asked suddenly. "How long did you sleep?"

"I never slept," Rillao whispered. "I was not one of the freighter's original passengers."

"But did you know the Empire—"

"I was brought here five years ago," Rillao said.

"—is defeated? Oh. You must. But the Republic stopped the slave trade!"

"Some exist who are content to allow that belief. It suits their purposes, to steal people in secret."

Chewbacca—Geyyahab! Leia reminded herself, Geyyahab and Lelila!—wrapped his huge hand around her upper arm. She leaned gratefully against his strength. But he, too, trembled.

Rillao stretched her right hand toward Lelila. A deep, badly healed, patterned scar disfigured her palm. A slave mark. Lelila had seen scars like that before, on the hands of people requesting medical treatment to have them removed. Before they asked for anything else, they asked to have the scars removed.

Lelila wondered if the brindled chestnut hand on her arm had also borne a slave mark.

"That's all in the past," Lelila said. "My equipment can't take the scar away, but as soon as we get back to civilization—"

Rillao closed her hand, folding her long slender fingers flat against her palm. There was nothing of a fist about her motion, but a move of concealment, protection.

"No," she said. "I have reason to keep that scar a while longer."

She pushed herself to her knees on the bunk, lurching clumsily in her weakness.

"How did you find this place?" she demanded.

The most important commodity Lelila and Rillao had between them to trade was information. Lelila decided to spend some of her currency.

"I followed a ship here."

The bedclothes shredded in Rillao's clenched hands.

"Did you kill it?" she said, her voice suddenly empty. "Did you kill the ship?"

"Of course not!" Lelila exclaimed. "Lie down, Rillao. You're too weak to get up."

"Did you—"

"Lie down! And I'll tell you what happened."

Reluctantly, Rillao lay back on the bunk. She pulled the shredded blanket with her, fraying its torn edge with her fingers.

"I followed the ship here."

"Through hyperspace? That's impossible!"

"I have a method, Rillao." It pained Leia to see Rillao flinch every time her name was spoken, but Lelila the bounty hunter took some comfort in having the upper hand. "Don't question me too closely."

"You saw the ship?"

"I did not. It was too far ahead of me. It came, and went."

"But you can trail it!"

"No. My method was . . . disturbed." She could not say that Rillao's own pain had created the disturbance. The Firrerreo might guess Leia's abilities. "The trail is gone."

Rillao slumped back. The moaning growl returned, but stopped abruptly as Rillao struggled to control herself.

"Do you know where the ship went?" Lelila asked.

Rillao shook her head. "It could have gone anywhere. Some places are more likely than others: where slavers, and others, hide, and wait, and gather their resources, and plan for the Empire Reborn."

"The Empire Reborn?" Leia scowled. "More deluded supremacists!"

Neither Leia of the New Republic nor Lelila the bounty

hunter understood why anyone would maintain loyalty to the old Empire, after its defeat, after the revelations of its atrocities. But, then, neither of them understood why Rillao wanted to keep her slave mark, either.

"The adherents of the Empire Reborn are powerful and wealthy. They have sworn a blood oath of secrecy and devotion." Rillao named several worlds where followers held power.

All the names surprised Lelila.

"And Munto Codru as well?" she asked.

"Munto Codru is a backwater," Rillao said, shrugging a dismissal. "And far too independent. Munto Codru was never amenable to the Empire. No one I ever heard of cared to hide on Munto Codru."

Leia put aside her concern about the Empire Reborn. Time to deal with it, after the children were safe. She had no attention to spare for anything else.

"Why did you think I'd killed the ship?" Lelila asked.

"Its owners have many enemies."

"Including you, I'd think," Lelila said.

Lelila the bounty hunter had no children trapped aboard that ship. She had no reason to shudder when she thought: How many people might want to kill it? Eventually, someone will succeed.

"Why did it trouble you so, Rillao, that I might have killed it?"

Rillao stared in silence at the shredded bits of blanket in her hands.

"Answer me, Rillao," Lelila said.

"My son is on the slaver ship!" Her voice broke. She wailed, with an eerie keening of desperate grief that lifted the hair at the back of Lelila's neck.

Lelila glanced back and up at Geyyahab. He blinked at her with infinite sadness, brushed past her into the cabin, and sat on the deck beside Rillao's bunk. He placed his huge brindled hand over Rillao's scarred one.

Lelila wanted to go to her, too, to embrace her and reassure her. But that was too much her other identity. Lelila the bounty hunter remained aloof.

She waited till Rillao's wail faded. Rillao's grief remained too intense to shut out. Geyyahab patted Rillao, crooning a purr that Lelila had never heard from a Wookiee before.

"Rillao," Lelila said, when both the Firrerreo and the Wookiee had fallen silent.

Rillao raised her head and looked her straight in the eye.

"We'll find him," Lelila said. "Your son. When I catch up to that ship, we'll find him. But you know more about the slavers. You must help me figure out where to go to catch them."

Han was badly winded by the time he reached Waru's dome, even taking the shorter public route.

Too much generaling, Han thought, and not enough work.

The field outside Waru's temple was deserted. Han paused beneath the filigree of the entry arch. For all he knew, it said "No admission allowed after the service has begun."

After the *performance* has begun is more like it, Han thought.

He did not care if the sign said "No admission." He plunged through the arch and across the courtyard. Instead of experiencing the silence as serene, Han felt oppressed by the brooding quiet.

"I'll talk in here if I want to!" Han said out loud.

He slipped into the theater.

The auditorium was filled, as before, with supplicants. They filled the seats, the resting pillows, and the aisles. Han had no way to get down to the front, where Waru held court. Standing on tiptoe, Han tried to look over the heads and backs and carapaces of the assembly. Finally he spotted Xaverri, standing near Waru's base. As far as he could tell, she was all right, though he did not much like the way she stood with her head down, her shoulders slumped.

If she collapses again, Han thought . . . What will I do? What *can* I do?

He scanned the huge room, searching for another way to reach the stage. But the auditorium was dangerously crowded.

Waru had accepted another subject for healing: an Ithorian family.

"Do you wish me to try to heal you, seeker?" Waru said.

Waru's voice filled the auditorium. Inclined to find everything about Waru suspicious, Han noted the difference between Xaverri's private conversation with the being and the public voice that drew everyone's attention more firmly to the ceremony.

"Then I will try to help you," Waru said.

Han snorted, then wiped the contemptuous expression from his face as a huge leathery being turned slowly to loom over him, gazing down with irritated distraction.

"Just a little allergy," Han said.

The being waved its ears and returned its attention to Waru.

Han could not reach the foot of the stage. The crowd was impassable. Han tried to keep an eye on Xaverri, for all the good it would do; at the same time he watched Waru's performance and tried to figure out the illusion.

A subfamily of Ithorians approached the altar. The quintet of tall, crooknecked beings carried a blanket-wrapped companion to Waru. The tallest of the Ithorians opened the blanket, revealing a youth, painfully thin. Its intelligent eyes blazed at the ends of its hammer-shaped head, and it struggled to remain upright. The adult family members petted it and whispered to the youth, perhaps promising that they would soon return to their herd-city, and helped the child lie down on Waru's altar. Their stereo voices warbled strangely in the theater.

The youth was pathetically weak. The family gave it into Waru's care and stepped back.

As before, the gold scales liquefied, flowed, and covered Waru's patient. Ichor dripped around the cocoon and solidified. Light glowed through the translucent covering.

But after that, everything changed.

Waru shuddered violently, crying out. The cry rose and fell, simultaneously: it climbed to a piercing shriek and descended to a rumbling roar. The high pitch screamed in Han's hearing, then vanished above his range. He felt as if his brain were being pierced by sound waves. At the same time, the low roar became an unsettling vibration. The walls reverberated at a low pitch that shook Han's bones.

It sounded, to Han, like a great cat growling in satisfaction over its prey.

The supplicants cried out in a horrified, keening wail, and fell to the floor before Waru, covering their eyes. Only Han was left standing. Even Xaverri knelt at the base of the altar, her head down.

Waru shuddered.

But this ritual was different. Han strained to see, but he was certain Waru had changed the procedure. Instead of expanding, the chrysalis clenched, as if it were squeezing the Ithorian youth.

Waru sighed.

The chrysalis exploded. Like the embers from a forest fire out of control, whipped by a screaming wind, brilliant sparks whirled up from the altar. The whirlpool of fire spiraled through the hall. Sweat burst out on Han's forehead. The air became hot and oppressive.

Han watched in horror.

Waru's scales fluttered, and smoothed.

On the altar, the Ithorian youth lay in a collapsed pile of awkward limbs. The youth's family huddled in a heap, holding each other, crying, afraid to look up.

"I regret," Waru said. "I regret. I cannot always succeed. Perhaps you waited too long to ask my help, or perhaps your offspring's time had come."

The Ithorian family climbed uncertainly to their feet, holding each other, silent.

"We honor you, Waru." Speaking Basic, the shortest of the Ithorians blinked sadly. The Ithorian's voice fell to a ragged whisper. "We honor you."

"I have exhausted myself," Waru said. "I must rest." The golden scales contracted together, closing the ichor-producing veins.

Acquiescing to Waru's demand, the Ithorian family wrapped its offspring in the blanket, now a shroud, and picked its way from the altar through the crowd. The people made way for them, then followed them out of the theater.

Han pressed himself against the rear wall of the theater. Sweat sparkled and prickled in his vision. He closed his eyes, trying to blot out what he had seen. People brushed past him, and finally the hall was silent.

"Come with me, Solo," Xaverri said.

He opened his eyes. She stroked his arm, gently, soothing him; he stared at her. Horror possessed him. He could not speak. He could barely breathe. Xaverri wrapped her fingers around his, and led him silently from the theater.

Behind them Waru hulked, and slept.

Xaverri and Han walked in silence through the courtyard. Even after they passed beneath the arch, they did not speak.

Luke ran toward them across the field, his robes flying. Threepio hurried after him, falling behind with every step.

Luke stopped in front of Han and grabbed him by the shoulders.

"What happened? Are you all right?"

"Waru . . . I don't know. I'm all right, but . . ." Han drew a deep breath, trying to collect himself.

"I felt—I don't know, a disturbance—" Luke let Han go and rocked back on his heels and raked his fingers through his hair. "What's going on, Han? I feel like I'm standing on quicksand, and I can't find solid ground."

"Somebody died," Han said softly. "A kid. Come on, let's go back to the lodge."

Without a word, Luke and Threepio—Threepio, without a word!—turned and joined them.

Han trudged up the path, with leaden feet.

When they were out of sight of Waru's dome, Xaverri drew Han from the trail. She took his hands and looked into his eyes. He tried to shut her out. He did not want to think about what he had seen.

"Now," she said, "do you understand why I think Waru is true . . . and dangerous?"

"Yes," Han said, his voice as hoarse as if he had been screaming.

The Ithorian family had given the youth into Waru's care.

And Waru had killed it. Killed it, and pretended effort and weakness and exhaustion in its benefit.

But I *saw* Waru crush that child, Han thought, and I couldn't do a damn thing about it.

Han had heard Waru's growl of satisfaction as the Ithorian youth's life passed into Waru's power.

"Yes," Han said. "Now I understand."

Chapter

8

Rillao's strength returned quickly. She sat up in her bed, eating stew as the unnamed one had: picking out the chunks of meat with her fingers, then drinking the sauce when the meat was gone. Beside the wide port, Lelila and Geyyahab sat with her and planned a strategy. Outside the ship, the hijacked ships orbited each other in a complicated dance, against a brilliant backdrop of stars.

Rillao watched the ship of the Firrerreo through the porthole.

"Lelila," she said, "when you found me, did you find anything else, anything . . . strange?"

"Besides a web feeding on your body? Besides a shipload of abandoned people? Something strange like *what*?"

"Like a small machine. You could . . . hold it in your hand. Perhaps it was on the table, or fallen on the floor?"

"No," Lelila said. "What was it?"

"Nothing," Rillao said. "Nothing of any importance."

Beyond the group of passenger freighters, the ship of the Firrerreo began to accelerate. It moved slowly out of the dance of ships, speeding up so gradually that its motion was nearly imperceptible. The acceleration would accumulate, second by second and year by year, until the ship plunged toward its destination at a measurable fraction of the speed of light. Rillao watched the ship. Starlight shone along its dark flank, picking it out with streaks of silver.

"You and your son should be on that ship," Lelila said.

"Yes . . ." Rillao replied.

"Will you join them, when you recover him?"

"I cannot think that far ahead. I can only think of finding him."

Lelila rose.

"Where are you going?" Rillao asked.

"To the other ships. To wake people, to ask them if they know where we should go. And to free them."

"That would be a waste of time."

"Freeing them?" Lelila exclaimed.

"Yes! They know nothing of their abductors. If you wake them now, you'll have to help them be on their way. It will take days."

"Do you expect me to leave them here, derelict?" Thinking that she had sounded too sympathetic, Lelila added, "If I free them, they're likely to be . . . grateful."

"They haven't the resources to be grateful," Rillao said. "They're refugees. Exiles. They have nothing you could want —unless you want their seed corn." She snorted. "And you can always come back and get that."

"How can you be sure no one here knows where our quarry went?" Lelila asked.

"Sit down, and I will tell you."

Unwillingly, Lelila sat on the edge of the chair. Her nerves tingled as if they extended beyond her skin. They made her restless and sensitive. If she tried to use the sensitivity, she slipped off into the despair that had gripped her previous identity. As soon as she had reached this wilderness of drifting, dying ships, her sensitivity had not only failed but punished her.

Lelila the bounty hunter craved action, any action, that would keep her from remembering.

Rillao closed her eyes, took a deep long breath, and began to speak.

"An evil man—I will tell you his name—seized the ships drifting here in this desert. He thought he had the right, because he was responsible for their existence. He was responsible for building them, for arresting and convicting the people imprisoned within them. Any world that defied the Emperor, he condemned.

"This evil man—I will tell you his name—even condemned his own homeworld. His own planet, Firrerre! And all his own people.

"He condemned people, and sent them into the wilderness to colonize new planets.

"In a thousand years he would seek them out, and plunder whatever they had built.

"For, you see, this evil man—I will tell you his name—believed the Empire would last a thousand years. He believed *he* would live a thousand years. He believed that when he returned to the people he had wronged, their descendants would remember him as a god. An evil and all-powerful god whom they must obey.

"For, you see, he was Procurator of Justice for the Empire."

Rillao's calm, storyteller's voice broke with contempt on the word *justice*. Lelila nodded, and Geyyahab, sitting on the floor beside the bed, rocked back and forth in grim understanding. The Procurator of Justice had been a shadowy, mysterious figure, never named or pictured during the Emperor's reign.

His actions had been anything but mysterious. Both Lelila and Geyyahab remembered the Empire's justice.

"But his plans went awry. The Empire fell! His power vanished. He fled. But he fled with his resources intact: wealth, and sycophants, and above all his own small planet, a worldcraft, which can travel between the stars.

"He chased down the passenger freighters he had dispatched into the void. He towed them into hyperspace.

"He would not wait a thousand years. He would plunder them now!

"He could have freed his former prisoners. He could have returned them to their homeworlds, to their families. He

could have submitted himself to the compassion of the New
Republic, which is said to be merciful—"

Lelila glanced at Rillao sharply from behind her curtain
of hair, seeking recognition but not finding it.

"—and perhaps he would have been forgiven.

"But this evil man—I *will* tell you his name!—did not ask
for the Republic's mercy. He towed the captured freighters
into hyperspace, and he brought them here. He left their passengers sleeping and unaware. He visits. He passes through
the ships like the vengeful god he wished to be. He chooses
children, and takes them away to sell them into slavery.

"Sometimes he wakes the parents and tells them he is
stealing their children. For the adults are rebels and he would
like to break them. Then he could sell them, too.

"He lives in luxury, planning the rebirth of the Empire.
Planning to rule over the Empire Reborn!

"His name . . . is Hethrir." She spoke the name with a
growl.

Rillao smiled with grim satisfaction when she revealed
the Procurator's name. She folded her hands, finished with
her story.

"Is that . . . is that what happened to you? He made
you watch while he stole your son?"

"It is more complicated than that," Rillao said. "My relationship with Hethrir is . . . unique."

"How could your people leave, knowing their children
had been stolen?" Lelila cried.

Rillao hesitated for some moments before replying.

"Their children were not stolen. My son is the only youth
of our people left alive. Hethrir did not force my people to
watch their children be sold into slavery. He took them away
from Firrerre, and he left their children behind. Then he destroyed our world. He made them watch while their children,
and all the rest of our people, died."

Rillao folded her hands in her lap and lay back on the
bunk, drained even of her anger.

Lelila could not speak. She was horrified by the evidence
of secret evil, an evil she believed had been vanquished. A
few remnants of the Empire remained, of course, causing mis-

ery when they struck, but at least they had the spirit to reveal themselves.

This evil had to be uncovered. Hethrir had to be hunted down and captured. This "Empire Reborn" had to be destroyed.

She pulled her knees to her chest and wrapped her arms around her legs and buried her face.

"And now, I think," Rillao said, "Hethrir has run out of freighter children to sell. Has he begun to steal them from the Republic's worlds? Are you trying to rescue one?"

Lelila hesitated, then decided to tell as much of the truth as she dared.

"At first the parents thought it was a kidnapping. For ransom."

"But no ransom demand arrived, so they hired you."

"Yes."

"And you are . . ." Rillao paused, choosing her words carefully to avoid offense. "You are new to this profession."

"This particular profession, yes."

"I will help you," Rillao said. "And you will help me."

"Yes," Lelila said.

"Take us to Chalcedon," Rillao said.

Rillao slept.

Tigris carried Anakin down the long tunnel to the worldcraft's landing field, following Lord Hethrir and eleven handpicked Proctors. The newest Proctor strutted at the end of the line. Tigris hurried to catch up, to even out the line by walking two by two.

"Nursemaid!" The new Proctor sneered at him. "How dare you walk beside me? Walk behind me, where you belong!"

Humiliated, Tigris fell back.

I hope you die, he thought furiously at the new Proctor. It's about time for a new Proctor to fail the purification ritual! I hope it's you!

Whenever a purification ritual failed, the Proctors were all sworn to secrecy about the death of their comrade. No one ever bothered to extract an oath from Tigris, so he could tell the new Proctor the risk, if he chose. He held the power close to him, cherishing it, but once again decided not to use it. He would be loyal to Lord Hethrir, even without an oath.

Tigris's arms ached from the weight of the child Anakin. The pain humiliated him. He had thought he was strong. He spent hours each day training with a practice sword. He trained during every bit of spare time he could snatch. Sometimes he snuck out of the dormitory in the middle of the night to practice, even though he had to fight to stay awake the next day, to be alert for Lord Hethrir's commands. He only wished the worldcraft's sleeping period always corresponded to the worldcraft's night. He liked to practice in the darkness, where no one could see him, where no one could taunt him about using only a homemade practice sword instead of a real lightsaber. The worldcraft's days and nights were so short that sometimes everyone slept during full daylight, and sometimes he was seen.

Anakin held tightly to Tigris's neck. The hot light of the worldcraft's tiny sun fell into the tunnel mouth. Silhouetted ahead of him, the Proctors followed Lord Hethrir onto the landing field.

The child can walk, Tigris thought. He *should* walk onto the Lord's starship. He should approach his destiny on his own two feet.

Tigris put Anakin down.

"No!" Anakin shouted. "No, no, no!"

He grabbed Tigris by the leg and clutched him desperately.

"Stop it, now," Tigris said. "You aren't acting at all dignified."

"Not walk!" Anakin screamed. "No!" He opened his mouth and screamed, a high-pitched cry that pierced Tigris's hearing.

"Be quiet!" Tigris said.

Anakin only cried louder. Tigris crouched down beside Anakin, gently disengaging the child's clenched fingers from his ragged brown robe.

"Little one," Tigris said more gently, "everything will be all right."

Anakin stopped screaming long enough to take a breath.

Tigris hugged the child.

"It will be all right," he said again.

Anakin flung his arms around Tigris's neck and sobbed quietly against his shoulder, hugging him fast.

Tigris tried to remember the last time another person had touched him. Lord Hethrir never touched him, even for discipline. The Lord's voice was sufficient to impose his will. Tigris recalled with desperate envy the times when the Lord placed an approving hand on the head of one of his Proctors, or pinned a medal or promotion on one's shoulder and shook his hand.

My mother was the last person to touch me, Tigris thought. I was ten, and she hugged me and smoothed my hair and told me she loved me. But all the time she was stealing my ability to touch the Force. And even Lord Hethrir has not been able to give it back to me.

The last person to touch me, Tigris thought with fury, was a traitor.

Anakin's sobs slowed and changed to sniffles. Tigris suddenly realized that Lord Hethrir's Proctors had crossed the field and disappeared into the starship. Lord Hethrir himself stood in the hatchway, waiting for Tigris and Anakin, watching with disapproval as Tigris spoiled the child with weakness.

Tigris jumped to his feet. Anakin clung to him, but his little hands slipped. He would have fallen if Tigris had not grabbed his wrist.

"No more crying!" Tigris said roughly. He pulled Anakin along a few steps. The boy hung back, struggling, his face puckering again. In the shadows of the starship's hatchway, Lord Hethrir scowled.

Tigris scooped Anakin up, ignoring the ache in his own arms, and carried him across the field and up the gangway. The hatch folded closed behind them.

In the presence of Lord Hethrir, Anakin quieted. He watched the Lord thoughtfully, intensely. Tigris felt proud of the little boy. Anakin recognized Hethrir's power, and acceded to it.

In silence, Lord Hethrir turned and led the way into his auxiliary starship. In the passenger compartment, the Proctors had already strapped themselves in. They pretended to pay him no attention, but one whispered, under his breath, "Nursie!"

Tigris flushed, but Lord Hethrir took no notice so Tigris pretended he had not heard the insult.

Hethrir gestured toward one of the couches. Tigris obediently disentangled himself from Anakin's arms, placed the child in the couch, and strapped the harness around him. Anakin started to fuss. Tigris took Anakin's hand, enfolding the small fingers. A stray thought flicked through his mind: the size of his own hand. His hands felt clumsy and disproportionately large for his body. He had been growing recently, but his arms and legs had not caught up to his hands and feet. His bones ached like an old man's, especially after he had trained for hours. He felt clumsy. He was hungry all the time.

He sat in the couch beside Anakin and reached with his free hand for the harness.

"Leave him and come with me," Lord Hethrir said sharply, and strode from the compartment.

Elated, shocked, Tigris leaped to his feet. The Proctors glared at him, offended and jealous. Anakin clutched his hand. Tigris pulled free and hurried after Lord Hethrir.

Anakin began to wail.

Tigris hesitated, glancing back at the crying child, then toward Hethrir.

The Lord waited impatiently at the control chamber. "Leave him!" he commanded. "Close the door. He must learn."

Tigris obeyed. He knew Anakin should learn to control himself, but the child was so little, and a few words of comfort served to quiet him much better than leaving him to scream himself to exhaustion.

Panicked, the child cried. Tigris wanted to return to the passenger compartment. But Lord Hethrir had never before allowed him to ride in the pilot's chamber of the starship. Surely one of the Proctors would quiet the boy.

If one did not, the child would have to comfort himself. Perhaps, if Lord Hethrir wished it, that was the right way to teach him strength and self-reliance.

Tigris followed his lord, wondering what this honor

meant. Perhaps Lord Hethrir had finally decided to allow him to be a helper.

Lord Hethrir gestured to the copilot's seat. Tigris took his place, his heart swelling with pride. It did not matter that he could not fly a starship. Perhaps Lord Hethrir planned to teach him.

"Never hesitate," Lord Hethrir said softly, "when I give you an instruction."

Tigris flinched. He clamped his hands around the armrests of the seat, so he would not tremble.

"Do you understand?"

"Yes, Lord Hethrir. But Anakin was so very upset—"

"Never hesitate when I give you an instruction."

Tigris fell silent.

"Do you understand?"

"Yes, my lord," Tigris whispered.

Lord Hethrir turned his attention to launching the starship, ignoring Tigris. Tigris could hear, faintly from the end of the hallway, the sobbing of Anakin.

The starship rumbled beneath them, then lifted off through the worldcraft's thin blue band of atmosphere. The bright blackness of space and stars surrounded them.

Lord Hethrir's silence stretched on like the starship's course through space. Tigris thought of speaking, then thought better of it. He watched Lord Hethrir fly the starship, he let his gaze rest longingly on the smaller lightsaber Hethrir carried, and he tried not to listen to Anakin's crying.

Finally even Anakin fell silent. The only sound was the engines' faint vibration, almost too low to be a sound.

Hyperspace leaped toward them and streaked around them. Tigris gasped. Hyperspace thrilled him. He wished, someday, to try to explore it, to put on a pressure suit and go out in it, though many said that was impossible. Some said it would drive one mad; some said it would drive one to death.

Back at his room at the lodge, Han sank into the couch. The glass doors to the terrace hung slightly ajar. Heavy, hot air flowed over him. Han was exhausted and distressed. He pushed the doors wide open and breathed the humid night scents of Crseih Station. He wished for the cool and fresh night air of home.

Threepio hovered worriedly nearby, fussing about having no food to prepare, nothing to serve, and no money to buy dinner with.

"There is not even a sip of wine or a cup of tea, Master Han," Threepio said.

"Never mind, Threepio," Han said. "It doesn't matter."

"Tea is always good after a shock." Threepio bustled away, hoping for better luck finding provisions in Luke's room.

After Threepio left, Luke shook his head. His silence had lasted all the way back from Waru's compound. Han's experience distressed him.

"You should never have gone to Waru alone!" Xaverri said. "You should have waited, as I asked you to. You should have returned with me, as I asked you to." She laughed bitterly. "But of course you never, ever did as I asked."

"Excuse the hell out of me!" Han said. "*You* were there all alone, I was worried about you!"

"I have been with Waru all alone—truly alone, not with a thousand supplicants looking on—almost every day for a hundred days. Waru trusts me. If you keep behaving this way, Waru will stop trusting."

"The Ithorian family trusted Waru, and look what it got them."

Sorrow swept over him, and terror. In his mind, the memory of the Ithorian family transmuted itself to his own family. Though he knew it would never happen, he could not wipe away the image of him and Leia, Jaina and Jacen, begging Waru for help and placing Anakin on that altar. Though the oppressive heat made him sweat, he shuddered.

He had risked his own life a thousand times. He had never felt vulnerable, as he felt vulnerable now.

The kids are on Munto Codru, Han reminded himself. Jaina is dismantling some chrono; and Jacen is making friends with some critter that we'll find out later is maybe just a little bit venomous; and Anakin is watching everything, taking in everything, looking for mischief to get into. Leia is watching over them, and Chewbacca is keeping watch over them all. They're fine, they're *safe*.

But he could not stop shivering.

"Did you *know* what was going to happen?" he asked Xaverri, in sudden fury. "Did you *know* Waru was going to murder that kid?"

"I knew—"

Han jumped up in shock, but Xaverri raised one hand, palm out, and stopped him.

"I knew another person would die. I cannot know when. I cannot know who. I did not know the Ithorian youth would die. It is impossible to know which subjects will die when they submit their lives to Waru. One can only attend, and watch, and wait." She sighed. "I would not have had you see that, without warning. I could have warned you, if you had waited—as I asked."

"Waru's a healer," Luke said reasonably. "No healer can succeed all the time. It's tragic, but people *do* die. Even young people."

"You didn't see what happened!" Han said. "Waru didn't fail. Waru planned what happened. Waru—" His voice broke. "Waru enjoyed it."

"Do you believe, now, that Waru is no fraud?" Xaverri asked.

"I don't know if Waru is a fraud or not," Han said. No one who ever wanted to commit murder for profit, or power, or excitement ever needed to invoke the supernatural. "And I don't care." He could barely keep his teeth from chattering.

How can I feel so cold, when it's so hot in here? he thought.

But Han knew the cold at his core would never disperse until he could stop what was happening.

"I do know Waru is evil," he said.

"You can't know that," Luke said. "Not this soon."

"Sure I can. I do. I *know*."

"How?"

"How should I know? I don't know! How do you know what you know when you know it?" Han paused, frustrated. "All I know is what I know!"

"I think you're jumping to conclusions," Luke said.

"I jumped to nothing," Xaverri said, offended. "I observed. I gained Waru's trust. I came to certain conclusions, and I requested your help."

"Where did that thing come from?" Han asked. "What *is* it?"

"When Crseih Station belonged to the Empire," Xaverri said, "the Procurator of Justice used it as his headquarters. He used it as a prison for enemies of the Emperor. He used it as a torture chamber for his own enemies. And he used it to perform savage rites. . . .

"It is said," Xaverri said, "when people breathe their secrets in the darkness, that Waru appeared in response to the Procurator's rites. It is said his sacrifices called Waru from empty space, and strengthened Waru with the lives of people.

"It is said," Xaverri said, her voice falling to a whisper, "that they forged a pact, an alliance, that when Waru is satisfied, Waru will reward the Procurator with absolute power."

A chill crept up Han's spine.

Xaverri folded her hands in her lap; she closed her eyes.

"The Procurator of Justice is *dead*," Han said.

Xaverri opened her soft brown eyes and gazed at him.

"He's one of the survivors? The ones you've been tracking, and watching?"

She nodded. "I have been trying to catch up to him for a long time. I have discovered that he comes here. When he does, I will be waiting."

"But Waru's a *healer*," Luke said.

"I need not tell you," Xaverri said gently, "that a healer bears the knowledge to kill."

"Do you have proof?"

"Han has seen the proof."

"Luke, I'm sorry this isn't working out the way you wanted," Han said. "But we have to stop this thing."

Luke simply gazed at him, as stubbornly defiant as he had ever been as a youth.

"If Waru's a manifestation of anything," Han said, "it's the dark side."

"No," Luke said. "Not the dark side."

"How do *you* know *that*?"

"I don't know." Luke smiled bitterly, ironically. "All I know is what I know."

"That's not much of an answer," Han said.

"I know what the dark side feels like. I know what it's like, to be in the dark side's presence. This isn't it."

Threepio returned from Luke's room. "Master Luke, we having nothing to eat."

"We'll go out, Threepio. Don't worry."

"We cannot go out, sir. We have no money."

"Then we'll worry about it tomorrow."

"Perhaps I should return to the *Falcon*, and retrieve some provisions."

"Go on, then!" Han said, unable to listen to Threepio for another second.

Threepio left, disappearing into the dark hallway.

"You shouldn't have sent him away," Luke said.

Han did not reply. He shivered deep and hard. The more he fought it, the worse it got. Xaverri rose from the couch beside him and went to Luke.

"Leave us for a bit, Master Luke," she said.

Luke hesitated. He glanced from Xaverri to Han, and back again.

"He will be all right," Xaverri said. "Only, please, leave us for a bit."

Luke's robe swirled around him as he left Han's room and returned to his own. The door closed.

Xaverri sat beside Han. She took his hand between hers. Her familiar warmth was the only relief in the world from the cold of Han's shivering.

"Solo," she said, "I understand. We will stop Waru, you and I together. He is powerful, but we will think of a way. Now you must sleep, you must rest."

She enfolded him in her arms. Unlike the heat of the station, the warmth Xaverri gave him reached his center.

His thoughts slipped back to the old days. The terrible shivering slowed, and slipped away, and ceased. Han fell asleep.

*   *   *

Lord Hethrir's starship tunneled out of hyperspace. Normal space opened, bright with stars. Tigris bathed in beauty.

The starship's shields formed, blocking out the intense radiation of the region.

A maelstrom of light blazed before them, barely dimmed by the shield: the cosmic whirlpool of a black hole's accretion disk burned before them.

"I will be glad," Lord Hethrir said, speaking for the first time since lifting off, "when I can travel in comfort. When I no longer need to hide my worldcraft from those lowborn thieves of the New Republic. I dislike leaving my home behind."

"My lord," Tigris said, "if I can be of service—if I can attend you—"

"No," Lord Hethrir said.

"I beg your forgiveness, my lord."

"It will be some hours before we reach Crseih Station," Lord Hethrir said. "I must—meditate. I must prepare for the child's purification."

He rose. Tigris fumbled for his harness, for he should not remain seated while Lord Hethrir stood.

Lord Hethrir gazed at him.

Is it my imagination? Tigris wondered. Or is his expression kindly? Of course, he is thinking about the offering. Not about me.

"You must sleep," Hethrir said. "You may sleep across my door."

Tigris was amazed. To sleep at his lord's door was an honor. A small honor, to be sure—not the same as being promoted to Proctor, or being permitted to serve him at table. But it was an honor nonetheless, the first one Lord Hethrir had ever shown him.

"Thank you, my lord." He bowed his head.

Lelila prepared *Alderaan* for flight. She fastened safety straps around Rillao, then she and Geyyahab and Artoo-Detoo secured themselves in the cockpit. Lelila engaged the drive.

Alderaan came to alert around her. It displayed her surroundings, picking out each of the disabled ships, charting a safe course past them. Lelila felt guilty about leaving them, but Rillao was right. A few days this way or that would make no difference to the sleeping passengers. A few days' delay for *Alderaan* might lose the children—all the children—forever.

She sent an unsigned message, an SOS from the stolen ships, to General Han Solo. Lelila the bounty hunter could not afford to think of asking the famous freedom fighter to come to her aid; she could not afford to think of the touch of his hand, the warmth of his body in the night, his grief and rage when he learned all that had happened.

Alderaan displayed its course to Chalcedon; Lelila accepted it. The ship powered forward. Lelila shouted out a cry of resolution. Beside her, Geyyahab roared in harmony. *Alderaan* exploded forward into hyperspace, plunging through the radial aurora.

Lelila and Geyyahab fell silent. They both felt better.

Han struggled against the terrible paralysis of sleep. Anakin was in danger. A great space-snake writhed toward the child, who watched with interest and a complete lack of fear. The snake metamorphosed into Boba Fett the bounty hunter, intent on kidnapping Han's children so Han would be in his power as well. A reflection glinted off Boba Fett's helmet, gold as sunlight. A scarlet vein of blood streaked through the reflection. The bounty hunter whispered a curse. The gold and red expanded, brightened, and transmuted themselves into the shape of Waru, the alien that even Threepio could not place. Waru whispered a promise to Anakin, and Han's child clambered to his feet and ran toward the being.

Han knew if he could run after Anakin, or shout, or move a single muscle, he could catch him, save him, but the paralysis gripped him. He knew he was asleep, one twitch the wrong side of wakefulness; if he had the power to do *anything* he could stop the terrible dream—

"Solo! Solo, wake up!"

The shaking released him. The nightmare dissolved just before Anakin reached Waru's altar. Han sat up with a great gasp of fear and relief.

Xaverri stopped shaking him, stopped holding him.

"A nightmare," Xaverri said. "A nightmare, not real."

Light and shadows fell through the open glass doors: strange light, stranger shadows.

"It could have been real, though," Han said.

"I know," Xaverri said softly.

He did not ask if she too had nightmares about Waru. He was still wrestling his own dreams. Besides, he thought he already knew the answer.

He was in bed—lying on his bed, to be more accurate, with his boots and jacket off and a light coverlet thrown over him. Xaverri sat on the bed beside him, on top of the coverlet.

"How'd I get here?" he said.

"I put you here, of course," Xaverri said. "Time has passed—neither of us is of an age to rest well, sitting up."

He remembered one night when their only choice had been to sleep sitting up, up to their necks in muddy swamp. They had slept in turns, holding each other, so they would not both slip beneath the surface and drown.

Xaverri smiled. "I did not offend your modesty," she said.

"Do you have a family?" Han asked suddenly.

Her expression hardened. "You *know* that I had a family before you met me! You know that the Empire—"

"I mean now," he said gently. "The Empire is a long time ago. Are you alone? Haven't you found someone?"

"I will always be alone," she said. "I will never again—" She stopped, and shook her head. "I will always be alone. If I had not made that vow, Solo, I would never have left *you.*"

"You're cheating yourself," Han said.

"In your opinion," Xaverri said. "But imagine. If your nightmare had been real—"

Han stiffened. He rejected the possibility violently, as if to accept it would be to bring it to pass.

"It was just a dream!"

"If your nightmare had been real, would you not protect yourself from experiencing it again? No matter how many years ago it had been?"

"It was just a dream!" Han said again. The knowledge of his complete vulnerability swept over him, even stronger than the night before. He imagined what it would be like never to hold Leia in his arms again, never to hug his children again, never hear them giggle, feel them cover his face with wet childish kisses.

They're safe, he told himself again. Safe on Munto Codru.

"Your experience was a dream, Solo." Xaverri rose. "Mine was real."

She left him alone. The door closed itself softly behind her.

Han threw the coverlet onto the floor and got up. In his stocking feet, he rapped on the door of Luke's room and entered without waiting for a reply.

All the windows and curtains were open. The white dwarf, the crystal star, shone at its zenith as it crossed the orbit of Crseih Station. The black hole, the burning whirlpool, began to rise. Invisible itself, it spun in the center of its violent accretion disk, which exploded with released energy. Light flooded the room from two directions. Gradually, the light of the accretion disk overwhelmed the light of the white dwarf, splashing intense illumination and stark shadows across the floor.

Luke sat crosslegged on the balcony, his back to Han. He did not speak.

Threepio straightened. The droid had set the table with ration packs from the *Millennium Falcon*. Washcloths from the bathroom served as napkins.

A tumbler of grotesque and contorted flowers formed the centerpiece. Generations ago, while Crseih Station was still being properly maintained, the flowers might have started out as some recognizable species. Over the years, as the radiation shields became less and less reliable, they had mutated and changed into thick-petaled monstrosities that resembled slices of raw red liver infected with chartreuse tumors.

"Master Han!" Threepio said. "Are you hungry? I've prepared a light brunch . . . if we can rouse Master Luke."

"I *was* hungry," Han said. "Till I took a look at those flowers. Space the decoration, will you?"

"But sir, they are quite intriguing—"

"They're the ugliest damned things I've seen since Öetrago." He sat down. "And they *smell!*"

"They are *flowers*, sir," Threepio said in a pained voice.

"They are *supposed* to smell. It was only my intent to bring some cheer into the room, and if I may say so, I had to bear our host's wrath to obtain them."

Oh, fine, Han thought, but did not say aloud, another charge added to our bill.

Han went to the terrace door. "Luke! Breakfast."

Han sat at the table and opened his unappetizing ration pack. When's the last time I replaced this stuff? he thought. He glanced at the date on the package and winced.

"Threepio, why didn't you bring some of the real food from the *Falcon*?"

"Because, Master Han, it was no longer fresh."

"Neither is this."

"Of course not, sir. It is preserved."

"This is ridiculous. I'll order us a decent meal."

"That is impossible, sir. Our host, the lodge-keeper, insists that we pay as we go."

Han sighed and resigned himself to a terrible, if sustaining, breakfast.

"Hey, Luke!"

Outside on the terrace, Luke rose slowly to his feet.

I can go out to the *Falcon* myself, Han thought, and get whatever's left over in the galley. It might not be right out of the garden, but it'll be better than this.

Luke's shadows fell across the table, shivering, darkening.

"Sit down—" Han saw Luke's face. "What's the matter?"

"Leave you alone for a bit? A *bit*?"

"Huh? What are you talking about?" Han asked, baffled by Luke's tone. "Oh—you mean what Xaverri asked you? Did you want to talk some more? Sorry, I fell asleep."

"And she didn't leave till this morning," Luke said with a dangerous edge in his voice.

"No, she—wait a minute. What are you suggesting?"

"Suggesting doesn't have anything to do with it."

"Now look, kid—"

"Don't call me 'kid'!"

Luke's hand slipped beneath his robe, where he carried his lightsaber.

"What the hell's the matter with you?" Han asked,

poised halfway between laughing and losing his temper. "What are you going to do? Chop me into little pieces because I spent a few hours alone with an old friend?"

He had not intended to sound defensive, but that was the way it came out. It offended him that Luke felt the need to chastise him for his behavior. It insulted him that Luke felt the need to remind Han of his vows to Leia.

"I don't know what I'm going to do," Luke said.

"Apologize. That would be a good start."

Luke glared, without replying.

"If you don't trust me," Han said angrily, "if you don't think Leia should trust me, why'd you come with me—or is that *why* you came with me?"

The ration pack crushed between Han's fingers, littering the carpet with protein crumbs.

"I'm going out," Luke said. "To try to cool down." He headed for the door. "And I hope I don't run into your 'old friend' while I'm at it."

Threepio watched them, standing stock-still.

"Leave Xaverri out of this!" Han said. "This doesn't have anything to do with her—"

Luke laughed bitterly.

"—it has to do with your opinion of me. Which obviously isn't nearly as high as I thought it was."

"I can't talk to you right now," Luke said. The door opened for him. "I *won't* talk to you right now." He plunged through the doorway, jerking the door closed behind him. But it refused to slam; it shut silently.

Han flung the crumpled ration pack on the floor among the protein crumbs.

"Blockheaded, arrogant, Jedi—Jedi *kid!*"

"Master Han!" Threepio said. "What in the world—?"

"It's too complicated to explain," Han said, as he left Luke's room.

"Did Master Luke not like his breakfast?" Threepio asked plaintively.

Chapter

9

Alderaan streaked through hyperspace. Lelila the bounty hunter sat in the cockpit, letting the fireworks display of hyperspace light lull her toward hypnotic sleep.

It did not help. Hyperspace remained empty of any perceptible trail. Lelila sighed.

Geyyahab her copilot joined her, and let himself collapse in the navigator's seat. The bandage on his leg displayed no warning sign of infection. Though the wound obviously pained him, he as obviously preferred to pretend he was all right. Lelila made no comment about it.

"You're a very handsome color," she said, admiring his black and silver striped fur, with the hint of chestnut beneath.

He touched the streaked brown hair hanging down before her face; he made a questioning sound, and looped a green strand around his finger.

"No," she said, "it's boring, is what mine is. But the color will do for the moment."

Her starship fell out of hyperspace and powered toward Chalcedon. Lelila transmitted a reservation to the landing field at their destination. The artificial-intelligence scheduler accepted her message.

Leia gazed at the planet and several expanded displays. It was rocky, all right. Several great volcanic peaks rose from the flanks of the world, deforming the sphere. It was hard to imagine how the planet maintained a steady rotation.

The world had an atmosphere that was barely, marginally breathable, thanks to the continuing volcanic activity. It had some weather, mostly dry violent storms, and erosion. It had some water. But it had no indigenous life. Here and there, scattered across the surface of the world, as far from the tremendous volcanic peaks as they could be, a few blue and green blots blemished the surface: two struggling colonies, and a way station.

"Why would anyone want to live here?" Lelila said.

Geyyahab did not try to answer her rhetorical question. He strapped himself in and impatiently motioned to Lelila to do the same. She complied, while she checked with Artoo-Detoo that Rillao, too, was safely secured in the medical couch.

Her ship landed, a graceful fish settling to the scoured bottom of a river. The landing field was solid stone, blackened by spaceship exhaust. No dust scattered from the jets' exhaust. A few other ships stood on the field.

Lelila jumped up when she heard Rillao. She hurried to join her. The Firrerreo had wrapped the sheet around her. She walked slowly, carefully. She had gathered her long striped hair and braided the ends together into a loose clump at the back of her neck. Her wounds had healed, leaving silver scars on her tawny skin.

"Do you have clothing?" she said to Lelila.

Lelila blushed, embarrassed not to have offered her any. "Your unnamed friend—"

"No friend of mine," Rillao snarled.

"—didn't wear any, I thought your people don't—"

"Nobody wears clothes in suspended animation," Rillao said. "Even if the Imperial overseers who put you to sleep leave you with any to wear."

Lelila took Rillao into her cabin and dug through the closet. Most of the clothing was out of the question; some would simply look ridiculous. Rillao was considerably taller than Lelila. Finally she found a splendid long green silk robe, meant as a lounging outfit. The fabric was heavy enough to be worn outdoors.

"Would this do?"

"It will suffice," Rillao said. She shoved her long arms into the sleeves and unrolled the deep cuffs to their longest length, tied the sash twice around her waist, and kilted up the skirts of the robe between her legs to form makeshift pantaloons. She tucked the ends of the robe in the sash. "Better," she said. "Let's go."

Geyyahab waited for them at the hatch.

"Please stay and guard the ship," Lelila said to him.

He growled in refusal.

"Someone's got to stay," Lelila said. "No, not me, I'm the only one who hasn't been knocked around." She felt the need to keep the Wookiee hidden as much as possible.

Why do you want to hide Geyyahab? Lelila the bounty hunter asked herself. So what if anyone sees him? He's just another brindled Wookiee . . .

She shook her head, fighting off a wave of confusion.

"Please," she said to him again.

He sighed loudly and scuffed down the corridor to the cockpit.

As Lelila and Rillao climbed down from the ship, the ground quaked and rolled beneath them. Lelila gasped and grabbed the edge of the hatch for support.

"Earthquake," Rillao said. "They're common here."

With the ground still shivering, she set off. Lelila hurried after her.

Soon they both slowed, for the air was thin and it had a bite. The volcanic trace gases hurt when Lelila drew them too deeply into her lungs. Rillao slowed to match Lelila's pace.

"That droid is following us," Rillao said.

Leia glanced back. A hundred paces behind, the little droid rolled toward them, making up the distance, beeping.

"That's all right," Lelila said. "The galley stores are low. We can buy food and some more medical supplies. The droid can take them back to the ship."

The quiet of the landing field gave way to the spaceport

bazaar. The noise of sellers and a small flute band roiled and tweeted around Lelila.

"What an impressive bazaar," Lelila said dryly.

Rillao snorted. "We aren't here for the bazaar," she said. She strode on, but, like Lelila, she soon had to slow down. She coughed. "Foul air," she said.

Several sellers offered their wares—fruit pockmarked with the acrid volcanic chemicals, vases and goblets and ornaments blown from local volcanic glass.

"Looks like mud," Rillao said.

A troop of Twi'leks danced in the shadows of the bazaar wall. Swinging their prehensile head-tentacles, they cavorted around Lelila and Rillao. One plucked a small harp, while another whisked the air above Lelila's head with a fan of insect wings. The wings traced pastel patterns, shedding glittery scales that stuck to Lelila's skin and caught in her hair to shimmer before her eyes. Rillao, too, glowed in the sunlight with a dusting of iridescent wing-scales. The dancers spiraled in toward them, circling closer till Lelila grew tense and angry.

At the edge of the bazaar, the dance troop left them as suddenly as it had appeared: the spiral dance reversed and widened, and the troop disappeared between a canvas tent and a portable geodesic dome.

Lelila followed Rillao into the cobblestone streets of the town proper. The buildings hugged the ground, low dwellings of black stone blocks, worked so carefully they fit without mortar.

With every step, Lelila wanted to stop and demand that Rillao tell her where they were going, who they were looking for. But she suspected that asking for more explanations would cause her to lose face in Rillao's eyes. She walked in silence, driven by desperation that she forced to the back of her mind.

The cobblestones gave way to rough glass brick. In this part of town even the houses were built of glass, the muddy native volcanic glass. The surrounding walls rose twice Rillao's height, a forbidding barrier. Lelila wondered if the volcanic glass could be made transparent enough to look through. So far she had not seen a single window.

Rillao stopped in the spun-glass arch of a recessed door-way. The glass strands looked like streams of dirty water. A pattern of parallel glass rods decorated the door. Artoo-Detoo caught up to them and pushed into the recess beside them, crowding the space.

Why don't they welcome us? Lelila asked herself. Then she thought, Who do you think you are, some princess who's welcome anywhere she cares to go?

Rillao drew her fingertips across the glass rods. Each one hummed a different note. The crystalline music shimmered around them. A moment later the door swung open.

The glass wall surrounded a huge shallow pool filled with polished agate gravel. Water flowed over the bright agates, sparkling and trickling like music. Cobbled paths twisted across the pool-bed, and above, a strange webwork of thick glass fibers—glass so clear and colorless that it disappeared at certain angles—rose from the pools, lifting into delicate peaks.

The ground shivered gently. The glass webworks quivered and hummed.

Several beings draped their boneless bodies and prehensile trunks across the webworks, lounging in the glass framework. A number of other, similar beings moved leisurely in the pools, splashing the shallow water on their skins or burrowing down into the agates till only their eyes and trunk-ends showed.

One raised a radial trunk (it had five) and sprayed water high in the air. The sun glanced off the droplets and created a rainbow. One of the beings lounging on the web shook the spray off its skin and hooted in protest through two of its trunks.

Rillao led Lelila and Artoo-Detoo past the ponds and between the supporting struts of the webwork.

The person who lives here must be very rich, Lelila thought, to be so profligate with water on a world that's mostly bare volcanic plain. And the person must be very brave, to build so high, with glass, in an earthquake zone.

The noon sun beat down through the webwork, surrounding Lelila with ethereal shadows and flecks of spectral color.

"These people look nothing like the people in the bazaar," Lelila whispered to Rillao. Beyond that, they were a species of being with whom she was entirely unfamiliar.

"Of course not," Rillao growled in an undertone. "No one is native to this world. Those were the peasants and traders. These are the bureaucrats."

They followed a winding cobbled path, walking carefully on the slick places where water had splashed. No one spoke to them or took any more notice of them than they took of the ground tremors. Several of the beings pushed the agate gravel into new patterns, new contours.

Artoo-Detoo bumped along behind, hooting in disgust at the design each time he had to navigate an acute angle of the pathway.

Lelila and Rillao reached the center of the agate pool, directly beneath the highest point of the glass webwork.

In a small deep agate nest, one of the boneless beings shifted back and forth. Water sloshed peacefully to its rhythm. Only two of its prehensile trunks projected, one high and taking in air, the other low and exhaling, occasionally dipping beneath the surface to blow bubbles.

Rillao sat on her heels beside the agate nest, and waited.

Powerfully disinclined to sit and wait, Lelila remained standing, gazing around curiously at the unfamiliar courtyard. She bent down and reached for one of the polished agates.

Rillao grabbed her hand. The Firrerreo's scarred fingers clamped down with surprising force.

"Have you no manners?" she whispered. "Sit down and be quiet and keep control of your eyes—and your hands!"

"Let go!" Lelila jerked her hand away.

Rillao's nails scratched her skin.

"Ouch!" One of the scratches cut deep enough to bleed. Lelila brought her hand to her mouth. She wondered if Rillao's nails contained venom or allergen. She thought, I'm a bounty hunter, where would I learn manners, and why should I be punished for not knowing any?

"Your eyes, and your hands—and your voice!" Rillao said.

All right, Lelila thought, I'm a bounty hunter, I can sit quiet and wait if I have to.

She glared at Rillao, who gave no sign that she owed Lelila either explanation or apology. Lelila sat crosslegged and let her hair spread around her. The ends fanned out on the cobbles.

I can still see, she thought with satisfaction, but now no one can tell where my eyes are looking. No one can tell where my eyes *are*.

So she sat beside Rillao and watched the boneless beings lounge and spout and push agates into new swirls and patterns. Every so often she glanced at the being in the central pool. It breathed and blew bubbles and occasionally caressed an agate or two with its prehensile limbs.

Rillao balanced on her toes, her forearms relaxed on top of her knees. Her eyes were closed. Lelila thought, This is hardly the time or place for a nap!

She felt agitated. Anger and impatience trickled across her like the water in the agate pool. Beneath the surface, despair lurked.

Don't get so involved in your prey, she said to herself. You're a bounty hunter, if this one gets away you'll always have another case to go after. Above all, you must stay calm.

A spark of light ignited at the back of her mind. She came to full awareness, full attention, thinking, I'm here, who's calling for me—

The being burst upward, all its tentacles extended and twisting, and landed with a great gush of water. The fountain erupted from the agate pool and splashed Lelila from the top of her head to the ends of her hair.

With a shout of surprise, Lelila pushed herself back from the edge of the path. Her hair was so thick that it had protected her clothing from being drenched. The spark of light vanished, forgotten.

The wave soaked the path. Water flowed around her. She jumped up and sat on her heels like Rillao, out of the wet.

Artoo-Detoo squealed and rolled backward and rotated its carapace back and forth, shaking off the water like a dog. Lelila grabbed the droid as its back wheels touched the edge of the path. It rolled a handsbreadth forward, no closer, and settled stolidly on the cobbles.

"Enough, cease!" the being cried, speaking through one

of its prehensile trunks. The central bulge of its body projected above the water and the ends of its tentacles writhed. Fine tendrils covered the tips of several of the tentacles (it had at least ten; ten was when Lelila lost count of the snaky limbs). Its mass of crystalline eyes swiveled toward Lelila and Rillao, like so many tiny antennae.

Rillao, who had endured the soaking without a sound or motion of protest, slowly opened her eyes.

"I have business, Indexer," she said quietly.

"Business! Speak to my assistants. Why are you here, disturbing my concentration?"

"To solve a difficult problem," Rillao said. To Lelila's wonder, the Firrerreo offered a compliment. "Only the Indexer can make suitable connections."

Mollified, the Indexer subsided into the agate pool.

"A challenge, you say," the Indexer said.

"A very difficult one."

"State your question."

"We are in the trade," Rillao said, in a voice flat and cold. "And we have been engaged to fulfill the requests of our employers."

"Ah," the Indexer said. "Employers of your own planetary group?"

"Yes," Rillao said.

"Wishing the same?"

"Yes."

Lelila struggled to decipher the code of the conversation. She wondered what difference the background of employers made. She started to say she was her own employer. The scratch on her hand gave her a brief, stinging twinge. She remembered Rillao's caution to keep control of her voice.

"That *is* a challenge," the Indexer said. "For you, that is to say." The faceted eyes clumped together in the direction of Lelila. "In the case of her, who knows? We will worry about her later." The faceted eyes returned their focus to Rillao. "I thought your people were extinct."

"Not . . . quite," Rillao said.

"I thought the Firrerreo did not participate in the trade," it said.

"We are highly adaptable."

"I see, I see. That is good—a good way to keep from becoming extinct. Ah, I *do* see, you wish to widen the gene pool."

Rillao remained silent.

"Or perhaps withdraw your people from the trade. Cause trouble, publicity—"

"All that concerns you is the shape of my money."

The code became clear to Lelila the bounty hunter. Rillao was asking to buy a slave.

Your life has been too sheltered, she told herself. It's a good thing that you've become a bounty hunter.

She glanced sidelong at Rillao, through the curtain of her damp hair. She felt herself blushing with furious anger and humiliation, to be described as a slave buyer to a slave procurer.

What does it matter, Lelila said to herself, what the Indexer believes you do for a living? What do you care what the Indexer thinks? Remember your job. Your job is to find the escaped ship. And if deception is the means for it . . . think of your reward when you succeed.

"The search will be costly," the Indexer said. "You must realize that. A great deal of data to be sifted for a small bit of information."

Rillao dismissed the cost with a gesture. She turned toward Lelila, who suddenly realized that Rillao had no money. Rillao had nothing.

"Pay him whatever he wishes," Rillao said to Lelila.

"But I don't—" She stopped, thinking, Of course I carry money. Why ever did I think I don't carry money?

Confused, distressed, she jumped to her feet.

Balanced precariously on her toes on the wet cobblestones, she swayed and nearly fell. Rillao gripped her upper arm, steadying her, shocking her out of her momentary hallucination of being two people. One, Lelila the bounty hunter, straightforward and phlegmatic; the other, a stranger, stark-eyed and dangerous with the power of her rage.

Rillao had caught several strands of her hair, along with her arm. Inadvertently she pulled them.

"That hurts," Lelila said. "Let go, I'll pay him." The enraged stranger vanished.

Rillao reluctantly withdrew her hand, staring at Lelila with a curious, intent expression.

Avoiding Rillao's gaze, Lelila turned toward the Indexer. "How much shall I pay you?"

"It depends on the search." The being reached up with several tentacles and wrapped them around the glass super-structure. The rest of the being's limbs burrowed down into the agates.

Lelila crouched down again to wait.

An eerie musical note of high, crystalline character ema-nated from the glass superstructure. The boneless beings lounging upon the glass hunched themselves into motion and climbed with careless fluidity toward the Indexer. Their mo-tion changed the pitch and intensity of the notes, creating an ethereal melody. The closer they moved, the higher rose the pitch. Rillao narrowed her eyes and raised her shoulders, as if to block the tune from her perception. After the sound passed completely out of Lelila's hearing, Rillao moaned softly, dropped her head, and slipped her hands over her ears.

All the beings in the Indexer's courtyard congregated nearby. Each one twined tentacles with the others, till their organic network cast an irregular shadow over the Indexer.

The Indexer's crystalline eyes focused into the pond; the Indexer's free tentacles sifted through the agate gravel. The stones rattled and scraped together; the water made them sound hollow.

"What's he doing?" Lelila whispered.

"Shh!"

Her toes and her knees ached but she did not want to sit down in the puddle. Her wet hair chilled her. She stayed where she was, her legs trembling.

A moment later, the Indexer relaxed from sifting through the agate gravel. The other beings disentangled themselves, and slipped back on twisting tentacles to their places in the ponds and on the glass framework. Whether they went back to their original positions, Lelila could not tell. The melody dropped back into her hearing, then stopped abruptly in mid-trill when the Indexer's tentacles dropped from the strands.

The Indexer's tentacles arranged themselves into a rosette

around the boneless body. The crystal eyes projected above the water.

One of the tentacles crept above the water and flattened out before Lelila, who slipped her hand into the pocket where she kept the money.

"What is the price?" Rillao said, her voice tight.

The Indexer named a figure. Lelila tightened her hand around the bills. The price was a significant fraction of their resources.

This is no time to quibble, she said to herself. She put a handful of credits onto the Indexer's prehensile trunk, which snapped into a coil around it and splashed back underwater. The tentacle burrowed into the agate gravel; the credits disappeared. When the Indexer's tentacle appeared again, it carried nothing.

"I found no one of your species, Firrerreo," the Indexer said. "Not a single one ever sold publicly in the trade."

Lelila jumped up, outraged. She nearly stumbled, for her feet had fallen asleep.

"Nothing!" she said. "You charged us for nothing!"

"I charge for my time, and my experience," the Indexer said calmly. "I cannot produce results that do not exist!"

"You could have warned us!"

The Indexer shrank back.

Rillao put her arm around Lelila's shoulder.

"Never mind," she said.

"But we've been cheated—!"

"Don't make accusations you cannot support," the Indexer said dangerously.

"The Indexer cannot produce results that do not exist," Rillao said. She sounded calm, not so much resigned as relieved.

Lelila was astonished that Rillao did not erupt in a fury, that she did not pounce on the Indexer, rend the tentacles, and fling them all over the courtyard.

"Thank you, Indexer," Rillao said quietly.

"Firrerreo!" the Indexer said suddenly.

"Yes, Indexer?"

"I found no *public* record. I would have no record of a private transaction."

Rillao tensed. Her fingers dug into Lelila's shoulder.

"I will tell you something I have heard, if you will promise to confirm or disprove the rumor for me."

"State your question." Rillao's voice was a low, ominous whisper.

"It is being said," the Indexer told them, "that the Asylum Station imagines it can compete with Chalcedon."

Artoo-Detoo warbled in distress.

"Asylum?" Lelila said. She knew no place called Asylum Station.

"I would have thought," Rillao said softly, "that the Republic would have destroyed that evil den at its first convenience."

The glittery faceted eyes of the Indexer oriented toward Rillao.

"Perhaps the Republic finds it useful," the Indexer said, and subsided into the water. Its skin mottled and it disappeared against the luminous earth colors of the agate nest.

Artoo-Detoo, anxious to escape the dampness, spun a quarter turn and bumped away along the cobbles. As Lelila followed Rillao from the courtyard, the smooth round stones rattled and shifted in the bottom of the pool.

Outside, on the street, Lelila frowned.

"Why would the Republic want to destroy Asylum Station?" Lelila asked.

"It's a place where the Empire tested its methods of coercion and death . . . on sentient subjects."

"But that would have stopped!" Lelila cried. "It would have stopped when the Empire fell. Wouldn't it?"

"I don't know," Rillao said. "I've been out of touch."

Outside the lodge, Han strode down the path.

He was furious. Furious at Luke for being suspicious in the first place, and for refusing to have a sensible conversation about his suspicions in the second.

Han still had feelings for Xaverri; he could not deny them. He would not. But he did not believe he should be chastised for them.

Am I supposed to forget that I ever loved Xaverri? Han

thought. I chose Leia, and she chose me. Because we loved each other. None of that has changed. I love her. I love her *now*. What I felt for Xaverri was . . . a long time ago.

He wondered if he should find Xaverri and ask her to stay away from Luke for the next little while. Or find Xaverri, then go find Luke and both tell him about last night. But that felt too much as if Han had something to apologize for.

He swore softly under his breath. He had no idea where Xaverri lived. He did not know where to look for her, except at Waru's compound. For the moment, he could not face returning there. He could not face seeing again what he had seen yesterday. He could go back to the lodge and ask Threepio where he had found Xaverri when he sought her out.

But he did not want to do that either.

That's quite a list, he thought, of things you can't do or don't want to do. Forget them all. Xaverri can take care of herself—as she's told you in no uncertain terms. And Luke may be angry, but he isn't stupid. If he was going to lose his temper completely, he'd've lost it back at the lodge, with me.

Choose a problem you *can* do something about, he said to himself, turning his steps toward the welcome dome, the taverns, the gambling dens. And while you're at it, start thinking —*hard*—about what to do about Waru.

Jaina opened the door cautiously and peeked outside. Her light glowed from behind her, casting her shadow all the way across the dark stone floor. She quickly let the light go out, afraid someone was watching.

She listened carefully. She heard a soft buzzing sound.

Is that a watcher droid? she wondered. She stepped back into her cell. She left the door open only the smallest crack. A watcher droid could see in the dark. It would sound the alarm. Then one of the Proctors would come and shut Jaina back in her cell. Maybe forever!

The buzzing sound did not move. And it really did not sound like a droid. Scared but determined, Jaina rubbed a few air molecules together to make a faint glow. She sent them out into the middle of the gathering hall.

A Proctor stood in the entrance of the corridor. He was supposed to be standing. But instead he was leaning. And he was asleep. The noise was his snore.

Jaina slipped out of her cell. Her door closed behind her. She let the light fade to almost nothing. She walked a few steps forward and stopped. She was scared. The Proctor might wake up, any second. If she turned around and went back into her safe cell she would no longer be afraid. She could light the air up, and it would warm her.

But if she did that, she would never find Jacen and she would never see Mama and Papa again and she would never know what had happened to Anakin.

Across the room, a faint line of light glowed in the darkness. Jaina crept toward it, her hands out in front of her in case she bumped into anything. The line of light shone out beneath one of the other cell doors.

"Jacen?" she whispered.

"Get me out of here!" he whispered.

"Shh!" It would be so much easier if they could *talk* at each other, in their minds. But if they did, Hethrir would know. Jaina was afraid even to try.

Jaina looked over at the Proctor. His head nodded forward. He snorted and nearly woke up. Jaina froze.

The Proctor muttered something. He slid down the wall and rested his forehead on his knees.

He started to snore again.

Jaina made some air molecules bump against each other. They made a soft humming, thrumming noise. Maybe now the Proctor would not hear her.

"Hurry!" Jacen whispered.

Jaina grinned.

The cell doors were latched, not locked. They could not be opened from the inside. They did not need to be locked on the outside. Hethrir never thought that one of the children might get loose and open all the doors.

Jaina grabbed the handle and pulled the door open.

The door *squeaked*.

"What? Who's there?" The Proctor stumbled to his feet.

Jaina jumped behind the door.

The Proctor ran over to the open cell.

"What's going on here? How did you open this door?"

"I don't know," Jacen said. "It just *opened!*"

Jaina could not see the Proctor but she heard him poking at the latch.

She pushed the door toward him as hard as she could.

The heavy wood banged against his head. He shouted and stumbled into Jacen's cell. Jacen ran past him and Jaina slammed the door so the Proctor was locked inside.

The Proctor started shouting, and pounding on the door, but Jaina did not pay him a single bit of attention.

Jacen grabbed Jaina in a big hug. Jaina hugged him back.

"Jasa, Jasa, I'm so glad to see you—"

"Jaya, I thought they'd take you away—"

"—but what about Anakin? And—"

"—this is the most awful place—

"—this school is so—"

"—*boring!* I think they're all liars—"

"—yeah, *liars,* because they said Mama and Papa—"

"They aren't dead!" Jacen said. "They aren't!"

"I know," Jaina said. "They just want us to think so."

They stood in a faint pool of light as Jacen's heated air molecules spun around at their feet.

The Proctor banged on the door again. "Let me out!"

"No!" Jaina said. She was glad she had not bashed in his head. Kind of glad.

Jacen grinned at her. His front tooth was loose too, but he had not lost it yet.

"Look!" Jaina said. "I'm getting a new tooth!" She stuck her tongue out of the space to show Jacen where her new front tooth was coming in.

"Me, too. Pretty soon, I mean."

"Let's go!" Jaina grabbed his hand and pulled him toward the darker darkness of the corridor.

"Wait! What are we going to do? What about the others?"

"We're going to climb out past the dragon and run away and maybe we can get far enough away to *think* at Mama and Uncle Luke." She had not thought about the other children.

"Maybe they want to come with us. Or run away themselves."

Jaina was impatient but she guessed Jacen was right. She

ran to the door beside his and pulled it open. She heated up some of the air so she could see.

"We're running away. You can run away or you can stay here!"

Behind her, Jacen ran to the door on the other side of his cell and opened it.

"We're running away! Do you want to run away too?"

Most of the other children jumped up from their floor-beds and ran out into the gathering room. But a few backed away into the corners of their cells. Jaina did not try to make them come with her. She did not have time. She left their doors open in case they wanted to change their minds.

Then she opened the last door.

"We're running away! Do you—"

Vram stared at her. Jaina stopped.

Hethrir locks Vram up at night, too! Jaina thought. He made him a helper, but he doesn't really trust him.

Vram had a bed and a blanket and a light. But he was *still* locked up at night.

"Don't!" Vram said. He was very scared. "Don't hit me, I'll tell Hethrir on you!"

Jaina was scared. All the other children were gathering behind her, excited, whispering, their happiness and hope collecting around them. She had not thought that any might run and tattle. She was not afraid one of them might. But Vram would, in his new rust-red tunic.

"Do you—do you want to come with us?"

"You'll hit me! You'll kill me!"

"I will not!"

He took a deep breath. "Help!"

Angrily, Jaina slammed the door shut on him.

Jacen grabbed her hand. Together, they ran into the corridor with their beacons of glowing air swirling ahead of them and behind them.

The other children followed.

The tiny sun was just setting when they reached the stairwell to the outside. Jaina ran up the stairs and raised her head above the edge. No one was watching. The playground was deserted.

"What about the dragon?" one of the other children whispered.

"I don't know," Jaina said. "Jacen, we can't use the multitool, the sun's going down!"

Jacen flicked a tiny swirl of heated air into existence, and concentrated it. It was much brighter than the light from Jaina's multitool lens. It bounced across the playfield. Jaina and Jacen ran after it.

"Dragon!" Jacen cried. "Hey, you dragon!"

The dragon jumped up out of the sand and roared. But she did not throw herself against the fence. She looked around and snorted and leaped into the air to try to catch the flametoy Jacen made for her. Then she hunkered down beside the fence and pressed her shoulder against the mesh.

Jacen rubbed her pebbly scales. The dragon rumbled.

I wish I could do that! Jaina thought. Pat a dragon, and make friends with it, like Jacen.

But she knew Jacen was a little envious of her for being able to take machines apart and put them back together again and make them better.

Jacen stood nose-to-nose with the dragon. The dragon snorted. Jacen snorted back. He stuck his hand through the fence and rubbed the dragon's heavy brow ridges. The dragon flicked out its tongue.

Jaina gasped.

"I think she's just tasting me," Jacen whispered. "If she's like the lizards back home."

"Tasting you! So she can eat you, maybe!"

"So she knows it's me. Let's go!"

"Are you *sure*?" Jaina asked.

Then the alarms started ringing and they did not have any choice.

Jacen scrambled up the fence and over the top. Jaina followed. The wire mesh scraped her hands. She scooted over and jumped down on the other side.

The other children swarmed up over the fence and jumped to the ground, but they stayed as far from the dragon as they could get.

The dragon slurped her tongue across Jacen's shoes.

"She just wants to be sure she'll recognize me," Jacen insisted. He slid onto Mistress Dragon's back. "Is this okay, Mistress Dragon? Can I ride you?"

She snuffled and raised her head, but she did not buck or roll over or try to rub Jacen off against the fence. Jacen dangled the light-toy in front of her.

"Come on, hurry!" Jacen held out his hand to Jaina. She grabbed it and jumped on the dragon's back. The dragon lurched to her feet, standing up with her back legs first and then her front legs. Jaina shrieked with surprise and grabbed Jacen around the waist. She would feel a lot more comfortable if the dragon was a landspeeder and she was driving it.

The other children ran to the dragon. Jaina grabbed their hands and pulled them up onto the dragon's back. Soon the dragon was covered with children. Most rode her back, but a few hung on to her legs, giggling.

"Is this still all right, Mistress Dragon?" Jacen asked. "Can we all ride you?" He glanced around at Jaina. "I don't think she minds."

"Hurry, let's go if we're going!" Jaina could hear shouts from back in the canyon.

She kept expecting Hethrir's power to loom over her. As soon as he knew they were escaping, he would fling her to the ground. He would throw his heavy cold blanket over her, like he had when she tried to protect Lusa. . . .

Jacen dangled his fire-toy in front of Mistress Dragon.

Jaina shivered.

"Be careful, Jasa," she whispered. "Be careful."

Swinging along through the sand, the dragon followed the point of light away from the fence and out through the canyon mouth. The fire-toy made the shadows move all around them.

Jaina wished Lusa was with them. She wondered how her centauroid friend could ride on a dragon. But then she thought that maybe Lusa wouldn't have to ride, since she had four feet to run on. She had wanted so much to run.

Jaina worried about Lusa, and about Mr. Chamberlain's wyrwulf.

Somehow, Jaina thought, *somehow* I'll find them and somehow I'll rescue them! I don't care what Hethrir does!

The dragon climbed a steep dune, lurching up the slippery sand. Jacen grabbed the dragon's neck and Jaina grabbed Jacen's waist and the child behind Jaina grabbed her waist. They all slid back a little. The dragon whipped her tail back and forth and up, holding the children on her back.

"I think she likes us," Jaina said, trying not to sound scared.

Jacen grinned. Then he looked serious. "Where are we going?"

"Away," Jaina said.

The dragon reached the top of the dune. She stopped and raised her head, nostrils flaring as she drank the wind.

Jacen leaned forward and whispered to the dragon. Mistress Dragon leaped from the ridge of the sand dune and slid down the slope. Everybody yelled with excitement. This was better than any amusement ride!

Mistress Dragon reached the bottom of the sand dune. She strode across the ground toward the stream and the forest. She could move very fast, when she wanted to.

Jacen fumbled in the front of his shirt.

"What are you doing?" Jaina thought he was scratching. "Did something bite you?"

"Bite *me*?" Jacen exclaimed.

"Someday something will."

"Nothing ever bites me!" Jacen said. He pulled his hand out of his shirt and showed her. In the starlight, a little creature wriggled gently in his grasp and looked around with bright eyes.

"What is it? Was it in your cell?"

"No . . ." He opened his hand a little. The creature stretched its two pairs of wings and grabbed Jacen's finger with its one pair of feet.

"It's from Munto Codru!" Jaina said. "It's a bat! You weren't supposed to play with the bats!"

"I wasn't *playing*," Jacen said. "I was *looking*. It's really *interesting*."

The bat yawned. Its sharp teeth glittered in the starlight.

"It's poisonous!" Jaina said.

"I was just *looking* at it," Jacen said again. "I didn't mean to bring it along, I mean how was I supposed to know some- body was going to come along and steal us?"

"What are you going to do with it now?"

The bat crouched in Jacen's hand, stretching its wings in four directions. Jacen touched the bat's wingtip with the tip of his finger.

"Let it fly," he said. "It's been all cooped up. It's bored."

Jacen raised his hand. The four-winged bat raised its head, sang a few notes, spread its wings, and vanished into the dark.

Mistress Dragon walked and walked across the sand. Jaina kept expecting a skiff to fly overhead. She expected Hethrir and his Proctors to land in it and make them go back.

But that did not happen.

Mistress Dragon kept walking. The little sun fell toward the horizon. They had been traveling all day. "All day" was only half as long as a regular day, but Jaina got thirsty, and then hungry, and then sore from riding.

In the distance, a stream glimmered in the starlight. The stream wound through trees and led to a forest. It would be easier to hide down there than out in the bare sand.

Mistress Dragon raised her head and sniffed the air. She put her head down again and walked even faster toward the stream.

Mistress Dragon's feet squished into mud at the edge of the stream. She stopped and snortled. She put her head down and Jacen slipped right off. Jaina grabbed Mistress Dragon's scales and held herself on. All the other children jumped off the dragon's back.

Mistress Dragon wanted to drink from the stream. Then she splashed in it. She waded out into the stream and lay on the gravel, like a new island. She lowered her head beneath the water and blew bubbles through her nose. She shook her- self.

Jaina fell off into the water. She struggled and splashed onto shore. She knew she should keep running, but she was awfully thirsty and tired and hungry. She drank from the stream.

The sky was turning from black to purple and then to pink and yellow and blue as the sun raced up. The trees cast cool shadows. All the bushes at the edge of the stream were heavy with berries. Just looking at them made her mouth water. But she was afraid to eat them.

I don't trust anything on this world, she thought. Except Jacen, and maybe Mistress Dragon. Hethrir said he was our friend, but he wasn't, he wasn't! And he said he was trying to teach us things we need to know. But he was lying then, too.

And even Tigris, who sometimes was not completely mean, had said Mistress Dragon would eat them.

Mistress Dragon settled deeper in the water, dunking the children hanging on to her sides. She stood up, making a huge splash. Jaina laughed. But she was still hungry.

Jacen ran up the bank. The four-winged bat landed in Jacen's wet hair. The bat chittered and sang. Jacen went straight for one of the bushes and grabbed a handful of berries.

"Jacen! They might be poison!"

He stuffed them into his mouth and ate them.

"Don't be dumb, Jaya," Jacen said.

"I'm not, *Jasa*!" Jaina said, emphasizing his nickname.

"Somebody built this place. Right?"

"Yeah. That's obvious."

"So somebody put stuff on it that's good to eat."

He handed her some berries. Jaina ate them. They were delicious.

Later all the children sat on the bank of the stream, full of sweet berries, and getting warm and dry in the sun. One of the little ones—Anakin's age—cuddled up against Jaina.

"Can we go home now?"

"Pretty soon," she said. "Pretty soon, I hope."

"I want my mumma," the little one said, sniffling.

"Me, too," Jaina said. She hugged the little one. Her lower lip trembled and she had to stop talking so she would not start crying in front of the others. She did not want to scare them. She was scared herself because she did not know what to do now. She looked over at Jacen and she knew he did not know what to do now either.

Jaina scooted over to sit right next to Jacen.

"We have to find a place those Proctors can't go," she said.

He nodded.

"What can we do that they can't?" Jacen said.

"Lots of stuff," Jaina said. She almost *reached* to lift a rock—

"Don't, don't, Jaina!" Jacen cried.

Even before Jacen said anything, she had pulled back. She was afraid Hethrir's power would loom up around her. And she was afraid he would *find* her, if she used her abilities to move anything bigger than air molecules.

"Lots of stuff, usually," she said sadly.

"We're little," Jacen said. "And they're big. It isn't fair."

"Yeah," Jaina said. "We're little. And they're big."

She pointed across the stream, where thick bushes grew down the far bank.

"I bet they couldn't go in those bushes. I bet *we* could."

Jacen grinned. "It would be like caves."

"And then we could sneak out when it's dark again, and try to find their spaceships."

"Or their message capsules."

"Or kidnap one of *them* and make them take us home!"

Jaina looked at Jacen skeptically. He was mostly joking. But they both wished it was possible.

"We better go."

"Hey, everybody!" Jaina said.

The other children stopped playing in the shallows of the stream or climbing on Mistress Dragon or eating berries from the bushes.

"We have to run away," Jaina said.

"Or those Proctors will come and put us back in jail."

One of the little ones came up to Jaina and hugged her around the waist.

"I'm tired, Jaya," the little one said. She sounded so much like Anakin that Jaina wanted to burst into tears. Jaina missed her little brother and she was worried about him even though he could be a pain sometimes.

"I know," Jaina said. "I am too. Let's go hide in the bushes and then we can take a nap. Okay?"

The little one kicked her toe in the dirt. "Yeah, I guess," she said reluctantly.

Jaina held her hand and Jacen held the hand of one of the

other little ones. They clustered together and waded into the stream toward the other streambank.

Mistress Dragon snorted and splashed, switching her long pebble-scaled tail in the ripples.

She stuck her head underwater and came back up with a big mouthful of water-weed. She munched it contentedly.

"You're very beautiful, Mistress Dragon," Jacen said, scratching her eyebrows. "But you're too big to come with us. Maybe you should go back to the desert and hide, so those Proctors don't hurt you."

Mistress Dragon settled down in the water till only her back and her eyes and her nostrils stuck out above the surface. She blinked. Her eyelids flicked water droplets onto Jaina's face.

"I think she thinks she's hidden," Jaina said.

Jacen hesitated, worried.

"We have to go," Jaina said. "We have to hide. She'll be okay, Jacen. Maybe they'll even think she ate us up and they'll give her a reward, they'll be so glad."

Jacen grinned.

The children all splashed through the stream and climbed the far bank and crawled on the wet mossy ground and slipped under the dense bushes.

Jacen found a sort of trail. He said an animal probably made it. Jaina hoped she did not run into the animal. She imagined that it probably had big claws and teeth.

But Mistress Dragon has big claws and teeth, Jaina thought, and she turned out all right.

Jacen untangled the four-winged bat from his hair and held it gently in his hands, looking into its sharp little face. The bat wriggled and Jacen let it go. It flapped away, flitting through the gold-green shadows beneath the bushes.

"It's going to look for a place for us to go," Jacen said. He had persuaded it, the way he persuaded Mistress Dragon, and the myrmins.

They crawled down the trail. Jacen took the lead and Jaina went last.

I bet there's all sorts of worms and stuff on this trail, Jaina thought. Yuk. I wish I was back home in the chemistry lab.

A few minutes later, Jaina heard voices and the hum of

landspeeders. She was scared that Hethrir and the Proctors were so close behind her.

We almost waited too long! she thought.

One of the little ones, crawling along in front of her, stopped and looked back.

"Jaina!" the little one whispered. "Did you hear—?"

"Shh! Hurry! Be real quiet and keep crawling!"

They crawled as fast as they could. Jaina could not see Jacen and she could barely feel him up ahead. She hoped the bat would find the way through the bushes. But what then?

Behind her, Mistress Dragon roared and splashed and thumped. The Proctors started yelling.

I hope Mistress Dragon stomps them! Jaina thought.

She caught her breath. She was afraid she would hear the hum of a lightsaber. She was afraid Hethrir would kill Mistress Dragon with as little thought as the Proctors had crushed the myrmins in their pants.

Mistress Dragon's huge splashes sounded farther and farther away.

Jaina grinned. Mistress Dragon is scared, too, she thought. She's running away. She'll be safe. But I bet she scared those Proctors first.

Jaina hoped Mistress Dragon found another succulent patch of water-weed.

"Look!" one of the Proctors yelled. "Footprints, on the far bank. Let's go!"

"Hurry!" Jaina whispered again, expecting every second to be dragged backward by Hethrir's power.

In front of her, the other children crawled as fast as they could.

The ground got muddier and muddier. The knees of Jaina's pants were soaked and filthy and so were her hands. The leaves of the bushes got droopier. But they fluttered away from her face, which was good because of their spines. She hoped the little ones in front of her were being careful about the prickles. Nobody had started to cry yet so maybe it would be okay.

Behind her, one of the Proctors yelled in protest.

"Ow! What are these, thorn bushes? I'm not crawling through thorn bushes!"

"You will," yelled the Head Proctor. "Or you'll be sorry!"

Jaina crawled faster. The voices sounded muffled. She was glad because she did not want to listen to them.

The trail suddenly opened out into a space beneath the bushes. All the children crouched at the edge of the wide muddy space. Jaina could see across it but she could not see either end of it. It was like the stream, only filled with mud.

Jaina crawled forward and joined Jacen.

"Where are we?"

"I dunno," he said. "A wallow, maybe. For the critters who made the trail. The bat led us here."

On the other side of the wallow, a huge tree rose up through the bushes. Its shadow darkened the gold-green of the shade beneath the bushes. Its roots twisted together, spreading out across the far side of the swamp.

"Look!" Jacen pointed. The little bat flitted across the swamp and into a dark place among the roots.

"It's like a tunnel," Jaina said.

"I bet it is. I bet it leads into the tree just like on Chewie's world!"

The bat flitted out again, hovered, and vanished into the darkness.

"How are we going to get over there?"

"I dunno," Jacen said. "I guess the bat forgot we can't fly."

"We better hurry," one of the other children said. "Listen!"

The Proctors sounded nearer. They also sounded mad.

Jacen took a big step forward into the mud.

He immediately sank in up to his knees. He tried to take another step but the mud sank under him. He sank to his hips.

Jaina slid down the bank and grabbed him. She almost *reached* for him—but shrank back scared that Hethrir would find them. She pulled at Jacen's hand, but he kept sinking. He looked scared.

Jaina sobbed with anger and fright.

But then the other children clustered around her, reaching for Jacen, grabbing his hands.

The mud sucked at him but the children, all together,

were too strong for it. They pulled him free and onto the bank.

Jaina hugged him. He panted, trying not to cry, trying not to make any noise that would alert the Proctors.

"You all saved me!" he whispered.

But they still had to get across the swamp.

A little at a time, Jaina thought. Then Hethrir can't stop me, he can't find me. A couple of molecules . . .

Instead of speeding up molecules the way she speeded up the air to make light and heat, the way she spun the sand into tiny wind-devils, she slowed the water molecules in the swamp.

She slowed them and slowed them and nearly stopped them.

A fine film of ice formed near the bank. The muddy water froze, crackling around water-grass, cooling the warm air around them. Beautiful frost patterns painted the surface of the ice.

Jacen saw what she was doing and helped her. Together, they froze a narrow path across the surface of the swamp.

Jaina crawled out onto it, very carefully. It creaked and groaned under her hands and knees, but she kept freezing little bits of water and the surface held. She hurried to the other side of the swamp.

She grabbed one of the thick, twisty tree roots and pulled herself off the ice. Her hands and knees were very cold and she was tired from slowing down so many millions and trillions and googolplexes of molecules. But she made it across! She motioned for the other children to follow.

One by one they came to her and clung beside her on the tree roots. The four-winged bat fluttered out of the hollow root and flitted back and forth.

Jacen came last. The ice was very weak now. It cracked and protested with every step he took. Jaina was so scared she could hardly keep the water molecules slowed down, even with Jacen's help. He was an arm's length from her when the ice cracked. Jacen fell face-forward in the freezing muddy water.

Jaina grabbed his hand and pulled before he could sink very far. He kind of swam and kind of crawled toward her.

There was no solid ground on this side of the swamp, just the mud and the tree roots. Jacen's whole front was covered with bits of ice and frozen grass. He flung his arms around Jaina. He was shivering. The little bat landed on his hair and trilled to him. Jaina held Jacen tight, trying to get him warm.

"The hollow r-root l-leads inside," he said. His teeth chattered. "All the w-way to the top."

"You follow the bat!" Jaina said. "It'll lead you. You lead us. I'll come last."

Jacen crawled into the hollow root. Jaina clung to the twisted roots on the bank as the other children followed Jacen into the tree. She helped the little ones. Some of them were scared and did not want to crawl into the dark. Jaina thought of making some glowing air to lead them, but she was afraid it might set the tree on fire. Besides, she did not think she could heat up air and keep water frozen at the same time.

Finally the last of the children crawled into the tree and disappeared.

The Head Proctor pushed his way through the prickly bushes. Jaina dove into the hollow, then squirmed around to see what the Proctors would do.

The Proctor's face was scratched and his pale blue jumpsuit was dirty and torn. He looked very mad. The other Proctors fought their way out of the bushes behind him. They had tried to walk, instead of crawling through the animal trail. They were all scratched and bleeding. Jaina looked at her hands. She was muddy, but that was all.

The Head Proctor saw the path of ice across the swamp. He frowned, and tested the surface with one foot, and stepped out onto the solid patch. He motioned to the other Proctors. They hung back until he yelled at them and ordered them to follow him.

Jaina waited till he was in the middle of the swamp and the other Proctors were strung out behind him on the ice.

Jaina dropped the water molecules. She felt them leap apart in the hot humidity of the swamp. The ice disappeared. Jaina fled into the hollow root, and she did not look back to see what was happening.

But she could hear the shouts, and the splashes.

She crawled faster. The inside of the hollow root was very

smooth, as if a thousand generations of wood insects had polished the surface.

She reached the end of the root. Above her, the other children climbed through the trunk of the tree. Their sounds echoed. The tree trunk twisted, around and around, and the twists formed a steep spiral ramp that led up into the darkness. Jaina thought she could see a tiny bit of daylight. She scrambled upward, following Jacen and the other children.

Chapter

10

Lelila heard something. It was a cry from a far distance, a call to someone else.

"What did you say?"

Geyyahab made a questioning sound. He had not spoken.

"I said nothing," Rillao said. "What did you hear?"

Lelila felt her mind tremble. She slapped the emergency controls of her ship, and crashed out of hyperspace.

Chewbacca howled in shock, and Rillao snarled something in a language Lelila had never heard.

"What are you doing? We must hurry to Asylum Station!"

"Look," Lelila said.

Before them lay a tiny star and a tiny blue and green and brown planetoid.

Artoo-Detoo trilled, Geyyahab made a gruff bark, and Rillao lunged forward in surprise. They all stared at the display. Lelila expanded it, marveling.

"It's artificial," she exclaimed. "It's too small to be natural. The star, the planet—"

"It's a worldcraft," Rillao said.

Chewbacca growled.

"No," Rillao said. "They are not mythical. I wish they were. I hoped never to see one. The Emperor caused a few to be created. He gave them as rewards, to the cruelest and most loyal of his officers. Tokens, he called them. His 'tokens' were a greater gift than a natural world." She trembled with tension. "It appears . . . he presented one to Hethrir."

Lelila put on a burst of speed. Her ship arrowed toward the tiny artificial planet.

Geyyahab hunkered over the controls, preparing for evasion. The worldcraft had survived so long by concealment, by being nothing but a tiny spark of light, always moving, always avoiding the spaceways. Yet it might have defenses. It might attack.

But the worldcraft made no challenge. As far as Lelila could tell, it was deserted. It spun beneath her. She sought a starship. She found a landing field, but it was empty. Its center glowed in the infrared with the heat of a recent departure.

Have they all fled? she wondered. But if they fled, what brought me here?

The starship slipped into the atmosphere, slowed, and changed to its soaring mode. It crossed a desert that gave way to a meadow, a stream.

Alderaan stopped, hovering low over the flowing silver water. A great lizard rose up from the ripples, snorting, flailing its tail.

"There!" Rillao exclaimed.

Beyond the stream, past a wind-rippled sea of low green bushes, a huge tree twisted upward at the edge of a marsh.

In the marsh, a group of people struggled in the mud. They looked like they had walked to the middle before they sank. Lelila could not imagine how they could have gotten themselves in such a predicament. She arrowed toward them, for they looked like they needed help. They were holding to each other, the ones nearest the shore desperately scrambling to reach solid ground, the ones in the center trying to clamber on top of their fellows.

Rillao's strong sharp fingers clamped around her shoulder.

"Leave them," she said. "They aren't the ones we seek. If we help them, they'll try to stop us."

"But they're drowning!"

"They might drown each other," Rillao said without sympathy. "If they helped each other, if they did not panic, they would survive. If we help them—they will kill us."

Geyyahab cried out with delight. He pointed to the branches of the huge twisted tree.

There, on a branch as wide as a garden path, a group of children stood high above the ground. They waved joyfully at *Alderaan*.

The ship lowered itself gently beside them. Lelila jumped up and ran back to the hatch. Rillao followed. They opened the hatch to fresh air, a gentle breeze, the scent of growing things, and the excited cries of welcome of the children.

Lelila's sight was blurred. She pushed her hair out of her eyes, but that did not help her see.

I'm crying, she thought. Why am I crying? I should be happy, I've found my quarry.

She blinked away the tears.

"Mama! Mama!"

Lelila the bounty hunter vanished as if she had never been.

Jaina leaped into Leia's arms, jumping across a sheer drop to the marsh. Chewbacca quickly moved *Alderaan* closer to the tree branch. Jacen took Rillao's hand and stepped gravely onto the ship.

Leia knelt and hugged Jaina and Jacen, then held them against her with one arm. She could not bear to let them go, even as she reached out to the children still standing in the tree. With Rillao's help, all the children climbed from the tree and into *Alderaan*.

"Mama, Mama! They took Anakin and they took Mr. Chamberlain's wyrwulf and they took Lusa, we have to find them before they cut off Lusa's horns!"

"We *knew* you weren't dead, Mama," Jacen said. "Is—is Papa all right? Is Uncle Luke—? Is Chewie flying *Alderaan*?"

Leia nodded. "Yes. Yes, they're all fine. Chewie's here."

"I knew it!" Jaina said. "I knew Hethrir told a lie. He told *lots* of lies."

"He's a mean man," Jacen said. "I don't want him to be my hold-father!"

"He is not your hold-father, children," Rillao said. "Is that everyone? No one left in the tree?"

"Wait!" Jacen said. He leaned toward the open hatch and whistled and chittered. Leia held him, afraid he might vanish, leap back into the tree, slip out of her arms ever again—

A tiny four-winged bat flitted into *Alderaan* and landed in Jacen's hair.

"That's everybody!" Jacen said. The hallway and both cabins were packed with children, all of them muddy and scratched, but all of them unhurt and excited, crying or screaming or shouting.

"I wanna go home!" one of the little ones cried.

Rillao closed the hatch. "We shall find your home, little one, and return you to it."

Jacen patted Leia's undone hair. "Mama, your hair's so long!"

"And it's such a different color," Jaina said. "I like it the old way!"

Leia touched her hair. She had forgotten it was down. She had forgotten the color-crawlers had changed it. She pushed it back from her face and twisted it into a knot at the back of her neck. She could not speak. She buried her face against their shoulders.

They hugged her.

Her hair fell down again. She left it loose.

"Mama, I lost my front tooth! I'm getting a new one! I'm getting grown up!" Jaina said.

"Both *my* front teeth are loose!" Jacen said.

Leia gasped in a long breath and held it, to keep herself from crying.

"It's okay, Mama. We're okay. All we have to do is rescue Anakin—"

"—and Mr. Chamberlain's wyrwulf—"

"—and Lusa!"

Alderaan hovered above the swamp. Chewbacca roared a question down the hall.

"Chewie!" Jaina ducked out of Leia's grasp, grabbed her hand, and pulled. Leia rose and let Jaina and Jacen lead her back to *Alderaan's* control chamber, slipping around and past the other children. Jaina and Jacen piled into Chewbacca's lap, hugging and kissing him. He enfolded them in his long arms and growled with joy and relief that they were safe.

"You're all *speckled!*" Jaina exclaimed. She laughed, petting his brindled fur.

"Be careful of Chewbacca's leg, children," Leia said. She was astonished that her voice was almost steady.

"Oh, wow!" Jacen said.

"What happened?" Jaina asked.

"He'll tell you later," Leia said. "For now we should save those people in the swamp."

"I think we should *leave* them there," Jaina said. "They aren't very nice."

"But it wouldn't be nice to leave them, either," Jacen said.

"We should make them tell us where Anakin is," Jaina said. "And Lusa, and Mr. Chamberlain's wyrwulf. And then we should drop them back in the mud!" She jumped out of Chewbacca's arms and ran to Leia again. "I'm so dirty, Mama! And hungry! We found some fruit. But the food Hethrir—he isn't really our *hold-father*, is he?—the food he gave us was *nasty!*"

Leia could not help but laugh. Jaina and Jacen filled part of the emptiness in her heart, though she still feared for her littlest one. She saw, with horror and fury, how gaunt the other children were. Hethrir had starved them, and would have starved *her* children, too.

"No more nasty food," she said. "I'll make something good for all of you. No, my sweeties, Hethrir isn't your hold-father. Our friend is right." She gestured toward Rillao, standing in the doorway. She introduced her children to the Firrerreo. "This is Jaina, and this is Jacen."

"What's *your* name?" Jaina asked.

"Jaina!" Jacen said, shocked.

"You may call me Firrerreo, little one," Rillao said. "When I know you better, perhaps I'll tell you my name."

"You look just like Tigris," Jaina said.

"Where did you see him?" Rillao asked, her voice so intense that Jaina took one apprehensive step back. "Is he here? Is he with Hethrir? Is Hethrir here?"

"Are you his mama?" Jaina asked.

"Yes, little one," Rillao said. "And I have not seen him in a long time. I miss him very much."

Leia grasped Rillao's hand. "We'll find him. Don't worry, we'll find him."

While they spoke, Chewbacca dropped *Alderaan* to just above the struggling, muddy mob, and loosed a cable for them to grab. He used Leia's ship as their anchor, and watched while they pulled themselves out of the mud. He could have pulled them out with the strength of the ship. But he did not.

Rillao hurried to the display and expanded it. She searched the group, then turned away, downcast.

"Tigris isn't one of those *Proctors*," Jaina said.

"Where is he? What is he doing?"

"He . . . I don't know," Jaina said. "Mostly he followed Hethrir around. And he took Anakin."

"Hethrir told him to," Jacen said.

Jaina glowered at Rillao. "He kept trying to act mean."

"But he wasn't, not *really*," Jacen said.

Alderaan swooped. Chewbacca herded the Proctors through the stand of bushes and across the stream.

"Make them go in the desert, Chewie!" Jaina said. "There's a place we can keep them where they can't be mean to anybody!"

The huge pink and black and tan lizard exploded from the center of the stream, flinging her head up, lashing her tail, roaring in challenge at Leia's starship. Water splashed in great sprays, like rain falling upward. Sunlight reflected through the droplets, cloaking the enormous lizard in rainbows. The creature lumbered across the stream, following *Alderaan*. It climbed the bank. Its claws left great gouges in the mud.

"Look, Mama, Mistress Dragon is coming, too." Jacen grinned. "I bet she got tired of taking a bath, and she wants to go back to her sand nest."

Mistress Dragon followed the Proctors into the desert. As she caught up to them, they tried to run. They all looked exhausted.

"Did my son tell you his name, children?" Rillao asked.

Jaina wrinkled her nose in deep thought. "No, that was Hethrir who told us."

"Hethrir . . ." Rillao said softly, dangerously.

The deck of the starship was cold and hard, even harder than Tigris's steel bunk on the worldcraft. At least back on the worldcraft he had a thin mattress and a blanket. Sometimes he slept without them, to toughen himself. Tonight, he wished he had them. A faint breath of warm air trickled from beneath Hethrir's door. A faint buzzing sound came with it. At first Tigris thought it might be a snore, but he banished the improper thought. Lord Hethrir had said he would meditate; he would naturally focus his attention with a chant.

Another noise came to him, from the passenger compartment of the starship. Anakin was crying again, with an exhausted sob. Tigris tried to ignore him, tried to disregard how hungry the child must be. He could not understand why the Proctors had not soothed him and fed him.

His own stomach growled. That was easy to ignore. He would not eat till Lord Hethrir bade him to.

But the Lord had not commanded him to remain here all night. He had merely given Tigris permission to sleep here, if he wished. Surely it would cause no harm to attend to the child. It was important for Anakin to be strong and alert when he was purified.

Tigris rose silently and crept down the dim corridor to the passenger compartment.

Except for Anakin, it was empty. All the Proctors had gone to their cabins to sleep or gamble.

Anakin's face was smudged and blotchy with crying. He stared warily at Tigris.

"Come along, little one," Tigris said. "You must be lonely, all by yourself. And hungry. Let's get you cleaned up, and find you some supper. We have to be quiet, though, so we won't disturb Lord Hethrir."

He unfastened the harness and offered his hand to Anakin. Anakin took it, slid down from the couch, and followed Tigris quietly and obediently.

A little later, they found fruit and bread and milk in the ship's galley. Anakin ate hungrily. With a mustache of milk, and crumbs on his chin, he offered Tigris a half-eaten slice of bread.

"Supper!" he said.

"No, thank you," Tigris said, strangely touched, reprimanding himself not only for being touched but for being tempted to take the bread and dunk it into the glass of milk and eat it. "That's your supper."

"Share!" Anakin said.

"No, thank you," Tigris said again.

"Anakin want cookie," Anakin said.

"Lord Hethrir doesn't eat cookies!" Tigris exclaimed, shocked.

Anakin pushed his lower lip out stubbornly.

"No cookies!" Tigris said.

"Papa," Anakin said. "Papa, Mama . . ."

He was about to cry again. Tigris wiped Anakin's face with the edge of his sleeve, hoping to distract him. He stopped sniffling.

"I want my papa," he said.

Tigris knelt beside him and gazed into his eyes.

"Anakin, little one," he said, "there's something you must know. Your mama and your papa don't want you anymore. Lord Hethrir saved you, adopted you. As he adopted me, and all of us."

Anakin scowled. He gnawed on a piece of fruit, thoughtfully and silently. He did not start to cry again.

"What is this? A picnic?"

Tigris leaped to his feet, startled and dismayed. Lord Hethrir stood in the doorway, elegant as always in his long white robes, though his hair was disarranged.

"I beg your pardon, sir," Tigris said. "The child—I thought—"

"Be quiet. Put the child back in his place. Your permission to attend me is revoked. You will stay in the passenger compartment with the child until the voyage is ended."

Hethrir left them, striding away. He had not even raised his voice, but Tigris trembled. Whatever good impression he had somehow managed to make, it was destroyed. He glanced at Anakin in irritation. Destroyed because of the child . . .

Tigris sighed. Much as he wanted to blame his disgrace on someone else, in good conscience he could not.

He turned to Anakin.

The child offered him a sticky piece of fruit.

"Supper?" Anakin said.

Tigris accepted the slice of fruit. He ate it. It tasted delicious.

In the passenger compartment, cut off from the sight of space and stars, Tigris and Anakin waited together while Lord Hethrir landed at Crseih Station, better known in the trade as Asylum.

Alderaan hovered above a low, massive compound, a windowless stockade of huge gray stones, built atop a hill. The Proctors trudged up the slope toward it, a dejected group.

Jaina pointed to a canyon that split the hillside below the stockade. "That's where we played, Mama," she said.

"And Mistress Dragon lives in the dunes," Jacen said.

"We never got to go in the house," Jaina said, gazing down at the stockade. "We were underground."

"In long dark tunnels!" Jacen said.

"And little tiny rooms. With no light!"

"Oh, my dears," Leia said softly.

Alderaan landed near the courtyard of the stockade. Leia disembarked, followed by Jaina and Jacen, all the other children, and Rillao and Chewbacca.

"Will you search the compound?" Leia asked Rillao and Chewbacca.

Chewbacca growled.

"And leave you here alone with them?" Rillao said in a tone of protest. She gestured toward the group of Proctors straggling into the courtyard. Mistress Dragon ambled along behind them.

The Proctors staggered across the cobblestones and flung themselves at Leia's feet.

"Madam, your mercy, we beg you!"

They looked as if they had been on a desperate campaign.

Their skin was blotched with insect bites. Their clothes were torn from the bushes and muddy from the swamp. Their feet were swollen and blistered from the tramp across the desert.

"I think I'll be all right," Leia said dryly.

"Very well."

Rillao and Chewbacca crossed the compound and disappeared down the staircase into the stockade.

Mistress Dragon lumbered in behind the Proctors, snortling and roaring. The Proctors shuddered and flattened themselves to the ground and lay very still, though their mud-stained blue uniforms gave them no camouflage against the stones.

"Please, my lady," whispered the Proctor with the most elaborate decorations on his shoulders and sleeves. "Save us from these plagues. Please don't feed us to the dragon!"

Mistress Dragon lay down near them with a great "Huff!" of breath. She lashed her tail. The Proctor ducked, flattening himself to the ground again.

"Beg the pardon of my—" Leia revised what she had begun to say. "Beg the pardon of all these children," she said. "Then I'll consider mercy."

It occurred to her that if Mistress Dragon decided to snack on a Proctor or two, she had no way of stopping the beast.

The Proctor lay still, facedown, humiliated. Then his terror and his discomfort overcame his embarrassment. He crawled slowly—keeping his head very low—to the children gathered behind Leia.

"I beg your pardon," he said.

"Promise that you'll never behave toward another being as you've behaved toward these children."

"I promise," he said.

"Now stand up, and remove that nonsense from your shoulders."

He balked at that, but she stared him down. He rose, glancing over his shoulder at Mistress Dragon (who closed her eyes and snored), then pulled away the jeweled patches from his uniform.

Each of the Proctors made a similar promise. The pile of insignia grew. While the Proctors watched, Leia handed their epaulets and medals to the children to use as toys and decorations.

"Where are the other children?" Leia asked the leader of the Proctors. "Where did Hethrir take them?"

"I don't know, madam," he said.

She could see a tiny flare of fear in him. He was not exactly lying, but he was not telling her the whole truth, either.

"Where *might* they be?" she asked, her voice a cutting edge. "The little child Anakin, and the youth Tigris—"

In the back of the group, one of the Proctors snickered nastily. Leia silenced him with a glance.

"And Lusa!" Jaina said.

"And Mr. Chamberlain's wyrwulf!" Jacen said.

The Head Proctor stared at the ground.

"It will go better for you, if you tell me," she said.

"The Lord Hethrir . . . he culled the group only yesterday."

"*Culled* them?" Leia felt her skin grow cold, and her heart angry.

"Only to sell, madam!" the Proctor said. "Then he departed—"

"To Asylum Station?"

"Yes, madam. He took the child Anakin. And *Tigris*—"

"Such contempt," Leia said with wonder at his tone of voice.

"Tigris is weak! The Lord Hethrir wouldn't even make him a helper!" The Proctor sneered. "He had to serve at table, and nursemaid the youngest children—"

"And you believe that task isn't fitting for a strong young Proctor?" Leia said easily.

"Children are useless until they're old enough to serve the cause of the Empire Reborn!"

"No one will serve the Empire Reborn," Leia said. "Not ever again."

Defiantly, the Proctor raised his arms and cried, "The Empire Reborn!"

If he had not been so pathetic, so young, Leia would have been angry. As it was, she glanced at the bedraggled Proctors and she glanced at the tired band of children who had bested them.

She laughed. The Head Proctor flinched as if she had struck him. And then, at least, he had the intelligence to look abashed.

"Now," Leia said, "we'll find a place for you where you'll make no more trouble."

"I know where to put them!" Jaina said.

Jaina led the way through long, dark tunnels to a huge, low-ceilinged room as oppressive as a cave. She flung open one of the doors that lined its walls and showed Leia one of the tiny dark cells.

"This is where *we* had to sleep! In the dark! So they should have to sleep—"

Appalled though she was by the cells, Leia put her hand on Jaina's shoulder. Her daughter fell silent and looked up at her, angry and confused.

"They asked for my mercy," Leia said. "And they asked your pardon—"

"They didn't really *mean* it," Jaina muttered.

"—and we won't treat them harshly. We mustn't take revenge, sweetheart. That isn't just." She looked over the bedraggled group of Proctors, realizing how young they all were. She addressed them directly. "However, we have no other place to keep you where you will be safe." Where you can't get into mischief, Leia thought. "You must stay in this hall, with the door locked. You may use the cells—if you like."

Leia knew from the stubborn set of her daughter's jaw that Jaina was far from satisfied, and Leia did not blame her.

"If one of them's *bad*," Jaina said, "and you *have* to shut him in—don't use my cell." She pointed at one of the doors, indistinguishable from all the rest. "Because I broke the latch!"

Leia knelt beside her and hugged her. "It was very clever and brave of you to do that."

"And I put sand in their pants and Jacen made the myrmins bite them!"

Jacen looked at the floor. "But the Proctors killed them. The myrmins," he said softly.

Leia hugged him tight. "Oh, my dear. My dear child." She held his face between her hands and kissed him on the forehead. "That makes them hero myrmins—doesn't it?"

He nodded, only a little comforted.

As Leia shepherded the children from the gathering hall, Rillao and Chewbacca met her.

"I found another group of children," Rillao said.

"Those are the helpers!" Jaina said. "They do whatever Hethrir tells them to, they're even meaner than the Proctors."

Leia exchanged a look of concern with Rillao.

These young helpers, Leia thought, may be much harder to liberate than my children, and the children who resisted Hethrir with them.

"And we found the cook and her assistants. Lelila, we must hurry, Hethrir is going to Asylum Station—"

"So the Head Proctor told me. The Indexer was right. But first we have to see to—"

She gestured around her, distressed. Her strongest desire was to fling *Alderaan* back into hyperspace and follow Hethrir.

But she could not leave the stolen children out here in nowhere by themselves. Leia hesitated, wondering whether it would be harder to persuade Rillao to stay behind, or Chewbacca.

Chewbacca whuffled.

"Oh!" Leia said. "Of course—"

"We will take them with us," Rillao said. "We will take the worldcraft."

"We'll take it away from here," Leia said. "But we'll send it to safety."

"A practical suggestion, Lelila."

"How long will it take to move it?"

"Only a few minutes," Rillao said. "In hyperspace, the worldcraft is as fast as any other ship. I will chart our course." She strode away, the green silk pantaloons whipping around her ankles.

For the sake of the other children, Leia forced herself into a fragile calmness. Only a few minutes, she thought.

Jacen looked up at her, his brown eyes wide. "It will be all right, Mama," he said. "We'll find Anakin."

Leia knelt and hugged him, hugged both her twins.

"I know we will. Very soon."

Jaina leaned against her. "I'm so hungry, Mama."

"Let's go find everyone some dinner," Leia said.

The group of children cheered raggedly.

Jacen led the way toward the dining hall. As they approached, a tall and massive six-legged being lumbered down the corridor toward them, tendrils wrapped around the handle of a great steaming cauldron. Leia recognized the being as a Veubg, from a culture she remembered with great affection.

"That's Grake," Jaina whispered. "Who threw us food."

The being stopped.

"What are you doing, Grake?" Leia asked.

"Taking the children's gruel to the Proctors," Grake said. "The Proctors' dinner is on the table for the children."

The children cheered and rushed down the hall. Chewbacca hurried after them, to be sure everyone got a share.

"Go," Leia said to Jaina and Jacen. "Go with Chewbacca and get some supper."

They ran after their friend.

Leia glanced into the cauldron Grake was carrying.

"This is dreadful," she said. "It looks like old dishwater. Whatever were you planning to do with it?"

"Give it to the Proctors," Grake said. "To see how they like it."

"That's out of the question." Leia stopped. "You said— this was the *children's* supper?"

Grake would not meet Leia's gaze.

"How *could* you serve this to children?"

"How could I not, madam?"

Leia waited.

"Lord Hethrir ordered it."

"You had the choice whether to follow the order or not!"

"I did not, madam."

"Because you needed the job? Because he'd be angry at you?"

"Because I'm a slave, madam. Because Lord Hethrir has the power of life and death and punishment over me."

Shocked, unable to speak for a moment, Leia gently took the cauldron from Grake. Then she put her hands into the mass of Grake's tendrils, and let the tendrils wrap around her fingers.

"I am most sincerely sorry for the manner in which I spoke to you," Leia said to Grake. "You are no longer a slave. You are free. I cannot take you home for a little while yet. But I will."

Grake trembled.

"Thank you, madam," she said, her voice soft and rough.

"Will you show me the kitchen?" Leia said. "And the laundry? There's work for me to do."

"What am I to do?"

"Whatever pleases you."

"It pleases me to cook real food for the children."

"You do understand that you're free?"

"I do understand, madam. That's why it pleases me."

"Thank you, then," Leia said. She smiled ruefully. "I've never had occasion to learn to be a good cook."

"Come along," Grake said patiently. "Never too late to start learning." She hesitated, glancing at the cauldron. "What about this?"

"We'll throw it out," Leia said. "And send bread, and fruit, and soup—real soup—to the Proctors."

"Because it pleases us," Grake said.

Tigris had passed his childhood on a remote, boring, pastoral world, kept from his destiny. Since Lord Hethrir rescued him, he had lived on the quiet worldcraft.

Tigris loved Crseih Station.

The welcome dome of Crseih always overwhelmed him with its noise and activity. People poked at him, plucked his sleeve, offered him sweetmeats and jewelry and a selection of robes, one of them a silky white one that he wanted more than he had ever wanted anything material in his life.

But as Lord Hethrir preferred, he walked without pausing, without allowing himself to be visibly tempted.

Anakin reached for one of the sweetmeats. The sweetmeat-monger drew the tray away, spiraling its wrinkly arms, and the tray, out of Anakin's grasp.

"Patience, small person," the being said. "You must pay, first."

"Pay?" Tigris asked, curiously. He knew the concept of

paying, but only in context of Lord Hethrir's political dealings and his involvement in the trade. Pay for food, for clothing? He tried to remember if he had paid for anything when he was a child. He had a vague memory of trading, of being given gifts, of his mother providing aid to one of the other villagers, then finding a bushel of fruit or a brace of game or a length of cloth on the doorstep the next morning.

"Yes, pay! You are not a beggar and I am not a do-gooder." The being extended an eyestalk and bent its eye up and down, regarding Tigris. "Or perhaps you *are* a beggar."

Lord Hethrir had not even paused. He strode away, followed by the phalanx of his Proctors. In a moment they would disappear into the crowd. Tigris scooped Anakin up and hurried away from the sweetmeat-monger. The being followed, bulging along with limber gracelessness.

"This is not a transaction of world-shaking magnitude," the being said.

"I have no account," Tigris said. "Nothing to transfer to you."

"No one makes a transfer to buy a sweetmeat! Where are you from, the planet of foolish people? All it requires is a coin of the least magnitude."

"Excuse me," Tigris said, slipping between two groups of beings and nearly getting tangled in their tentacles. He had not realized, before interposing himself between them, that they were engaging in some unexplained interaction.

The sweetmeat-monger caught up with him on the other side of the group of tentacled beings. Tigris wiped slime from his face and his sleeve.

"I see you *are* from the planet of the foolish people," the being said. "You aren't safe to be around, even to make a sale. Your pardon, small person," it said to Anakin, and disappeared.

Tigris rushed through the crowd, heedless of giving offense, trying to catch up to the end of the marching Proctors. His lord walked quickly. A path opened before Lord Hethrir. But Tigris had to edge through. He did his best not to run into anyone else. He wished Lord Hethrir were unaware of his moment of distraction, his fascination with the material things being offered to him at the entryway.

Especially the white robe.

He knows what's happening behind him, Tigris thought. He always knows.

He labored after Hethrir, Anakin growing heavier and heavier in his arms. Hethrir never looked back.

The children ate with desperate appetite. It broke Leia's heart to watch them. She sat in the dining hall with Jaina and Jacen, unable to eat anything herself. She cautioned the children not to eat too quickly, or too much. She feared that nevertheless there would be upset stomachs tonight.

"I want to go home," said one of the little ones. "I want to go home!" Soon all the children were clamoring for their homes, their families.

Leia knew exactly how they felt.

As Leia calmed the children, Rillao entered the dining hall.

"We'll take you home soon," Leia said. "I promise. For now, a nice hot bath and a nice warm bed. How does that sound?"

She saw a few trembly lips and teary eyes; they wanted to go home *now* and Leia did not blame them.

She only hoped their families could be found. Had Hethrir murdered their families in order to steal them? Were they all from the passenger freighters? Or—were their families the people Winter had gone to meet, who thought their children had run away?

Rillao perched on the bench beside Jaina.

"The worldcraft will enter hyperspace soon," Rillao said softly to Leia. "Before morning, we'll reach Asylum Station."

Hethrir strode into a lodge in a quiet park. The only sound was the ripple and splash of the water in the pools and streams of the lobby. Tigris followed. Anakin wriggled to get down. Tigris let him free, gratefully, then had to hurry after him as the little boy headed straight for the irresistible ponds. He crouched down and splashed at the edge of a still circle of water, patting the surface to spread ripples.

"My lord." The rainbow whirlwind wavered into view, hovering above one of the streams. "All is ready for you."

"Have my guests arrived?" Hethrir asked.

"Yes, my lord," the whirlwind host replied. "They will gather to meet you when—"

A purple humanoid droid clattered into the lobby.

"I simply do not understand," the purple droid said, "why you're being so disagreeable about this situation."

The purple droid followed a service droid, gesturing as he spoke. The service droid's large carrying surface bore a couple of small valises, a scattering of opened and unopened emergency ration packs, and a battered bunch of ugly flowers without a vase.

The carrying droid rumbled a reply comprehensible only in its indifference.

"Halt!" said the host. Its rainbow colors brightened in a threatening manner.

The service droid lurched to a halt. The ugly flowers scattered on the floor.

"What do you mean, performing an eviction through the front door?"

"This is *quite* absurd!" the purple droid said. "We are no more than hours late with the rent. My human companions will return soon and pay you! They are *very busy* people!"

The service droid snatched up the spilled flowers with its pincers, breaking the stems and littering the floor with crushed petals. The petals oozed pale fluid. Lord Hethrir watched without expression. The Proctors stood in perfect array, but the droid's distress amused them.

"Mr. Threep!" Anakin shouted. He ran to the purple droid, bouncing with excitement. Tigris bolted after him but could not keep him from fastening his arms around the strange droid's leg.

"Master Anakin?" the droid said. "Master Anakin! Whatever are you doing here? Where are your brother and sister? Where is Prin—your mother?"

"Bring the child back," Hethrir said.

"Who are you, sir?" the droid asked Hethrir. "I have not been instructed that you are permitted to attend Master Anakin!"

"You have mistaken this child for someone else. You are in error. Perhaps you need your brain circuits wiped."

Tigris hurried to Anakin and managed to pry his little hands from the droid's knee. The droid tried to interfere, but Tigris fended him off. Anakin shrieked wildly. He kicked at Tigris's shins.

"Ow!" Tigris said. "Don't, Anakin, come away, leave the Mr. Droid alone. Your pardon, sir."

"Who are you, young sir? What are you doing with Master Anakin?"

As soon as Tigris freed Anakin from the droid's legs, Lord Hethrir strode past him, drawing his lightsaber.

The lightsaber flamed wildly. Its energy blade arced through the droid's head and body. The handle back-flashed. Sparks pierced the air, searing it into ozone. Lord Hethrir shouted a curse—his high-pitched shout startled Tigris even more than the failure of the lightsaber—and dropped the handle. The blade seared a fissure into the smooth flagstone, flashed to brilliance, and faded.

Tigris had never seen anything like it.

The droid, frozen in place, toppled onto the stone floor with a great metallic clank. He shivered violently, then fell quiet. Purple paint flaked from him, revealing patchy bits of gold.

Anakin screamed and struggled. "Mr. Threep! Mr. *Threep!*"

Tigris scooped him up and held him, despite his crying and kicking.

"It's all right, little one," he whispered. "Shh, shh."

Confused and angry and exhausted after the long trip and the long confinement, Anakin lapsed into frustrated sobs.

"Fetch my lightsaber," Hethrir said to Tigris.

Frightened but resolute, Tigris bent down awkwardly, holding Anakin in one arm, and picked up the pommel of the lightsaber. He was sure it would explode; instead, it felt dead in his hand. He offered it to Lord Hethrir, but the Lord ignored him.

"I do beg your pardon for this unforgivable disturbance," the whirlwind host said to Lord Hethrir. "The droid clearly has twisted circuits. It already tried to defraud me!"

"Secure the droid," Hethrir said. "It's dangerous. Later perhaps we will wipe it and recycle it."

"Very well, my lord," the whirlwind said.

The service droid wrestled the collapsed droid onto its carrying surface and rolled away into the shadows.

Anakin stared at the service droid, and at the comatose purple and gold droid, with wide, frightened eyes.

"Mr. Threep," he whispered.

Lord Hethrir put one hand on his forehead and gazed down at him.

"It can't be of use to you, little one," he said. "We're the ones who will take care of you."

In the Proctors' large, airy dormitory, Leia and her comrades moved the beds together to form a sleeping platform big enough for all the children. The cupboards held extra blankets and comforters, enough for everyone to be toasty warm even with the windows open.

Rillao and Artoo-Detoo went to handle the worldship's controls during the entrance into hyperspace, while Chewbacca and Leia tucked the children in. Jaina and Jacen sat on the sleeping platform but did not get under the covers.

"I want to stay with you, Mama," Jaina whispered. "Me, too," Jacen said.

"You aren't too sleepy?"

Jacen shook his head. Jaina yawned.

"I have to go over to *Alderaan*," Leia said. "Would you like to come with me, and sleep in my cabin?"

Both twins nodded energetically.

"The ground is going to shake," Leia said to all the children. "Just for a little while. It means the worldcraft is moving. There's nothing to be scared of. Chewbacca will be right here with you."

The children snuggled contentedly under their blankets.

Chewbacca crooned a cradle song from his homeworld. As Leia left the dormitory with Jaina and Jacen, several of the little ones climbed out of bed and scampered to the Wookiee, to cuddle against his brindled fur. He put his arms around them all, and continued his wordless song.

Leia smiled. Children took to Chewbacca instantly.

Leia took Jaina and Jacen to her cabin and tucked them into her bunk and sat with them. Jacen's four-winged bat fluttered up to the ceiling, landed against the wall, and clung there.

Alderaan shuddered beneath them. The worldcraft and its tiny sun pulled at each other, accelerating, and the ground quaked and rumbled.

Jaina sat up, excited, and Jacen patted the bulkhead beside him.

"It's like taking off!" Jaina said.

"Exactly like," Leia said.

The worldcraft transited into hyperspace. The shuddering stopped. Jaina wriggled back down under the covers.

"We're going to rescue Anakin, aren't we?" she asked. "And Lusa—before they cut off her horns!"

"Yes," Leia said, hoping she was telling the truth. Now that they were in hyperspace, she looked and listened for Anakin. She could find no trace of him.

"I missed you so much, Mama!" Jaina said, holding her hand.

"I missed you, too, my darling. Do you know I followed you through hyperspace? I could feel you calling to me. I almost lost you—but then I heard you again."

Jaina flung herself into Leia's arms. "Every time we tried to use the Force, Hethrir stopped us! We tried to use the barrier! To protect Anakin. But he stopped us! I know I wasn't supposed to do anything else, without Uncle Luke, but I thought—we tried—he's still stopping us, but we could do *little* things—"

"It's all right, Jaina. It's all right. I'm so proud of you both."

She tucked them in, pulling a warm blanket up around them.

"Mama?" Jaina asked.

"Yes, sweetie."

"Can you make him stop?"

"Make who stop? Stop what?"

"Jaina and I can't hear each other," Jacen said, "like Uncle Luke taught us."

Leia frowned with concern.

"Sweetheart, why not?"

"Because Hethrir won't let us!"

"But he isn't here, darlings. He's nowhere near, he can't touch you."

Both children stared at her, wanting to believe her but afraid.

"He still can," Jaina whispered.

Leia closed her eyes and opened herself to the widest range of her perceptions.

She found nothing. She *reached*, as far as she could. She could feel her children's fear, she could feel what they had experienced while Hethrir controlled them. Her heart trembled, near breaking.

"He isn't here," she said again. "You're safe now."

Jaina and Jacen hugged each other. The glimmer of their barrier shone around them, then vanished like a spark, beneath the waterfall of their fear. Hethrir was gone, but he had left behind him such fear that Leia could not touch it.

Leia scooped her children up and hugged them. Jaina and Jacen held her desperately tight.

Rillao ran into the cabin, her hair flying and her eyes wide.

"What are you doing? Who are you? Who—" She stared at the children, then turned her gaze to Leia. "You are Jedi," she said.

Leia shook her head. "No," she said. "I'm untrained, the children are just beginning their training— How did you know?"

"You just gave me the worst headache I have ever suffered in my life."

"Make Hethrir go away, Mama," Jacen said.

"He's gone, dear one. He can't touch you now."

But Jaina and Jacen stared at her, unable to believe Hethrir had no distant control over them.

Rillao sat on the bed beside Leia and her children. With the tip of her finger, she stroked Jaina's hair, then Jacen's, delicately. They both looked up, wide-eyed, frightened and fascinated.

"Your mama is right," Rillao said. "Hethrir has no power to touch you anymore."

Rillao spoke softly. As she spoke, as she stroked the children's hair, the strands of terror within Jaina and Jacen disappeared beneath her touch.

Leia watched, astonished.

"Better, now?" Rillao asked.

Jaina and Jacen hesitated for a moment, as if they had been shut away from sunlight for so long that they could not believe its return. Then Jaina laughed aloud and Jacen smiled. They leaped up. They grabbed hands and spun around and around; they grabbed Leia's hand, and Rillao's, and drew them into their circle. The children's barrier spiraled up around them all like a glowing whirlwind. Their laughter filled the room.

They fell down, deliberately, laughing and giggling. Leia fell down beside them and hugged them.

Rillao sat on her heels nearby, watching, with a silent smile.

"Thank you, thank you!" Jaina cried. Jacen watched Rillao gravely. "Yes, thank you," he said.

"You're welcome." Rillao turned to Leia. "We must speak."

"Yes. We must." Leia gathered up the twins. "You're getting so big!" she said. She put them back into her bunk and tucked them in again. They were exhausted, but calm. She kissed them and sat beside them. In a moment they had fallen asleep.

Rillao had left the cabin. Leia found her in the copilot's chair, staring out the forward port, into the worldcraft's sky, her face illuminated by the lights of hyperspace.

"Who are *you*?" Leia asked. "You're a Jedi, aren't you? A real Jedi Knight."

"I was," Rillao whispered.

Leia sat in the pilot's chair and turned toward the Firrerreo.

"Tell me."

"I was a student . . . of Lord Vader."

"But—" Leia protested.

Rillao stopped her with a gesture. "He taught us in secret. Even after the Empire declared our people subhuman, and destroyed us, he kept me . . . and one other."

"And when the Empire fell, you both fled." Leia spoke coolly, holding herself under tight control so she would not reveal her horror. Rillao, a pawn of the Empire?

"It is not quite that simple," Rillao said. "When we were young, just beginning our studies, we both . . . we fell in love.

"Lord Vader believed we would produce a child with extraordinary talent, one he could bend to the use of the Empire."

"And . . . did you?" Leia asked. She thought, This could be the cause of the rumors Luke is investigating. What is my brother facing? A youth as talented as Anakin, trained by my father, Darth Vader, Dark Lord of the Sith . . .

She shivered.

Rillao smiled gently. "We produced a child. An ordinary, sweet child. Tigris . . . I was so happy when I realized he had no talent for the Force."

"Happy!" Leia exclaimed, simultaneously shocked and relieved.

"Even before our child, I became . . . a disappointing student to Lord Vader."

"But *you're* extraordinarily talented," Leia said. "How could you be disappointing?"

"Can't you guess, my friend?" She smiled, fiercely this time, showing the sharp tips of her unusually prominent canine teeth.

Leia waited.

"I was not tempted to the dark side," Rillao said. "It repelled me. I had no desire for power over other people. I could not understand Lord Vader's compulsion to gain it, any more than he could understand my desire to escape it."

"At the end of his life," Leia said, "he would have understood."

"Then perhaps he found peace. I am glad. But when I knew him, he was driven. He had no patience for my weaknesses. Lelila, I am possessed of a gift. I can heal, and strengthen, and soothe."

"As you healed and soothed my children," Leia said.

Rillao nodded. "Lord Vader forbade me to exercise my healing talents. In turn, I resisted his instruction. Both Lord Vader and my lover found me undependable."

Her quiet breathing deepened, and she closed her eyes.

"I could not bear it," she said. "Lord Vader treated me with scorn. My lover . . . ceased to love me. His feelings for me did not vanish. I could have borne that. I could have borne hatred in place of love. But contempt . . ."

She paused for so long Leia was afraid she would not—could not—complete her story. Leia placed her hand gently over Rillao's.

"What happened?"

"Lord Vader appointed my lover—you understand that he is the one whose name I spoke to you, you understand that he is Hethrir?—Procurator of Justice. He charged him with the destruction of our world, and the abduction of a freighter full of our people."

"Your own world! His own people! How—" But she knew how. It was not even rare.

"He did it to prove his loyalty, his loyalty above all to the Empire. He thought, if he proved himself, the Empire would declare him human after all." She laughed bitterly. "I wondered, after our world died, why anyone would *want* to be considered human."

Leia nodded. After the destruction of Alderaan, she had wondered the same thing.

"Before our child was born, I fled. After the child came, I hid us on the smallest, meekest, most backward worlds. Lord Vader had great hopes for my son, and I feared what he might do when he discovered my son could not fulfill his ambitions."

"Neither could his own," Leia whispered. "No, never mind, it's too complicated to explain, I didn't mean to interrupt you."

"When the Empire fell," Rillao said, "I thought perhaps we were safe. I did not know what had happened to my lover. I grieved that he was dead. I grieved for my world, ruined by the arrogance of the Empire. I grieved for my people, sent I knew not where into space to a far destination. My child and I lived happily. As happily as we could, alone. I could not even answer my child's questions about his father. I practiced my craft, but in secret.

"And then," Rillao said softly, "I discovered that I need not have grieved for my lover's death. The one I had loved discovered us. He had been seeking us constantly. He has vast resources. He foresaw the fall of the Empire, and he prepared for it. We struggled." She looked away, ashamed. "He overcame me."

"You'd practiced healing. He practiced for war."

"He overcame me," Rillao said, turning aside Leia's excuses for her. "He imprisoned me. He took our child. He has had our child for *five years*."

And, Leia realized, Hethrir had imprisoned Rillao in the passenger freighter, under torture, for five years.

"What did he want of you?" Leia asked softly, meaning, He could have killed you cleanly, but he chose to torment you, for all that time.

"He wanted to win me back, of course," Rillao said. "Or break me to his will. It made no difference to him, I think, as long as I surrendered to his bidding. He wanted a partner, or a pawn, to strengthen his rule of the Empire Reborn." She stretched out her hands, spread her long fingers, turned her hands over to reveal the scarred palms, and clenched her fists. "And he wanted our child to be his heir. To the Empire Reborn *and* to his dark power."

She smiled again, but her eyes were full of tears.

"My sweet son . . . I fear what Hethrir has done to him, in five years. He cannot fulfill his father's ambitions for him. He cannot gain, for Hethrir, full access to the dark side. He could be a fine scientist, or an artist, or an explorer-diplomat. He cannot be a Jedi."

"And you haven't even seen him in five years!" Leia exclaimed in sympathy. She tried to imagine missing Jaina and Jacen for five years. She did not think she would survive.

"I have seen him," Rillao said. "He came to the chamber with his lord. He called me traitor, and weakling, and fool."

She scrubbed the back of her hand across her eyes, dashing the tears away angrily.

"I must find him, Lelila," she said. "Perhaps he's already

lost to me . . . lost to himself. But perhaps Hethrir has not yet extinguished his sweetness. What your children said of him gave me hope."

"My name isn't Lelila," Leia said.

"You need not tell me—"

"It's Leia. And when we rescue Ti—when we rescue your son, and mine, we'll go home to Coruscant. You'll have a safe haven. You'll have colleagues. Luke—my brother, Luke Skywalker—will be so excited to meet you!"

To her astonishment, Rillao dropped to one knee before her, awkward in the cramped pilot's cabin.

"Princess Leia of Alderaan," she said. "Freedom fighter, destroyer of the Empire, and founder of the New Republic. I pledge you my loyalty. I should have recognized you—"

Suddenly shy, Leia began twisting and plaiting her hair into a messy heap on top of her head.

"I was traveling incognito," she said.

Chapter

11

Leia hugged Chewbacca when he boarded *Alderaan* and came to her cabin to assure himself that Jaina and Jacen were safe.

Under Grake's watchful eye, the other stolen children slept on the worldcraft, which was programmed to travel to Munto Codru. There, the children would be safe, and the work of finding their homes and families could begin.

"Will you stay in my cabin with Jaina and Jacen?" Leia asked Chewbacca. "I don't want to leave them alone."

Chewbacca snorted a question.

"Yes," Leia said. "You are an excellent navigator. But Rillao knows the route to Asylum Station."

Chewbacca growled his opinion of a navigator who had not flown for at least five years, but the growl was just for show. He laid one huge hand gently on Leia's head, and sat on the end of the bunk where the twins were sleeping.

Leia hurried to her pilot's seat. She lifted *Alderaan* off the worldcraft. The worldcraft vanished into the brightness of hy-

perspace, on its way to refuge. Leia gave the controls over to
Rillao.

They were on their way to Asylum Station, and Anakin.

Han strolled happily along the quiet path. What a great
evening. No one bothering him, the razor edge of his concentration sharpened rather than dulled by the excellent ale,
nothing to worry about, nothing to *think* about, playing cards
on instinct and nerve. Winning.

He felt terrific.

And he knew what to do about Waru.

The lobby of the lodge was deserted. He was rather disappointed. If the host had shown up and harassed him for the
rent, he could have laughed and thrown hard cash money at
the whirlwind's feet. No, not feet. Whatever the whirlwind
used instead of feet. He could have pitched the credits into the
host's twisty gullet.

He slipped on the flagstone floor and nearly fell.

What the—? he thought. I'm not *that* drunk.

He glanced at the spot that had tripped him up. A
cracked floor tile was littered with thick, ugly flower petals.
He had stepped on one and it had squashed under his heel.
The petals looked like they came from the same flowers
Threepio had pilfered for the breakfast table.

Probably the cleaning droid mistook them for garbage
and took them away, Han said to himself. Then dropped them
on the floor.

Han climbed the stairs two at a time. He would give the
rent money to Threepio. Only fair to let the droid pay the
host, since Threepio had been the one to explain and excuse
their being late with the payment.

He felt cleanly and completely tired. He looked forward
to sleeping late. By afternoon, evening anyway, Luke would
have cooled off.

And I've cooled off, too, Han thought. If the kid doesn't
jump down my throat again, everything will be fine.

His code would not open the door to his room.

"Hey!" He banged on the door. "Let me in!"

After a moment, the door-screen lit up with the image of a beautiful woman, wrapped in a robe, her hair disheveled.

"This is no time for trading," she said. "Come back at a civilized hour. We'll go to my ship and I'll display the new merchandise."

"Trading? Merchandise? Huh? Who are you? What are you doing in my room?" He thought, If Luke sees her, I'll *never* be able to make him understand about me and Xaverri. I'll never get him to believe this is a misunderstanding.

"This is my room, sir, and I am sleeping in it."

Peering close, he rechecked the room number. No, he had made no mistake.

"I've been here for days!" he said. "My stuff is in the closet!"

"*My* things are in the closet. Go away. I have called the host." The door-screen faded away and she would not reply to Han's knocking, or his shouts.

A couple of large droids trundled toward him, one from each end of the corridor. They looked like Artoo-Detoo on growth hormones. With a pincer maneuver, they herded him toward the stairs, bumping him roughly despite his protests, then trundled on thick treads after him, one before him, one behind.

In the lobby, the lodge's host waited for him.

"What's going on?" Han said. "Who's that in my room? Where are my colleagues? Where's our stuff?"

"My establishment has been reserved by a conference," the host said. "You and your colleagues have consistently been late with your rent, so I required them to find other shelter."

Han threw a handful of credits at the host. The credits fluttered through the whirlwind image and scattered over the pool's surface.

"There."

"Too late."

The two overgrown droids nudged up against Han's back and pushed him toward the door, rolling over the crushed flower petals and releasing a powerful cloud of their fetid odor.

"Wait! Hold on!" Han pushed at the droids. He had no

effect. Their pressure increased and their progress continued unhampered.

"Dammit, where did my friends go?"

"I do not know," the whirlwind said. "Furthermore, I do not care."

The droids bumped Han outside so roughly that he nearly fell on the steps. The door slammed shut behind him. Catcalls followed him through the darkness.

In the warm damp night, Han swore.

Where did they go? he wondered. They didn't have any money. . . .

As Han walked, the crystal star dawned. First dawn and second dawn no longer occurred in opposition, second dawn blasting first sunset out of the sky. The crystal star had plummeted past Crseih Station, falling closer to the black hole. It rose, creating first dawn. Nearly in conjunction, the blazing whirlpool of the black hole exploded over the horizon.

Between the interference of the burning whirlpool and the haphazardly effective barriers of the radiation shields, Han's comlink was unreliable. He tried to reach Luke or Threepio, but received no answer.

He tried to force himself to think clearly.

Of course: they must have gone back to the *Falcon*. Too much trouble to come and find me, not that I exactly left word where I'd be. I'll have to go all the way back to the landing field. . . .

He tramped back down the path.

Suddenly the light around him dimmed a bit. Han glanced upward.

The white dwarf plunged behind the accretion disk of the black hole. For a moment, communication cleared slightly. Han called the *Falcon*.

No one answered except the *Falcon*'s automatic systems. No one had entered the ship since Threepio fetched the emergency rations. Neither Threepio nor Luke had left him a message.

As Han tried to call Luke directly, the white dwarf appeared from behind its companion. The interference increased again, blasting Han's connection to the *Falcon*.

Could Luke have gone back to Waru? Han thought.

Maybe he doesn't even know we're thrown out of our room. Maybe Threepio went to find him. . . .

The daylight brightened again.

Instead of soaring outward from the black hole, the white dwarf sailed around in front of it. Its eccentric elliptical orbit had changed phase, to an orbit nearly circular. The black hole drew the crystalline white dwarf closer. As the crystal star spun around the black hole, a stream of glowing plasma ripped from its surface. The dying star whirled around the black hole, plasma surging from it as it spun. The two stars formed a double whirlpool of light.

As the binary rose higher in the sky, the strange harsh light mottled the dome and the ground. Han blinked, wishing for a clearer, warmer, more ordinary light. He did not even want to know the strength of the X-ray flux.

Threepio was right about the radiation, Han thought.

Han reached the welcome dome, where the lights of the signs and shops obliterated the burning of the black hole. The welcome dome was as active, bright, and noisy now, at double-dawn, as it had been at star-dusk, and at midnight.

Han sighed. He was not interested in anything the welcome dome had to offer. All he wanted was a few hours' sleep. Instead, he trudged away toward Waru's compound, thinking, Haven't these folks ever heard of public transportation?

Alderaan's molten skin shivered beneath the assault of X rays as it dove into the strange system.

Asylum Station spun in space, a chaotic cluster of irregular, cratered asteroids, held together with communicating tunnels and gravity fields.

Leia frowned. She had never been to Asylum Station, yet she recognized it. There could not be two such strange stations.

"It's Crseih!" she exclaimed, as Artoo-Detoo whistled the same conclusion. "Crseih Station!"

"Yes," Rillao said. "Its real name is Crseih. In the trade, it is known as Asylum. Do you know it?"

"My husband and my brother are here," she said. She felt both hope and joy. "If Anakin's here, Luke will know it!"

She might land on Crseih Station and find her little boy waiting to meet her, safe and free. She imagined him running toward her, imagined his arms wrapped around her neck, imagined hugging him to her.

She imagined the empty spot in her heart, filling with his presence.

She tried to reach Han, to contact the *Millennium Falcon*, but the same radiation flux that had prevented her calling him from Munto Codru now blasted her communications out of the sky. Crseih Station was cut off from the rest of the galaxy by the frenzy of the double star.

"Be patient," Rillao said. "Soon we will find out. Soon we will know."

"You sound like my brother!"

Leia sighed in distress. For all she knew, Han and Luke had finished their investigation—their vacation—and headed back home before Hethrir brought Anakin to Crseih.

Near tears, Leia caught her breath. She pressed her hands against her eyes and extended her perceptions as far as she could.

She felt nothing.

She let her hands fall.

Rillao, beside her, patted her shoulder gently.

"We're still a distance from Crseih," she said. "Let's not distress ourselves quite yet."

Leia saw that Rillao had searched for Tigris, as Leia had searched for Anakin, and failed to find him.

Leia shook herself and tried to take Rillao's advice.

Before Leia, beyond Crseih, a binary system blazed. A white dwarf star plunged around a whirlpool of glowing debris. The black hole within the whirlpool ripped at the surface of the white dwarf, drawing star-stuff into explosive destruction.

Leia gazed at its wild beauty.

"This is the oddest system I've ever been in," Leia said, searching for something to distract her attention. "The oddest, and the most violent."

Artoo-Detoo beeped, and a geyser of information burst into the air above his carapace. He warbled with excitement.

Leia deciphered Artoo's display of information.

"He says they're odd indeed," Leia said.

Artoo amplified a portion of the information and pushed it toward her.

"Dying?" Leia exclaimed. "The *star* is dying?" Leia looked closer, interpreting what Artoo showed her. "*All* white dwarf stars are dying. The star—it's *freezing*."

"A freezing star?" Rillao said skeptically. "I think your droid is joking with us."

"Artoo has a lot of good qualities," Leia said, "but he doesn't have much in the way of a sense of humor. What's happening is, the star's so dense it's nothing but a quantum plasma. It's very, very old, so old it's stopped burning. It's giving up its heat to the universe. Freezing into one huge quantum crystal."

Leia heard a whimper from the far end of the companion-way. She jumped up and ran from the cockpit to her cabin, to her children. Chewbacca sat beside them, looming over them protectively.

Jaina and Jacen awakened, Jaina with a cry, Jacen pale and silent.

"It's all right, dear ones," Leia said. She and Chewbacca hugged them. She wished she had left them back on the worldcraft, safe and sound, yet she was desperately grateful to have them with her.

"Is Hethrir back?" Jaina whispered.

"No," Leia said. "He's nowhere near. I'll never let him near you. Did you have a dream? A nightmare?"

Jaina nodded somberly from the safety of Chewbacca's arms.

"My head hurts, Mama." Jacen held Leia tight.

Leia rocked him, crooning. After a while, they fell back into uneasy sleep. Leia tucked them in; Chewbacca fastened a safety guard around them.

Alderaan was about to land on Crseih Station.

*   *   *

Tigris entered the meeting hall of Crseih Station's travelers' lodge. The long stone pews were filled. Shimmering white velvet backed the dais upon which Lord Hethrir would stand. Against the brilliant white, Hethrir's gold and red hair would blaze like flame, and his dark eyes would burn.

Tigris recognized most of the people who waited for Lord Hethrir. Lady Ucce sat in the place of honor reserved for the most generous donor to the Empire Reborn. Lord Qaqquqqu sat among Lord Hethrir's lesser supporters. Many of the guests had visited the worldcraft, either as members of the trade or as supplicants for Hethrir's favor. Others had been promoted from Proctor to Empire Youth and sent out to work in secret on behalf of the Empire Reborn. Their reunion was unique in Tigris's experience. The Youths set themselves off with their pale uniforms, their medals, their elegant long coats.

Every free person at the meeting was devoted to the memory of the Empire, and to Lord Hethrir's plan for the Empire Reborn.

They had never before gathered like this. Something new and strange was happening. Tigris was proud to be involved, no matter how small his part.

A child of a nonhuman species accompanied each guest. All the guests, of course, were human. It was the place of humans to restore the Empire and to regain their power.

Tigris saw the centaur child who had joined Anakin's sister in defying the rules of Lord Hethrir's school. In fact, many of the slave children in the room were from the group that Lord Hethrir had just culled and sold. It seemed odd to Tigris that the guests would want to be attended by slaves so young and untrained that they had to be leashed. Some still cried for their mothers. But it was not Tigris's place to criticize Lord Hethrir's guests.

Keeping his silence, holding Anakin's hand, Tigris looked for a place to sit. The meeting room was very full.

The Proctors gathered just outside.

"Rise!"

Tigris hurried into the last pew, pulling Anakin with him. All around, the guests rose and bowed their heads. Tigris stared at the floor, waiting for Hethrir's permission to look up again.

Lord Hethrir's retinue of young Proctors marched through the doorway and up the aisle and fanned out on either side of the podium.

Lord Hethrir swept in.

"Were you planning to keep my lightsaber?"

Tigris straightened up, startled by Hethrir's low and dangerous voice. The Lord frowned down at him.

Tigris paled. The pommel of the lightsaber lay heavy in the pocket of his ragged robe. He fumbled for the saber and gave it to his lord. He should have followed Hethrir to his room and returned the saber immediately. Instead he had calmed Anakin. He should have left Anakin to cry himself to silence. The child must, after all, learn to control himself.

Hethrir strode down the central aisle and took his place on the podium.

"You may be seated," Hethrir said.

But one of the guests remained standing.

Tigris recognized him. His name was Brashaa. He was an undistinguished member of Lord Hethrir's following. How dare he defy Hethrir's command?

Hethrir looked down at Brashaa, with every evidence of welcome. Tigris thought he detected a hint of amusement in Lord Hethrir's expression. Amusement, and contempt. Brashaa was a notorious miser. He was not even attended by a slave. Instead, he dragged Anakin's pet after him on a heavy chain. Lord Hethrir had given Lady Ucce the ugly black six-legged creature for free. It panted and whined. Slaver dripped from its heavy, pitted fangs. Lady Ucce must have made a great profit by selling it to Brashaa.

"What is it, Brashaa?" Lord Hethrir said.

"My lord. For many years now you have promised action. We grow weary of concealing ourselves from usurpers of the New Republic."

Anakin saw the fanged creature. He jumped off the pew and would have run toward the monster if Tigris had not held him back.

"Sit still, little one," Tigris whispered.

"Anakin want woof!" Anakin said.

"Shh."

Lord Hethrir said nothing in response to Brashaa. He waited, silent and dangerous, until Brashaa gathered the courage to continue.

"My lord, we tire—desperately—of treating nonhumans as equal beings. We must act soon, before our children are too much affected by egalitarian propaganda, before our generation is too old to act—to fight!"

"I think you do not trust me, Brashaa," Hethrir said.

"I trust you with my life and with my wealth, my lord. I only mean—"

"I suspect you doubt me, Brashaa."

"Not at all, my lord. Not for a moment."

"I wonder if you are a traitor, Brashaa."

"My lord!" Brashaa protested. He grew pale with dread and regret. Tigris felt sorry for him, and horrified that the man had questioned Lord Hethrir.

"Leave us, Brashaa. You have no part in this meeting. I cannot trust you to hear my plan."

Brashaa stared at him, speechless even to defend himself. He hesitated, as if he hoped Lord Hethrir would repeal the sentence he had pronounced.

Lord Hethrir stared at him. Brashaa's face reddened. He gasped for breath. All around him, people withdrew, afraid that to stand too close would mean contamination.

A trickle of blood leaked from Brashaa's nostril.

Anakin clambered up on the seat of the pew and stared, wide-eyed and silent. Brashaa dropped the chain of the fanged creature, who watched its owner as intently as Anakin.

"I beg your forgiveness, my lord!"

Lord Hethrir simply gazed at him.

The traitor staggered toward the center aisle. Lord Hethrir's followers made way for him. No one reached out a hand to help him.

"Your forgiveness, my lord!"

Lord Hethrir would never let him live, after such a challenge. Tigris looked away, ashamed of his own weakness but unwilling to watch another man die.

And yet Brashaa did not fall. His footsteps sounded toward the back of the meeting hall.

"Your forgiveness, my lord!"

Tigris turned just in time to see Brashaa flee out the doorway.

The fanged creature looked around. Its ears perked up. Its chain rattled. No one moved to restrain it.

Tigris turned toward Lord Hethrir. He was shocked by his lord's strained face. Hethrir's complexion was even paler than usual, gray in contrast to the brilliant white of his robes and the soft white velvet.

He *did* mean Brashaa to die! Tigris thought. But something—something went wrong. The way Lord Hethrir's lightsaber went wrong . . .

Anakin plopped himself down on the seat beside Tigris.

"Bad mans, Tigis," he said solemnly.

"Shh, little one." Tigris hoped Lord Hethrir did not hear. Anakin clutched Tigris's hand in his grubby little fist. Tigris did not draw away. Confused and unhappy, trying to put aside his disloyal ideas, he thought: *Lord Hethrir erred.*

The fanged creature skulked down the aisle. Everyone ignored it. Instead of running away, or following its master from the hall, it settled itself at Anakin's feet.

"Shoo!" Tigris whispered.

"Hello, woof," Anakin said. The monster leaned its ugly head against Anakin's knee. Anakin scratched the black fur behind the creature's ears.

Hethrir's guests had returned their fascinated attention to their lord. Hethrir recovered himself. He smiled benevolently, as if he had let Brashaa live on purpose.

"Does any one of you have a question," he asked kindly, "before I tell you of my plan?"

No one spoke.

At Anakin's feet, the wolf-creature whined.

Hot and sweaty in the oppressive heat, Han trudged toward Waru's calligraphed building. He was so tired that the calligraphy leaped and spun and rewrote itself in his vision. He was traveling against the traffic; Waru's supplicants danced along the path.

The service must be over, Han thought. Fine. Maybe I'll meet Luke and Threepio coming out. Maybe they'll meet me halfway. Maybe Xaverri is around here somewhere, too, and we can clear everything up all at once.

The idea of entering Waru's presence again gave him the creeps. If he never had to see the damned thing again, he would be perfectly happy.

One of the supplicants stopped Han. "Waru has dismissed us, seeker," the scaled and feathered being said to him. The feathers ruffled; the scales turned tan, then pure bright yellow. "You will have to come to a later service."

"It's okay," Han said. "I'm meeting someone."

The feathered being patted his shoulder in a friendly manner and continued down the walkway.

Han passed the end of the line of departing supplicants. Luke and Threepio were nowhere in sight.

Han crossed the silent courtyard, whistling defiantly, and entered Waru's building. His shadows disappeared. He paused in the cool foyer and listened. A single voice spoke, the words and timbre jumbled by complicated acoustics. After a silence, a second voice replied. Han recognized the second voice: Waru.

He stepped into the theater.

At the foot of the stage, Luke stood with his shoulders slumped, facing Waru.

"I am tired, Luke Skywalker," Waru said.

Oh, *fine*, Han thought. He's told that guy who he is!

"You think of me as a tireless benefactor, a limitless healer. But I am a living being, and I tire like all other living beings. My other followers have acquiesced to my request that they depart. Can you not show me the same courtesy?"

"I'm afraid if you don't help me, I'll die."

What the—? Han thought.

Waru gave the impression of a deep sigh. "Very well. I will help you."

Luke stepped up on the altar.

"Luke!" Han yelled. As Luke stretched his arms to Waru, placing his palms on the limpid gold scales, Han sprinted toward him, his boots pounding the floor. He reached the altar and leaped up beside Luke. He grabbed him and pulled him away. Luke struggled, blindly reaching for his lightsaber. Han wrestled with him and pulled Luke's arms behind his back. Once Luke got his hands on the lightsaber, Han knew he could not win.

"Stop it!" he said. "You're not going to use the lightsaber on me and you know it!"

Then he got a look at Luke's face, pale and drawn and intense with pain, his eyes staring, and he was not so sure.

"Leave him," Waru said. "He has asked my aid, and I have offered it."

"No, it's too much to ask," Han said. "We'll come back when you're rested."

Wait a minute! Han thought. I'm trying to be diplomatic —while I'm *dragging* Luke out of here?

"He has the right to determine his own fate," Waru said. The low voice flowed like silk. "To choose to try to save his life."

"There's nothing wrong with him, dammit!"

Han jumped off the edge of the altar, pulling Luke with him, barely managing to keep his balance. Luke stumbled against him, going limp. Han expected a trick. He expected Luke to *will* the lightsaber into his hand. Instead, he found himself half dragging and half carrying Luke away from Waru's altar.

"He is very ill, very weak," Waru said. "Bring him back to me. If he can be healed, I will heal him."

Without replying, Han pulled Luke to his feet.

"Give me some help here, brother," he muttered.

Beside him, Luke staggered upright.

"Please, Han," he whispered. "Help me . . ."

"Bring him to me!" Waru's words shook the chamber.

Han slung Luke's arm over his shoulder and kept going toward the exit.

"No," Luke whispered. "No . . . please . . ."

Han went cold. Luke was begging not for escape, but to return to Waru. Han refused to let him go.

"I've saved your life before, kid," Han muttered. "You owe it to me at least once."

He dragged Luke out of the theater and through the silent entryway and into the open field. The disintegrating stars dazzled him. His eyes watered and his vision blurred. The black hole blazed and the crystal star pulsated, high in the sky. Their brightness increased, battering the strained radiation shields. Han shivered.

But Han had a lot more things to be uneasy about right now than the stars in his sky.

He wrestled Luke around and headed toward Xaverri's secret path.

Tigris listened, rapt, to Lord Hethrir's speech. He had been speaking for hours. Like the others, Tigris was fascinated, hypnotized, by the Lord's voice and his powerful message.

Only Anakin was immune to the power of Lord Hethrir's voice. The little boy had clambered to the floor and curled up with the six-legged fanged creature. They slept soundly on Tigris's feet.

"Today, I will consolidate my power," Lord Hethrir said.

"Today, I will be refined like precious metal from the rough ore of earthly existence.

"Today, I will be reborn—like the Empire, whose reincarnation I have conceived and incubated.

"Today I will bring forth—the Empire Reborn."

His followers gazed at him, stunned by his audacity. Then, all together, they leaped to their feet and cheered.

Tigris, too, started to rise. But if Tigris got up, he would wake Anakin. Anakin might begin to cry, and disturb the Lord's triumph.

Besides, Tigris's feet had gone to sleep.

Some of the slave children were whimpering and crying. But their behavior was not Tigris's responsibility. Anakin's was.

Tigris stayed where he was, hoping he was far enough in the back, far enough in shadows, so his failure to stand up and acclaim the plan would never be noticed. A whole roomful of people was standing, shouting, waving, applauding, between Tigris and Hethrir. Perhaps, for once, the Lord would not know everything Tigris did.

Anakin looks so peaceful, Tigris thought. I wonder how he can sleep, in all this noise?

He smiled fondly at the little boy, curled up on the floor among the fanged creature's six legs.

I wish he was always so peaceful! Tigris thought. I wonder what it would be like to have a little brother like Anakin? I wonder what it would be like to have a brother or a sister or a family at all? Why was my mother a traitor? Who was my father, and why did he abandon me?

Anakin opened his eyes. He blinked, sleepily, saw Tigris smiling at him, and took his thumb out of his mouth to smile back. He clambered up on the seat beside Tigris. He reached into his pocket with his sticky hand and pulled out a sweetmeat with one bite taken out of it. He offered it to Tigris.

Tigris laughed softly. "Thanks," he said. He broke off the least battered end and ate it. It tasted as good as the slice of fruit Anakin had offered him, back on the starship. "Where did you get this?" he asked. It looked like one of the sweetmeats the vendor had offered them in the welcome dome, which they could not buy because they had no money. Anakin just grinned and ate the rest of the sweet.

Tigris wiggled his toes so his feet would wake up. His skin prickled. The fanged creature snorted, woke, and stretched.

The meeting hall suddenly fell silent. The people sat down. The slave children huddled at their feet. Hethrir stood above them, his arms extended. The wide sleeves of his white robe spread like wings, the edges shining with silver light. Tigris hurriedly swallowed the last crumbs of Anakin's gift and wiped his mouth on his sleeve and urged Anakin to sit up straight. Instead, Anakin burrowed against his side.

"Anakin, go to sleep," he said.

"Come with me," Lord Hethrir said. He descended from the podium and strode down the aisle, looking neither right nor left, paying no attention whatever to whether anyone was following him.

For, of course, they did follow him. Two of his Proctors

ran before him to open the door, while his guests spilled into the aisle behind him and followed him out of the lodge and trooped down the path. They pulled the sleepy slave children along with them.

"Don't sleep yet, little brother," Tigris whispered. "Come on, we have to go." He gathered the child into his arms and stood up. Now that the excitement of Lord Hethrir's speech was fading, Tigris felt as tired as Anakin.

"Hey, nursemaid!" One of the Proctors pointed at Tigris, jeering. "You'll get left behind!"

The Proctors followed the crowd, laughing, letting the door slam shut behind them. Tigris had to balance Anakin on his hip and wrestle the door open wide enough to slip through. The wolf-creature trotted after him, dragging its chain.

Clenching his teeth, Tigris held his head high.

Leia, Rillao, Chewbacca, Jaina, Jacen, and Artoo-Detoo rode Crseih's landing field tractor to the station.

What a raiding party we make! Leia thought. *A raiding party disguised as a family outing.*

She looked for the *Millennium Falcon,* but could not see it beneath the multitude of irregularly shaped radiation shields.

I could ask after it, she thought, *but I don't want to give myself away.*

"Does the landing field have a registry of ships?" she asked the driver.

"Such a list will be stored."

"How can I look at it?"

"You will not."

"Why not?"

"The company will protect its information."

Jaina snuggled against Leia, clutching her multitool in one hand and a smart camping blanket from *Alderaan* in the other. She said the camping blanket was for Anakin when they rescued him. But Anakin did not have the habit of sleeping with a camping blanket or carrying one around. Jaina had, when she was younger, but her blanket was back home on

Coruscant. When Winter asked if she wanted to bring it on the tour, Jaina had said she was not a baby any longer and did not need a blanket except for camping, and besides, maybe it was lonely for the other camping blankets.

Leia had no intention of teasing her daughter about carrying the cuddly blanket.

Leia's comfort was the touch of her children, and the hope that all three would be safe in a short time.

Jacen petted the little four-winged bat, which peeked out from beneath his shirt. The bat made Leia nervous, mildly venomous as it was. If it bit Jacen, he would have a terrible itch. But if it had been going to bite him, it probably would have done so long since. Leia had learned to regard Jacen's explorations with a certain Jedi-like calm that drew very little from Luke's lessons in meditation. She was working on the same reaction to Jaina's habit of dismantling household machines.

Leia was traveling incognito, as Lelila, though this time without abandoning her real identity in the personality of the bounty hunter. She doubted her position as Chief of State of the New Republic would provide her much esteem on Crseih. Her hair swirled wild and long and free.

Rillao carried herself so proudly, she looked so regal in the emerald tunic, that it was possible to overlook how rumpled the tunic, and how tired and drawn Rillao was. The tunic covered most of her scars.

Chewbacca still limped; a bandage wrapped his leg. But he had bathed, and combed his brindled fur. The new silver and black streaks curved into smooth patterns. He was the most presentable of the biological members of the party.

Jaina and Jacen were clean and well dressed. They no longer wolfed down every meal and snack. But an aura of intensity and distress possessed them both.

Among them all, only Artoo-Detoo looked and acted exactly as Leia expected him to.

Jaina pulled at Leia's sleeve.

"Mama!" she whispered, excited. "That's one of the ships!" She pointed across the landing field toward a shiny gold spacecraft beneath a custom-made radiation shield.

"Which ships, sweetheart?"

"The ships that came to the worldcraft—right before Hethrir took Lusa away!"

Leia and Rillao looked at each other. Leia saw hope in Rillao's eyes, and felt hope in her own heart.

"We have to go rescue Lusa, Mama!"

Could it be this easy? Leia wondered. But . . . if Anakin is in that ship, why can't I tell?

"Driver," she said, "we would like to visit that ship." She gestured toward the gold spacecraft.

"You will pay more," the arthropoid driver said.

Chewbacca growled. Leia patted his arm gently.

"That's acceptable," she said to the driver.

No one in the ship replied to the driver's signal. The crawler pressed its entry tunnel up against the ship's gold surface. From a distance, the gold ship appeared featureless. Close up, Leia could see its many gilded ports, peering mysteriously at her.

"Be careful, Mama!" Jacen said. "Mean people took Lusa!" Jaina whispered.

Leia knocked on the outer shell of the spaceship. Her heart sounded just as loud, beating with anticipation and fear.

Nothing happened. Leia waited, then knocked, louder, on one of the ports. She cupped her hands around her face and tried to peer inside, but the gilding was so strong that she might be imagining the shadows inside. She knocked a third time.

The seamless gold surface parted irregularly, softly.

"Patience, gentle, patience! What do you want?"

"I'm—"

It would be so easy, Leia thought, if I knew Anakin and the other stolen children were in there. But if they were—I'd know it. Wouldn't I? It would have been so much easier in the old days, when we *knew* . . .

"We are looking for a child," Rillao said.

"That's right," Leia said, following Rillao's direct approach, the same approach she had used to the Indexer.

"Human?" the voice said. "You *are* . . . human?" A hairy protuberance with a starburst of fleshy tendrils pressed through the opening and wriggled, sensing her. "Or do you prefer transspecies?"

"We're looking for Lusa!" Jaina said. "She has four feet, not two! She's red-gold, with white spots, and she has *horns*. Horns!"

The furry starburst inclined downward and inspected Jaina.

Jacen pulled at Leia's sleeve. "Mama," he whispered, "Anakin isn't in the gold ship."

"He—he isn't? But Jaina said . . ."

Jacen shook his head gravely. Leia thought back over what Jaina had said, and Jacen was right. Jaina had never said her friend Lusa and Anakin were together. The Proctor she had questioned had let her think Anakin might be on Crseih Station. But he had not said it was certain.

If I cannot find my little one, she thought, I'll go back to the worldcraft and—

"I mean," Jacen said, "I don't *think* he's there." He frowned. "Everything's so *weird*." He looked up at her, trusting and hopeful. "Can't *you* tell where he is?"

"Is Lusa here?" Jaina asked the wriggling starburst.

"I cannot say, young gentle. You must speak to my mistress, Lady Ucce."

Leia stroked Jacen's hair. The force of her disappointment shook her to her core.

"Where is Lady Ucce?" Leia asked.

"You may inquire after her at Crater Lodge."

The gold skin of the spaceship healed over smoothly. Leia knocked again, then slapped her hand angrily against the ship's skin.

But no one answered her.

Chapter

12

Leia's raiders entered the lobby of Crater Lodge like a party of vacation tourists. They stood alone among the pools and streams and black flagstones. A repair droid buzzed and whined over a long ragged scrape that marred one of the tiles. The droid ignored them.

Jaina and Jacen stared around, curious. The four-winged bat clambered out of Jacen's shirt and flitted off into the dimness.

"Hello!" Rillao called.

"You are rather late." A waterspout appeared above one of the still pools, rippling its surface. "You will have to hurry."

"Are you speaking to me?" Rillao asked.

"Yes—are you not a member of the Lord's retreat?"

Rillao barely hesitated. "I am," she said.

"May I register your name?"

"If you know the Lord," Rillao said, "you should know better than to ask *my* name."

Leia did not need Jedi abilities to feel the tension emanating from Rillao. Her abilities had taken leave of her, as far as

she could tell, leaving behind them nothing but a dull headache. She wondered if Rillao was having the same disori-
enting experience.

"Your pardon," the waterspout said.

"Granted. The Lord has arrived?"

"Arrived, and departed with his followers. But if you
hurry you may catch them."

"I shall need a guide."

"You will not."

Rillao gave the waterspout a quizzical look. The waterspout spun peacefully.

"You need only ask. For Waru."

"Very well."

"I will see that your servants are taken care of."

"They travel with me," Rillao said.

"Ah." The waterspout shivered, then steadied.

The Codru-bat swooped over the water, dove, splashed,
and flapped upward again, a tiny fish caught in its claws. It
hovered, snacking on the tasty morsel.

"This is *not* the dining room!" The waterspout's tone
sharpened with anger and disbelief. "Those creatures are val-
uable—they are expensive! They are part of the decor!"

Chewbacca snorted.

"I'm sorry!" Jacen said. He held up his hand and the bat
nestled into his palm. "He was hungry."

"Put the fish on our account," Rillao said. "Let's go."

Outside, Rillao asked the first person she encountered
where to find Waru.

"This path. That airlink. You will see." The being blinked
a circle of wide eyes. "But revered Waru is resting. He has
asked for peace and time."

"I see," Rillao said. "Don't worry. We'll just look."

She strode down the path. Leia and Chewbacca and the
children followed.

They had left the park dome before Leia noticed that
Artoo-Detoo was not accompanying them through the airlink.

Where did he go? she wondered.

She could not turn back to look for him now.

*   *   *

The ground rose beneath Han's feet. He toiled up the hill. He was getting no help at all from Luke. But even exhausted and overburdened as he was, he was less out of breath than he would have been if he had tried this hike when he first arrived on Crseih Station.

"Let me go, Han," Luke said. "Please. Let me go. I have to see Waru!"

Han dragged him behind a boulder, off the path, and dropped him on the ground. Luke huddled in the dust, his head down, digging his fingers into the dirt.

"What the *hell* do you mean," Han said roughly, "asking that—that *thing* to heal you? After what I saw it do? And *you* aren't even *sick!*"

"I am! Something's happening to me, Han, something terrible. Can't you *see*—?"

"I see you're behaving like a jerk," Han said. "Why'd you tell Waru who you are?"

"Han . . . I'm losing my abilities. My connection to the Force. I can't maintain my disguise. People started recognizing me. When we talked about Xaverri—I couldn't know if you were telling me the truth! I feel like I'm deaf and blind, like my heart's been ripped out of my body." He ran his hands through his hair, pushing it into complete disarray. "I don't know what to do!"

"Don't give yourself to Waru!" Han said. "You don't even know what's wrong. Maybe somebody put lizards in your bed—"

"There aren't any ysalamiri here," Luke said.

"—or maybe your lightsaber has blown a fuse—"

"It doesn't *have* any fuses—"

"—or maybe it's something in the water! Or the air. Or the light!" Han wiped his sleeve across his forehead. The material of his shirt came away soaked with sweat.

He sat down in the narrow shadow of a massive boulder.

Luke started to object again, then subsided. He sat cross-legged, thoughtfully, resting his elbows on his knees. He ducked his head and combed his fingers through his hair and pulled his hood up to shade his face.

"We've had plenty of vacation," Han said. "Luke, this isn't the old days. We don't have to solve every problem and win every fight on our own. If you're sick, we'll go back to Coruscant and get you well again."

And figure out what to do about Waru from a safe distance, Han thought. This isn't like the old days at all. In the old days, I always knew who the enemy was, and I only had one response. Now . . . everything's more complicated.

"I want to get out of here," Han said. "This place gives me the creeps."

"But the Jedi—" Luke said. "Waru—"

"There aren't any lost Jedi here," Han said gently. "It was all Xaverri's reports, and her reports are all about Waru. Not Jedi. *Waru.*"

Luke hesitated. "Yeah." His voice sounded sad, and confused.

"Let's go collect Threepio and Xaverri and blast off out of here."

"Xaverri?" An edge of anger replaced the confusion in Luke's voice.

"Yeah—you don't expect me to leave her here, if I can get her to leave. Do you?"

"What do you need *her* for?"

"What's got into you?" Incensed, Han grabbed Luke's robe and pulled him to his feet.

Glaring furiously, Luke pulled away and flung up his hand, palm outward. Han felt the touch of the Force in the center of his chest. He jumped backward, thinking, I can't move fast enough—I'm dead!

The touch vanished and Luke crumpled to the ground. Han hurried to his side and knelt beside him.

"I'm sorry," Luke said. "I'm sorry, I don't know—"

"I loved Xaverri," Han said. "I *loved* her. I won't deny it. I can't. If she hadn't left me—I don't know. It doesn't matter, Luke. Can't you see that? I promise you, brother—what Xaverri and I were to each other years ago has nothing to do with what Leia and I are to each other now."

Luke broke his own gaze, looking away, looking down. "I'm sorry," he said. "I had no cause to say what I said to you. To refuse to listen to you. It's just that yesterday—"

"I saw a child die!" Han shouted. "And it was like I could see my own kids in that thing's power!"

"You needed somebody to talk to," Luke said. "I understand that. But I could have—"

"You *can't* understand how I felt." Han doubted he could make Luke understand what he was trying to tell him. "I'm sorry, Luke, but you couldn't. Xaverri could. Her children— the Empire murdered them." Han jumped to his feet and strode away a few steps, fighting to control himself. "We've got to get out of here."

Luke remained silent.

Han returned to him and helped him to his feet. His friend did not resist him.

"Where's Threepio?" Han asked.

Luke shrugged. He was shaking. Han looked at him with concern, thinking, He really *is* sick. I've got to get him away from here.

"It beats the hell out of me where he could have gone," Han said. "He isn't at the lodge." He glanced toward the secret path, not looking forward to the trek through the mutant forest.

Xaverri ducked out of the concealed entrance. She walked toward him.

"Xaverri!"

She raised one hand to acknowledge his greeting. Her expression remained neutral. He had almost forgotten the way their last conversation ended.

Helping Luke along, Han went to meet her. When he stepped out of the shade, the light hit him like a wave of hot water. He stopped before her, hoping she would take his hand. She simply gazed at him, in silence.

"We're leaving," he said. "You're right about Waru. About the danger. We're taking the information back with us. To decide what to do."

"I am glad to hear it," she said in a neutral tone.

I'll find the Ithorian family, Han thought. They're New Republic citizens—I'll try to persuade them to press charges in a New Republic court. Then I can have Waru arrested, and tried—even if the Ithorian family won't agree, there must be some victim of this monster who's come out of its spell. . . .

"Come with us."

Her lips twitched in a quick smile.

"Xaverri, in the center of government? The center of law? I could never fit there, Solo. I could never survive."

Han grinned. "You might be surprised."

"Perhaps. But I think I will not risk it." She glanced at Luke, who stood gazing at the ground with his hood pulled far forward.

"Skywalker," Xaverri said. "Why are you so melancholy?"

He raised his head, but the starlight shone in his eyes. He flinched and ducked down again. Xaverri frowned and leaned against a rock spur edging the trail. She gazed at Waru's retreat.

At the far end of the dome, a group of people entered from the main connecting path. They strode toward Waru's compound. First came a marching phalanx of youths in blue uniforms. Their chests shone with medals, their shoulders with bright epaulets. They led the way for a tall man in a shimmering white robe. Older youths in long white vests flanked the tall man. A more unruly crowd of richly dressed people brought up the rear.

Han leaned on the rock beside her to watch.

The blue-uniformed cadre stood guard on either side of the filigreed archway. The white-robed man walked alone into Waru's compound.

Xaverri's whole body tensed. Han glanced at her.

"What—?"

"I know him," she whispered. "It is the Procurator of Justice."

Han snapped around, following Xaverri's gaze. The other followers were entering the compound.

Then Han saw, at the back of the crowd, a human youth, or one of the smaller species of sentient beings. He held the hand of an even smaller person, a child by the way he walked. They vanished between the two lines of guards.

Han froze.

"Luke," he said.

Beside him, Xaverri turned toward him, startled by the tone of his voice.

Han's heart crashed against his ribs. "Xaverri . . ."

"What's wrong, Solo?"

"That's Anakin," he whispered.

He vaulted over the rock and onto the steep slope. Ignoring the path, ignoring the prickly mutant plants that ripped at his clothes, he stumbled and slid down the hillside. Pebbles rolled and clattered, avalanching beside and around him, making so much noise, raising so much dust, that he had no idea if Luke or Xaverri were following him.

Anakin vanished into Waru's retreat.

For a moment, just a moment, Leia could imagine she was taking a quiet walk with Jaina and Jacen. They held her hands, trusting. Then the emptiness of Anakin's loss drained her again, leaving a cold and hollow spot in her heart.

"Can you catch any hint of Tigris?" Leia asked. "If Anakin is there . . ." She sought desperately for a sense of her child. She felt as if she were shouting as loud as she could, in a canyon so large she could not even hear the echoes. "If they're here—then what?"

I've spent years bringing back the rule of law, Leia thought. Putting the rule of justice in place of the rule of terror. But there is no law here. No justice.

"I'm not completely without resources," Rillao said. She strode onward without looking at Leia.

"But we aren't armed. And you said . . . you told me . . ." Leia hesitated, reluctant to bring up a subject that caused Rillao pain. "Wait, please." Jaina and Jacen could not keep up, so Leia picked up Jacen and Chewbacca carried Jaina.

"I told you he overcame me, five years ago. Yes."

"All his guards are with him. And he must be armed!"

"He is. With his lightsaber . . . and mine."

"Then—"

"Lelila, you must have noticed! It's as your boy said." She glanced at Jacen, and brushed his tangled curls from his forehead. "Everything is *weird* here."

Leia nodded.

"The Force is disturbed, disarranged. I open myself to it, and it will not touch me. I cannot heal—so Hethrir cannot destroy. Our worlds have turned to chaos."

They exited the airlink and came out at the top of a long slow slope, above a graceful building.

"I could not use my lightsaber if I had it," Rillao said. "But neither can Hethrir."

Leia frowned, confused. "Why not?"

"Because Hethrir's lightsaber can only be empowered by the Force," Rillao said. "Mine is built to the same design."

They walked through an airlink and came upon a peaceful vista, a wide valley spreading below them.

Rillao stood on the hill above a graceful building surrounded by archways and gardens. One by one, youths in pale blue uniforms passed through one of the arches, crossed a courtyard, and vanished into the building.

"We have found him," Rillao said softly.

"His guards, anyway," Leia said. "They'd be easier to recognize with mud on their uniforms."

Leia put Jacen down and turned to Chewbacca. He growled in refusal before she even spoke.

"It's important!" Leia said. "I expected Artoo to stay with the children, but he's disappeared! Please, Chewie! Someone's got to keep watch out here. In case . . . in case we fail."

Jacen clutched Leia's leg.

"Mama, don't go away again!"

She knelt beside him. "I have to, sweetheart. I have to go get Anakin. I'll be back soon." She steadied her voice. "I promise."

Chewbacca sat on his heels, hugging Jaina in one arm, and gathered Jacen to him.

"Hurry, Lelila," Rillao said as Leia rose. Below them, the last of Hethrir's Proctors disappeared inside Waru's building.

Rillao and Leia hurried down the hillside path.

Leia heard a scattering of gravel, the scuff of boots on steep ground. She turned.

Partway around the dome, Han plunged down the slope, heedless of the trail. Luke and another person followed close behind.

"Han!"

Leia ran to meet him. She pushed her hair back from her face; it flew behind her in the wind of her speed. Han slid to a stop in a small avalanche of gravel and dust. Astonished, he enfolded her in his arms.

"Leia—what—?" He touched her hair, her painted eyebrow, her cheek.

"I found Jaina and Jacen," she said. "They're all right." She pointed up the hill, where Chewbacca stood with the twins, watching unhappily but stoically. "But Anakin—we think Hethrir brought him here!"

"Anakin *is* here," Luke said. He glanced at Rillao, then looked at her more closely. She met his gaze coolly.

"He's inside," Han said. "We saw him— What *happened*?"

Leia grabbed his hand and ran toward Waru's building.

The crowd swept Tigris into its excitement. Hethrir's guests gathered around the stage, below the great gold altar of Waru's form. Their lord faced it; the Proctors fanned out on either side of the entryway, standing along the back wall, watching and alert.

"Hello, Ally Hethrir."

Tigris surreptitiously watched the new Proctor, amused by his surprise: The altar spoke! It moved! Its gold scales rippled and surged.

In Tigris's arms, Anakin watched, wide-eyed and silent.

"Hello, Ally Waru."

"What have you brought me, my friend?" the golden being asked. Its form changed and expanded. Scarlet flesh swelled between the shining scales.

"What you required," Lord Hethrir said. "I will give you a gift. And you will keep your promise to me. You will open me to the limits of the Force."

"What have you brought me?" the being asked again, its voice soft and wondering. "I have waited a long time. I am tired. I am lonely."

Hethrir's guests pressed forward, whispering, "My lord, take mine, take mine."

The children at their sides drew back fearfully, but the

guests held them tight. One of the guests struggled to keep the red-gold centaur child from scrambling away and fleeing. The child's hooves clattered and scrabbled on the smooth stone floor.

Lord Hethrir gazed over their heads. He gestured to Tigris.

Tigris edged through the crowd. At first they resisted him —he was only Tigris, in his grubby robe, nursemaid, figure of ridicule. He wished Anakin's ugly pet would lead the way, instead of tagging along at his heels. Lord Hethrir's followers surely would move aside for those dripping fangs.

Then Lord Hethrir gestured again, and the followers noticed that he wanted Tigris.

They parted, making a path for Tigris and Anakin.

They knelt on the stone floor. Tigris was thrilled.

If only Lord Hethrir would purify *me*, Tigris thought. I know I could serve him better. I could truly aid the cause of the Empire Reborn.

He stopped before Lord Hethrir, his vision blurry with tears of hope and desire.

"Give the child Anakin to me," Hethrir said. "I will present him."

Anakin clutched at Tigris's neck, hiding his face. Tigris took a moment to soothe him.

"Do not hesitate when I give you an order," Hethrir said softly, and for the first time in all the years Tigris had known his lord, and honored him, he heard fury in his voice.

Anakin held tight.

"Let go, Anakin." He tried to disentangle the little boy's hands from his neck, from his striped hair. "This will be wonderful, I promise you. You're such a lucky little boy."

Anakin trembled, trying to exert his unschooled abilities. But even his light had faded. Lord Hethrir must have him completely in his power. Tigris managed to pry Anakin's hands loose.

Tigris wished the Lord's control extended to making Anakin do what he was told.

Anakin looked into Tigris's face, and put one hand on Tigris's cheek. "Tigis crying," he said.

Embarrassed, Tigris ducked his head, trying to wipe his face on the sleeve of his robe. But with Anakin in his arms, it was too awkward. He put Anakin down and wiped away the humiliating tears. Then, holding Anakin's hand, he took the little boy to Hethrir.

"No, Tigis," Anakin said. "No. Please?"

Hethrir took Anakin's hand and led him toward Waru. Anakin hung back, straining toward Tigris with his free hand. Anakin's creature tried to follow, but Tigris grabbed it by the collar and held it back. It strained forward, whining softly.

All the followers of Hethrir watched, envious that Anakin was to be purified, while the children they had brought were overlooked.

Anakin plopped to the floor, sitting down hard, refusing to move.

"Get up, child," Hethrir said. "Approach your fate with honor." Lord Hethrir dragged him a little way.

Anakin kicked, and screamed, and his face turned scarlet. Hethrir scowled, picked him up, held his feet from kicking, and approached Waru.

Lord Hethrir placed Anakin, still screaming, on the gold scales of Waru's base.

"I have brought you what you wished," Lord Hethrir said. "The most powerful child."

He paused.

"I have brought you the grandchild of Darth Vader."

Tigris watched, his feelings a strange mixture of jealousy, regret, dread, and horror. No wonder this gathering differed from all the others. No wonder Lord Hethrir did not make Anakin go through the training required of helpers, and Proctors, and Empire Youth. Anakin would ascend in one step to the highest level.

Or he would die in the purification ritual.

Behind Tigris, the terrified centaur child reared and screamed and tried to escape. Her hooves slipped and scraped on the stone.

The fanged creature pulled forward till its collar slipped from Tigris's grip. It ran after Anakin, howling piteously.

And Tigris thought: None of Hethrir's guests brought any of their own children.

None of the children has any choice. It isn't fair! I would choose—

Waru rippled its scales. They shimmered, liquefying.

Anakin sank into the molten gold, shrieking in terror.

"Tigis! Tigis!" The little boy stretched his arms toward Tigris.

I would choose to give myself to Waru, Tigris thought. I don't care about the danger! But Anakin *didn't* choose.

Tigris darted forward, grabbed Anakin, snatched him from the altar of Waru's body, and turned to run.

"What are you doing?" Hethrir cried.

Waru rose, its body elongating enormously, scarlet ichor flowing from its flesh. The being roared, a cry of protest, and anger, and desperation.

The roaring shriek of the strange gold being overwhelmed Leia's cry when she saw Anakin. A youth pulled her little son away from the writhing gold creature. The youth stumbled backward, trying to flee. Mr. Iyon's wyrwulf crouched at the foot of the altar, growling.

Leia ran toward the youth, toward Anakin. Han was right behind her.

Leia ran through the crowd, through the ragged path the people had left clear when they knelt. Some were struggling to their feet. All the adults were human, but the children with them were of many other species.

Leia and Han reached the youth who had rescued Anakin.

"Papa! Mama!" Anakin cried. His face was streaked with tears, flushed with anger and terror. The youth—This must be Tigris, Leia thought, oh, my, he looks like Rillao!—was crying, too.

Anakin struggled from Tigris's grasp. He leaped and fell into Leia's arms. She hugged him with desperate gratitude. She held him against her, kissing his sticky face. Han touched Anakin's hair, gently, with wonder.

"It's all right now, sweetheart," Leia said. "I'm here, Papa's here—"

The golden being stretched itself toward them. Leia had never seen anything like it. She backed away, bumping into Han. He, too, backed away, holding Leia and Anakin.

Anakin scrambled over Leia's shoulder and flung his arms around his father's neck. Han held him gently, radiant with relief and joy.

A white-robed man—Hethrir, Leia thought—grabbed Tigris by the collar and shook him.

"You fool! Wretched, worthless fool!"

"Waru!" Luke ran past them all, passing Tigris, leaping onto the altar.

"Luke, no!"

He's empty-handed! Leia thought. He's attacking—defending—without even his lightsaber!

"Stop!" Hethrir cried.

Luke leaped onto the dais, onto the border of gold scales.

"Waru!" Luke said.

"What do you want, Skywalker?" Waru said, its voice rumbling. "I am in pain, I have no gifts to give my followers."

Hethrir stared at Luke in confusion and anger. Then his expression changed to astonishment and recognition.

"Skywalker!" Hethrir said. "Waru, take *him*. Luke Skywalker is a trained Jedi. He is Vader's *son*!"

The great gold being loomed. Luke faced it, completely open, his arms spread wide. His boots sank into the liquefying gold. The gold being's form widened. It formed a concave surface, with great rough wings curving forward to surround Leia's brother. Luke's reflection in the scales was distorted, inverted, misshapen.

"Yes," Luke whispered. "Take me."

The being roared again, but its voice was softer, a great sigh of satisfaction.

"Luke!" Leia cried.

Before she could react, the gold wings collapsed, falling onto Luke, inundating him. The gold scales liquefied, surging forward like waves, pulling back like the tide.

Luke disappeared.

"No!" Leia cried, horrified. This was all too much like seeing Han trapped in the carbon-freeze—

Anakin was safe in Han's arms. Han stared at Waru, the joy in his face turning to grief.

Leia brushed her fingers quickly against his cheek. Han looked down at her.

Leia turned toward the roiling, clenching mass of molten gold that imprisoned Luke.

She ran after her brother.

Leia dived beneath the surface of the golden sphere.

Leia swam in golden light, her hair fanning all around her. At a great distance, she saw Luke, straining and twisting between great rippling shields of solidified gold. She plunged toward him. He wrestled futilely. She remembered his time in the regeneration tank, where he slept, and dreamed nightmares, and struggled to escape.

Leia's breath burned in her lungs. She was afraid to breathe, afraid of drowning in the thick and honey-colored light. But she had no choice. She gasped, and the warm thick radiance poured oxygen into her lungs. She exhaled, and breathed again. It was hard work, but she was not drowning.

The gold shields twisted and danced between Leia and Luke. She tried to push one aside, but it turned edge-on to her and slashed at her like a blade. Her sleeve ripped. Leia tumbled backward, then kicked upward, outward—she could hardly perceive gravity in the strange environment—and avoided one of the shields. Another whirled toward her. She met it with her boots. She kicked it. It shattered. Its fragments shattered again, and disintegrated into fine glittering gold dust, and disappeared.

She slid between two other shining plates, and reached Luke's side.

"We can't stay here, Chewie!" Jaina cried.

"Mama's down there, and Papa too, and Uncle Luke," Jacen said.

"We have to help them." Something was wrong, she knew it. But she could not tell what. Her head hurt so much.

Chewbacca's growl turned to a cry. He was as upset about being left out here, as anxious to go inside and help, as Jaina and Jacen. He had already moved halfway down the hill, as Jaina and Jacen pulled at his hands, but there he stopped.

Mama left him here to protect us, Jaina thought. To protect the children.

The dome reverberated with a mournful howl.

"Chewie! That's Mr. Chamberlain's wyrwulf!"

He glared down the slope, whuffling with indecision.

Another child screamed.

"It's Lusa!" she cried. "Oh, Chewie, please—!" She pounded at his leg, desperate, trying to make him go down the hill, trying to make him let her down. He glanced down at her. She stopped. She saw that she had hurt him, and she was horrified at herself for hitting him. "I'm sorry! I'm so sorry!" She patted his fur, trying to straighten it around the bandage. "But it's Lusa, they're cutting off her horns, please, we've got to hurry!"

She pulled out of his grasp and ran.

Chewbacca roared. He grabbed Jaina and stopped her. He lifted her, and Jacen, onto his shoulders, and he loped down the hill with amazing speed.

Chewbacca crossed beneath arches and entered the building. He had to push his way into the theater past a line of Hethrir's Proctors, who barred the way of a crowd of people fighting to get out. The people were in fancy robes and jewelry. They all shoved and shouted, in a panic. Chewbacca pushed straight through them. Jaina was afraid of the Proctors. But they could not even turn on their lightsabers! Jaina could not use her abilities, either. But Chewbacca was not afraid of them at all. He walked through their line and hardly even slowed down.

Everyone was shouting and screaming and running around. All the children Hethrir had sent away were right here, crying in fear. Even though they had no place to run, they were all trying to run away.

Except Lusa. She was running, but she was not running away. She ran right up to one of the Proctors and turned her back on him and kicked him so hard with her back feet, with her cloven hooves, that he fell down. He lay on the floor, groaning. Mr. Chamberlain's wyrwulf followed, watching curiously.

Jaina laughed with delight. "Lusa!"

The noise was so loud in the theater that Jaina did not know if Lusa could hear her. Jaina could hardly hear herself.

Chewbacca never paused. He strode to the front of the theater, where Papa stood holding Anakin. They were both safe, and both of them were crying.

"Anakin!" Jaina shouted with joy. "Papa!" She reached down from Chewbacca's shoulder to touch her father, to make sure he was real. "Don't cry! You're not dead, I *knew all along* you weren't dead! Where's Mama? Did you see Mama? Where's Uncle Luke?"

Nearby, Tigris looked confused and hurt and unhappy. The Firrerreo stood between him and Hethrir.

She launched herself at Hethrir. She grabbed him by the throat and knocked him down.

Papa put Anakin into Chewbacca's arms.

"Take care of the kids," he said.

Jaina had never heard Papa's voice sound like that before. He looked at Jaina, and at Jacen, just a quick look that did not even last a second.

"I love you," he said. "I'll always love you."

He turned around and ran away and leaped up at a huge quivering gold sphere.

He disappeared beneath its surface.

"Papa!" Anakin buried his face against Chewbacca's fur and bawled.

It was so beautiful—! Jaina wondered if Papa would come out of the sphere all covered with gold like Threepio.

Lusa ran up beside Chewbacca. "Jaina! Isn't this fun? It's fun to kick Proctors."

"I'm so glad to see you! They didn't cut off your horns!"

"No—but they were going to feed me to that monster, that monster can eat people."

"F-feed—?" Jaina whispered. She stared at the gold sphere where Papa had disappeared, and she was afraid she knew what had happened to her mama and Uncle Luke.

*   *   *

Tigris fell back against the dais. Waru's transformation roiled and shook above him. Shock paralyzed him. He had not ever expected to see his mother again. Hethrir had told him she was dead. She had been executed for betraying the Empire. For refusing to support the Empire Reborn. And Tigris had been glad.

Before him, she fought Hethrir bitterly.

He should help his lord. But he could not move.

Hethrir snatched his lightsaber from beneath his robe. Instead of turning itself on at his command, it reacted with an electronic screech and an assault of sparks and ozone. Hethrir cursed and dropped it. It spun across the floor and crashed into the wall. It shattered, melting the stone beneath it.

Rillao clawed at Hethrir's face. The second, smaller lightsaber fell from his belt. Rillao leaped away from Hethrir. They faced each other, panting, scraped, bleeding. Rillao feinted, and when Hethrir leaped to the attack, she ducked away from him and grabbed the fallen lightsaber.

She did not engage it. She slipped it beneath her robe. In her moment of inattention, Hethrir leaped onto her back. She staggered. He choked her with his arm, and when her knees trembled, Hethrir bared his sharp teeth. He would bite her spine, snap it, paralyze or kill her—

"No!" Tigris shouted. He grabbed Hethrir's robe and pulled him back. The Lord's teeth snapped together, biting air, gashing his own lip. Rillao escaped his grasp and fell forward, panting.

"Foolish boy! Foolish! She's a traitor!" Blood gushed down his chin.

"Please don't kill my mother, my lord."

Hethrir snorted in disgust. "She's a traitor! She betrayed the Empire—she betrayed you!"

Rillao struggled to her feet. "You are the traitor," she said.

Tigris glared at her, furious. "How *dare* you say that to Lord Hethrir!"

She looked at Tigris sadly, then faced Hethrir again. "You could not tell him, could you, Hethrir?"

"Do not speak my name!" he said.

To Tigris, she said, "He is a traitor to you."

Tigris shook his head, confused.

"Hethrir is your father."

Han swam toward Leia and Luke, flailing through the thick light. He swam forever, until his muscles ached.

Waru was far larger inside than outside. The creature's circulation whirlpooled around a central point of darkness. It looked like the black hole and its accretion disk.

Han wondered, Could the black hole open a portal to another universe? Is that where Waru came from?

Nothing could escape the black hole's gravity . . . but the singularity distorted time and space around it—

None of that mattered. All that mattered was getting to Leia, to Luke. They swam back to back, fending off creatures that looked now like knife blades, now like streamlined predators with hides of molten gold. Han plowed through the ring of attackers, succeeding in his blind rush because Waru's predators were so intent on the prey at the center of their circle.

"Han—!" Leia's warm fingers wrapped around his. He melded into a circle with his love and his friend. They swam, back to back, kicking, twisting, fighting.

The whirlpool swept them around and pulled them inward, toward the point of utter darkness.

"Swim!" Han yelled. He knew—How do you know? he asked himself, and answered, I don't know, I only know what I know—that if they touched the darkness, they were doomed forever.

He thought he could hear the ghosts of the people Waru had killed.

He kicked, a swimming kick. He tried to propel himself and Leia and Luke away from the center, out of the maelstrom, to Waru's molten skin. Leia joined his efforts.

But Luke floated between them, strangely quiescent, holding them back.

"Give yourself to me, Skywalker," Waru said. "I'll show you—I'll open you to the greatest power you can imagine."

Luke slipped away, diving toward Waru's trap.

* * *

"It's lying!" Leia cried. She felt her brother falling. He drew her with him, *tempted* her with him.

He slipped away from her. She swam after him. The whirlpool drew them deeper.

"It's the truth," Waru said. "*I* am truth."

The siren song of Waru's voice soothed Leia's fears. Her fingers slipped from Han's grip, and when she tried to find him again, the golden light blinded her.

The whirlpool held her hand.

Chapter

13

Jaina rode Chewbacca's shoulder, with Jacen beside her. Chewie hugged Anakin close against his chest with one arm. With his free hand, the Wookiee grabbed one of the Proctors by the scruff of his neck and shook him. The Proctor grabbed his lightsaber but Jaina was not even afraid of it. She knew it would explode as soon as he tried to turn it on. He did, and it flashed sparks and burned his hand and fell to the floor in pieces. Jaina was glad.

Chewbacca shook him again.

"I yield!" the Proctor screamed. "Please, stop!" Chewbacca shook him again and let him fall. The Proctor cowered on the floor.

All the children were running around, shouting and screaming, holding on to the Proctors' legs, sometimes biting them, tripping them and running away. Lusa and Mr. Chamberlain's wyrwulf played with them together. Lusa rushed up and turned to kick, while the wyrwulf crouched behind the knees of the Proctor. The Proctor would step back and fall over the wyrwulf. Lusa and the wyrwulf laughed and howled and ran away.

If the Proctor did not step back, Lusa kicked him. Sometimes she kicked even when she did not really have to.

The Proctors had bullied some of the guests into a corner of the theater. Jaina did not know why they were trying to keep the guests inside. Maybe Hethrir wanted to feed them to the gold monster. A lot of the guests had escaped, leaving the children behind.

The Proctors could have escaped if they had let all the guests run away. They might even have won the fight. There were a lot more of them than of Jaina's friends. But without the use of their lightsabers, and without Hethrir to tell them what to do, they were lost.

Chewbacca picked up another Proctor and shook him and dropped him on the floor. When he tried to stand, Chewie picked him up and shook him again and held him higher and dropped him again. He stayed where Chewie put him.

The person who had come down the hill with Papa and Uncle Luke let several of the Proctors rush her, then spun and ducked out of their way. When the Proctors ran into each other, she grabbed their arms and twisted them and made the Proctors fall down. She ripped their sleeves to the elbows and tied their arms together behind their backs. She ripped their pants halfway up their legs, and tied their knees together.

Chewbacca and Papa's friend advanced on the last two Proctors. The Proctors brandished the handles of their useless lightsabers. Jaina was glad the Proctors could not turn their lightsabers on in this strange place. But she was sorry too, because it meant *she* could not do anything to help.

I wish I had four legs and hooves, she thought. Like Lusa! Or big fangs like Mr. Chamberlain's wyrwulf!

The last two Proctors dropped their lightsaber handles and fell to their knees.

As Papa's friend bent to tie them, Jaina slipped from Chewbacca's back, climbing down his fur, and ran to Lusa. She embraced her. Lusa bent down and hugged Jaina, and rubbed her forehead, and her horns, against the top of Jaina's head. Lusa's horns had broken through their velvet. Now instead of being soft red-furred knobs, Lusa's horns were transparent, as bright as diamond, cool and ridged and smooth.

"Thank you, Jaina. Thank you, thank you," Lusa whispered.

Jaina started to cry.

A few of the guests tried to sneak out of their corner. Chewbacca snarled at them. They cowered away from him.

Unafraid of Chewbacca's roaring, the children all clustered around him. Papa's friend joined them.

"Do you remember me?" she asked Chewbacca. "I've changed, but I'm Xaverri."

He snorted in surprise, then put one huge gentle hand on her shoulder. She patted his wrist.

"Papa," Anakin wailed. "Papa, come back!"

They all turned toward the molten sphere. Anakin stretched out his hands, yearning toward the shining surface.

There was no sign of Papa or Mama or Uncle Luke.

"We have to rescue them!" Jaina said. She ran toward the golden sphere. Lusa leaped in the air and followed.

Chewbacca roared in distress. He ran after Jaina and scooped her up. She struggled, but he hugged her and she cried against his rough fur.

"Chewie, what are we going to do?"

He faced the dais and roared.

Anakin shouted again. "Papa! Mama!"

"Uncle Luke!" Jaina and Jacen cried. "Mama! Papa!"

"Solo!" Xaverri shouted.

Lusa joined them in calling out, and the wyrwulf howled again. The other children crept around them and gathered around Chewbacca's feet, and they yelled too.

Tigris stared at Hethrir, stunned. "My father—?"

"A traitor, *and* a liar," Hethrir said. "What do you expect, from someone who would abandon her oath to the Empire? To Lord Vader. To me!"

"What of your vows to me?" Rillao asked sadly.

"You gave up any right . . ."

Tigris realized that his mother was telling the truth. Hethrir had been caught in a lie. Tigris had never before seen him at a loss for words.

"Were you so disappointed in me," Rillao asked, "that you couldn't acknowledge our son?"

"Our *son*," Hethrir said, with pure contempt, "deserved no acknowledgment. He can never fulfill my legacy. He is *ordinary*."

Tigris's face burned with humiliation.

Hethrir turned away from Rillao, from Tigris, and leaped onto the dais.

"Waru! The time has come! You have Skywalker! Keep your promise to me, Waru! Make me omnipotent!"

Tigris tried to follow him, but Rillao grabbed him and held him and stopped him.

"Let me go!"

"He isn't worth your loyalty! He isn't worth your life!"

Han struggled to keep his grip on Leia's hand, struggled to swim up out of the whirlpool.

"Swim!" Han shouted. "Please, Leia, I love you, swim!"

But she was captured by Waru's promises, by Luke's fascination. Her fingers slipped from his hand. Her beautiful hair waving around her, hiding her like a cape, she dove and descended into the golden light.

"Leia!" He dove after her, toward the cold darkness.

Leia basked in the siren song of Waru's promises. The melody distracted her from the voice calling behind her. She followed Luke toward—

"Mama, Papa, Uncle Luke!"

She hesitated. The whirlpool pulled her into a spiral. She slowed, trying to remember what those words meant. She swam a few strokes as the wordless assurances of Waru drew her deeper.

"Mama! Come back, Mama!"

She remembered the sound of Jacen's voice, her joy when he kissed her cheek, her wonder and delight as he and Jaina grew and changed and learned.

"Mama!"

She remembered the glow of Anakin's spirit.

Leia stopped, floating, spinning dizzily. The gold light opened beneath her, and pressed her down from above.

"Papa! Mama! Uncle Luke!" Chewbacca's roar pushed the children's voices through the light.

Below her, Luke hesitated in his headlong plunge. He was very close to the point of darkness. If he touched it, he could never escape. He would be destroyed.

"Luke," Leia whispered. "Luke, we have to go back."

Han appeared beside her, shining in Waru's radiance. He took her hand.

"Luke—!"

"Leave him to me," Waru said. "Leave him, and I will free you."

"No!" Leia cried. "Give him back to us, why do you want him?"

"He can help me return to my home." Waru's voice softened. "Won't you help me? You know what it is to miss your home. I can see that. I've been away so very long."

Waru's voice was so sad that Leia let herself drift closer, deeper.

"How can we help you?"

"Leia!" Han tried to draw her back. "Don't listen!"

"His power can help me open a portal—"

Luke raised his head. His eyes were empty.

Leia gasped. She barely recognized him as her brother.

She knew that if he helped Waru, he would be destroyed. She tried to reach him, tried to pull him up out of the whirlpool. He struggled against her.

The darkness opened, expanding, reaching hungrily after them, swirling at Luke's feet.

"Uncle Luke!" Jaina cried.

Luke shivered. He closed his eyes. He shook his head.

When he opened his eyes, he looked confused, but he was Luke again.

"Where—? What—?"

"Come with us!" Leia said.

Luke kicked fiercely. Leia and Han pulled him.

They escaped the night by a hairsbreadth. Holding Luke in her arms, Leia gasped with relief.

They all fled, plunging away from the pursuing night, fighting their way through Waru's illumination. The whirlpool burst into chaotic eddies and erratic spirals, knocking Leia back and forth as she fled.

She reached toward the shimmering golden surface. Her fingertips brushed it, broke it, reached through into the air.

Leia fell out onto the dais, drawing Han and Luke along with her. She lay on the stage, panting for breath. She staggered to her feet and slid off the stage, wanting only to get away from Waru's touch. Luke lay collapsed behind her. She helped Han drag him from the altar.

Jaina and Jacen and Anakin ran to her and launched themselves at her. She knelt to hug them, tears streaming down her face. Chewbacca loomed over her. Han swept Anakin into his arms, and Luke picked Jaina up. Leia stood, still hugging Jacen, and Chewbacca wrapped his arms around them all.

The children were safe.

Waru's voice filled the theater. "You did not keep your promise, Hethrir. You did not give me the child. You did not give me the Jedi. I owe you nothing. I am hungry, Hethrir, I am hungry and lonely and dying, and I want to return home."

"No—!" Hethrir cried in terror.

The golden surface expanded, quick as a snake's strike. It broke over Hethrir, surrounded him, engulfed him.

Hethrir disappeared, leaving nothing behind but a scream.

Something happened. All three children whimpered. Lusa jumped straight up in the air. Rillao flinched, and Luke moaned, and Leia felt as if a gong were ringing in her head. It was as if for an instant the Force had disappeared from the universe.

The feeling vanished, leaving Leia breathless and shaken.

Unaffected, unaware of the disturbances raging all around him and tearing at the fabric of space-time, Tigris broke free of Rillao and jumped up onto the stage after Hethrir. Rillao lunged and grabbed his ankle. She held on to him with tenacious desperation. Xaverri ran to help her.

"Let me go!" Tigris struggled. Rillao was too shaken to hold him. He broke away just as Xaverri reached for him.

Rillao cried out in despair.

Tigris flung himself against Waru's golden shell.

The gold yielded, then rebounded, flinging him away. Waru's shell rang, a great low-pitched bell. Tigris fell to the stage.

The ringing slowly faded.

The only sound was Tigris's anguished sobs.

Waru's golden shell solidified.

It began to contract.

Rillao and Xaverri drew Tigris from the stage.

"Tigris," Rillao said, "my sweet son—"

"Leave me alone!" he snarled. "Never say my name! *Never!*"

He ran a few steps, then stood, shaking, with his shoulders hunched.

"Mama?" Jaina said.

"I'm all right, sweetheart." Leia looked into Han's eyes, and smiled. She hugged Jacen, she held him with one arm and touched Luke's face with her free hand, then squeezed Chewbacca's arm, as he held all his human friends, his Honor Family, in a protecting embrace. "We're all all right. We're going home."

Jaina surveyed the theater from the vantage point of Uncle Luke's shoulder.

"All those Proctors escaped!" she said. "And the other people, too!"

Once the Proctors were tied up, the guests had fled. Xaverri had tied the Proctors with their uniforms. They had ripped the cloth, untied each other, struggled free. They had all run away. Bits of light blue uniform and the dead handles of lightsabers littered the floor.

Jaina was wrong about *all* the Proctors. One was left, the one who had just been promoted. No one had stopped to untie him, and he had not been able to free himself. He struggled, but could not rip his knotted uniform.

"We should go after them," Papa said.

"They're no threat, without Hethrir," Xaverri said. "The ones you must worry about are those Hethrir placed within the Republic." She smiled wryly. "But I suspect they will soon find themselves unemployed."

"We'll deal with them," Papa said. He sounded mad. "The guests, too, the damned slavers! They all ought to be in jail!"

"I will tell you where to find them," Xaverri said. "Soon. When I am done with them. When you complete an important task: return these children to their homes." Her smile vanished. Her voice was shaking. "These children still have homes."

"Xaverri—" Papa said.

"Good-bye, Solo." She turned to Mama. "Good-bye, Princess Leia. I'm glad to have met you."

"Good-bye," Mama said. "Thank you, Xaverri."

"Good-bye, Xaverri," Papa said.

She strode away without another word, walking up the slope of the theater. She paused long enough to cut loose the last tied-up Proctor, to fling away his lightsaber, and then she walked out of the theater without looking back.

The Proctor staggered to his feet. He looked so funny, with the arms and legs of his uniform cut off, that Jaina laughed. He glared at her, but there was nothing he could do. He glanced after his lightsaber, but he was too frightened to retrieve it. Stumbling, awkward, he fled.

On the stage, the gold sphere contracted to the size of a ball. Hethrir must be squished up inside it.

Jaina felt safe.

Leia feared for no one for the first time in too long. She worried about Rillao and Tigris, reunited, yet separated by Hethrir's lies. But she could not bear more fear.

"Let's go home." Han stared at the diminishing sphere that had been Waru. "This place gives me the creeps."

"It gives me a headache," Rillao said. "I do not like this system at all. It is . . . disconnected."

Leia went to her brother. She set Jacen on the ground and reached up for Jaina, still on Luke's shoulders.

"Come down, sweetheart," she said. "Your Uncle Luke is tired." Jaina dove into Leia's embrace and hugged her tightly, then jumped down and wrapped her arms around Luke's waist.

"You lean on me, Uncle Luke!" she said.

Luke looked gray with fatigue and pain. "Thank you, Jaina," he said. His gaze kept returning to Waru's sphere.

"What did it want from us?" Leia asked. Waru whispered to my brother, she thought, and told him—tempted him . . .

"It was stranded," Luke said. His gaze was haunted. "It could only gain energy by annihilating the Force of our universe with the anti-Force of its own."

"And Waru reached the Force . . ." Leia said, horrified.

"Yes. Through people. By *destroying* people."

"Lusa said it *eats* people," Jaina said.

"The Ithorian child," Han said.

Luke nodded. "But Waru didn't always kill its victims. Sometimes, if it was satiated, it would feed the power back. It really could heal people, or strengthen them. That's what happened to Hethrir's Proctors if they survived—if they were reborn. And that's what Hethrir wanted for himself. To have his connection to the Force strengthened and refined. It is . . . a very tempting offer." Luke shook his head as if flinging off a memory. "Hethrir had to satiate Waru before he'd risk himself. He needed someone stronger than he was, someone Waru would prefer—yet someone Hethrir could control."

"Anakin," Leia whispered. Han smoothed Anakin's dark hair, holding him protectively.

"Anakin get down!" Anakin said. Reluctantly, Han let him down. Anakin ran to Luke, and gazed up at him.

"Waru didn't care what Hethrir wanted," Luke said. "Waru needed enough power to rip a path through space-time back to its own universe. Like an electron and a positron. Bring them together, and—" He clapped his hands together. "Annihilation. Unimaginable energy." He closed his eyes. "Hethrir thought he'd be able to tap into that power. And . . . for a moment, so did I."

"Is it gone for good?" Han asked.

Luke nodded. "And Hethrir, too. Waru wanted to go home."

Leia could not make herself feel the least sympathy for Waru.

Luke drew Jaina and Jacen and Anakin into an embrace. He kissed them each on the forehead.

"Thank you, young Jedi Knights, for calling me back."

"You're welcome, Uncle Luke," they said.

"Hey," Han protested. "Don't Leia and I get any credit?"

Luke hugged the children, and smiled.

Leia and Chewbacca gathered the stolen children together. Rillao put her arm around Tigris. He shrugged it off angrily. He tried to pick up the gold sphere that had been Waru, but he could not lift it, he could not move it. He ran out of the theater, leaving Rillao behind. Leia took Rillao's hand and squeezed it, hoping to give the Firrerreo some comfort.

"Oh, Lelila," Rillao said. "My sweet son . . ."

"Give him time."

"Yes. And peace, if we can find it."

"I'll help you," Leia said. "Luke can help—"

"No!" Rillao gripped Leia's hand intently. "Tigris has been too much under the influence of Hethrir. He cannot counter it. He must be left alone, to find himself. If he returns to me, it must be of his own free will."

Leia's eyes filled with tears of sympathy for the distress in Rillao's voice.

"I know a place where you can rest, and think, and talk, and play—a refuge, for as long as you need it. A place of peace."

Rillao tensed. It was not the custom of her people to accept charity or even sympathy. Leia was afraid Rillao would snarl, "Who asked you for your help?" and stalk stiffly away.

"My family owes yours so much!" Leia said sincerely. "We'll always be in your debt, Firrerreo." *I'll never speak Rillao's name in public again,* Leia realized. *I'll never again use that power over her.* "Please let me repay you a little."

Rillao hesitated. "I accept, Lelila," she finally said.

Rillao glanced at the altar. The sphere contracted to half its size, to half its size again, and again. Each contraction happened more quickly. The sphere was the size of an orange, an egg, a marble. It blurred.

A grain of golden sand lay on the altar. With a blaze of energy, the *pop!* of air filling a vacuum, it disappeared.

Rillao shivered and turned away.

"Come with me," Leia said.

"Very well, Lelila."

Together, they walked into the light of the crystal star.

Tigris had run halfway to the hill, and then he had stopped. He sat on the ground with his back to them, his head down. Rillao watched him from a distance.

Leia passed through the archway of Waru's retreat. Heat and brilliance hit her. Her knees trembled with exhaustion. She sat abruptly on the ground. Jacen ran to her, worried, and cuddled in her lap. She held him, smoothing his unruly hair. Rillao sat on her heels beside them, gazing toward her son.

The sky beyond the dome amazed Leia. The crystal star orbited the black hole, closer and closer, crashing through the glowing whirlpool. Gravitational stress was ripping it apart. The black hole pulled a swirl of glowing star-stuff from the dwarf's surface and spun it into the accretion disk, which blazed more and more brightly. Leia had to look away, before it dazzled her.

Mr. Chamberlain's wyrwulf flung itself at her feet and gazed at her with wide gold eyes, panting.

Free for the first time in—how long?—the stolen children ran and shouted and played. Lusa leaped in a capriole, jumping high in the air and kicking her hind feet.

Han sat behind Leia.

"Are you okay?"

She nodded, too tired to speak.

Jaina nestled in her lap next to Jacen. Anakin ran over and cuddled with his brother and sister. Leia hugged them. Han put one arm around them all, and stroked Leia's hair. Leia leaned gratefully into Han's warmth and strength.

"We'd better get out of here," he said. "But first we have to find Threepio."

"And Artoo," Leia said.

"Speaking of," Luke said.

Artoo-Detoo and See-Threepio descended the trail, Artoo rolling and bumping along at full speed, Threepio walking as fast as he could.

"Mistress Leia! Master Luke, Master Han!"

"Mr. Threep!" Anakin jumped up and ran toward Threepio and grabbed him around the leg.

"Master Anakin!" Threepio said. "I'm delighted to see you well!"

Anakin stood on Threepio's foot to ride back to Leia. He shrieked with delight.

Both droids slowed when they saw Tigris, but the youth did not react to them. Artoo rolled on by; Threepio passed him with a curious glance.

Anakin jumped off Threepio's foot and ran to Tigris. He grabbed Tigris's grubby shirt and pulled him toward the others. Tigris shrugged, pulling his shirt out of Anakin's hands.

Mr. Chamberlain's wyrwulf loped after Anakin. The heavy chain attached to its collar clanked and rattled.

Threepio reached Leia and Han. "We must hurry, Master Han!" he exclaimed.

"Where have you *been*?" Han asked. "And what happened to you?"

Threepio's new purple varnish had crackled all over like the glaze of an antique pot.

"A strange man—he was with that boy—" Threepio gestured toward Tigris. "Master Anakin was with him! When I requested an explanation, why, the man struck me! With a lightsaber! I was of course completely disabled. I was lucky not to be dismembered! Master Luke, if this is the caliber of the people you are looking for, I beg you not to try to find any more of them!"

"Don't worry, Threepio," Luke said.

"They imprisoned me! Artoo discovered me, and resuscitated my circuits—"

Artoo-Detoo trilled emphatically.

"—but no time for that!" Threepio exclaimed. "Artoo has made an ominous discovery!"

"I'm not sure we can stand another ominous discovery," Han said indulgently. "Can it wait till after supper?"

"I fear not, sir. The white dwarf star has cooled into a perfect quantum crystal. Very rare—unique, to my knowledge! As the black hole increases the amplitude of its resonance—"

"The crystal star is resonating?"

"I beg your pardon, Master Luke?"

"The crystal star is *resonating*."

"Indeed it is, sir—I believe I said as much. The resonances destabilize its orbit. The crystal star is in danger of falling into the black hole at any moment."

Threepio paused to be sure everyone knew what this meant.

Everyone did.

Threepio continued anyway. "When that happens—the violence of the explosion, the density of the X-ray flux . . . No living being, biological or mechanical, will survive."

"How long have we got?" Han demanded.

"The possibilities are never *all* calculable, I regret to say," Threepio said.

Artoo whistled insistently.

"I believe I said *that*, too," Threepio retorted. "It is clear to everyone that we do not have much time."

Leia shooed Jaina and Jacen out of her lap, and jumped to her feet.

"Children!" she called. "Come along! It's time to go home."

None of the stolen children begged to be allowed to run and play a little longer. Even Lusa, who had run all the way around Waru's retreat at a dead gallop and passed Leia on the way to making another circuit, slid to a halt. She pranced and danced in place.

"Home!" she said. "Home!"

The stolen children set off up the hillside, shepherded by Chewbacca and Threepio and Artoo. Chewbacca looked like a pile of children, for he carried them on his back and in his arms. Two of the little ones rode his feet, delightedly clutching his fur and squealing with each stride. The rest of the children jockeyed for a place as near to him as they could get.

"Let's go, love," Han said to Leia. They held hands and walked toward the hillside trail. Rillao and Luke and the twins followed.

As they approached Tigris and Anakin, Tigris unfastened the collar and chain from Mr. Iyon's wyrwulf. He rose and threw the collar away, as hard as he could.

Mr. Iyon's wyrwulf sat on its haunches and gave its neck a good scratch with both feet of its central legs.

Rillao stopped a few paces from Tigris.

"My son," she said gently. "We must leave."

Tigris glared at her. "No."

"This system will die soon."

"I don't care!"

Leia joined them. "Then it doesn't matter," she said, "whether you come with us or not. So you might as well."

Tigris glanced at her, quizzically.

"Tigis come home!" Anakin demanded.

Tigris laid his hand on Anakin's dark curly hair. "I have no home, little one."

"Cookies!" Anakin grabbed Tigris's hand and pulled.

Tigris raised his head and looked his mother in the eyes. "You didn't steal the Force from me, did you?"

"No, my sweet," she whispered.

"I never had any abilities at all, did I?"

Sadly, she shook her head.

"Wait a minute!" Han said. "Kid, you saved my son's life. Maybe you can't use the Force. So what? Neither can I, and it hasn't held me back."

"Who *are* you?" Tigris said.

Han laughed, surprised. "Maybe my disguise is better than I thought. I'm Han Solo."

"I was taught to hate you." Tigris added thoughtfully, "As I was taught to hate my mother."

"That's too bad," Han said with genuine regret. "I'm grateful to you. Thank you for bringing Anakin back to us."

"And I was taught to respect you—" Tigris said.

"That's a start—"

"—as an enemy."

Han grinned his lopsided grin. "A weird start, but a start all the same. Come on, kid. Let's get out of here."

"I don't have any choice, do I?" Tigris said belligerently.

"Not a whole hell of a lot," Han said.

With a show of revulsion, Tigris trudged after the other children. Rillao watched him go, her shoulders slumped. Leia put her arm around her new friend.

"It *is* a beginning," she said.

"Yes, Lelila. A beginning."

Han made a choking sound. Startled, Leia looked up. He was doing his best not to laugh at Tigris.

"Han!" Leia said. "Stop it!"

"Okay," he said, his voice strangled. He controlled his laughter by force of will, and grinned crookedly at her. "I don't know what he *does* think," he said, "but I *don't* think he wants to die."

Even Rillao brightened at that. "I believe you are right," she said.

"Luke?" Leia said. Her brother was staring at Waru's retreat. Leia had the irrational fear that he would run back inside.

"Resonance," Luke said. "That's *it.*"

"What?" Han asked.

"The resonance. Of the crystal star. It's disrupting the Force—that's what's been happening to me."

"To me, too," Rillao said.

Luke spun toward her. "You—a Jedi?"

She drew the inactive lightsaber from inside her robe. She did not try to engage it, but she fastened it to her belt in its proper place.

"I see that you found your 'small machine,'" Leia said.

Rillao nodded solemnly, then glanced at Luke.

"Perhaps, when we have left this place, we might spar a bit. Though I am badly out of practice."

Luke managed a smile. "I'd like that."

Han thought: We have three hours to get out of here. Three hours, more or less. It's the "less" that bothers me. Like Threepio said, the possibilities are never *all* calculable.

"What about Crseih?" he said to Leia.

"What about it?" she replied.

"When the star goes—the station will get blown to dust."

"Subatomic particles, more likely," Leia said with some satisfaction.

"Leia!" Han protested.

"She is right," Rillao said. "This place is best destroyed."

"People live here," Han said. "A friend of mine lives here."

"Warn her," Rillao said.

"If I can find her," Han said.

"If Xaverri does not survive," Rillao said, "it will be a shame."

Leia relented. "We'll warn *everyone*. Of course. But surely they keep watch on their own star. Surely they know they have to evacuate! This is *supposed* to be a research station, after all."

"Whatever was done here," Han said, "you can hardly call it research."

Leia slipped her hand into his.

"How could I *not* know about the trade?" she said. "I thought everything was going so well, and all along the Empire still terrorized people, in secret—!"

"You sent Winter to investigate—"

"I never talked to people who might have been affected. Back on Munto Codru, I spent a whole day talking to officials and ambassadors, and when I asked about the people still waiting to talk to me, I let myself be told they didn't have anything important to say."

"Sweetheart," Han said. He put his arm around her shoulders and drew her close. She leaned against him and embraced him, and they walked close together. "You've been working yourself half to death—you expect too much of yourself."

"I could say the same of you," Leia said fondly.

"And I could say *I* should have known about the trade."

"But—"

"I learned a lot about Hethrir and his followers from Xaverri," Han said. "They're careful and they're wary and they have enormous resources. Plunder from the Empire . . ."

"All the more reason to find them."

"Yes. Now."

"I always like to have an important project," Leia said dryly.

Han chuckled, his laugh part self-deprecation.

They walked up the hill in silence, and passed into the airlink.

Han leaned toward Leia and whispered, "Did I tell you how much I like your hair that way?" He twined his fingers in the long, smooth strands.

Her free hand flew to her head.

"I forgot it was down!" she said.

She decided to leave it that way.

Han surveyed the landing field. It was a cacophony of departing starships, shipowners arguing with field personnel, residents seeking a passenger berth.

"Looks like *some* people are paying attention," Han said.

As Leia and Chewbacca divided the children into two groups, one to board *Alderaan* and the other to depart on the *Millennium Falcon*, Han hurried over to See-Threepio.

"Can you get in touch with Xaverri?" he said. "She never *would* tell me where she lived, how to reach her—"

"I have already done so, Master Han," Threepio said. "In fact . . ." He pointed to a derelict-looking ship rising off the field with a precision and speed that belied its ugliness. "I believe that is her ship now, on a course for hyperspace."

Han relaxed, and grinned. "She always did like deceptive appearances."

"Papa!" Anakin, riding on top of Han's shoulders, kicked his heels against his father's chest. "Look at Mr. Chamberlain's woof!"

The great fanged wyrwulf lay on the field, curled up, its nose hidden by its bushy black tail, all six limbs pulled in close beneath it. Han strode over to it and sat on his heels beside it.

"Hey, fella, are you all right?"

The wyrwulf opened one eye halfway, whined, and curled up tighter.

Leia hurried over. "Oh, my," she said.

"Do you know what's wrong with it?"

"Nothing," she said.

"Strange kind of nothing."

The beast was sweating heavily. Its sweat was thick and blue. It flowed out over the wyrwulf's fur, matting it down.

She smiled. "I think that when we get back to Munto Codru, we'll bring a little boy or a little girl to Chamberlain Iyon, in place of his wyrwulf."

"What?"

The blue sweat solidified on the wyrwulf's body, forming a rubbery coating.

"It's metamorphosing," Leia said. "When it wakes up again, it will be self-aware—a Codru-Ji child."

The blue sweat flowed down over the wyrwulf's face. The wyrwulf snorted; the sweat covered its nose and mouth. The rubbery blue coating formed a seal.

"Help me carry it onto the ship."

Luke joined them. "It looks like I feel," he said.

"You do look a little blue," Han said.

"I'll be all right as soon as I get out of—"

Luke fainted.

Jaina waited for liftoff in *Alderaan*. She held Uncle Luke's hand. Jacen sat on Uncle Luke's other side. Between them they kept watch over him. If they could just get away from this system! Mr. Threepio had tried to explain about the resonating star, the quantum crystal. Jaina did not understand why the white dwarf star did not look like a big jewel, a huge diamond in space. But she did understand that it was why she could not use her abilities. She understood that it was making Uncle Luke sick. That it would also make her and Mama and Jacen and Rillao, and Anakin especially, sick, if they did not leave soon.

"Almost ready, now," Mama said, her voice disembodied. She was up front in the cockpit with Rillao. Papa and Chewbacca were over on the *Millennium Falcon*, with Threepio and Artoo and Anakin and most of the other children. Tigris was on *Alderaan*, but he might as well be anywhere, or no place at all, because he would not speak to anyone.

Lusa and the wyrwulf's chrysalis lay on Mama's bed in the other cabin. Lusa was scared. She had not been on very many space flights. Jaina wished she could be with her.

"We're all ready, Mama," Jaina said.

"How's Luke?"

"He's . . . he's very quiet, Mama."

The engines whispered.

"Leia, is Artoo with you?" Papa's voice sounded fuzzy through the comlink.

"No, I thought he was on the *Falcon*," Mama said.

"*What?* Okay, you get Luke out of here, I'll take one more look around for him."

Han could not lift off without Artoo-Detoo.

The radiation shields withdrew. Above *Millennium Falcon* and *Alderaan*, the sky was free.

But Han could not leave without the droid.

He jumped up with a curse. "Did *you* see where Artoo went?"

Chewbacca snorted a negative.

"I just don't know what to do," Threepio said. "That Artoo-Detoo never does as I ask—never does as expected—"

"Where did he go?" Han demanded.

"I believe—though I could be wrong, he does sometimes give me inaccurate information—"

"*Where?*"

"He went looking for the engine controls of Crseih Station."

"I ought to let him get vaporized along with the rest of the blasted place—"

Han jumped up and headed for the *Falcon*'s exit ramp.

"If I'm not back in fifteen minutes—"

Chewbacca's roar drowned out his words. Han grinned. Chewbacca was not about to leave without him.

With a musical beep and warble, Artoo-Detoo lurched from the landing field to the *Falcon*'s entry ramp, and rolled toward him.

"About damn time!" Han said. "We were going to leave you behind."

Unperturbed, Artoo whistled and rolled on by. Han and Threepio followed the little droid into the *Falcon*.

"What did you say?" Threepio said, outraged. "What do you mean, you don't care if you miss the flight? Do you want to get vaporized? Why, we've waited so long looking for you that we might be vaporized no matter what!"

Artoo-Detoo whined and wheeped.

"Why—why, I must say, that was very clever of you."

Han threw himself into the pilot's seat and strapped in. "Let's get out of here."

The *Millennium Falcon* came to life around him.

"Artoo-Detoo has arranged," Threepio said, "for Crseih Station to follow us out of this system so it will not be vaporized. Many of Lord Hethrir's guests are still on board . . ."

"And they'll be easy to round up," Han said.

The *Falcon* rose above the battered landing field of Crseih Station, and soared into space after *Alderaan*.

Leia headed for the hyperspace point, but her attention was behind her ship, back on Crseih Station and the *Millennium Falcon* and the tumult of elemental forces that would soon explode. The crystal star raced around the black hole, faster and faster, closer and closer, with more of its surface stripped away into great glowing streamers of burning plasma.

Leia's head ached fiercely, as if her brain vibrated in time with the star system's resonance. Rillao, too, looked pale and ill.

"Hold on," Leia said, as much to herself as to Rillao. "Just a little while longer, and we'll be away from this place."

"Yes," Rillao whispered.

In the distance, Xaverri's ship vanished into hyperspace. Leia was curious about her. She wanted to talk to her, to learn more about the times in Han's life that he usually avoided discussing. Strangely enough, she did not feel jealous of Xaverri.

I always believed, if I met her, I'd think she wasn't good enough for Han, Leia thought. But she was. And I'm glad.

She watched intently for the *Millennium Falcon*.

Where *are* you? she cried in her mind.

"Mama?"

"Yes, Jaina?"

"I think . . . I think you better hurry . . . Uncle Luke . . ."

The burning whirlpool spun furiously, ripping the glowing crystal's surface to ribbons. The whirlpool blasted out X rays, gamma rays, intense light. Leia closed her eyes, trying to force away the pain.

"Han!" she cried, but no transmission could penetrate the primordial cacophony.

Suddenly, against the brilliance of the dying stars, a point of darkness appeared and expanded.

"It's the *Falcon!*" Leia said.

It streaked toward *Alderaan*. Leia accelerated, wild joy overcoming the resonating pain. The *Millennium Falcon* raced *Alderaan* toward hyperspace.

In the far distance, the crystal star spiraled inward. Nearer, Crseih Station plunged into motion, its engines shuddering it into flight.

The face of the crystal star reached the event horizon of the black hole.

The crystal star shattered. Ripped apart by unimaginable forces, it disintegrated into atoms, into stripped nuclei and electrons, into subatomic particles. As they fell toward the black hole, energy burst from them. The radiation fueled a pressure wave of gas and stripped atoms that exploded outward, to sweep away anything in its path.

On *Alderaan*, Leia felt the disruption in the Force before the storm could reach her; she knew she must escape before the light and the X rays and the pressure wave *could* reach her.

Hyperspace flared open before her. Her ship blasted toward safety, the *Falcon* at its side, Crseih Station just behind.

The disruption of the crystal star lifted from Leia's shoulders.

She was free.

She was going home.

Leia piloted *Alderaan* from hyperspace into the normal space of the star system of Munto Codru. Then she waited, anxiously.

The *Millennium Falcon* appeared.

"Han!" Leia said.

The transmissions became clear once more. Han replied from *Millennium Falcon*.

"We made it," he said.

"Are you all right? Is Anakin?"

"He's okay. I was worried there at the last—but he's okay now."

As Han spoke, Crseih Station dropped into existence a few light-seconds away. It slipped into orbit around Munto Codru's sun. Following Artoo-Detoo's instructions, its engines turned themselves off. The outlaw station, and all its inhabitants, were stranded.

Hethrir's worldcraft spun serenely, surrounded by every ship in the Munto Codru system, as Leia's advisers and the Munto Codru officials rescued the lost children and began the work of returning them to their homes.

Leia unstrapped herself from *Alderaan*'s pilot's couch and hurried back to the twins. They were excited, exhausted, as bright-eyed as if they had a fever. She hugged them and kissed them.

"You're so brave," she said. "So smart, and so brave. I'm so proud of you."

She took Luke's hand. It was cold and slack.

"Luke—"

"Uncle Luke!" Jaina said. "Wake up!" said Jacen.

Rillao joined them. "Let me help," she said.

She sat on her heels beside Luke. He did not stir.

"Do not leave us now," she said. "You were in the influence of the crystal star, but you survived. You were in the influence of Waru, but you survived."

She stroked his forehead.

"Come back to us, Jedi."

Luke's eyelids fluttered.

"Are you going to let a little thing like a rip through space-time slow you down?" Rillao asked.

Luke opened his eyes. He looked at her, and smiled.

On the other side of the cabin, in silence, Tigris watched his mother.

Lusa clattered down the companionway and skidded around the corner.

"Are we home yet?" she asked.